Game of Chance

SANDRA CUZA

ONE—LOS ANGELES

*C*alypso Laskar sipped her club soda and leaned against the silk-covered wall watching the guests who, in glittering formal dress, crowded the large drawing room. An arm snaked around her narrow waist, and she felt a gentle squeeze. Twisting slightly, she regarded her husband, Seth, with luminous, walnut-brown eyes.

"What're you doing here all alone?" he asked anxiously.

"Observing the gala and wondering why you didn't have a party like this when you and Jackson founded the company," she replied with a smile that revealed the faintest hint of a dimple in one cheek. "Just look at it." Her hand, with its oval, crimson nails flashing, swept through the air indicating the brocade draperies, marquetry tables, rare Salor and Konya carpets, the collection of miniature Dutch porcelain and English glass objects, velvet sofas and needlepoint chairs. Her eye lingered on an exquisitely molded, small gold bear shimmering in the circle of illumination provided by a concealed spotlight, and her smile broadened.

Seth relaxed. "It's pretty grand, I'll admit, even for San Marino."

Yes, thought Calypso, still smiling, even in this exclusive, super-rich area dotted with spacious and elegant residences, it was an outstandingly beautiful home. Like Starr Bailey, their hostess, it was perfect and coldly impersonal, certainly nothing she envied.

"How about a walk outside?" Seth asked, frowning at the totally unnecessary blaze in a Venetian marble fireplace. "The heating's natural and Starr must have had an army of gardeners working around the clock."

Calypso shook her head, setting the gold spirals that swung from her ear lobes in motion. In each earring, two stones were anchored by loops of gold; one was a round, glittering diamond and the other a chameleon of color that now, in incandescent light, was the shade of ripe raspberries but would become a blue-green when struck by sunlight. These were alexandrites from Calypso's native Brazil, arguably the world's most costly and rare gemstones; Calypso wore them constantly, not for their material value but because they reminded her of home.

"Not right now. I'm curious about your new partner," she replied, pushing the mass of kinky hair behind both ears.

"Who is late."

She shrugged, her honey-toned skin glistening in the overheated room. "Back home, no one's on time."

"Wheeler is not Brazilian and this isn't proper American etiquette." Seth's diction was very precise, as though he'd studied elocution, a quirk Calypso no longer noticed.

"Sweetheart, the Morrisseys aren't here either," she said mildly. She knew financial men were punctilious about every detail but this was a *party*.

"They're here, just hard to spot in this mob of socialites, wannabees, hangers-on and prospective clients." Seth grinned. "Out of four partners in the firm, only one's missing and *he's* the guest of honor."

Calypso nodded. Although she preferred small parties

with close friends, her students or university colleagues, large business galas were ordeals she endured for Seth. Talking to people she didn't know and would probably never see again about economics or local political problems with an interested, solidified smile was exhausting.

"You never told me much about this new man except that he's a geologist with a good education. What's he like?"

Seth paused thoughtfully.

"Wheeler? He's quite a talker. Very charismatic."

Calypso glanced quizzically at the kind, even-tempered man she had married three years ago. They were colleagues at Claremont University, where he taught business and she was the assistant professor of Latin American Studies; closest friends and devoted lovers, Calypso still occasionally felt they were sometimes oddly out of sync. Brilliant in his field, Seth had managed to straddle both the educational and industrial worlds, juggling the classroom, navigating easily through tangled academic politics and maintaining independent business consultancies. He and Calypso had built a close and loving relationship and yet there were occasions, such as now, that she could sense her husband holding back.

Directly opposite, a uniformed maid crossed the black and white marble foyer floor and opened one of the heavy, double oak doors. A young woman, whose slightly plump body was wrapped in a skin tight, black sequin dress with spaghetti straps, stepped hesitantly over the threshold and gazed around the entrance. To the left, a broad staircase with an elaborate wrought iron balustrade curved grandly upward and out of sight; the woman's eyes followed it, chin tilting toward the ceiling. She stared at the enormous chandelier, its dozens of swaying crystal prisms reflecting muted shafts of light onto the peach colored walls.

Just behind her, a man slipped a proprietary arm around the woman's waist and gestured toward the drawing room. He was very handsome, with finely cut features, black hair touched with grey and a tanned, obviously trim body inside his perfectly cut suit that indicated either a great deal of time spent in outdoor activity or a gym.

"That's Wheeler," announced Seth in a pleased tone, taking his wife's hand and leading her toward the couple. As they moved across the room, Calypso found herself studying the new member of the firm and wondering again why he'd been offered a job. As far as she knew, Bailey International didn't need a geologist.

Without waiting for an introduction, Wheeler dazzled Seth and Calypso with a brilliant smile. "Hello, guys. This is my fiancée, Maybelleen Stockley. You must be Calypso." His eyes, for the briefest moment, were riveted to Calypso's alexandrites. Automatically touching an earring, she was seized by an instinctive distrust and dislike for the new partner. Wheeler gestured expansively toward Seth. "And this is one of my new partners, Seth Laskar."

"Pleased to meet you both, I'm sure." Maybelleen's high, clear tones seemed to float above the crowd as she smiled, first at Calypso and then Seth.

Maybelleen liked everyone, in varying degrees of course. Some people required more patience and understanding than others and occasionally, like now, she felt instant bonding. Her best friend Blossom called it intuition. Shaking hands with Seth and looking into the alert, brown eyes that nearly matched his slightly graying hair, Maybelleen felt a warm companionship spread through her body, as though they had been buddies for years. Not that he was in any way remarkable. Of average height, weight and build, the man's friendly, all-American face was only slightly lined, although he was most certainly in his forties. He reminded Maybelleen very strongly of Daddy.

"Welcome, Wheeler," said Seth, shaking the other man's hand. "I thought you might not make it to your own party."

"Sorry about that but Maybelleen took a long time to get ready."

His companion widened her very blue eyes, the lids heavy with lavender color and long, black false lashes and tilted her head to one side.

"The very idea... I was right on time, but you got lost."

Wheeler's smile hardened slightly and he winked surreptitiously at Seth: "Whatever you say, Goldilocks." Calypso's dislike intensified.

"Wheeler told me that you both teach at college." Maybelleen addressed both Seth and Calypso.

"Seth is also on the Auditing Committee of AT&T's Board," added Wheeler.

"I don't know how you manage so much." Maybelleen tilted her head and looked upward. "Wow, this is some house, isn't it? Like the Disneyland Hotel," she breathed. Calypso smiled warmly. The pair didn't seem to match but this was an interesting lady.

In unison, the quartet turned toward a woman gliding toward them through the crowd of guests. At least six feet tall with long, ash-blond hair worn in a casual coil, an impersonal smile illuminated the woman's perfect features as she appraised the new arrivals with shrewd, yellow-green eyes.

"I'm Starr Bailey." Her voice was husky, sensual. "Welcome to our home."

Her skin was smooth, buffed copper. Everything about Starr seemed to be flawless; her manicure, her slender figure with exactly the right curves, the mulberry-colored lace silk pullover worn over a matching silk slip-dress, her emerald-cut diamond necklace. Normally placid, Maybelleen nervously fluffed her platinum hair with two fingers, wondering if her rhinestone cocktail ring was too large or the long, black, sequined sheath, second-hand and just like one worn by MM, too tight.

The game was all Starr's, Calypso thought, her facial

muscles beginning to quiver under the strain of an easy smile. Ravishing, impeccably groomed and dressed, their hostess used her physical appearance to intimidate all but the most intrepid. Silently, Calypso prayed that Maybelleen would hold her own.

"I'm Wheeler Webb, this is my fiancée, Maybelleen, and thank you for this wonderful party. Jackson's a lucky man to have such a beautiful home and family." His intent gaze brushed the perimeters of flirtation.

"You're too kind," she purred. An older man with a receding hairline and well-trimmed gray beard appeared at Starr's side and clasped her unresponsive hand in his. The two were just about the same height.

"You must be Ms. Stockley. I'm Jackson Bailey, Starr's husband."

"And the president and founder of the consulting company," added Wheeler.

The flesh around Starr's mouth tightened for an instant as Maybelleen vigorously shook Jackson's free hand. "Pleased, I'm sure. Call me Maybelleen."

"Maybelleen," Starr mused, stretching her neck regally. Lights glinted on her golden hair like a halo. "That's an unusual name."

"I was named for Mama's sisters May and Belle but this is just a little more elegant." Maybelleen's eyes twinkled.

"Interesting." Starr's tone conveyed anything but interest. "And your mother's name?"

"Babe."

Calypso jumped in before Starr had a chance to speak. "Unusual, but not as odd as the names we have back home. Laerte, Jader, Euzanir, Iranir, Tralli, Ewerthos, Claucirlei, to name just a few." Calypso was uncomfortably aware that Wheeler was again furtively studying her earrings.

Maybelleen lifted her eyebrows. "Mama will just love hearing that." She gazed around the room through a screen of false eyelashes. "This house is so beautiful. I bet even

6

movie stars don't live like this."

"I was a movie star," Starr responded. Calypso glanced quickly at her husband; they had heard this before. More than once. "And a top model, but I gave it up for my husband and children and my current business, which is working with other celebrities." Starr slid out of her husband's light grasp, gesturing toward another woman. "Piper and I were just talking about the absolutely legendary party on the 14th floor of the Hilton in London when I was on location in Morocco." Her smile was radiant. "Every star, director and producer was there and it went on for four weeks. I partied for one wild, wild night but I was back on the set next afternoon. And I knew my lines. Now, let me find Giles with the drinks."

With a shimmer of silk and the hard glitter of diamonds, Starr vanished into a vortex of guests. Wheeler's resonant voice filled the uncomfortable silence.

"I'm a very lucky fellow. I've admired Jackson's business achievements for a long time, and consider it an honor to be invited to join the company. Now I find that we're also a glamorous group with a movie star in our midst."

The silence deepened. A knot of anger squeezed Calypso's stomach. She had always liked Jackson and was acutely aware that Starr's obsession with herself, embellishment of modest theatrical achievements and compulsive spending habits had created a disastrous domestic situation. She turned to Wheeler.

"I'm afraid I don't know very much about you, Mr. Webb, except that you're a geologist. Are you from Los Angeles?"

"It's Wheeler to my friends." He smiled broadly, revealing very even, intensely white teeth. "No. I lived in Seattle as a child but we left when my parents were divorced."

"I thought you moved when your father died," commented Jackson.

"He died shortly afterward."

"Wheeler's had a really, really sad life," said Maybelleen, twisting a lock of platinum hair around one forefinger. "I'm so lucky to have both my parents and two brothers, although right now, Bobby and Jimmy are in the navy fighting for our country."

"Where are they doing this?"

"Hawaii."

"Let's go into the garden," suggested Jackson. "I think I saw the elusive Morrisseys sneak out there."

With a gracious gesture, he indicated French doors at one end of the room. Led by Calypso, they moved across the room and into a garden illuminated by torches and lanterns. Water trickled over a mossy rock garden to the right, splashing gently into a pool filled with water lilies and rimmed with hyacinth. Directly to the left, a curved, white wooden pergola sheltered a round stone table and a grouping of white wooden chairs, two of which were occupied. After stepping across the threshold, Jackson glanced at the seated pair.

"I thought I saw you hiding out here. Maybelleen this is my cousin Virginia Morrissey and her husband Pete, our public relations man."

"Pleased, I'm sure." Overhead, lacy ebony patterns, woven against an indigo sky, swayed as a warm breeze stirred the thick leaf and branch canopy.

Pete leapt to his feet. Free-form gold cuff links, just a shade too large, gleamed against pristine white cuffs as he straightened a colorful Hermes tie. Tipping his head so that his long black lashes cast shadows on prominent cheekbones that were hollowed by flickering imitation candles in the white chandelier overhead, he stared at Maybelleen with deep brown eyes. Placing one hand over his heart, he declared, "Beautiful. You must be Marilyn Monroe's daughter. Granddaughter, I mean."

Calypso was torn between embarrassment and laughter. The man was a perfect fool but, like most narcissistic buffoons, was intensely happy with himself.

Maybelleen giggled. "A lot of people tell me we look alike. I hope it's not true."

Gallantly, Pete stepped forward, took her right hand, and bent to kiss it. Straightening, he pierced her with a warm, intimate stare. "Why not?

"She's dead."

Both Calypso and Virginia chuckled. The latter stood and stretched out her hand to Maybelleen, her slight figure and pale, almost translucent skin, emphasized by her long, black crepe-de-chine dress. Although she saw Virginia only occasionally, and always at company functions like this, Calypso liked the witty, sharp-tongued woman and wondered again why such a sophisticated, well-educated woman would marry a lecherous simpleton some twenty-five years her junior. In fact, she thought, of the four partners, only she and Seth seemed well-matched and happy with one another.

"Welcome to our dysfunctional group," Virginia said. "My spouse meant that you closely resemble Marilyn Monroe when she was twenty-something."

"Thank you I'm sure."

Virginia turned to Wheeler.

"Nice to meet you. Maybelleen...and ......Wheeler?" It was a question.

"Like in wheeler-dealer," explained Maybelleen.

"It's an old family name," he said. "The pleasure is mine."

Virginia smiled and seemed about to comment then changed her mind. Again aware of Wheeler's gaze that briefly, but intently, focused on her earrings, Calypso stepped closer to Seth, brushing his fingers with hers. After slicking back a strand of dark brown, wavy hair that had fallen over one temple, Pete stared attentively at Maybelleen's ample chest.

"What were you two doing out here all alone?" asked Seth, looking at Virginia.

"Drinking and quarrelling," she answered.

Jackson laughed into the pall of embarrassed silence that had seized Seth, Wheeler and Calypso. "Virginia, I cannot imagine you arguing with anybody," he commented easily.

The cousins smiled comfortably at one another. Her sleek cap of red hair glinted as Virginia tilted her head and lifted both finely arched eyebrows. "Hard to believe, but true."

Ignoring them all, Maybelleen stepped to the edge of the pergola, pressing one bejeweled hand to her throat. "This is truly the most gorgeous garden I've ever seen in my entire life," she exclaimed.

After giving Calypso a sly and meaningful wink, Pete stepped to Maybelleen's side and leered lasciviously at her breasts. "But not nearly as gorgeous as you."

"Let's move toward the dining room," Jackson suggested, gesturing toward the house. "I'm sure it's nearly time for dinner."

Calypso sighed. Her appetite seemed to have faded.

In the Bailey's large dining room, several round, linen-covered tables sparkled with crystal, silver table ware and porcelain. Sprays of rare orange and yellow orchids graced the center of each table, their faint, exotic scent overpowered by drifts of clashing perfume and after-shave from the seated guests. Dining chairs were upholstered in a floral fabric that matched both the pattern on the carpet and the room's only non-glass wall. A low murmur of conversation, as soothing as a distant chirp of crickets, thickened the air.

"This is all so ritzy," breathed Maybelleen, leaning forward and sniffing the centerpiece. "Especially this room."

Starr smiled and daintily slid one tiny shrimp onto her fork.

"Thank you. I entertain often and smaller tables are

infinitely the most practical. More intimate, don't you think? I asked Rudolfo Bassi to design and paint the wall and then I had the fabric and carpet hand-loomed in a duplicate pattern. Rudolfo's Italian, of course, just as my family is."

Maybelleen stretched out one hand and stroked the painted wall.

"Wow. It looks exactly like some wallpaper I saw at Sears." A tiny frown marred Starr's smooth forehead for a fraction of a second. "Was it cheaper to do it this way?" Her hostess fiercely stabbed another shrimp.

"What kind of work do you do?" Calypso asked Maybelleen. Grateful for her tact, Seth gently squeezed his wife's knee under the table.

"I'm a mechanic." Maybelleen flipped one errant curl behind her ear. "Wheeler and I met when he brought his car into the shop for a check-up, and I found he needed a new alternator and an oil change."

"That's an unusual occupation for a woman," observed Virginia.

"She's a great mechanic," enthused Wheeler. "A real artist."

"I just love fiddling around with engines, although my parents don't like it one bit. They think I should get married and be an Avon lady."

There was a moment of collective concentration on the shrimp. Ignored, Pete ogled all the women at the table, including his wife.

"I think everyone should do what makes them happiest," said Calypso, "just like the men who love this new project." Smiling, she half turned toward Seth. "Selfishly, I'm hoping I can tag along on some of their trips home."

"Where's home?" asked Maybelleen.

"São Paulo, Brazil."

Puzzled, Maybelleen looked at her.

"Where is that? I've never heard of it."

"In South America," explained Calypso softly. "The country's as big as the United States and the climate is like California, but Brazilians love to dance and laugh and have fun, spend time with their families." Her voice trailed away and Seth squeezed her knee again.

"I love to spend time with my family too. In fact, I live with them." Maybelleen looked at Seth. "Do your folks live close by?"

Calypso and Seth exchanged quick glances.

"No, I lost my parents at an early age," he answered carefully. Calypso reassuringly stroked the back of his hand with her fingertips.

"Oh, I'm so sorry." Maybelleen shook her head in genuine sadness before turning her attention to Jackson. "Could you tell me what exactly is this project? Wheeler never really explained."

She thought Jackson looked just like Santa, with his rounded features, rosy cheeks, brown eyes and gray beard. He only needed to trade in his tux for a red suit and stocking cap and say "ho-ho" a couple of times to be St. Nick's twin.

Starr flung her wrists aloft in a fragile, helpless gesture. Virginia bent toward Jackson and rapped her knuckles severely on the tablecloth.

"Tell us very simply."

"I'll try. It's a little complicated but basically we've got a company called California Consultants."

Starr raised her brows and patted her lips with a linen napkin.

"My old firm, Bailey, Inc. worked for years with the Defense Department and different security agencies in operations that used satellite tracking technologies. I developed a system based on infrared technology that can identify heat distinctions between land, animals, fires and such and differentiate between the bodies of animals and humans. We worked..."

"You mean you spy on people?" Maybelleen was clearly

dismayed.

"I wouldn't put it quite like that. Surveillance keeps our country strong."

"Snooping is not very Christian." Maybelleen's tone was thin but very firm.

"It's Republican," commented Calypso.

"And sometimes necessary," added Wheeler, giving Maybelleen's shoulders a sharp little hug which she interpreted as affection. "Crime detection is a strong defense."

"So is the military. My brothers are keeping our country strong," she said.

"I'm sure they are."

"When he was vice president of Engineering for SEC Technologies , Jackson developed the system that tracked down Che Guevara." Starr spoke with a touch of pride. Calypso folded her fingers together, stared hard at the centerpiece and forced back a wrathful retort regarding life under a dictatorship.

"Che who?" Maybelleen tilted her head inquiringly.

"Way before your time, my dear," Jackson remarked.

"Maybe not. I was born in 1981."

Despite her captivating and youthful appearance, Starr was heading directly for the half-century mark in age and dragging her feet at every birthday. At this reminder of time, she shot her twenty-two year old guest a look of resentment. Busy cleaning her salad plate, Maybelleen missed it, although Calypso and Virginia were more observant.

"We had a lot of business during the Cold War, but it's slowed down considerably since then," Jackson continued. "California Consultants was founded recently, after I won a bid to engineer and specify a satellite system over the Amazon Basin in Brazil that will link up with existing programs in more developed parts of the country. Of course, once I generate the system requirements, I'll identify the appropriate vendors. Eventually, it'll be possible to monitor all kinds of things in the area—aviation, illegal mining activities, brush fires, pollution—with weather stations and meteorological data centers for research and forecasting, a communication center..."

"Enough," announced Starr firmly. "I think she has the picture."

Lifting his graying eyebrows, Jackson's face bunched into happy, rounded contours.

"Sorry. I get carried away sometimes. Anyway, although I've got an MBA, earned in youthful days when I was stalling for time and looking for a job, I'm basically an engineer. With Seth's financial skill, Pete taking care of public relations and Wheeler on board as our geologist we're a perfect team."

We'd better be, Jackson thought, anxiously. Right now his income was precarious, with very few clients and investments that had soured along with his marriage. Unlike many other fifty-five-year-old men, Jackson had no desire to trade Starr for a fresh, new spouse but he hoped that an injection of money could repair their increasingly shaky relationship.

"Brazil sounds so romantic," mused Maybelleen.

Pete leaned forward. "You deserve romance, Marilyn Maybelleen," he purred.

She giggled and turned toward Virginia. "Isn't that the cutest? I've been called a lot of things but Marilyn Maybelleen is a new one."

"He's an original," remarked Virginia dryly.

Calypso was once again aware of Wheeler's focus on her earrings. She twisted in her chair and asked, "Is something wrong?"

"Aren't those alexandrites?" he asked.

"Yes, they are." Her muscles relaxed slightly and her hostility eased. After all, he was a geologist.

"Jeepers, I thought they were rubies," said Maybelleen, "but I only know rubies, emeralds and diamonds. And amethysts."

Calypso smiled, warming to the other woman's lack of pretense, aware of Maybelleen's very slight lisp. "Alexandrites are very rare. Although you can't see it now, they change color. In daylight, these are a bluish green color we call *pavão* at home."

"My goodness! I've never heard of jewels like that."

Attention was totally focused on Calypso's earrings. Wheeler's authoritative voice broke the stillness.

"Those stones are extremely scarce and very, very expensive. Alexandrites were first discovered in Russia and then Sri Lanka, but now they're only found in Brazil. In the State of Minas Gerais, to be exact."

"Wheeler Webb, you are so smart!" exclaimed Maybelleen enthusiastically.

"Geology was my field of study at the University of Nevada," he said modestly. "That's how I got into real estate there and then in Montana and Idaho."

"Seth probably told you that he grew up in Montana with an old aunt. Maybe you know some of his cousins," Jackson said.

"Montana's a big place," commented Seth in a flat, clipped tone.

"That's a fact," agreed Wheeler pleasantly.

Calypso could feel her husband's tension and her muscles clenched in nervous sympathy. Although he had never explained his aversion to the subject, Seth reacted to any attempted discussion of his family with silence or short, brusque replies. Her mind churned frantically in the brief hush that engulfed the table and then she turned to Maybelleen

"Did you know that the office is moving to Jackson's coach house out in back?" she asked.

Two maids scurried around the room clearing the salad plates, their progress closely watched by Starr. Maybelleen anxiously fluffed her hair with two fingers and turned to Wheeler.

"You used to have a beautiful office and a secretary.

Will you still have them?"

"Maybe."

Calypso saw the tiny frown that creased her husband's forehead. "What's the matter now?" she whispered.

Seth bent in her direction. "This is the first I've heard about Wheeler's real estate background," he murmured, "but then I don't know much about his personal life, except that he had a nasty divorce not too long ago. It seems his wife had an affair with another man and cleaned out his bank account and stock portfolio, then tried to put him in jail on bogus charges."

Loosely Catholic, Calypso believed absolutely in the sanctity of marriage and disapproved of divorce and philandering, activities that were often intertwined. Despite her vague dislike for the man, Calypso grew indignant thinking of the suffering and humiliation Wheeler must have endured.

"That's outrageous," she said.

"Absolutely." Seth straightened and dusted at minute crumbs before turning to Maybelleen. "Wheeler tells me you have a cat."

"Yes I do. Punky. He goes everywhere with me except dinner parties."

The main course was served, wine and water glasses refilled.

"When I was a boy I had a pet mouse named Sir Galahad."

Maybelleen's azure eyes widened and her delighted tinkle of laughter rolled through the room. Heads turned in their direction.

"You did?"

"I kept him in a cardboard box lined with tinfoil underneath my bed and nobody else knew about him. We were pals. I'd read to him and make up stories I thought he'd like. For a long time I wanted us to go camping in the mountains or to the beach together."

"And did you?"

"No." Seth's jaw muscles clenched as he recalled with unwelcome clarity the frantic struggle for money and the violent family arguments before the death of his father and the disappearance of his mother.

"And what happened to him?"

"He died." Seth still remembered the misery he had felt at the loss of his pet. Maybelleen reached over and gave the man an understanding pat on one hand.

"He sounds real nice."

"I don't suppose you cooked this delicious meal yourself?" Wheeler addressed the hostess with a warm smile.

"Of course. So few people in L.A. understand real Italian food."

"Anybody can make mashed potatoes," stated Maybelleen. "Even my brothers."

"You mean *Puré di Patate*. These are not hill-billy spuds." For a few silent moments the entire table seemed to focus on their plates. Then Maybelleen shimmied her shoulders briefly, the black sequins on her gown sending sparks of light in all directions, and encompassed them all in a broad grin.

"My parents would love this." She picked up her fork and cut a piece of meat. "So would Blossom. Mmmmm. I just adore meat rolls."

"*Asticciole alla Calabrese*," corrected Starr. "Who's Blossom?"

"My best friend. He and I go line dancing at least once a week at the Buttons and Bows."

All but Jackson and Calypso stared at her blankly.

"Line dancing? Is that like a floor show in a club?" asked Starr.

Both Jackson and Maybelleen chortled gleefully.

"A floor show? No, ma'am. In line dancing we all wear cowboy clothes, line up to face the audience and dance to country & western music. Without partners. It's real hill-billy stuff."

17

Pete perked up at the mention of cowboy outfits. He loved opportunities to dress up; it was the reason he was so fond of sports. Ice hockey, skiing, tennis, baseball and paintball all required special costumes that magically transformed the wearers into new personalities. He was always a star, master of the world once he'd donned his athletic gear, no matter how he played. Not, he mentally amended, that he ever turned in a less than magnificent performance, although his teammates sometimes failed to appreciate him.

"It's a tricky series of steps and routines that have to be memorized," Jackson volunteered. "A little bit like a musical comedy."

Starr wrinkled her nose in a charming suggestion of distaste. "How do you know?" she asked.

"I've always liked country & western music, and I watched line dancing in my undergraduate days. Never did it myself, though."

Starr turned toward Wheeler. "Jackson grew up in Kansas in a very unsophisticated family."

Virginia smoothed the high rolled collar that concealed tiny neck wrinkles. "That's untrue. His father was a lawyer in the State Legislature and his mother was president of the Junior League and Garden Club."

Starr lifted one languid hand dismissively. "Of course you *would* defend your cousin."

Her ivory skin flushed a dull rust color as Virginia leaned toward the hostess. "Just correcting a deliberate crock of shit."

"Do you have other hobbies?" Calypso asked Maybelleen.

"Oh, yes. Motorcycles. I have a yellow Harley with a jumpsuit and helmet and boots to match and I take lots of fun trips with the other Motor Maids. Punky comes along in his basket."

"Motor Maids?" Seth puzzled. Starr had forgotten to arrange her face and was clearly gawking at her guest while

Virginia's eyes sparkled in amused sympathy.

"My biker club. Only ladies allowed."

"The line dancing sounds great to me," Wheeler said with a warm smile, running one finger lightly up Maybelleen's bare spine. "I'd like to try sometime, sweetheart." If both Jackson and Maybelleen liked country & western and line dancing, it would be wise to show an interest.

Calypso glanced surreptitiously at the firm's newest partner. He was charming, extraordinarily good-looking and obviously intelligent, the kind of man that normally had to fight off lots of eager women. Maybelleen certainly looked easy enough, but Seth told her that after five dinner dates, a greenhouse full of flowers and a lot of movies, most of them old classics that she said she and her family adored, Wheeler had been awarded just one kiss on the cheek. The old hard-to-get game, only she had a very strong inkling that Maybelleen wasn't playing. The two women exchanged smiles.

"You should all come with us," Maybelleen urged the others.

"I'll go," volunteered Calypso. "It's similar to folk dance in other cultures and supposed to be quite a lot of fun."

Wheeler shifted his attention and glanced briefly at the alexandrites, giddy at the sight of many thousands of dollars hanging from Calypso's ear lobes. Thank you, he murmured to a God in which he did not believe, for guiding me to that course at the Gemological Institute. All those hours of study, plus the supplementary time spent in library research and prowling the museums might just pay off big time. A tiny plan began to curl around the edges of his brain as he lifted his eyes and smiled at Starr.

"This is truly one of the most interesting and unique parties I've ever attended," he said. "Garlands and kudos to a beautiful and talented hostess."

Nodding her head, Starr graciously acknowledged the compliments.

Outside, a trio of musicians stood at the edge of a polished wooden dance floor, softly playing a Jobim tune. Through the plate glass wall that curved around three sides of the dining room, guests enjoyed an unobstructed and dramatic view of the pergola, coach house, large oval swimming pool, and illuminated formal garden that stretched into the shadowy distance. Wheeler stared thoughtfully through the glass, tapping one finger in time to the music, and then turned again to Calypso.

"I haven't tried a samba for years, although I used to be a pretty good dancer. Would you be willing to risk a number later on?" He looked at Seth. "With your permission, of course." He stretched his arm around Maybelleen's shoulders and ran one finger gently up the side of her neck. "And yours."

"Certainly," replied Seth easily. "Calypso could samba all night, but I've never really learned how."

"Me neither," trilled Maybelleen, turning to Jackson. "But if they play a country tune, I'll teach you how to line dance. You too, Calypso."

"Unfortunately, I don't believe that opportunity will arise since this is a South American musical group," offered Starr smoothly.

"That's okay," responded Maybelleen cheerfully. "I bet I can learn to do a samba real quick."

"Oh my," mused Calypso. The evening was showing signs of becoming memorable.

TWO—LOS ANGELES

Several days later, Jackson escorted Wheeler into the coach house that had served as his study for years and was now his only office. With casual care, Wheeler checked out the dark paneled walls hung with turn of the century faded sepia photos of Los Angeles, floor to ceiling bookcases crammed with volumes and files, and a leather topped desk over which a thick layer of papers in sprawling stacks had been strewn. On one side of the room, green leather armchairs and a matching sofa were grouped around a polished marble coffee table. The office was masculine, tasteful and looked very expensive to Wheeler.

With a nod, Wheeler acknowledged Pete, who stood looking out the window at the swimming pool, and also Seth, seated at the desk piled with papers.

"Morning, partners." Wheeler grinned boyishly at Jackson. "You've got the shortest commute of anyone I know. This is a great set-up."

"It's handy. One of the reasons we bought the property, in fact," Jackson responded. "When I worked closely with the government, I had a place in D.C. as well as our old downtown office. I traveled a good deal then, but I still did a lot of my work at home. It was more convenient."

Across a broad expanse of closely cropped grass, they could see Starr as she emerged from the pool and blotted her bronzed body with a large white towel. Pete stopped rattling the coins in his pocket and smoothed his hair with cupped palms, leaning forward until his forehead touched the glass. Aware that she was being watched, Starr draped the terry cloth over one shoulder, then picked up a cellular phone and dialed. Turning, she walked toward the house with the phone clamped against one ear, her one-piece bathing suit, legs cut to the hip and back slashed almost to the base of her spine, exactly matching her hair and fiercely reflecting the sun's rays. Silently, Wheeler and Jackson had joined Pete at the leaded glass windows and all three watched as Starr disappeared behind the drooping tangle of grape vines covering the pergola.

"She never stops," Jackson commented softly. Suddenly aware that the other two had been openly gawking at his wife, he turned abruptly and faced his partners. When he spoke, his voice was professional and almost impersonal. "I hope neither of you regret the decision to give up our downtown office. Since the Brazilian project is all we've got right now, this seemed a practical move."

Seth and Pete had other sources of income, and perhaps Wheeler did too, but Jackson's share of the office rent, unfortunately, would have come right out of his nearly empty pocket.

Seth looked up from his laptop. "As I've said, it's a brilliant idea." Jackson, who no longer noticed the CPA's carefully mannered speech patterns or his insistence on business attire, even on informal occasions, flashed Seth a look of gratitude. He could always count on his long-standing friend and partner for support.

"Sure. We can always go back later on." Wheeler didn't sound entirely happy. Easing onto the sofa, he looked at a partially opened door on one side of the room, then asked, "Do we have a secretary?"

"I've always used a computer and a tape recorder here.´ responded Jackson as he settled onto an armchair. "I suppose we can get someone, if you think it's necessary." He glanced in exasperation at Pete, who was still gazing out the window, then gestured toward Seth. "Let's hear Wheeler's idea, shall we?"

Seth stood, straightened his cuffs and brushed a thread from his jacket before moving to one of the leather chairs.

"It's going to make us a fortune. We are going to be very, very rich and it's not going to take long either." Wheeler sat forward, laced his fingers together and stared at the other two. "Of course this is strictly confidential. "The man was just a shade too emphatic. Frowning slightly, Jackson leaned forward and poured three tumblers of ice water from a crystal pitcher, his eyes catching Seth's before settling upon Wheeler.

"In my line of work, I've always dealt with classified information," Jackson replied tartly. "What have you got?"

"An original concept: something that would work in tandem with the satellite project but will be much more profitable." Wheeler's voice tightened with excitement.

Neither Jackson nor Seth moved. A young, shapely maid in a black uniform emerged from the house; Pete again slicked back his hair, stepped to the doorway and slouched casually against the jam, his eyes riveted on the attractive servant.

"This is the perfect plan for making tax-free bucks." Wheeler glanced at Pete, who was clearly far more interested in the maid than the business at hand, took a sip of water and looked fixedly at the other two partners. "I got the idea when I saw Calypso's alexandrites. Those stones now come from just two mines in Brazil, the Malacacheta and the Hematita, both in the boonies north of Belo Horizonte, but actually there's a lot of very quiet exploratory digging going on all over that part of the country."

Both of his California Consultants partners listened intently.

"Everybody knows there are more deposits. They're the jackpot and we've got the winning ticket." Wheeler paused and looked at the other two expectantly. Immobile and unsmiling, they returned his gaze. "The satellite system is the perfect cover."

"What do you mean?" Jackson asked uneasily.

"Well, as you both know, our company won a consultant's contract to identify needs, develop expectations and qualify vendors that can build, install and implement the systems required by the Brazilian government." His voice was strong and reassuring.

"Our responsibilities also include making sure that the systems perform at or above specification," Jackson added.

"Of course. Our involvement as consultants in such a large and important project is very beneficial for the status of our firm. And extremely profitable. I propose that we fulfill our responsibilities efficiently and I also propose that we consider the possibility of identifying other opportunities, as long as they don't diminish the services required by the Brazilian Armed Forces."

A cautious frown creased Jackson's forehead as he nodded slowly.

"Well then. Alexandrite deposits are just under the earth's surface, five, ten feet down at the most, in very specific geological conditions consisting of seven layers of earth and rock, usually granite. The system we're designing includes sophisticated satellites that can spot and identify terrain where deposits are likely to exist. Since our services include evaluating the pictures taken over Brazil, for the first three weeks of operation we can involve the collection of data to be assessed by a spectro analyzer, which will allow us to identify, with a high degree of probability, new and untapped alexandrite deposits."

Radiating confidence, he paused. Seth shifted on his

seat and Pete waved at the maid, who promptly vanished into the house. The frown hadn't disappeared from Jackson's face as he planted both elbows on the arms of his chair, placed the tips of his fingers together and stared at Wheeler.

"And?" he asked.

"And once we determine the areas with a greater than ninety percent chance of having alexandrites, we buy up these properties through dummy companies and tie up the mining rights." His rich, smooth bass voice enunciated each word clearly and emphatically. "To avoid charges of breaking confidentiality agreements and breeching other conflict laws, no one else can know what we're doing".

Seth's lips thinned into a grim line and he shook his head disapprovingly. Jackson continued to stare at Wheeler as though observing a life form from another planet. Undeterred, Wheeler continued.

"We'll be rich." He held up a cautionary hand. "I've done my homework on this and found out that, in Brazil, the federal government owns all mining rights. We could get a license, like everyone else does, without buying the property, but the Hematita mine was invaded by thousands of licensed prospectors that robbed and killed and tore up the place. It's been periodically opened and closed by the police for years and there's always secret digging going on. That's not for us. We'll buy the land, which brings us ten percent of the total mined profits, and acquire the mining license as well, so we completely control all the earnings."

Evidently tired of waiting for the maid to return, Pete moved inside, propped himself against the wall and surveyed his colleagues with apparent boredom.

"Why hasn't anybody else thought of this?"

"Maybe they have, but up until now the Brazilian satellite system has been limited to telecommunications services."

Jackson nodded. "That's right. It's incomplete and not terribly refined. Otherwise our company wouldn't have been hired."

For a few moments, the room was absolutely silent.

"Well?" Wheeler's persuasive voice was filled with confidence. "How about it?"

"It's totally unethical," Jackson said.

"And?"

"We're not sure, but probably illegal." Jackson's tone was sharply edged. "And I've never, in all my business dealings, resorted to dishonest or corrupt practices." A few gray areas in the past, he thought, but nothing outright criminal.

"There's nothing corrupt about this." Wheeler's rich voice deepened. He placed one hand over his heart as though taking a pledge. "I would never encourage anything that jeopardizes the objective of the client."

"Don't shit a shitter," Jackson said curtly. "This is shady, at best."

"It depends on your point of view."

"Let me spell something out for you. The ownership of the project is the Brazilian government, so they should determine who gets the profits."

"Jackson, nobody gets hurt or even loses because no one else knows about it. This is a win-win situation. What I'm suggesting is that we use our brains and equipment to succeed. Make money big-time. Guys, this is not a dress rehearsal, it's the only life we've got and we'd better make the most of it."

It was exactly the right note. Jackson looked at Seth.

"What's your feeling?"

Seth stood up, adjusted his small gold cuff links and walked to the far window. In silence, he observed a number of gardeners pruning, hacking, trimming and weeding as they busily coaxed a casual riot of rich colors from the flower beds and severely disciplined the formal garden. Behind him, Wheeler's self-assured voice filled the room.

"Hey, we can't let this one go by. We'll be dropping

major, major bucks and I don't mind admitting that my ex-wife has me by the short and curlies. . Besides taking everything I've worked for all my life and then dumping me for a real bozo, she'll have the sheriff after my ass if I don't cough up alimony on time. I'd never dream of doing anything criminal, but this might give us all a little breather."

Jackson slowly drank his glass of water then doodled in the wet ring it had left on the marble. It was a serious temptation. Whatever she might say to the contrary, Starr's dazzling career as a teenage model had long ago tapered down to some infrequent appearances in mail order catalogs, and her foray into movies had stalled after two mediocre performances as a bit player. Profits from her brilliantly successful business, Starr's Stars, in which she advised celebrities about dress, hair and make-up, were unshared and went directly into her own private account. Basic living expenses, never small, had leapt astronomically since Starr had learned that, if this job panned out, they would be spending half the year in Brazil where she could cultivate new clients. Despite his urging to economize, she still indulged in designer clothes and hosted parties where countless dollars were spent entertaining her current and prospective customers. Over the years, their relationship had soured, but he couldn't afford a divorce from this self-centered, still-beautiful woman that he had once idolized. Jackson desperately needed money, possibly more than the project would produce, and this proposition just might be the answer.

"Seth?" he repeated.

Just then, Starr emerged from the house in a yellow trouser suit, black vest, very high yellow heels and a wide-brimmed straw hat. The cellular phone was again pressed to one ear while she gestured vigorously with her free hand, occasionally twisting and signaling to the uniformed female servant that trailed in her wake. Seth returned to his chair while Pete pivoted and took one step outside.

A humorless smile curved Jackson's lips as he watched his wife pause beside one of the stooping gardeners and point to a plant with one yellow pump, covering the phone as she addressed the workman. What was she up to now? Planning another party maybe, or setting one of her clients straight about how many diamonds could be tastefully worn at one time. Or maybe someone was frantically seeking information about the correct season for patent leather shoes. Whether shoulder pads were really in or out. Whatever it was, Jackson knew he was excluded from the picture and it was probably his own fault for spoiling and pampering Starr and their two adult children for years. And now he was sinking in financial quicksand. He turned back to his partners.

"Seth?" Jackson stared directly ·at his old friend. "Wheeler's got the energy to really get us going."

"I don't buy it. We can do just as well in the long run by sticking to our original plan—not as big a haul maybe, or as fast, but without the unnecessary risks."

"Seth, my man, life's a risk." Wheeler's voice was calm and persuasive. "Just getting up every day is a dangerous proposition."

Seth felt a cold flash of unaccustomed anger. Long ago he had used this exact same logic to convince himself that wrong was right. It was another time and place, a well-buried secret, but he still felt regret almost every day for that past mistake.

On the other hand, old habits die hard, if they expire at all. For the first time in years he felt the nearly forgotten surge of adrenalin and the squeeze of excitement at the prospect of risk and illicit profit. This wasn't criminal, he rationalized, just dishonest. With an effort, he smothered the thought and silently rubbed his palms together.

"I'll have to think about this one," Jackson said.

"We're making a decision here, Pete," Wheeler called.

Pete twisted and smiled at his partners. "Whatever you guys want is fine with me."

The company president lowered his eyes and shook his head almost imperceptibly. He and Virginia were not only cousins but life-long friends and, when she had asked him to hire Pete, her physically beautiful, empty headed boy-toy, he hadn't been able to refuse. Thank God Pete's duties were limited to public relations, of which there were practically none. Raising his head, he looked quizzically at Seth.

"It sounds pretty good to me," said the CPA. "But you're the president, Jackson, and we aren't going to do anything without your endorsement. It's really up to you."

THREE—SAN FRANCISCO

Virginia Bailey Fremont Morrissey threw off the peach-colored satin sheets and slid from the bed she shared with Pete. In an effort to perform some kind of conjugal duty, Pete had spent more than one pre-dawn hour in very skillful foreplay, which had also been the end play. Casting a glance at her reflection in the gilt-framed mirror, Virginia shook her head unhappily. Thanks to the miracles of cosmetic surgery, near starvation, and a punishing exercise program, her figure was still lean and mean, giving not the slightest hint that she was fifty-two years old. She yanked an exquisite Alencon lace negligee from the padded clothes dummy and thrust her arms into the bat-wing sleeves.

She spoke to the figure in bed. "What do you think that short garden hose of yours is for, anyway?"

Virginia paused in front of the mirror and adjusted her expression, lifting the corners of the lips and widening the eyes to smooth out any incipient wrinkles, then turned from side to side to inspect the make-up she always applied just before retiring. Pete had never once seen her bare face which meant, of course, that she had to devote many daytime hours to creaming, cleaning, masking and otherwise reviving her tired epidermis. Plus regular visits to Dominique's Salon for professional treatment. Why on earth had she ever married a twenty-eight year old? Because he made her feel young and attractive and looked good on her arm, of course, the same reasons old men married younger women. God, it was a lot of work with almost no returns.

On rare occasions she wondered why Pete seemed to function sexually with other women and no longer did with her. These flashes of candid introspection were usually followed by the suspicion that the twenty-four-year difference in their ages might be the reason for Pete's failure to perform. It was a nasty thought, rapidly banished. Meanwhile, she worked very hard at her appearance and badgered and belittled her husband, which only worsened the situation.

Shifting her gaze to the bed, she caught sight of Pete's handsome, classic profile outlined against the pillow and felt a rising wave of anger although she was uncertain whether it was directed at herself or her impotent husband who had the crust to lie there with his eyes peacefully shut. Her carefully composed face dissolved into hard crinkles as she cinched the gros-grain belt tightly around her waist and advanced on the canopied bed.

"Wake up when I'm talking to you!"

Obediently, Pete sat bolt upright, surrounded and overwhelmed by peach satin, and propped himself against the quilted headboard. Virginia was momentarily stunned by the sheer beauty of her second husband, a tender sentiment that invariably ended when Pete opened his mouth.

"I'm sorry, Ginny."

"Don't call me that. I've told you a hundred times I hate it."

"I'm sorry. Maybe I had too much to drink last night."

"Then the answer's simple. Go on the wagon."

"What?"

"Don't drink." Her hands clenched into fists. "Get up."

"But it's only five-thirty."

"Many people do their best work early in the morning. Certainly you don't if you think your talent lies in the bedroom, but the office is another story, I hope."

"Ginny," he announced, "you don't seem to understand that in the public relations world I'm a legend in my own mind."

Virginia closed her eyes for a moment, then slowly opened them and stared at her husband.

"Legend in my own time, is the expression. And the only legendary thing about you is that sick caterpillar." She pointed toward his groin with one scarlet nail.

"Ginn...Virginia, I'll make love to you any other way you like, you'll be amazed at—"

"Can it, hotshot. You're a wonderful lover and a lousy screw, and I'm becoming a virgin again. Not good, baby doll, not good."

"But I can't help it," he protested.

"Don't give me that. What do you do with your girlfriends?"

His brown eyes under the straight, dark brows grew larger in the sculpted face as he struggled out of the enveloping peach satin womb. Manfully, he batted away the last of the sleek fabric and stood, his magnificent, perfectly muscled body broiled a deep olive from long hours in a tanning salon.

"Girlfriends? Virginia, how could you think I'd want someone else when I've got the best right here?"

With dignity, Pete stepped into his dressing room, emerging a moment later wearing a paisley print silk smoking jacket, white ascot and gray silk pajama bottoms. Her husband's elegance fueled Virginia's rage. Pete mouthed a kiss, dropped one eyelid in a sensual and conspiratorial wink, and then padded out of the massive bedroom with its peach swag draperies and matching chaise lounge. He was an inveterate blockhead, she thought, watching him swing down the hallway and turn into his study. And about as sly and subtle as a hippopotamus... For sure he was calling one of his girlfriends right now, thinking no one had a clue when, in fact, only the blind and deaf in Los Angeles were unaware of his affairs.

Striding past the closed door of the study, Virginia threaded her way through the living room to the large, salt-water aquarium. Installed in a bookshelf and designed to be viewed from both the drawing room and the study, the glass tank was surrounded by an imperceptible pocket of air that made eavesdropping easy. Scowling, Virginia pressed one ear to the edge of the glass, hearing Pete's rich but hushed baritone.

"Marlene?" The desk drawer squeaked open and Virginia peeped cautiously through the water, watching as Pete took out a mirror and positioned it on his desk with one hand while holding the telephone receiver with the other. "I *do* know what time it is, but I couldn't sleep. I've been thinking of you all night." He squinted into the mirror examining his crop of morning whiskers then peered under his chin for signs of aging. "I told you, we don't share the same room. We don't share anything." Flaring his nostrils he peered into each then scrutinized the top of his nose. Frowning, he rummaged in the drawer for tweezers. "When? Just say the word and I'll be there." Pete tilted his head, removed a few stray hairs from his eyebrows and tossed the implement back into the drawer. "No, tonight I've got a Board meeting, but how about lunch tomorrow? Great; I can't wait."

He mouthed a noisy kiss into the receiver, replaced it in the cradle, then picked it up and dialed again. "Karen darling, I couldn't sleep thinking about you..."

Virginia's derisive snorts misted the glass and scared the fish but failed to capture Pete's attention. Thoughtfully, she returned to the peach tiled bathroom with the round, sunken tub and long, marble-topped dressing table.

Walking to the winter garden at the far end of the room, she crossed her arms over her chest, leaned against the wall and stared bleakly at the espaliered pear and peach trees. A cloud of blooms, barely visible in the pale, morning light, obscured the branches and supporting wooden trellis.

When she'd married Pete she'd known he was narcissistic and weak, but she hadn't suspected complete witlessness. Now she was wasting her time and the money that she'd inherited and parlayed into a small fortune; she needed to either cut her losses and dump Pete or somehow turn him into an asset. Unfortunately, even with Jackson's help, transforming this sow's ear into anything else was clearly an impossible task.

After she was orphaned at age three, Virginia had been adopted by her very rich, exceedingly severe and demanding grandmother in San Francisco, where she'd grown up as an overweight girl with beautiful hazel eyes, milky skin, red hair and, aside from Jackson, few friends. Although he didn't know it, that camaraderie had been a lifeline, a gift she could never repay.

Irritably, Virginia glowered at the pear tree, wishing she'd listened to her cousin's advice in the past, wishing Starr were more approachable, wishing she were twenty-eight again and had just met her first husband Ferguson, wishing Pete would die and bestow widowhood on her. Maybe she should try prayer. After all, she deserved to be a widow and Sneaky Pete would be justified in passing to his Greater Reward, which was most likely a place stuffed with nubile young women panting for a muscular eunuch with limited intelligence.

Virginia leaned her forehead against the glass and closed her eyes, remembering how happy and hopeful she had been just a few months ago, when she swallowed her pride and called Jackson with a proposal. The world had seemed to blossom and her life along with it.

Sourly, she recalled that very fateful day. She was

exultant, tossing the receiver from one hand to another, her face bisected by a broad smile. She would sell her house in San Francisco, leave her beloved native city and move to Los Angeles, cow-town of the state, so that Pete could have a chance to grow up. Her smile faded. The tiniest voice had whispered that a move of five hundred miles and a new job might not solve problems that they carried with them. She'd quickly pushed the thought away.

Humming tunelessly, Virginia stepped into a shiny, long-sleeved, red and white striped leotard and matching tights, slapped a clay mask on her face and moved into her mini-gym to try to condition those slightly sagging muscles and aging flaps of skin. Settling herself on the stationary bicycle, she lowered her head and torso over the handlebars as though in a race, her feet churning frantically as she thought about her future. Sweat trickled down her scalp, a welcome and gratifying sign that calories were burning away on her not-so-firm thighs. She pushed her muscles to the very limit. She smiled, savoring Jackson's promise.

Suddenly, the mirrored door flew open and Vince Soto, her driver, stepped inside, speechless and stunned into temporary immobility. Then he opened his mouth and guffawed. "What have you done to your face? It's all blue and sticky like those Monsters from Outer Space. And that little plastic shower cap!"

"Get out, you fool," she yelled, her face burning with embarrassment under the herbal mask as she struggled to dismount. "Go screw yourself, or one of your grease ball girlfriends."

Clumsily she disentangled herself from the machine, catching one foot on a pedal and stumbling as she lurched forward. Vincent wasn't supposed to come in here to check the equipment until later in the day. And he knew better than to barge into any room unannounced. Soberly, he backed into the corridor and shut the door.

"I know you were raised in a chicken coop, but those

of us that live outside of Brown-town knock on closed doors," she yelled.

"Sorry."

The reply was muffled but Virginia distinctly heard another brief cackle. She glared at the door, wondering whether she'd made a mistake eight years ago when she'd plucked him from a street fight a few moments before the police would have swept him off to the pokey.

Her vision focused sharply on her reflection in the mirror. No wonder Laughing Boy had killed himself at the sight. She looked like a scarecrow, an old hag with an artificial face and figure draped in skin that was sagging faster than the plastic surgeon could shore it up. A few more years and she'd be totally unable to bend, smile or frown. And that hair! Dyed to her natural brick-red hue in order to cover grey streaks, it had been cut and shaped into a sleek cap that was elegant, fashionable and somehow far too young for her.

Her hour of exercise ruined, Virginia moved into the bathroom where she systematically cleaned and massaged her face, applying toner, concealer and Wrink-fill, just as she'd done twice a day for years, but her mind wasn't on the job at hand. She'd increased Granny's legacy through clever investments but the shrewdest by far was the vineyard she and her first husband, Ferguson Fremont, had founded. All her money, time and energy had gone into the punishing but rewarding physical work that both she and Ferguson adored. It had been an era of total happiness. Grimly, she focused on her current spouse, and the plan that she hoped would force a change in his lifestyle.

Showering quickly, she stepped into a lavender track suit with embroidered flowers on the front and opened the door to the bedroom. Vincent lounged against the wall cleaning his nails with a switch-blade.

"This is my boudoir, slum crumb, and when I want you in here, I'll ask."

He grinned, folded up the knife and scratched an armpit under his uniform jacket. "I thought you called."

"You were mistaken. However, since you're here, you can go to the garage and bring the suitcases. All of them."

Vincent pushed away from the wall, throwing his employer a sloppy, half-salute, then waving toward a stack of suitcases beside the door.

"Already done..."

Puzzled, Virginia gently massaged the skin under both eyes.

"How did you know I wanted them?"

"I heard you begging Cousin Jackson to give Sneaky Pete a job."

"You eavesdropped on me?" she asked, dropping her hands to her sides.

"I was just in here tidying up, helping Blanca, and your voice came through that door loud and clear."

"Because you had a glass and one ear pressed to it, no doubt."

"Want to hear what you said? I got an audio-graphic memory."

"Not particularly."

His voice warbled into a high falsetto. "Jackson, I have a favor to ask. It's about the man I married last year." Vincent's voice returned to normal. "I can just see the dude sitting there counting on his fingers and wondering if he'd lost one or two husbands along the line." Before Virginia could interrupt, he closed his eyes and his voice rose again. "Pete's so charming, Gumps is lucky to have him in their advertising department. Of course the salary isn't as high as he'd like, but a place that's so prestigious has dozens of applicants that would take the job for nothing. And since he's at the top of the line right now, he can't expect any more advancement."

"That's enough, Vincent," she warned.

"He's an ambitious man, Jackson," Vince continued. "Hard working and honest. He's from an old San

Francisco family and has a top education."

"Did I say that?"

"Every word, Toots. I take it that *Cuz* came through?"

"That's right. Pete's going to be the public relations man for California Consultants since he's stuck on Grumps' corporate ladder."

"Nix, sweetheart. No, no. This is me you're talking to, remember? Sneaky Pete's old man got him that job because they didn't want him working as a model, and Sneaky went along with it because he can chase tail, go to parties and take it easy. He's not stuck. He's roosting."

"Life's about to change."

"When?"

"Just as soon as I can get the movers over here."

Moving back into the dressing room, Virginia stared resentfully at the foam of pear blossoms. The tree represented beauty, youth and robust health, the best in life. In contrast, her life was a mess, and she didn't have the least idea of what to do about it.

In San Marino, Jackson closed his office door and sifted through the stack of mail that the maid had just delivered. Dropping the others onto a chair, he carefully slit one of the envelopes and opened a letter from his bank manager. After studying the paper for a long time, he crumpled it in one fist, sank onto the leather sofa and closed his eyes.

And in Claremont, Calypso pushed the term papers she had been reading to one side and, frowning, slowly lowered the mobile phone to the desk. Marvin Beale. Who was he and why did his rare phone calls upset Seth?

FOUR—LOS ANGELES

*C*alypso and Seth moved cautiously across the boardwalk fronting the imitation clapboard facade with its rustic wooden awning and stopped facing the *Buttons and Bows* swinging doors. Eyebrows lifted in alarm at the muted thunder of canned country-western music, shouts and cheers emanating from the building, Seth fiddled nervously with his gold cuff links.

"Wow," he said. "You sure this is a good idea?"

Calypso tweaked the perky polka-dot bow tie her husband wore as a concession to the informality of the occasion and gave him an affectionate hug. "It'll be fun. Besides, we promised Maybelleen."

"And Wheeler, too."

Calypso lowered her head and, through thick, black lashes, gave him a hard look. "Maybelleen seems so sincere, even if her brothers *are* in the military. She could do a lot better than Wheeler."

"I don't know why you have it in for him. You hardly know the man." Seth glanced at the building. "Anyway, I'm not much of a dancer."

Her face soft with love, Calypso kissed her husband,

slipped one arm around his waist and guided him toward the door. "Then we'll just have a drink and watch. And we can leave whenever you want."

Pushing past the door, they were rocked by a renewed volume of noise, underscored by a hollow, rhythmic stomp that rattled bottles and glasses and jiggled the round, wooden tables. The cavernous room was packed and, after a quick glance around, Calypso's body began to sway. Brazilians love crowds, adore music and dancing and staid Claremont, more closely resembling a small New England Village than a California university town, offered nothing like this.

"Come on," she urged, clasping Seth's hand.

Slowly, they shuffled through thick sawdust, weaving through and around the dense crowd as they maneuvered toward the far end of the room where figures on a platform seemed to be bobbing up and down. Everyone wore cowboy outfits, a multitude of voices were raised in shouted attempts at conversation, and the costumed bartenders moved in a blur of speed, frantically attempting to satisfy the mob of demanding customers.

"There she is!" Seth pointed to the raised plank stage, source of the heavy stomping, where lines of men and women faced the room, and occasionally one another, and performed intricate dance steps. Dressed in snakeskin boots, a fringed shirt, flouncy flowered skirt and a cowgirl hat, Maybelleen was in the front row.

"What? I can't hear you." Calypso looked at the dancers, and then a smile flashed across her face. "There's Maybelleen!"

Catching sight of the couple, Maybelleen waved energetically then twisted to mouth a few words to a very tall dancer on her right whose boots, shirt and hat matched hers. The man's long, platinum blond hair was caught in a ponytail, several thin metal bands glinted on one wrist and a silver conch belt cinched the waist of his very tight jeans.

"Who's she talking to?" shouted Seth.

"What? I still can't hear."

"Never mind."

The music ended and, as a new piece boomed forth, Maybelleen, followed by her dancing companion, bounced down from the platform and hugged Seth and Calypso.

"I was so afraid you wouldn't make it. Mama and Daddy came with us and guess who else is here?" Clearly audible, her reedy voice soared right over the din.

"Who?"

"Punky." Suddenly, her aquamarine eyes widened. "Oh, excuse me. This is my very best friend, Blossom Strong."

"Pleased to meet you both," Blossom rumbled in a bass voice as he shook hands with the couple.

He was at least six feet-three, lean but large-boned with a direct, level gaze that Calypso liked. "You and Maybelleen look like professionals up there," she commented.

Smiling easily, he shrugged. "We practice a lot."

Arm in arm with Blossom, Maybelleen forged a path through the crowd, heading straight for a large, round table tucked into a far corner of the room where an older couple sat holding hands and drinking beer. Asleep in his basket, a cat occupied the center of the table. A few feet from the table, she suddenly stopped, clutching Blossom's arm and staring toward the door.

"Look who's here," she breathed, addressing no one in particular.

Following her gaze, Calypso saw Wheeler and her friend Gil Givens pushing their way through the crowd. Grinning, Wheeler waved and jostled his way to Maybelleen's side where he gave her a quick kiss on the cheek.

"What a surprise!" Maybelleen exclaimed, turning toward the other three. "Don't those western clothes make Wheeler look exactly like John Wayne in *Rio Bravo*?" Squaring his shoulders, Wheeler gave the black cowboy hat a manly tug and contemplated wearing the outfit on a daily basis.

"Just my old Montana clothes," he responded modestly, nodding a greeting to Calypso and Seth.

"How'd you know we'd be here?" Maybelleen asked Gil.

Gil stepped forward, placed his mouth close to her ear and yelled truthfully, "I eavesdropped on your telephone conversation."

Her clear laugh tinkled gaily.

"Gil Givens, you're always teasing. Fellows, I want you to meet my best friend, Blossom Strong. Blossom, this is Gil, the airline mechanic I told you about and my wonderful boyfriend Wheeler."

"A pleasure," Blossom rumbled in his hearty baritone.

While Wheeler stared with glazed eyes, Gil stretched out his right hand. "Nice to meet you."

"Isn't this perfect? Mommy and Daddy are here too," pealed Maybelleen joyfully, leading the group to the table. "Look who I found," she announced, sweeping one arm toward Gil, Wheeler, Calypso and Seth.

"These are my parents, Steve and Babe Stockley, and that's Punky in the basket. Let's all sit down for a minute and get acquainted."

Blossom lowered himself carefully onto one of the light wooden chairs that looked more rickety than western. Calypso and Seth followed suit while Wheeler suddenly rocketed into action, pumping hands, smiling, holding a chair for Maybelleen and signaling the waiters. Acoustics had improved in this remote spot and conversation was possible; Calypso wondered whether this was an advantage.

"Glad you folks could join us," Steve said. "Maybelleen's talked an awful lot about you and we always want to meet her friends." He lit Babe's cigarette, then one for himself. "Beer okay for everyone?"

"Just fine," answered Calypso, sneaking an amused look at her husband, who normally drank only the best Scotch and now seemed to either be in a state of shock or mentally concentrating on intricate mathematical problems. She reached over and straightened his bow tie which, along with the evening, was askew.

"This place is great. Just terrific," Wheeler purred. "And in a Santa Monica strip mall, can you believe it?"

"Blossom found it," said Steve, ordering a round of beers and an ice tea for Maybelleen.

"You did?" Wheeler turned to Blossom with diminished enthusiasm, certain he detected a hint of mascara on the man's long lashes. Blossom carefully crossed his legs and folded his manicured fingers together. "You work around here, then?" Wheeler persisted.

"No."

The air quivered.

"Blossom's a supervisor at the Pasadena Post Office, even though he's the only white person there. He's in charge because he gets along with everyone," said Maybelleen, patting Blossom's large hand.

"Everyone at the post office," corrected Blossom, unbuttoning his cuffs and rolling up the sleeves of his shirt to expose muscular arms abundantly covered with dark brown hair. "My, it's just stifling in here."

Wheeler smirked meaningfully at Steve and Babe, both of whom smiled coolly back. Punky opened his eyes, stretched luxuriously and curled up again. Seth slid his chair closer to Maybelleen and leaned forward.

"You're a great dancer. Both of you are," he amended.

"Well thank you, Seth. It's lots of fun and I just wish Mommy and Daddy would give it a try," she said.

"I'm going to learn," Wheeler declared a shade too loudly, draining his beer and gesturing for another, "unless the guys have to wear blouses and ponytails." He tilted his glass toward Blossom's shirt and raised one eyebrow. "Blossom and I buy lots of outfits together. Some for bowling at Bertie's Alley and others for line dancing. We even have matching hair," Maybelleen said in a tone that was remarkably close to tartness.

"I have a lot of trouble with the roots," Blossom boomed.

Babe Stockley gave his hand a comforting pat.

"We all do, dear."

Calypso noticed that Seth was not only drinking his beer but doing so fairly quickly.

"Blossom's like a sister, isn't he Daddy?" Maybelleen persisted.

Steve lit another cigarette and nodded. "More sense than most sisters, I'd say."

Puzzled, Wheeler looked at Maybelleen and her parents, then at Calypso and Seth, receiving impersonal smiles in return. Absently, he stroked Punky who hissed quietly and nipped him on one finger. He recoiled in shock.

"Punky, that was very naughty," Maybelleen admonished mildly. Punky flicked his tail vigorously and closed his eyes. For a fraction of a second, Maybelleen wondered if her cat hadn't perceived a hidden, negative quality in Wheeler but then a new tune thundered through the room.

"They're playing my song," Maybelleen exclaimed joyfully.

"They are?" Wheeler and Gil asked cautiously.

"Of course. This one's called '*Maybelleen You've Got To Be True*,' and we always dance to it, don't we Blossom?"

"Sure do."

"But not this time because it's special having us all together."

Babe blew a few smoke rings while Wheeler glowered at the cat and sucked his wound. Clearing his throat for attention, Gil announced, "I have some good news, Maybelleen."

"What is it?"

"I told my boss what a terrific mechanic you are and how you've worked on bikes and cars, and then I went to the shop steward and talked to him. You'll have to go in for an interview and take a couple of tests, but I've found a place that will train you as an airplane mechanic. When you're certified, you can apply to my boss. Maybe he'll take you on as an apprentice."

Maybelleen's crimson lips formed a perfect 'O' and her eyes, outlined by extra-long false lashes, widened and glittered tearfully as she absorbed this unexpected news.

"Good for you," rumbled Blossom. "Congratulations." He knew better than anyone how desperately Maybelleen had longed for just this chance.

"My daughter the airline mechanic," mused Babe contentedly. Years ago she herself had wanted to be a nurse but there was no money. Over time, her goal had dimmed in an endless procession of hairdressing salons where she worked as an assistant beautician, handing the stylist bobby pins and clips and pretending she was slapping surgical instruments into a doctor's hands.

Balancing a large metal tray crowded with empty glasses aloft on one hand, a passing waiter paused. Someone's been watching a lot of old cowboy movies, thought Calypso in amusement, studying his black shirt, imitation leather vest, red paisley neckerchief and something that looked like a red checkered tablecloth tied around his waist as an apron.

"Can I bring you folks something?"

"You bet," exclaimed Steve, elated. "Bring us another round." Eyes bright with affection, he turned to his daughter: "You done us proud, May."

Flushed with excitement, Maybelleen shook her head. "I haven't done anything yet."

"But you will."

"I think it's just wonderful when you can have dreams come true," said Calypso, remembering the thrill and sense of disbelief she had experienced when, shortly after earning her doctorate, Claremont had offered her a teaching position.

After a moment, Maybelleen jumped to her feet and rushed around the table, dispensing hugs and kisses. Straightening, she raised her arms and face joyfully to the ceiling, staring at a swaying, pseudo-Tiffany chandelier directly overhead and whispered, "Thank you."

Stretching both arms wide, she shimmied exuberantly for a moment, the fringes on her blouse flying wildly. "Yippee," she cried, before perching on her chair once again. Leaning forward, she gazed reverently at Gil.

"It's what I've always wanted, to be an airline mechanic! We can share lunch pails and thermoses and belong to the same union and wear matching overalls. Blossom can come to pick us up after work sometimes, and we'll all line dance." Maybelleen failed to notice that Gil suddenly looked quite bewildered. "Daddy, isn't this simply wonderful?"

"Darn tootin'," Steve agreed, lighting Babe's long, thin cigarette.

Ignored, Wheeler now stood up and addressed Steve.

"And I have some news, too. This is really terrific, but I came here for a specific reason."

"To line dance?" said Maybelleen. "And meet Mama and Daddy?"

All attention was now focused on Wheeler, who allowed the suspense to build. Calypso suspected that, thumbs hooked into his leather belt, he was

searching for a subject that would outshine Gil's news. Seth stared at his two new beers, wondering how soon they could go home.

"All of you except Blossom must be aware that I want to make Maybelleen my wife."

Involuntarily, Calypso and Seth swiveled to stare at one another in shock, as Calypso's face contorted in confusion and she mouthed the word, "What?" Seth lifted his eyebrows and shoulders in a puzzled shrug. Stunned gasps from others around the table were nearly drowned by a sudden warble from Patsy Cline and the soulful echo of a harmonica. When the music seemed under control, Wheeler continued.

"We've gone on some serious bike rides, bowled and watched a whole lot of movies together over the past few months. I am determined to have this woman by my side for the rest of my life, but not without the approval of her parents." Slowly and dramatically he turned to face Maybelleen. "You are the only woman who's said you'd be with me when I hunt, ski and play tennis." He was wise enough not to add that she was also the only one he'd failed to maneuver into bed. Wheeler pivoted to face Steve and Babe. "I want to give your daughter a comfortable and stylish life."

Forehead wrinkled, Seth stared at his partner. Undeniably charming, effervescent and full of original ideas, Wheeler could be breathtakingly unpredictable. This was a perfect example and it offended and disturbed the accountant's sense of order and planning.

"Wait a minute, you haven't asked me." Maybelleen's wispy voice cut underneath the thwack of a banjo.

Blossom bent toward his best friend and Calypso heard him whisper, "Eighty-six him. The guys's a phony."

Maybelleen tilted her head in alarm and whispered, "You think?"

"Absolutely, girlfriend."

Calypso wished she knew Maybelleen well enough to add her voice to Blossom's, but these were new acquaintances and she didn't dare. Besides, she was foreign and, in spite of her nearly perfect English, there was a chance she had missed a nuance, misinterpreted a phrase or didn't understand the cultural background of one or all of them. Silently, she strained to hear the rest of the conversation.

"You could be wrong," Maybelleen said hopefully. "He's very polite. Good looking and smart. And he has a beautiful office. I have strong, warm feelings when I'm with him, too."

"So? You also have strong, warm feelings toward Punky who is polite, good looking, smart and is sleeping in his beautiful office right now."

Blossom scowled at Wheeler. Wheeler tried to reciprocate in kind while smiling at the rest of the group.

Maybelleen's laugh lifted over Patsy Cline's highest note. "But Blossom, I think I'm probably in love with him. I mean Wheeler, not Punky."

Blossom shook his head. "You've known him for less than a year."

Wheeler advanced on Mr. and Mrs. Stockley, removed his hat and squatted awkwardly beside Steve. "Sir, will you permit me to marry your daughter?"

It took Maybelleen's father only two seconds to make up his mind. "Bet your boots, Wheeler. You seem to have your head on straight and I know you make my daughter happy. Babe and I got married three days after we met and that was twenty-five years ago. Go for it, son."

Beaming, Wheeler struggled clumsily to his feet, clapped the cowboy hat back onto his head and adjusted the small, black silk square tied around his neck. At the sound of Steve's stern voice, he froze.

"But only on two conditions."

"Conditions, sir?"

"The wedding has to be in the Pasadena Methodist Church where our family worships every Sunday." Wheeler opened his mouth to speak but Steve held up a warning hand. "You know we believe in the Ten Commandments and we read the Bible together every evening. I want Maybelleen to start her married life on the right track, like her Mama and I did."

"Of course we'll have a church wedding," responded Wheeler eagerly. "And you can depend on me to be very religious once I know what the Methodist rules are."

"God," mumbled Gil sacrilegiously.

Calypso frowned and gripped her husband's hand. "*What* is going on? I thought we came to keep Maybelleen company and learn how to line dance."

"Don't ask me. Maybe Wheeler's still on the rebound and she thinks he's romantic and adventurous. Or something... I don't know either of them that well but I do know one thing."

"What?"

He grinned, leaned to the side and rubbed his cheek against Calypso's. "I've been saved from the dreaded line dance."

Involuntarily, they both glanced toward the platform where heads bobbled up and down in time to the music, then turned to one another and smiled.

"Isn't he wonderful? So respectful and mannerly to Mommy and Daddy," Maybelleen whispered to a sullen Blossom. Studying her friend's face, Maybelleen fluttered her lashes in concern and covered Blossom's large hands with her own. "Now don't be like that," she pleaded. "I know you're very smart about people and situations but this time I think you're worried about our friendship. I love you dearly, Blossom. I hope you know you'll *always* be my best friend, no matter what."

Blossom shook his head, the blond ponytail swinging from side to side, and wordlessly squeezed Maybelleen's hands in his own.

"There's just one other item," Steve announced. "We have to move house before the wedding."

"Move?" Wheeler was baffled.

"I guess Maybelleen didn't tell you that moving's kind of a hobby with us. We get restless every six or eight months, and it's about that time again."

"You like moving?"

"Does a dog have fleas? We just load up the furniture on one of the trucks I drive and take it someplace new. We've lived all over. Bell Gardens, Van Nuys, Cerritos, Hawaiian Gardens, East Pasadena, Alhambra, Norwalk..." Wheeler's face reflected alarm as his future father-in-law listed the most dangerous, impoverished areas in greater

Los Angeles. "Kids went to at least ten schools, but it didn't hurt them none. They enjoyed making new friends, didn't you, Maybelleen?"

"Yes we did, Daddy."

"Then I hope we can move you soon, Sir, and book the church," said Wheeler.

"That's the ticket. Let's get this show on the road," agreed Steve, taking a swallow of beer. He grinned at Wheeler and waved the glass. "The Methodist Church don't approve, but I figure beer's the same as soda pop."

Wheeler nodded and moved toward Maybelleen, his arms lovingly extended. "Say the word, Maybelleen. Say you'll marry me and we'll live happily ever after."

Blossom glared at the groom-to-be.

"God," Gil muttered again.

Fingers intertwined, Calypso and Seth stared blankly at the others.

"Can I still be an airline mechanic?" Maybelleen asked anxiously.

"Anything you want, sweetheart," Wheeler responded.

"Then I accept your proposal." Maybelleen's voice was high and thin but very firm. By showing old-fashioned respect and courtesy toward her parents, Wheeler had won her over.

After a toast and another beer, Calypso bent close to Seth, her face clouded with concern. "I think we should go." Only too happy to comply, he nearly leapt from the table.

As her husband started the car, Calypso fastened her seat belt, and then gazed straight ahead through the windshield. "I think you should reconsider this whole Bailey telecom deal."

Seth was startled. "Why?"

"You're a serious accountant with a fine reputation and you're an excellent teacher. You've also been successful as a consultant with Jackson, but the minute Wheeler got into the picture it all changed."

"How? What are you talking about?"

She shrugged helplessly, turning toward her husband. "I can't explain it, but I have a bad feeling. Everything's just slightly wrong and out of focus."

He smiled reassuringly. "Woman's intuition, is it?"

"This is not funny. We both love our work, do it well and have a wonderful life together with no real problems. I can feel it beginning to shift."

For a moment he was tempted to give in, agree to her demands, and then he felt once more that long-buried flare of excitement at the idea of high risk and illegal profits. Reaching out, Seth gently pushed a few errant tendrils of curly hair behind her ears, and then stroked her cheek with one finger.

"I'll admit this is an odd situation, but don't worry. Wheeler's absolutely solid, and the project is going to work one hundred percent."

FIVE—LOS ANGELES

*V*irginia and Calypso emerged from the upscale Marketplace Grill on Sea Breeze and stood for a moment, stunned by the fierce, early afternoon sun. Slipping on her wraparound sun-glasses, Virginia frowned and peered irritably up and down the street.

"Where *is* that blockhead? All he has to do is answer his cell and drive the car."

"I'm sure he'll be here soon," Calypso murmured. "Thanks for lunch. I had no idea there was such a wonderful restaurant in Venice; I guess I'm pretty isolated out in Claremont."

A horn tooted and they spied Virginia's yellow Bentley rounding the corner and speeding toward them. Virginia's scowl vanished.

"Actually, some of the best restaurants in L.A. are here in Venice. This whole area used to be an appallingly seedy beach slum."

"So I hear."

"We'll have to bring you in from the sticks more often."

The women smiled easily at one another. Much as she

enjoyed joining Virginia in occasional lunches and forays to museums and galleries, Calypso loved living in Claremont. It had bistros, not elegant restaurants, and small shops instead of malls, and was quiet, leafy and tranquil. And she never thought of it as the sticks.

Virginia's Bentley glided to the curb and Vincent hopped out. With a dramatic flourish, he opened the back door and bowed. Stifling a grin, Calypso slid in, followed by Virginia. Vincent slammed the door, skipped around the car, bowed, tipped one finger to his cap and stationed himself behind the wheel.

"You certainly took your time, Vince. I want to ask you a question."

"Speak, Toots."

"Have you never heard of respect? I'm your employer. And I think I detect the faint odor of a marijuana cigarette in my Bentley. Am I right?"

"Is that the question?"

"Just answer."

"I had a little toke while I was waiting for you to finish your chow-down. Just to keep me warm and pass the time of day."

"It's over one hundred today so next time you're hit with a chill, turn off the air conditioner, open the window and bake. I have this unreasonable fear of dying that surfaces when I know my driver's stoned out of his gourd."

"Gotcha, sweets."

Her chocolate-colored eyes sparkling with amusement, Calypso looked out the window. Initially, she'd been shocked by the insults Virginia and her driver hurled at one another and embarrassed to be a witness to such mutual humiliation. However, in the months following Pete's initiation into the consultancy, she and Virginia had become friends and she'd discovered that this verbal jousting was a game expressing, in a peculiar way, reciprocal confidence and affection.

Calypso's eyes fastened on the driver. Dark, with a carefully trimmed mustache and hard, brown eyes that had probably seen everything, the twenty-eight-year-old chauffeur was short and deceptively slight. Virginia had told her he was also quick, strong and totally unprepared for gainful employment or useful leisure time unless both of those projects happened to include gang activities or driving, stealing and/or repairing a car. Right after her divorce eight years ago, Virginia had put him to work fiddling and tinkering with her car as well as serving as her driver/handyman.

It seemed to be a happy arrangement. According to Virginia, Vince's salary per year was more than he'd expected to earn, legally, in his entire lifetime. The man was often impudent and cocky but he had half the underworld up and down the California coast at his fingertips and, with him outside her door, under her car or behind the wheel, Virginia confessed that she felt safe and almost happy. Over the years, which Calypso surmised must have been quite lonely, Vince had become Virginia's trusted friend and her closest confident.

Now, dressed in the gray uniform which he considered a spiffy symbol of authority, Vincent piloted the car through afternoon traffic with expertise and aplomb. Virginia leaned toward Calypso and muttered, "Thank God he doesn't have a joint stuck over his right ear." She failed to add that it was another mark of rank and status in his peer group, and one he was very reluctant to relinquish.

"We going to Miz Webb's place now?"

"Right, Vince. That's where we going." Virginia turned to Calypso. "She didn't mention a time? Like morning or afternoon?"

Calypso shook her head. "Just said to drop by and see her new house."

"Well, I don't normally *drop by* but I'd like to see both her and the house." Virginia paused. "Maybe she knows what the men are up to."

"Like I said, they're probably busy getting this project off the ground."

It was a hope, not a belief. Over lunch, Virginia had confided misgivings about the Brazilian undertaking based on Jackson's uncharacteristic stress, preoccupation and short temper. Although Calypso had dismissed her friend's concerns, she herself had begun to notice signs of tension and detachment in Seth as well as a strange reluctance to discuss anything concerning his new business. The car crept down Pacific Avenue, part of heavy beach traffic that must be permanent since today wasn't a holiday nor was it summer. On the right, tiny one-story clapboard shacks, most with plate glass windows displaying bathing suits, surf-boards, bicycle parts and tacky souvenirs, separated the street from the beach. Calypso inched her window down, hoping to smell the ocean but instead sucked in a lung full of air saturated with the odor of slightly rancid grease and frying hamburger meat. Wincing, she rolled up the window. In Boiçucanga, where her family had a beach house, you heard the birds, felt the salt breeze and smelled the sea.

As the line of vehicles inched forward, Calypso studied the mob that crowded the pavement, jostling one another for space, clambering in and out of the shops. Most wore bathing suits of some sort and many were shoeless; all had on sun-glasses. How strange, she thought. In Brazil everyone was barefoot and in bikinis on the beach but the minute they stepped off the sand, feet slid into sandals and women wrapped themselves in kangas, or sarongs. She had been startled by the "no bare feet" and "shirts required" signs posted on the entrances of restaurants, pharmacies and clothing shops in Venice. She breathed a soft sigh. And just when she thought she knew all about her adopted country.

Reaching the traffic light, Vince swung left on Venice Boulevard and accelerated. Brushing invisible dust from her ivory silk suit and tossing her fox stole over one shoulder, Virginia snuck a covetous peek at Calypso's long beige linen skirt and finely embroidered batiste blouse. She wondered, not for the first time, how her friend always managed to look casual and just right for every occasion. During the fat part of her life, which was most of it, Virginia had dressed in shapeless and voluminous jumpers and overalls. It was only when she pared down to emaciation that she discovered the joy of clothes but, after so many years spent avoiding the thought and sight of her own body, she had an uncertain sense of fashion. Despite a zealous pursuit of Vogue and Elle, she was never sure whether the ensembles she put together were elegant and unusual or simply odd. Virginia's apparent dedication to shopping masked a constant search for the perfect outfit which, of course, she never found.

"A little hot for the dead animal, ain't it?" Vince asked, winking at the furry scarf in the rear view mirror. "You'll probably melt into a puddle of butter like that Black Sambo dude."

Virginia adored furs. She owned several and used them year round anywhere and everywhere, including the grocery store, despite the fact that Los Angeles temperatures rarely dropped below fifty degrees. In San Francisco, she thought wistfully, the climate had been much more cooperative, but she didn't intend to mold her life to California weather.

"I'm perfectly comfortable. Go up Doheny onto Sunset."

The chauffeur stopped winking and stared at her for a moment in the mirror.

"You want I should drive to Hollywood instead of the Webb's house?"

"You're very perceptive."

He was puzzled. "What for? You want a quick poke or something?"

Refinement wasn't his big point. She shot a glance at Calypso and caught the flash of the latter's broad, quickly smothered smile.

"No, Casanova. Remember, I *am* your *employer*, not one of your low-life mall-dolls."

"No assassination, huh? Man, you cut me up so bad."

"The word is assignation, Vince. And please remember, we have a guest in the car who is a cultured university professor unaccustomed to gangster-speak. Not that it's any of your business, but she needs to pick up a book or two at Pickwick's on Sunset."

"Please don't go out of your way for me," protested Calypso. "They always mail my books."

Virginia dismissively waved one perfectly manicured hand. "It's not out of our way at all, just a different route. And you can browse and see your friends. *Lots* more fun than the mail..."

"Well, thank you very much," Calypso said. Virginia was, she reflected, a very thoughtful and kind person, despite her tough, occasionally aggressive exterior. Over lunch, Calypso had mentioned Pickwick's, an independent bookshop owned by two of her Chilean friends, and spoken of the small support she tried to lend by purchasing books from them through the mail rather than patronizing chain stores in Claremont. In spite of Virginia's claim, Calypso knew this detour was definitely out of their way, one that would be a real treat for her.

In silence, they turned onto Doheny and began a gradual ascent. Vincent maneuvered the car onto the Strip, a section of Sunset Boulevard lined with chic night clubs, fashionable bistros and elegant shops. The street was luxurious, expensive and an odd contrast to the homes, some lavish and others modest, that dotted the nearby hills. Minutes later, Vincent swerved toward the curb, stopped abruptly and Calypso jumped out of the car.

"I won't be a minute," she promised.

As she hurried toward the door of Pickwick Books, Vince twisted around in the driver's seat. "You don't want to trot along with our cultured guest?" he asked.

"I want to have a little chat with you. What do you think of my husband?"

His black eyes were trained on hers: "You mean Mr. Morrissey?"

"That's right; my *current* spouse. The guy you usually call Sneaky Pete."

She saw the flesh around her driver's eyes puff up and knew he was enjoying a silent guffaw.

"It's not funny, Laughing Boy. Just tell me what you think."

"Truth, huh?"

"Yes. You've heard that word before, I suppose."

"Okay, boss-lady; you asked for it. I think the guy's a real asshole. A triple plus, number one bastard who's in love with himself and thinks he has to screw everything that wears a skirt to prove how macho he is."

"I know all that," she said impatiently, "but do you think he has any good qualities?"

"Not really."

"What about the company? Can he do any actual work here?"

"Nope. Toots, the day Sneaky Pete met you he hit the jackpot, and when you wrestled Cuz Jackson to the ground so's he'd hire Mr. Morrissey, that dude knew he had the Big Bentley for life." He turned to face the steering wheel again.

Virginia contemplated the back of her driver's neck. Brash, uncultured and uncouth, Vince was shrewd and very perceptive when it came to reading people. Intuitively, she felt he was absolutely right about Pete, whom she'd met in San Francisco when, recently lean through the miracles of plastic surgery and diet, she was divorced and lost and he was a practicing Lothario employed in Gump's advertising department. He was the kind of knock-out male she needed, at that time, to have on her arm, and his spinelessness meant she could mold him as she pleased. That's what she'd attempted, although it certainly hadn't worked.

Vince suddenly opened his door, bounded out of the car and around to the curb where he flung open the back door. Calypso, smiling broadly, and weighted by an enormous and obviously heavy bag, slipped inside. As Vincent returned to the driver's seat and started the car, she tipped the bag so that Virginia could see the contents.

"That was great fun. I have absolutely no sales resistance when it comes to books."

They both stared at the volumes.

"How'd you find so many so fast?"

Calypso laughed: "Practice."

At the end of the Strip, Sunset Boulevard broadened into a thoroughfare that stretched, dipped and wound through Beverly Hills, between gated estates, under large overarching trees, past The Beverly Hills Hotel and UCLA and on toward the beach. As they swept into a curve, Calypso gazed at a huge faux-English Tudor mansion on the right, shaded by leafy trees and protected by a high iron fence; at the top of a rise, a miniature version of Versailles loomed beyond a stone wall. Who would want to live here, she wondered, thinking of her own Claremont home, a comfortable nest into which she burrowed. Virginia frowned slightly and stroked the red fur.

"Ferguson phoned me."

Unsure whether she or Vince was being addressed, Calypso made an encouraging noise in her throat. Vincent seemed to have no such doubts.

"Yeah? You still got the hots for him after all those husbands and years." It was not a question.

Virginia inhaled sharply. "No, I don't, and it's one other husband and not that many years," she stated defensively. Calypso decided to keep her ears open and her mouth shut.

"Count again. So what's he want?"

"Me to go into business with him; this time in Baja."

"Do it. The dude's straight arrow and when you stop

being bossy, you're pretty much like him. You both laugh a lot, love the country and hate those politician pricks. Play your cards right and you could marry him again."

Vince was sometimes far too astute.

"I *am* married, Dr. Freud, and I didn't ask for a character analysis. In case you've forgotten, we separated because he wouldn't leave the cabbage patch and come back to live in San Francisco. A city that I think is divine."

Irritation didn't quite cover the traces of wistfulness in her voice. Calypso stared out the window as Vince's uniformed shoulders lifted in a shrug.

"Whatever... I notice you're not in Frisco now."

"Only tourists and illiterates call it Frisco, as you well know. Let's start again. I want you to train your great brain on whether you think it's practical for me to undertake a very time-consuming project one hundred fifty miles from here."

Vince shrugged again: "Why not? You don't do nothing else."

Her criminal driver had echoed Ferguson, a gentleman by anyone's standards, who managed unintentionally, in their friendly and very correct phone conversations, to make her feel that her life was trivial, superficial and sleazy. Suddenly, Virginia swiveled toward Calypso.

"How about it? What do you think?"

Startled by the unexpected question, Calypso felt her face flush. She knew all too well how idle and bored her friend now felt and had long suspected that Virginia's only real happiness had been with her first husband. However, like most Brazilians, Calypso disliked confrontation and had always taken great care to avoid offending others; when she spoke, her words were carefully chosen.

"I think it's your life and you should do what you want."

Virginia snorted disdainfully and Calypso was sure she heard a chuckle from the front seat. Rebuffed, she sank into the corner.

Vince turned off Sunset and headed into Santa Monica Canyon, the road now a shady, two-lane affair that dipped and rose, twisting between high hills covered with scrub and leafy trees. Homes were scattered, set well back from the street, and often partially hidden behind dense thickets, huge trees and profusely blooming, climbing vines. Virginia addressed the back of Vince's head.

"Before we get there, do we know anything more about the Webbs? Other than the fact that they were married not too long ago in the Pasadena First Methodist Church."

"Dude comes from Vegas."

"Wonderful. Do we address him as Capo Wheeler?"

"He lived somewhere else, too. Montana, maybe..."

"I know all that. What about Maybelleen?"

Virginia saw her driver's eyelids crinkle with laughter. "I only seen her once but she looks like that dead chick Marilyn Monroe only fatter and she rides a yellow Harley Davidson."

"Sometimes you're absolutely useless."

Easing toward the right, Vincent stopped beneath an enormous oak tree that shaded both a redwood ranch-style house and a smooth, dark green lawn that sloped gently toward the street. A pleasant clutter of flowers bordered the driveway, outlined the flagstone path leading to the door and filled a bed along the front of the residence. Vince switched off the engine and opened his door, pausing to frown at the ground.

"Hey, they got no sidewalks, like in Tijuana."

"North of the border, a lack of pavement is found in wealthy areas, my friend. Such as Carmel."

He chuckled, stood up and opened the back door. "Get real, boss lady. Lotsa streets in East L.A. got no sidewalks. Houses are dumps with dirt floors and corrugated roofs and no phones or indoor toilets and the people got squat for jobs and cash."

Calypso stepped out, followed by Virginia who tossed the fur over one shoulder.

"I'm not interested in your relatives' living arrangements, or their fortunes. And stay off the funny tobacco."

As Virginia rang the bell in the recessed entryway, Calypso studied the olive-toned double doors with inset strips and panels painted a grey-blue. Interesting, like the muffled music and laughter they could hear inside. The door opened and the strains of country & western music swelled.

"Hi, Maybelleen; I hope we're not interrupting your afternoon."

"Of course not; I'm so glad you could come for a visit," Maybelleen said. "I'd give you hugs, but I'm afraid you'd get all dirty."

Although her hair and make-up were perfect, a crumpled and stained plaid work shirt, and jeans liberally streaked with grease and tied at the ankles over battered Doc Martens cloaked Maybelleen's slightly plump figure. Wiping her hands on a rag, the new Mrs. Webb stepped back and waved her guests inside. Unwillingly, Virginia remembered the old days when she and Ferguson had worked long hours in the vineyard, both of them grimy, exhausted and completely happy.

"This is beautiful," Calypso exclaimed, stepping into the entryway.

Directly ahead, the foyer opened onto an enclosed garden filled with flowers and shrubs that extended to a swimming pool at the far end. Two sides of the courtyard were paved with flagstones and shaded by a beamed, redwood roof; to the left, a glass door to the living room stood open.

"Thank you. Starr Bailey helped me decorate." Virginia clamped her lips together disapprovingly. "I've been tinkering with the Harley over there," Maybelleen continued, waving toward a partially disassembled yellow Harley Davidson on a large canvas tarp. "I wanted to do it in the driveway, but Wheeler said the neighbors would think we're hicks."

Wheeler was probably right, Calypso reflected.

"Virginia, I want you to meet my best friend, Blossom Strong. He's a supervisor at the Pasadena Post Office, but this is his day off and he's practicing some line dancing steps."

Blossom, blond hair in a ponytail and wearing tight, black leather trousers with a white matador shirt, moved toward the visitors. For a few seconds he and Virginia scrutinized one another, she taking careful note of the high cheekbones, cleft chin and, most of all, the hazel eyes that somehow reminded her of Ferguson's. As she extended her hand, they smiled cordially at one another.

"It's a pleasure." He turned to Calypso. "So nice to see you again, Mrs. Laskar."

"You must call me Calypso."

"I just love your fur," Maybelleen said, staring at the animal's tail which seemed to be stuffed into its mouth. She examined one of several paws that drooped limply on Virginia's shoulder. "It's amazing that they could leave his head and little feet attached."

"Yes."

"Come see the house," she said eagerly. "It's just so gorgeous, the best place I've ever lived. I don't ever want to move. We have real roll-up bamboo shades and a covered porch that Starr calls a dining terrace and music piped all over the house. And two built-in ovens in the kitchen!" She smiled at her visitors, her eyes twinkling behind the fake eyelash screen.

"We'd love to see it all," responded Virginia as the group moved toward the glass door. "I imagine Wheeler can't wait to get home every evening."

"He's just so busy, I don't think he even notices the house," she responded, the happy lilt in her voice gone. "He's hardly here on weekends."

"Oh really?" asked Virginia softly. "Maybe he's under some stress. I wonder, Maybelleen, has he mentioned anything lately about what's going on in the business? Anything unusual?"

Maybelleen thought for a minute then slowly shook her head. "He really never talks about work to me except to say that we are going to be very rich."

Calypso stared through the tinted window of Virginia's luxury automobile at the tawdry streets of the Hollywood flats, dismay clearly written on her face. Lined with sex shops, discount clothing stores and adult film theaters, they were jammed with both predators and victims day and night. Boy and girl runaways from small towns all over America arrived penniless and friendless to be captured almost immediately outside the Greyhound station by cruising "talent scouts" for erotic publications and films. Older men and women with tired, sad eyes who had seen it all and knew the score, stood in doorways hustling money, drugs and people, selling anything available including bodies that, by age thirty, looked two decades older and bore both visible and hidden scars. Weaving in and out of decaying buildings, buying dinner from the hot dog stands and hoping every day for nothing, they had tried and failed and now, skimming the edge of poverty and usually out of legitimate work, they lived in the dark, dismal singles apartments that crammed the area from Franklin to Melrose. I am incredibly lucky, Calypso mused, mentally comparing this stark scene with small, lush Claremont and her own comfortable, tree-shaded home.

"Vincent, why did you choose this particularly unsavory route?"

"I thought a cultured university professor might like to deal with the real."

"You thought wrong, Einstein. Slums are *not* us."

"You wanna see East L.A., Toots? Maybe catch a shoot-out?"

"Mrs. Morrissey, to you chum, and we want to go directly home."

It was a city of desperate, worn-out failures, crumbling stucco buildings and mildewed dreams. Calypso watched a young woman in shorts and a tank top conversing with an imaginary friend at a bus stop and felt intense pity for everyone in sight. Propelled by ambition and starry hopes, they'd hit Hollywood like meteors and exploded on impact, their dust unnoticed in a city whose appetite for fresh talent and beauty was both infamous and insatiable.

Calypso looked at her watch, then at Virginia. "I really have to start back soon or I'll get caught in rush hour traffic." Greater Los Angeles was sliced, diced and defined by innumerable, intersecting freeways and broad, major thoroughfares, all of which were clogged with SUVs and sports cars and were impassable in early morning and late afternoon.

"Come for a cocktail and drive home later." Her voice was wistful.

"I'd love to, but I can't. Traffic doesn't slow down till eight or nine."

"Next time then..."

As they waited at a red light, a man dressed in a duck costume complete with head, tail and large yellow feet, pushed a shopping cart filled with clothing across the intersection. An aging crone that emphasized her vague resemblance to Elizabeth Taylor with garish make-up and harshly dyed black hair planted herself directly in front of the duck and lifted her skirt to shoulder height. Although she wore no underwear, the man passed her without a glance.

"Screenwriters can't even think up this shit," exclaimed Virginia sharply, leaning forward to tap the driver's seat. "I just told you to get us out of here."

Calypso stared at Vince's profile, suddenly aware that his eyes were trained on a car in the right hand lane. Following his gaze, she saw a lowered, two-tone Trans-am filled with Latino men of Vincent's age, all of them wearing white undershirts, hair nets low on their foreheads, gold chains and tattoos. The driver nodded to Vince, flashed him a gang sign which was returned and then, just as the light changed, accelerated noisily, peeling rubber. The car spun left in front of the Bentley, crashed against the left front fender of a shiny, red BMW waiting at the intersection, and then sped away.

"My God, Vince, your relatives should only be allowed out with keepers."

Traffic stopped, creating a perfect gridlock. Vehicle doors opened and eager witnesses emerged, scampering toward the damaged car. The driver, a tanned, freckle-faced woman wearing a skimpy chartreuse jump suit that accentuated her absolutely perfect figure, leapt out to scrutinize her fender, joined by a gathering number of spectators who gravely studied the dent. Considering the force of impact, it was relatively small.

Unable to move, Vince turned off the engine. Reaching into the glove compartment, he pulled out a switch-blade and what appeared to be a collection of traffic tickets. Opening the knife, he began slowly shredding tickets into the ashtray. Virginia stared hard at the woman, her forehead knotted.

"I've seen her somewhere. Does she look familiar to you, Calypso?"

"No." Actually, Calypso thought she was indistinguishable from most Southern Californians; blond and tan with blue eyes.

"Maybe she's one of your club buddies that speak with fringed tongue."

"That's *forked* tongue, Vincent," she corrected. "Go back to remedial English class."

The woman straightened and looked around accusingly, her thunderous glance resting briefly on Vincent. The concerned citizens clustered around her gestured, pointed, and conferred with one another, mouths busily flapping, as she scowled wrathfully at the small dent. Lips compressed and a hard glint in her eye, she finally stamped to her car, got in and slammed the door. Magically, the crowd dispersed and traffic began to move.

Snapping the knife closed, Vincent slipped on his mirrored sun glasses and started the car. Snatching his cap from the passenger seat, he jammed it onto his head and swung the car right on Third. The scenery changed almost immediately. Vast homes with meticulously manicured lawns and clipped hedges appeared on either side of the broad boulevard and those few pedestrians in sight were comfortingly dressed either in the pastel uniforms of the exclusive Marlborough School for Girls or the starched whites that denoted domestic servitude.

Virginia noticed none of it. She turned to Calypso, looking through the other woman as she searched her memory.

"I *do* know that woman. I just can't remember how or where."

From Virginia's tone, Calypso doubted that the association had been a pleasant one.

SIX—LOS ANGELES

*H*is fingers tightened on the window sill as Jackson watched five chicly dressed women emerge from the dining room and drift down the pathway toward the gate and into the street beyond. In the office behind him, Wheeler was on the phone while Seth reviewed spreadsheets. In the adjoining room, a secretary prepared papers and documents for the Brazilian lawyers and authorities. It was urgent that Jackson himself contact their Brazilian engineer and discuss the presentation they were scheduled to make to a prospective vendor, but he couldn't seem to move. He wasn't able to take his eyes off the evidence of Starr's increased extravagance despite his desperate pleas for her to at least cut back if not eliminate the entertaining altogether.

The women paused to admire a carefully tended rose garden and then Jackson saw his wife appear, stunning in a navy blue pinstripe suit over a V-neck white blouse, her arm linked with that of an internationally renowned actress. Her head tilted in a laugh, Starr strolled to the gate with her guests, waved them off, then strode back toward the house, her face set and determined. Physically, she is exquisite, Jackson thought with a flash of anger as she disappeared into the dining room. Since the day they first met, she a freshman on a dance scholarship at Northwestern University and he an MBA candidate, he had tried to make her happy. And for a while, it had worked, or at least he thought so. Jackson couldn't remember when the slow, subtle erosion of their relationship had begun, nor could he pinpoint the reason, but both he and Starr knew their marriage might now be past salvation.

"Be right back," he said, turning toward the door.

Seth glanced up, annoyed.

"Jackson..."

"I know. We're on a tight schedule."

Frowning, Seth watched his partner cover the lawn with quick strides. A workaholic, Jackson was sincere, brilliant and principled; Seth felt honored to count him as a friend. But now he was wobbling, unable to commit to or withdraw from Wheeler's scheme, which meant the entire operation was rudderless and floundering. He bent over the spreadsheets again, listened to Wheeler's rich tones, and his scowl deepened.

"Trust me, Ted, you can't go wrong by investing in California Consultants. We're not some fly-by-night outfit; this is a deal backed by the Brazilian government." Mobile phone clamped to one ear, Wheeler slumped forward in a leather armchair, his free hand aimlessly twirling a magazine on the coffee table. "Absolutely dead certain to make millions, and I guarantee that you will be a rich man." He paused again, listening. "Taking out a loan on your plane would be the smartest thing you've ever done. Put those wings to *work*." A smile crept over his face. "Fantastic, Ted. Just give me a jingle when you've got the cash."

He clicked the off button, tossed the phone onto the sofa and raised both fists in the air.

"Another investor—and this one are kicking in big

bucks!"

Seth swiveled around to face Wheeler.

"We never agreed to bring in more partners."

"Who's talking partners? We're just accepting loans, which we'll pay back with lots of interest."

"*If* we're successful... Did Jackson authorize this?"

"I mentioned it to him and he didn't actually say anything, which I took as an affirmative."

"He may not have heard you correctly." Seth's enunciation was precise, his tone cold.

Wheeler raised both hands, palms out, as though to ward off a blow. "I know, I know, but we can't do business without money."

"The Company has funds," Seth stated, neglecting to add that the finances were very shaky, the dollars few.

"Just trying to help," Wheeler said, flashing his partner an engaging grin and retrieving the phone.

The accountant turned back to his books. Since Wheeler had joined them, Seth's feelings of accomplishment and satisfaction in their work had vanished, replaced by a vague uneasiness that everything was slowly spiraling out of control.

Jackson skirted the pool, slipped into the dining room and watched as the maid cleared dessert plates from a table covered with linen cloths embroidered to match the rose-patterned china. Crystal bowls filled with roses of the exact same shade had been placed in the center of the table and on the sideboards; after a moment, Jackson bent to sniff an arrangement. Hothouse. And expensive, especially when there was an entire rose garden less than twenty feet away. Anger curdled his stomach.

"I thought you were working."

At the sound of his wife's voice, he turned. Leaning against the wall, Starr held a large, open notebook.

"I was, but I need to speak to you."

A tiny wrinkle creased the smooth skin between her dark brown, arched eyebrows and her full under lip curled in a slight pout, a signal of impatience. She raised one hand to smooth a stray strand of hair, now retaining its ash blond tone with the help of chemicals.

"I'm very busy."

The odd, yellow-green eyes that had won her national fame as a teen-age model flashed sparks visible even at a distance.

"Is this a new table cloth? How about the china?"

"Not totally new."

"We cannot afford this. None of it. The food, the maid, certainly not new porcelain and custom embroidered linens. My work right now is absorbing almost all our savings, with practically nothing coming in." His voice was firm, betraying none of the smoldering irritation that spread through his body.

Stubbornly, Starr raised her smooth jaw. "That's not my problem, Jackson. I'm not just sitting around, you know. I work hard at my company, but I need to entertain. It's one reason Starr's Stars is so successful. If you'd paid attention, you would have noticed that the guests today were important celebrities who would forget me in a hot minute if I allowed it."

His tone hardened.

"Starr, please. Most of the people in this town have no style, and they know it. That's why they've depended on you to help them buy clothes, put on make-up, figure out their hair-do's and weed out their closets ever since you thought up Starr's Stars. They need your talent, not lavish parties."

Starr crumpled a notebook page in one fist, her breath coming in indignant, shallow gasps. "Much of my success depends on word of mouth. I learned that as an actress when I was a household word and was mentioned in the columns."

His forehead began to perspire. "You had small roles in two bad films." He was shocked to hear himself expressing a truth that had always been shrouded in fantasy but, anxious and angry, he was unable to stop. "You're enormously successful, but as the owner of Starr's Stars, not as an actress."

Tossing her sleek, blond hair dramatically over one shoulder, Starr flung her notebook on a table. Her throat ached with tears. As a young model she was a triumph, and as creator of Starr's Stars a brilliant meteor. But a model's career is very brief and recent competitors had stolen some of her wealthiest business clients. Loss of customers reversed Starr's fabulous income, and cash flow was now a waterfall of debts and obligations, a fact carefully hidden from her husband. When she spoke, her tone was defensive.

"The films weren't that bad and my career slowed down because I couldn't devote myself to full time acting. I put my family first."

The maid stopped working and listened intently to the escalating quarrel.

"That's bullshit." Jackson stepped tentatively forward. "Look, Starr, I've always given you everything you wanted, but now I need your help to make this new Brazilian project work. The very least you can do is cut out the extravagance. You might even contribute to some of the household expenses for a change."

If she believed just how precarious their finances were at the moment, she'd leave, Jackson thought, which might not be a bad thing. He watched Starr grip the back of a chair and twist her fists in opposite directions, as though wringing a cloth or choking her husband.

Contribute, she thought? In the best of times she'd never shared her income, and now the only donations she could make were a lot of unpaid, overdue bills. If he knew the state of her bank account, he'd be out the door in a second, and she'd be destitute.

"I can't," she said truthfully.

"Of course not. You spend my money and keep yours. I'm asking."

She hated him.

"Well, don't. Just because your grandmother was a socialite and you think your family is important doesn't make me your servant," she shrilled.

"Starr, I'm not—"

"Your father was just a Kansas lawyer, and that means he was a bumpkin driving a car instead of a tractor. No wonder the summers you spent at Granny Bailey's in San Francisco were the high points of your life." The words tumbled out in a rush of sarcasm. "Virginia and I went boating in Golden Gate Park, climbed the walls of Coit Tower, rode cable cars and spent a lot of time staring across the water toward Alcatraz while hoping to see an escaping convict. We had such fun. The good old days."

At that moment, he despised her. Exhausted, Jackson stared numbly at his wife and took a deep breath.

"That's way off the subject. We're talking about you sharing some of your earnings." His voice was husky. "The ones that always go straight into your own bank account."

"I've already said no."

"Your mother is one of this country's most famous milliners, and your father's no slouch with his chic Michigan Avenue tailor shop, but they both started out dirt poor in Sicily and they've always put their money in the same pot. Lucia and I had a chat about it once."

"Lucia?"

"Mrs. Gasparotti, your mother."

Shocked, her chartreuse eyes widened.

"You talked to my mama about our money?"

Jackson looked upward, as though silently praying for deliverance.

"How dare you? Stick to what you know, which is mostly Tyler, Kansas. Tell me for the thousandth time about good old Scouts and fishing and camping and the town's only swimming pool and its sole movie theater and the exciting bike rides around Courthouse Square. And about Daddy Dan, Tyler's only lawyer and Mommy Sybil, who never worked so she couldn't be expected to contribute actual bucks, but she was a busy, busy member of the Garden Club and Bridge Club and president of the Junior League. And the Methodist church every Sunday and golf..."

"That's enough, Starr."

Deliberately brutal, she hurled words as sharp as razors.

"It certainly is. But don't forget that you and both your sisters left and never went back, so the picture can't be as rosy as you remember," she shouted.

The maid slunk along the wall and vanished into the kitchen, closing the door with enormous care. Jackson stared dispassionately at his wife.

"The rosy picture, Starr, was my family. It was close and loving and my parents taught me about honesty and loyalty, bravery, kindness—all the worthwhile values—through the way they lived."

"Oh, yes, honesty and kindness from a lawyer. That's a hot one."

"And you know very well I've always felt guilty about leaving them alone in Tyler."

"They certainly didn't have to stay."

"Tyler's their home."

"A life of Junior League rummage sales and Country Club dances. Hard to leave," she snapped. "The problem is that you want a family just like the one you had in Tyler, and it hasn't happened. And kindly do not mention my income again." She retrieved her notebook. "I have work to do."

It was a curt dismissal.

Jackson shoved both hands into his trouser pockets and, for a moment, rocked silently from toe to heel and back again while he studied his wife. Ignoring him, Starr sank onto one of the dining chairs and began work in the notebook, flipping pages, writing and drawing quick sketches while trying to bring her erratic heartbeat under control. Slowly he turned and left the dining room, stopping on the flagstone walk to close his eyes and lift his face to the sun.

She was absolutely right. He wanted a kind, loving family. Instead, he had two non-communicative, adult children living in Seattle, a wife indifferent to him and his needs and a critical financial situation. Despite the fact that his life was in shambles, Jackson suddenly felt the easing of invisible shackles. With nothing left to lose and a very real chance to solve his financial problems, he was truly free to throw himself wholeheartedly into the shady scheme that Wheeler had concocted. He paused for only a moment. Nothing to lose, he thought uncomfortably, but the life-long principles he could no longer afford to keep.

SEVEN—Claremont

Calypso dug out her keys, dropped the heavy book bag on the porch, and leaned against the ornate railing, enjoying a moment of perfect peace and contentment. She loved this clapboard house with its wide porch, beveled windows and hardwood floors almost as much as she loved the half acre of ground on which it was built, and the university town of which it was part. Located an hour east of Los Angeles on the fringes of the California desert, Claremont was composed of quiet, safe streets, huge old trees with interlaced branches, and spacious wooden homes.

"Hi, Mrs. Laskar."

Grinning, the red-haired boy pedaled his bike across the lawn, wheels crushing dried leaves, and braked beside the porch steps. Carefully, he handed her the evening paper.

"Thanks, Billy."

Wistfully, she watched him ride back to the sidewalk and then execute a wheelie in front of the Geary home next door. In Sao Pedro da Aldeia, a small village north of

Rio where Calypso and her family had often vacationed, the adult paperboy rode a horse. Billy couldn't be more than ten. Tossing the paper next to the Geary front door, the boy righted his bike, bent over the handlebars and pedaled furiously down the street.

With a sigh, Calypso picked up her bag and paper, traced the delicate lines of the oval, stained glass window in the front door with one forefinger, and let herself into the empty house feeling a vague but familiar unhappiness. She loved her job as Associate Professor at Pomona, one of the linked Claremont Colleges, but Calypso thought that a family was only complete with children. In the two years that she and Seth had been married, she had been unable to conceive.

The doctor had said to give it time and keep trying, but she was thirty-three years old; many of her graduate students were younger than she but already had children in kindergarten or older. Seth, usually so perceptive and sympathetic, not only failed to understand her anxiety but seemed quite delighted with their present relationship, which he often described as wonderful and perfectly balanced. He was willing to accept parenthood if and when it happened, but he absolutely refused to undergo tests, discuss adoption or consider extreme measures such as artificial insemination. Calypso found this rigidity upsetting.

Raising the windows in the living room to admit the late afternoon breeze, Calypso caught a glimpse of her image in the large mirror over the fireplace and stared critically. With olive skin, brown eyes, fragile bone structure, long, bushy dark brown hair, and a casual but stylish sense of fashion, she was typically Brazilian in appearance, but no one in the States ever pegged her correctly. In her undergraduate days at Smith she usually identified as North African, Mexican, Black or Italian, and was often the target of racial remarks that left her puzzled and hurt before she toughened up. Even though she couldn't vote, these nasty episodes had prompted her to join the Democratic Party with its precept of ethnic and religious equality and, together with some other faculty members of this conservative group of colleges, she spent many Saturday mornings as a volunteer at the local Headquarters.

Her glance strayed to the framed wedding photo on the mantelpiece and she smiled broadly. Leaning forward, she mouthed a kiss toward Seth's image, and then blew it another kiss just as the telephone rang. Her eyes still clinging to the photograph, she moved across the room and picked up the receiver.

"Hello?"

"Dr. Laskar?"

"Yes."

"This is Marvin Beale." After a slight pause, the voice prompted, "I'm with Price Waterhouse in Chicago; I used to work with your husband."

Her fingers tightened around the telephone.

"Of course... How are you, Mr. Beale?"

"Good to go. Is Seth around?"

"I'm afraid you've missed him. He's in Brazil for at least another week." Calypso was unable to control the slight quaver in her voice.

"Oh?"

"He has a new business that takes him there quite often."

In reality, it was so often that the Company had rented a house in São Paulo.

"Lucky guy... How come you're not with him?"

"I teach." He was far too inquisitive. "May I give Seth a message?" Her tone was chilly, her words clipped.

"Yes, if you would be so kind. A couple of months ago Price Waterhouse decided to open a branch in Helena, Montana, and they sent me to set it up because I'm a state native. Problem is, I was born and raised in Butte, and it's my only area of expertise, especially after being away for so long. Seth's from Helena, though, so I tried to look up his folks just to say hello and chew the fat and see if they could give me some unofficial information about the city. That's valuable in case we decide to expand in the state. But I couldn't find a trace of his relatives. I thought maybe Seth could point me in the right direction."

Calypso smoothed her crinkled hair.

"His parents died in a traffic accident when he was about eighteen."

"I know that. Poor guy came to Chicago afterward to live with an aunt, and then she passed away too. I just thought there might be some family or old friends around. I sure would like to pick a few brains."

Slowly, she shook her head. "Seth hasn't mentioned anyone, but if he calls, I'll ask him. Where are you staying?"

"Until tomorrow night I'm at The Biltmore, and then back to Montana."

"Well, if I have any news, I'll let you know."

"Thanks. I'd appreciate it."

Slowly, she replaced the receiver and moved back to the old fashioned, carved stone mantel. Lifting the wedding photograph, she held it to the light and traced Seth's image with her forefinger. Even in the photograph, kindness, intelligence and honesty seemed to radiate from the all-American face that was not notable either for excessive attractiveness or lack of it. Staring at the streaks of grey in his straight hair, her lips thinned and she tapped the photograph thoughtfully against her open palm as she recalled that first phone call from Mr. Beale so long ago.

Not long after their wedding, she and Seth were cooking an elaborate gourmet dinner for themselves when they were interrupted by the telephone. Slicing mushrooms, peeling and seeding a cucumber and only vaguely aware of the conversation, Calypso heard her husband discuss a business matter and reminisce about Montana. Suddenly, his voice tensed and altered pitch. Forgetting her kitchen tasks, Calypso watched Seth pace rigidly from the wall phone to the butcher block and back, his face a study in anxiety. Later, smiling and sautéing the chicken, he explained that he and Marvin had relived an old high school football match between their alma maters that was so exciting it still left him nervous and stressed.

Calypso was neither reassured nor convinced. From her one-sided listening post, she knew he was telling the truth and the discussion did seem to concern a game that took place many years ago, which only added to her confusion. Seth was dependable, unshakable and completely level headed; there was no reason he should have been so uncharacteristically and visibly upset by a football game that took place decades earlier, especially since he wasn't a sports fan.

It was an incident that she had nearly forgotten but now the memory returned forcefully, dredging up other buried questions about his family. With the exception of his pet mouse, Sir Galahad, he never talked about his childhood, told funny anecdotes or complained about his parents; it was as if the rodent was his only relative. During their courtship, Calypso had approached the subject with great delicacy, hoping to learn more about Seth through knowledge of his background, but mention of his family seemed to bring him such pain that she stopped inquiring. But not wondering. After all, he was fifteen years her senior and, at forty-eight, he'd had plenty of time to recover from almost any adolescent trauma.

She looked at her watch. A quarter to six. Feeling vaguely irritated, she dialed the number of the elegant mansion the partners had rented in São Paulo. On the fourth ring she heard Seth's soft voice informing her that he was unable to pick up the phone and inviting her to leave a message.

"Where are you?" she whispered, torn between worry and anger. "It's nearly midnight Brazilian time. And don't tell me you're in Minas Gerais again. Marvin Beale called and wanted to know if you had any family he could look up in Montana. Call me when you get in."

Replacing the receiver, she stared at the wedding photograph. Theirs had always been the perfect marriage, with trust, love and understanding on both sides. Now, he was spending more time in Brazil than in Claremont, frequently incommunicado in the state of Minas Gerais. If the trips were to Rio, Brasilia or even Salvador or Recife, it would be perfectly normal, but there were only mines, agriculture and old colonial towns in Minas. And, since the company project was satellite surveillance in the Amazon Basin, this just didn't add up.

Calypso poured herself a glass of wine, retrieved her book bag and moved into the small study that she and her husband shared. Automatically spreading out tomorrow's lecture notes, she gazed thoughtfully at Seth's half of the room. Flanked by an entire wall of bookshelves crammed with volumes they had both collected, her husband's leather-topped Italian desk was nearly bare, with only a small brass clock, a framed photograph of Calypso and an agate paperweight precisely arranged on the right hand side. His computer and printer, both carefully draped with protective plastic covers, rested on a wheeled table nearby. Calypso's own large and unattractive metal filing cabinet, close to her cluttered writing table, was in constant use while Seth had no files in evidence.

Abandoning any intent to work, Calypso moved to her husband's swivel chair, sat down and opened the center desk drawer. A smile of affection illuminated her face. Her students would say Seth was anal retentive, but Calypso found his meticulous organization an endearing quirk and an odd reassurance of the stability she found so important. Note pads were precisely stacked, pencils and pens grouped according to color and exactly aligned, and staples, clips, tape and push pins neatly housed in labeled plastic boxes. As in his life, everything was in order.

Calypso hesitated only a moment before opening the right hand desk drawer, which she knew contained the few personal files that were not kept at his office. Although Seth had never indicated that this was a private area, it was the first time Calypso had opened the drawer and she felt like a snoop. Resolutely, she leafed through the manila folders in suspended metal frames, each carefully labeled, wondering why she felt so guilty when she was only searching for information about her husband's family. Surely that couldn't be off limits.

Tax reports, receipts for utilities and telephone payments, mortgage payments, stock reports and bank statements had been arranged by date; nothing unexpected, interesting or informative. As she replaced the household inventory file, a folder titled only 'Bank-N' caught her eye. Removing the file, she opened it, puzzled by a stack of deposit slips from the Daly City National Bank. All the very large amounts were identical and the recipient was someone named N. Drefan.

For a moment, Calypso stared at the papers, unable to breathe. Who was this person receiving large, regular checks from her husband, and why had it been concealed from her? Heart thumping painfully, she sifted through a sheaf of bank statements covering the past five years and methodically arranged by date. Scanning the debits, Calypso unhappily confirmed that the Drefan payments were monthly, automatic withdrawals. There was no doubt that Seth had maintained this secret for a long time.

Darkness closed in, the streets lights came on and still Calypso sat, her thoughts muddled and confused, anger competing with grief as she studied the shifting, lacy leaf shadows on the wall. Her secure, happy life comprised of mutual trust and devotion had been jarred and, until her husband offered an explanation, nothing would be quite in focus.

Seth didn't phone. At four, which was ten in the morning in Brazil, Calypso called the São Paulo office of California Consultants and was told by the secretary that all directors were out of town for several days and couldn't be reached. Calypso made herself a cup of Brazilian coffee and sipped it moodily. Drefan. She would certainly have remembered the name had Seth ever mentioned it.

Restlessly, she moved through the house feeling agitated and unnerved, wanting more than anything else to call her parents and sister in São Paulo, yet knowing this would be the worst step she could take. Like most Brazilian families, hers was very close and they would not only strive to comfort her, which might involve a group arrival on her doorstep, but they would also speculate, or offer advice, snoop, pry and align themselves very firmly on her side of the marriage. Her loving and well-intentioned family might create a problem far more serious than these bank statements warranted, especially if there was a reasonable explanation.

But she needed to speak to someone who would listen sympathetically, give her a hug, pat her hand and help dispel this jittery sense of betrayal that had settled over her like a sticky web. Aside from Seth, there was no one. Her university colleagues were associates from whom she had deliberately distanced herself in order to maintain a professional relationship, and there had been little time, and less self-confidence, to develop friendships among the wide variety of potentially interesting people she had met through her activities with the Democratic Party. Socializing had primarily been dinners and outings with Seth's friends and associates and their wives, as well as some wonderful lunches and excursions with Virginia and Maybelleen, whom she now knew quite well. Not well enough, however, to discuss Seth, his apparent deception and her uneasy state of mind.

At exactly ten o'clock that morning, she closed her office door, picked up the telephone and dialed a number, nervously aligning the edges of her notes and rearranging her pens as she listened to several rings on the other end of the line.

"Daly City National Bank."

"I need to speak to the bank manager."

"Mr. Klein's secretary hasn't arrived yet. May I tell him what this is about?"

"No."

There was a tense moment of silence.

"Who is calling?" The voice had assumed a hard edge.

"This is Dr. Laskar."

"Oh, I'm sorry, Doctor." Servility had replaced animosity. "Are you Mr. Klein's personal physician?"

"Yes, I am." Calypso lifted her eyes to the small crucifix on the opposite wall and crossed herself apologetically.

"I'll put you right through."

And she did.

"Arthur Klein."

Calypso's pulse began to throb in her throat. "Good morning, Mr. Klein. This is Dr. Calypso Laskar, Seth Laskar's wife, speaking." Her words tumbled out in a frantic, uncontrolled rush.

"Yes? What may I do for you?"

"You may know that Seth and his partners are in the outback of Brazil for an indefinite period of time, and I must deliver a very urgent message to someone whom he regularly supports."

The silence was profound. Calypso felt her face grow hot and damp.

"How can I help?"

"I've misplaced the address and phone number, but I have the account number." She stared at the bank slip that was pinched tightly between one thumb and forefinger. "It's 65-7204/2998, and the surname is Drefan," she blurted.

"Norma Drefan's account. I'm familiar with it, Doctor, and I understand your predicament, but I'm afraid I can't be of assistance."

Norma? Her breath was ragged and she felt tears gathering behind her eyelids.

"Why? All I need is the address." Oddly, her voice

sounded perfectly normal although her free hand was pressed rigidly against the desk.

"Banking regulations prohibit dispensing that information unless the holder of the account, in this case Mr. Laskar, gives us written permission. Which of course he hasn't. It wouldn't solve your problem anyway since we simply transfer the deposits to an account in another bank."

Calypso cleared her throat.

"Which bank?"

"I'm sorry."

Calypso felt amazingly calm and very cold.

"I can assure you, my husband will be too. He may even be tempted to bank elsewhere."

"Mrs. Laskar, to me you are just a voice on the phone, and an unknown one at that. I would be more than happy to change the documentation on this account, but I need authorization. At the moment my hands are tied."

"Thank you for your help," she intoned icily.

Carefully replacing the receiver in the cradle, Calypso stared blankly at the framed photo of Seth and herself taken on their honeymoon in Rio. A friendly tourist had snapped the picture with their new panoramic camera as they stood at the feet of the gigantic statue of Christ on Corcovado Hill. Far below, the polished sheen of Guanabara Bay on one side and the choppy sparkle of the Atlantic Ocean on the other were raggedly edged with a strip of sand backed by a checkerboard of lush green forest, shimmering lakes and tan buildings. Crumbling favelas clung precariously to huge rock mountains that divided the city into sections unified only by tunnels invisible from this highest point in Rio. It had been a perfect day and the newlyweds looked eternally enraptured, her head on his shoulder and their arms interlaced.

Calypso turned the photo face down. So much for infinite bliss.

EIGHT—São Paulo, Brazil

*I*t was not quite summer; the fierce annual storms that brought power outages, floods and death had not yet begun and traces of winter coolness still lingered in the unusually clear air. Flowering trees in raucous shades of orange, magenta, scarlet and gold arched high overhead in a lush, colorful umbrella that occasionally shook violently as a family of noisy monkeys leapt and swung through the branches. The strains of a popular Carnival samba song floated from a small, white vendor's cart which, parked in deep shade on the sidewalk, offered ice cold green coconuts, their tops neatly sliced with a machete, allowing the clear liquid to be sucked through a straw. A flock of chartreuse parrots, invisible in the lush foliage, was momentarily outlined against the pale blue sky as the birds burst from a tangle of leafy boughs and swooped toward the horizon, then plunged once more into a copse of tall trees and were immediately concealed.

With a cheery wave, lavender-suited Maybelleen drove her matching Suzuki motorcycle past five stunned sentries and entered the heavily guarded Chacara Flora residential compound in São Paulo. With Calypso seated behind her, hair fluffing out beneath helmets, they cruised along, skillfully negotiating uneven, cobblestone roads that wandered between tall, concrete walls topped with razor wire. Some of the most luxurious private homes and villas in the city were located in the Chacara and protection of this property was a high priority.

"Isn't this just beautiful?" Maybelleen called over her shoulder.

"It certainly is," Calypso replied, hoping the muted boom of the slowly turning engine would hide the note of fear in her voice.

"And your family was so amazing having us all to dinner last night. Don't you miss them?"

Under her helmet, a tiny frown creased Calypso's forehead. "Of course, but we visit back and forth from time to time."

"It's not the same thing, though, as having your family around the corner."

"No."

Maybelleen's bike was the only vehicle in sight as, lustily belting a stanza of *Glory to His Name*, she turned left, passing a jogger who stopped to stare.

"Oi," she called. Slang for "hello" that was almost never used to address strangers, it was her only Portuguese word and one that Maybelleen thought sounded very friendly. She used it all the time.

A few moments later she paused beside a lake which, shaded by dense shrubbery and tall trees, was filled with water lilies and ducks. Hoping for an edible handout, the latter began a noisy and rapid advance toward the Suzuki. Maybelleen twisted toward Calypso.

"Could you lift Punky from his basket, please?"

Calypso leaned down and unfastened the lid of a wicker basket strapped to the side of the bike. Scooping up the cat, she handed him to Maybelleen.

"See the duckies, Punky?"

His body hanging in a limp, boneless arc, Punky glared at the lead fowl and uttered a small, warning growl.

"Naughty boy," she admonished. "You'll frighten them."

Calypso replaced him in the basket, secured the lid and Maybelleen revved up the engine. At the end of the street she turned past open gates into a driveway that wound up a knoll and curved around a circular swimming pool flanked by a two story house that the partners had rented. After parking the Suzuki in shade, the women dismounted and freed Punky. Maybelleen stripped off her helmet, shook out platinum curls and, followed more slowly by Calypso, moved toward a patio that seemed to be carved from one side of the house and vaguely resembled a miniature Hollywood Bowl.

"Oi, everybody," she called in a high, thin voice to Pete, Jackson and Seth. Wearing tennis shorts and white polo shirts, the men were seated at a long garden table covered with papers and ledgers and responded to her greeting with half-hearted waves. Calypso slipped onto the bench next to her husband and lightly rubbed his back with one hand while shamelessly studying the papers in front of him. Everything looked legitimate but, when she'd questioned Seth about the frequent visits to Minas, he'd been vague and evasive, saying only that it was one of the states to which their satellite system would be linked.

Maybe she was too suspicious. Brazilians were inordinately jealous and possessive when it came to emotional attachments but, until now, Calypso had always felt herself free of this cultural trait. There was no doubt, however, that their relationship had shifted and slipped; trust was now conditional and loving intimacy had been replaced by guarded congeniality and secrecy. At one point Calypso had decided to confront her husband and had bluntly asked for information about Norma Drefan but, before broaching the subject, decided to once again check the dates and amounts of the bank deposits. When she tried to open Seth's desk drawer, she found it locked. Was it previously accidentally open or had her husband learned about the phone call? Tension in the home increased; their romantic involvement flattened into polite civility.

In the concrete hollow of the patio, Virginia, snugly cloaked in a white sheet, sat rigidly in a director's chair while Blossom snipped, clipped and teased her hair.

"You're doing a beautiful job, Blossom," said Maybelleen. "I'm so glad you could come down with us. The Post Office is just so kind and understanding it's no wonder you gave up hairdressing to work for them." Tossing her own platinum curls saucily over one shoulder, she looked at Virginia. "Blossom is the best beautician in the world. We met when he cut my hair and..." she glanced at her parents and Gil Givens, her friend and airline mechanic mentor, who were drinking beer at a round marble table and stage-whispered, "...bleached it a little."

"Added highlights, darling," Blossom corrected, snipping delicately before leaning back to study his work. "Remember the terminology."

Holding up two large hand mirrors, Blossom moved slowly around the chair, allowing Virginia to view all sides of his handiwork.

"You've just shaved off twenty years, hasn't he, Mr. Stockley?"

Steve Stockley peered at Virginia, then nodded vigorously.

"Bet'cher boots."

"It's absolutely gorgeous," Pete announced, flexing his pectoral muscles under the polo shirt. As Blossom glanced toward him, Virginia's husband fixed him with a provocative stare and tantalizingly rotated one shoulder. Pursing his lips in disgust, the hairdresser bent intently over Virginia's head.

"Of course," he said, "we'll have to do something about the color. I see you've been dying it back to the shade of your childhood, but now that you're more mature, we need a soft, sophisticated tone."

He straightened, passed a mirror to Virginia, lifted his hands gracefully, then tilted his head to one side and smiled. Observing her image in the mirror, she had to admit she looked a lot younger. Prettier, too. Her eyes snapped with joy.

"Isn't he wonderful?" Maybelleen persisted. "So smart and thoughtful. Even though he's very busy at the post office, he still does my hair."

Swatting the air with a tennis racquet, Wheeler strode briskly from the recessed bar to the pool and back, cellular phone pressed to one ear.

"It's amazing. I've never been out of California before and now I'm in a foreign country where they can't even understand me," Maybelleen continued. She bent down to hug her parents. "I'm so happy we're all here together. Do you like the house, Daddy?"

"Too damn big; it's like a mausoleum."

Secretly, she agreed with her father. "Wheeler loves it. He's never lived in a small place, you know."

Gil flashed her a look of disbelief. "When you met him he was living in my guest room in Encino."

"That was a favor because you're his special friend." Gil's eyebrows arched toward his hairline and his gray eyes widened. "Anyway, we can always move," she said serenely.

"That's the ticket," exclaimed Steve enthusiastically, rubbing his hands together and winking at Babe. Maybelleen ambled toward Blossom, who was meticulously snipping a few stray hairs from Virginia's temple.

"When you're ready, let's all play cards. Gin Rummy, maybe, I like that."

"Because you always win," Blossom rumbled, scowling at two errant red strands.

Wheeler finished his phone conversation and whooped

excitedly.

"Guys, guys, we've done it. We've been officially picked to develop the surveillance system for the Amazon region. And we'll be paid five and a half million for our services."

"How's that?" asked Steve in mild confusion.

Pete leaned across the table and stage-whispered to Jackson, in a voice that reached the hollow patio, "That's what happens when you give big bribes to politicians."

Her breath flattening to shallow gulps, Calypso felt Seth's back muscles stiffen under her hand. Jackson stared hard at Pete. "Those are campaign contributions, remember? We don't use the word bribe—ever."

"But they were..."

Wheeler strode to the table and, bending down, spoke in a low, soothing, voice.

"Listen, Pete, we need to spread around a lot more *campaign contributions* and some attractive side deals to certain members of the US Department of Commerce so they'll be sure to loan Brazil the money for the project. After that happens, we can identify Globaltrac as the best vendor."

"And we own 45% of Globaltrac," crowed Pete.

Doodling on a piece of paper, Seth glanced at the younger man and shook his head slightly, then glanced at his wife. It was a look of apology, of pleading and it explained more than words could have. Calypso dropped both hands in her lap and stared at the four men, her nerves taut and her throat dry.

"Is that legal?" she asked.

"Calypso," Wheeler answered, his earnest brown eyes fastened on hers, "believe me, I would never do anything unlawful. This is a very complicated, very involved business deal that'll make us all super rich."

"I thought we were already rich," piped up Maybelleen.

"Richer."

Calypso wasn't reassured by Wheeler's confident tone, nor did she entirely believe any of his words other than those dealing with wealth. Although she was not a businesswoman and knew very little about technology of any sort, she had grown up in Brazil where *dando um jeitinho*, or finding a way, was standard procedure. And the way that was found was often very creative, very illegal, and extremely lucrative. Occasionally, after a building collapsed, it was discovered that the contractor had used building materials obtained from demolitions and very sandy cement; from time to time mayors of cities with appalling roads and defunct schools were found to have millions in foreign bank accounts; and scandals involving judges, mayors and police captains were not unusual. No one on an elevated socio-economic plane ever served jail time—that was reserved for the very poor—and the money the rich had pocketed was never replaced. Yes, she knew about *jeitinhos*, and this deal had the same feel and smell.

Her eyes followed Jackson as, twisting a pencil between his fingers, the company president stood up, walked to the edge of the polished concrete terrace and stared out over the grounds. Starr was inside planning a cocktail reception for the new Consul General, which would be held here on the terrace in three weeks. He'd thought, for just a minute and a half, that spending time in Sao Paulo where they were strangers in a foreign land would cramp her style, but she'd immediately joined the American Society, volunteered as a Board member and was hosting a number of dinner parties. Nor had she relinquished her position as Hostess of Los Angeles. Expenses continued to escalate and now he had actively collaborated in a scheme that was distinctly unethical and very probably totally illegal after a lifetime of fairly clean business practices. His life had rocketed out of control.

Calypso quietly joined Jackson and studiously perused the lush garden. "You don't look happy," she observed.

"It's hard to get used to new business practices." And immorality, he added silently.

"I imagine it is," she sympathized, "especially in a foreign country. At least now you have a chance to spend some time with your cousin."

Jackson smiled. "Which hasn't happened for years—not since those summers in San Francisco. I adored her because she was so cosmopolitan and never made me feel like a Kansas yokel." He could still remember the painful shyness that Virginia instantly dispelled. "We laughed a lot, shared secrets, and got into mischief that would have shocked Grandmother. We were best friends even though buddies were supposed to be the same gender."

Calypso turned her attention from the verdant flora to Jackson.

"Virginia told me she loved you because she was fat and ugly and unpopular and you never seemed to notice."

"I didn't. Funny, I don't remember her that way at all."

Shifting gears, she said, "I understand you men have made quite a few trips to Minas. I didn't think that was in your surveillance area."

Jackson's breath caught and, for a moment, he felt his right eyelid twitch. Twisting toward Calypso, he smiled easily before answering, wishing to God he could be entirely truthful, feeling guilty in advance for the half-truth he was about to tell.

"We have...and it isn't. Not exactly. It's a border state, and we have to check out a number of properties."

Calypso searched his face for a moment then slowly nodded. "I see."

Maybelleen crossed the terrace and joined the pair, hooking one arm through each of theirs. She angled her head toward Jackson, blue eyes glinting in the sun. "Jackson, you are one of the nicest men I've ever met, but all you do is work and that's not healthy. When we get back, I want you to come on Sunday to the Pasadena Methodist Church with me and my family."

"I was raised a Methodist but I've kind of dropped out of the fold."

"Well, you just drop right back into it with the Stockleys. Promise?"

He paused, lured by the memory of Sundays in Tyler when the entire Bailey clan filed into the First Methodist Church for Sunday school and services. Afterward, they gathered for a huge chicken dinner followed by darts, croquet and horseshoes for the adults and roller skating, jump rope and hopscotch for the children. In the evening, they all trooped back to church for a prayer meeting, a gospel sing-along and an Ice Cream Social. Life was predictable, comfortable and very secure. He felt enormously sad.

"Starr's Catholic."

"Oh, we don't mind one bit. She's very welcome too." Unnoticed by either of them, Calypso swallowed a smile. Maybelleen blinked, her false eyelashes casting shadows on her cheeks. "I think everyone deserves a fair chance, including Catholics. That's why I have all kinds of friends that I love dearly."

Jackson glanced quickly at Blossom. "Yes, I know." He reached a decision, haunted by the memory of that former, happy life. "Tell you what. I can't speak for Starr, but I'll come to church first Sunday we're back."

"We'll go as one big family, with Mama and Daddy. Wheeler will be so happy."

That's very doubtful, Calypso thought, watching Blossom dust Virginia's neck with a soft, thick brush.

Suddenly, Maybelleen straightened and shimmied briskly. "Wheeler," she called.

"What?" Beside the table, her husband served an invisible ball to an imaginary opponent.

"I almost forgot. Just before I left L.A. there was this funny message on the answering machine from a woman named Patsy Adams in Las Vegas."

Only Calypso seemed to notice the tennis racquet freeze in mid-swing and Wheeler's deeply tanned face drain of color.

"She said it was hard work to track you down but now she's going to wring your neck and hopes she doesn't have to come all the way to Brazil to do it. I'm sure it was a joke. Do you know anybody named Patsy Adams?"

All eyes focused on Wheeler who, healthy color restored, was again practicing his serve. Grinning boyishly, he shook his head and briefly lifted both shoulders in a shrug. "Not to my knowledge, but I meet all kinds of people, and when you're a company executive the nuts gather around." He smacked the air.

"That's what I thought." Maybelleen stepped forward and bounced toward the patio, silvery curls shimmering. "I'm going to get the cards."

Covertly studying his athletic partner, Seth tapped softly and thoughtfully on the table. Years of wariness and caution, covering his tracks and analyzing every future move, had honed his instincts to a very fine point. Although he had always regarded Wheeler as an egotist with some excellent ideas, Seth was now positive that the man had a darker side—perhaps one as hidden and unsavory as his own.

Calypso's eyes shifted from Seth to Wheeler and back again, feeling her world tilt and shift, as though balanced on the summit of a sand dune. Patsy? Could Norma Drefen have some connection with Patsy Adams? And for how long and in what context had her husband known Wheeler? Until this moment, Calypso's disquiet and unease had focused on the business but now she wondered if the problem wasn't much more personally threatening.

Calypso turned the photo face down. So much for infinite bliss.

NINE—Santa Monica

*P*ete Morrissey leaned across the linen tablecloth, fingertips just touching those of his lunch companion, loafers toe to toe with her lizard-skin, stiletto-heeled pumps. The diffuse restaurant lighting emphasized the cleft in his chin, the sensual lips and the tender, loving deep brown eyes which were focused intently on tanned, freckle-faced Sally Jacobson's hazel ones. As she finished her sentence, he nodded, allowing a small smile to illuminate his face and gouge a deep dimple in his right cheek.

"Did you understand?" she asked.

"Not quite," he purred in the liquid baritone he had once hoped to use as a television anchor person and now reserved for seductions. "You're so distractingly beautiful that I can't concentrate on anything else."

"Please try," she ordered with a note of impatience. "This is a service for your country that we're talking about."

"America doesn't deserve to have a DEA agent like

you." He paused and stroked her slender, well-manicured fingers, unperturbed when Sally withdrew her hand. "Although, it was a smart move on the government's part; I'll bet those drug dealers and dopers all say, 'I give up. Take me, please.'" Pete lifted his chin slightly so that the planes in his face were accentuated and his cheekbones pronounced. It was a move he'd practiced in front of the mirror numerous times. "And that's what I say. Susan, take me, please."

"Sally."

He didn't miss a beat. "But Susan could be our private code."

He slipped out of his left loafer, trapped one of her feet between both of his and began to gently inch up her ankle with his left foot. Lifting her free foot, Sally brought the pointed heel down forcefully on his instep then crossed her legs and finished her glass of wine as he gasped for breath.

A converted warehouse that had been white-washed, layered with balconies, and partitioned with mirrors, palm trees and waist-high walls, Vicolo West was one of Venice's most popular restaurants, despite the fact that it was a block from the beach and offered almost no available parking. Waiters strode between the tables, trying to serve at top speed while conveying an aura of California laid-back cool. The ceiling was high, the area packed and no one was interested in Pete and his friend. At least, that's the way it appeared.

"I prefer Sally," she said briskly. Facial bones, cleft chin and dimple forgotten, Pete grunted in pain, and leaned down to tenderly rub his foot. "Let's go through it one more time," she offered. "When the Brazilian telecommunications system is in place, I want you to set up a ten-second lag between the time information is collected and the time it's transmitted so we can route everything through DEA headquarters and track suspicious movements in the Amazon. We'll also learn first-hand what the Brazilians are doing."

"But something that technical isn't my specialty."

"Of course it isn't. Pick an engineer on the crew to do it."

Face still twisted in agony, Pete poked his wounded foot to one side and bent to peep under the black sock, his head colliding with the knees of a scurrying waiter. Sound was suspended for a moment as clients focused on the lurching waiter and swaying tray on which were balanced three teetering martinis. As Pete straightened, his head bumped the underside of the tray; drinks flew, gin and vermouth showering nearby patrons, glasses shattering noisily.

Sally jumped to her feet, using both hands to brush her raw silk designer suit that was now saturated with very dry martini. Injury forgotten, Pete snatched up his napkin, rose gracefully and began blotting her bosom.

"Right after lunch I'm going to call my lawyer and sue that guy," he assured her in deep bass tones.

Her face grim, Sally pried the linen from Pete's grasp and lightly slapped his hand. After a few more futile attempts to dry her jacket, she dropped the soaked napkin and slowly sat down, an action that was precisely duplicated by Pete. For a moment she stared at her lunch companion with obvious distaste; then her expression cleared and she leaned forward confidentially. Sally's voice was little more than a murmur. "I cannot stress enough the importance of secrecy. You must never mention this plan to anyone."

He ventured a smile then lifted his chin and gazed at her through long, thick lashes. "What about my partners?"

"Under no circumstances! You know how important it is to perform this service for your country, but they might not see it that way."

"Jackson's been a spy for years."

Sally studied him with the same veiled amazement that she would bestow on an award-winning hog at a state fair.

When she spoke, her voice was kind and patient. "Allow me to correct you. Mr. Bailey was never an operative. He was involved in international surveillance on a very high, non-spook level, and naturally would try to take control. And credit. However, the DEA has more confidence in your ability, courage and patriotism. It's that simple."

Pete tilted his handsome head to one side and exhibited his dimple.

"You're right; I'm fearless and bold, just like Tarzan, only I'm better dressed. I love our flag and the Pledge of Allegiance." Placing one hand reverently on his chest, Pete's eyelids drooped to half-mast and seemed to undergo a palsied flutter as he peeped amorously at his companion. "They say Brazilian women are the world's most beautiful, but you are much more fabulous, Su...Sally."

All around them busboys swept and mopped while waiters offered fresh table linen, dry plates and apologies to the customers. Their unhappy server shook out a napkin and eased it over Sally's lap. Pete's patriotic hand fell, his eyelids flew open and so did his mouth.

"You've got one big lawsuit coming down the pike, butterfingers." Pete tilted his chin and directed a masterful, dimpled smile at Sally who stifled a deep sigh.

Elbows bent, Sally's fingers were interlaced forming a support on which her chin rested. For just a moment, she scowled wrathfully across the table, a hard glint in her eyes, and then her face smoothed into a pleasant, bland facade.

Seated at a corner table on the balcony, Virginia, Calypso and Maybelleen peered intently at the couple. Although her two friends wore casual clothing, Maybelleen had dressed very carefully, choosing an extremely tight white linen suit with large, yellow polka dots, bright yellow sling-back pumps and matching hat and handbag; she was now the recipient of many covert glances. The trio had picked Vicolo West, a new, very chic establishment on Ocean Avenue in Santa Monica for this lunch, an event that had become a bi-monthly occasion. Not until they were seated upstairs and perusing the menus had Maybelleen's azure eyes spotted Pete on the main floor.

"What a piece of shit," Virginia murmured. "What do women see in him?"

Calypso silently wondered the same thing. Her back rigid, Maybelleen strained to see through the thicket of eyelashes then turned slowly toward Virginia.

"The same thing you did, I imagine. Maybe she's a new secretary, or someone important visiting from Brazil."

Virginia frowned and stared down into the room below, studying the small woman with the delicate, perfectly oval face that missed true beauty through a ski-jump nose and heavily freckled skin. "I've seen her before but I can't remember where. Anyway, she doesn't look like the secretarial type to me, and in Brazil women are seldom important enough to send abroad."

"What else could she be?"

"A girlfriend."

Startled, Maybelleen turned for another look.

"But he's your husband. He can't have a girlfriend." Her voice carried clearly to the couple seated at the next table. Virginia snorted.

"At least they're not lovers. I speak from grim experience."

At the nearby table, conversation was abandoned.

Calypso leaned forward on her forearms, her errant hair forced into a pony-tail, and stared at the couple. It was an elusive, wispy memory but she, like Virginia, knew she had seen Pete's companion before. She watched the woman brush liquid from her suit jacket and sit down, an image hovering on the edge of recognition. And then Pete barked something at the waiter, the woman's fingers laced together into a bridge on which her chin rested and, for a moment, she glared hatefully across the table. Calypso's memory shifted into focus.

"Virginia, that's the woman in Hollywood—the one that had her car rammed the first time we went to see

Maybelleen."

Absently sipping her spritzer, Virginia narrowed her eyes and scrutinized Sally. Turning her attention to Calypso, she slowly nodded. "You're right. That's the same woman, but who is she and how does my devoted spouse know her?"

"The world's a very small place," commented Maybelleen sagely.

Virginia chuckled humorlessly. "Indeed it is, especially when it comes to Pete and the ladies. He seems to know them all."

At the adjacent table, two pair of eyes rolled toward Virginia. Maybelleen stood up.

"What are you doing?" asked Virginia.

"I think we should go down there and introduce ourselves. How else are we going to find out who she is?"

"A brilliant plan," commented Calypso, wishing that it were Seth and Norma down there in the pit. She still hadn't found a way to broach the subject of her husband's infidelity, and the longer she waited the more impossible it had become to ask him outright. This was so much easier, so much more civilized, an encounter in a public place with two friends. Carefully, she placed her napkin next to her plate and looked questioningly at Virginia. "Shall we?"

Across the restaurant, Pete fumbled for Sally's hand, inadvertently knocking over his wine glass. Cabernet drenched her apricot silk jacket, the white table cloth and the recently cleaned floor. Smothered giggles rose from the surrounding tables while waiters exchanged stony, unamused glances. A muscle twitched in Sally's jaw and the freckles on her smooth, blanched face seemed to deepen in color. Pete gracefully smacked his forehead with the fingertips of his right hand, an elaborate gesture he had once seen in an Italian movie and considered very continental. "What can I say?"

Sally stood up: "I certainly hope your efforts for your country are more skillful than those at the lunch table."

101

Flinging her napkin down, Sally gripped her lizard skin bag and strode toward the entrance. Dismayed, Pete jumped up, tipping his chair backward into the path of a waiter, and dashed in pursuit. Halfway to the door, he paused to lower one eyelid in a sly wink at a handsome waiter and then to peep down the cleavage of a tall, luscious blond headed in the opposite direction. Pivoting, he collided with a palm tree.

"Wait!" he called, batting at the fronds. Sally marched past the oyster bar and disappeared from sight.

Disappointed, Calypso murmured, "Too late."

Virginia shook her head slowly from side to side. Shifting her gaze to the now empty table, she twisted the thin, gold wedding band on her finger. "I must have been temporarily insane when I married him."

Maybelleen sat down and took a sip of heavily sugared ice tea, her drink of choice. "You were just blinded by love."

Scowling, Virginia retorted, "Blinded, but not by love. The Brazilians have it right when they call him Peachy."

Maybelleen shook her head, the yellow, wide-brimmed hat flopping.

"That's unkind, Virginia. We both know Brazilians can't say American names very well, but they do their best. Isn't that right, Calypso?"

Smiling, Calypso nodded. In Brazilian Portuguese, proper nouns were not customarily allowed to end in a consonant; when this inadvertently happened, a corrective, verbal 'y' was usually tacked onto the offending word or name. Thus, Pete became Peachy, Dan was Dany, Helmut became Elmúchee and picnic transformed into picky-nicky. Even the airline, Varig, was pronounced Varigy. Although, she mused, this was not at all an inflexible rule. Look at Robinson, which was pronounced Hobison. Funny, she'd never really thought about this before.

"And Peachy sounds kind of cute, although he certainly was having a bad day today," said Maybelleen, pulling

Calypso sharply from her reverie.

Virginia stared at Maybelleen in disbelief.

"If you knew Peachy a little better, you'd know he was having a great time even if his friend wasn't having such a wonderful experience."

Listening, Calypso's mind again began to drift, circling back, as it always did lately, to Seth. He was out of town again, presumably in São Paulo, which could very well be true since the partners didn't always travel together. On the other hand, he might be in L.A. or Santa Barbara or New York, lunching at this very moment with Norma, who would be elegant, sophisticated and beautiful. And then where would they go? To a museum? Or back to a hotel? Furious with the persistent jealousy and suspicion that had recently colored her imagination, Calypso forced her attention back to the table.

"Let's pay the bill and go back to the Harley dealer for your new bike," Maybelleen suggested. She turned to Calypso. "Sure you don't want to get one too?"

Smiling, Calypso shook her head. "I like riding on the back of yours."

"Well, you can't join the Motor Maids and go on trips if you don't have one," Maybelleen said with a tinge of asperity. "Virginia's going to get a pretty pink bike with colors to match since she's so beautiful herself."

Their neighbors swiveled around for a better look. Virginia smiled with pleasure and flushed slightly. Her hair was now a sophisticated shade of ash blond and she had added ten pounds to her thin frame, a combination that served to soften her appearance if not her tongue. On a daily basis, she was astonished when her mirror assured her that, for the first time in her life, she was quite stunning.

"I'm not dressed for a motorcycle," she protested.

"Oh, pooh, just hike up your skirt. Nobody cares."

"I care. We can shop for the Harley tomorrow, but now we'll stick with the car even if you don't especially like the Bentley."

"How can you say that? I adore it," Maybelleen chirped indignantly. "When I make a lot of money as an airline mechanic I'm going to buy a brand new Bentley engine for our coffee table so I can put it together and take it apart in my free time, sort of like a puzzle." She shimmied briefly with excitement, her azure eyes snapping behind the heavy veil of false lashes.

"Isn't a car engine a little large for living room decor?"

"Of course not! I'll just get a super-big table." She looked at her left hand, and then held it up so the diamonds encircling her fourth finger sparked a rainbow of lights. "You know, I have trouble remembering to take off my ring when I'm working on motors. I wanted to ask Doug to get me a plain gold one, but Daddy said changing wedding rings could bring bad luck. What do you think?"

Both of the other women stared silently at their own left hands. Calypso certainly hadn't replaced her wedding band—she couldn't remember taking it off a single time—and yet her marriage was rapidly crumbling. She lifted her head and smiled cynically at Maybelleen.

"We make our own luck. And I don't think the ring makes a bit of difference."

TEN—Claremont

Calypso opened another window in her living room, then turned to watch Jackson and Virginia push her Tabriz carpet further into one corner. With an effort, Virginia straightened, picked up a magazine from an end-table and fanned her face and neck before collapsing onto an armchair. Normally, Calypso never thought about the age of her friends or colleagues, but Virginia's fatigue was a reminder of the fact that, appearances notwithstanding, she and Jackson were a good deal older than the others. Returning to the center of the room, Calypso took her place near Maybelleen.

"We're getting pretty good at the Alpine. Let's practice it one more time." Her face flushed and glistening with perspiration, Maybelleen shimmied briefly, sending the long fringes on her suede vest flying in all directions.

"Boys," she called to Pete and Wheeler who slouched on the sofa downing rounds of Hennessey, "come dance with us and have some fun."

"I'm having a ball just watching you people trying to

get it right," her husband replied. "I'm a surfer, a skier and a tennis player, remember. I can't handle line-dancing."

"You should learn something new. Would one of you please skip to the second track on the next CD? It's Garth Brooks' 'Take Off the Edge,'"

Pete immediately sprang to his feet and raced across the room to the CD player that was located close to the dining room. Bestowing a dimpled smile on Guadalupe, the young Salvadoran maid who was clearing the table, he murmured,

"Can I help you with anything?"

"Music, Peachy," Virginia called sharply, hoisting herself out of the armchair and moving toward Maybelleen.

Clasping her hands behind her back and planting her tooled, snakeskin cowboy boots a foot apart, Maybelleen spoke over one shoulder to Virginia, Calypso and Jackson, who now stood in a row behind her.

"I'll call this time, but remember when we dance at the Buttons and Bows there won't be any caller. Don't be nervous."

Reluctantly, Pete turned his attention to the CD player and, suddenly, the country singer's voice bellowed through Calypso's living room. The four dancers sprang into action as Pete leaned against the wall, again staring intently at the maid.

"Fan right, fan right, fan left, fan left, heel toe, heel home right, heel toe, heel home left, heel knee, cross heel home right..."

Her shoulders dipped and swayed, her broomstick skirt billowed out in a circle and her feet stamped authoritatively on the hardwood floor as Maybelleen shuffled, bounced and spun in perfect harmony to Garth Brooks' accompaniment. Frowning in concentration, her friends collided with one another, hastily corrected their steps and occasionally paused to become reoriented before making another attempt.

"Isn't this fun?" Maybelleen's glistening, vermilion lips parted in a happy smile as she whirled and twirled in a blur of flying fringe and tossing curls. Garth's smooth voice hovered over the finale and, executing a quarter turn, Maybelleen stomped saucily, ending the dance with dramatic panache. Her students groaned in exhaustion, staggered to the sofas and flung themselves onto the soft cushions.

"That was wonderful," said Maybelleen. She stared hard, first at Pete, then at Wheeler. "If you lazy fellows would join us, we could line up for the Southside Shuffle."

"Not me," said Wheeler. Still ogling Guadalupe, Pete failed to respond.

Calypso lifted her long, kinky hair, tightly corkscrewed with sweat and body heat, off her neck. Seth had been in São Paulo—or at least not in Claremont—for nearly a week. Already tired of being alone, she had invited the others for dinner and a line dance lesson. This is worse than a workout at the gym," she said, sympathizing with Virginia. "I guess I'm just too old."

Jackson reached over and squeezed the hostess' hand. "What rubbish! I wish I'd had a young, beautiful professor like you in my college days."

Although his tone was light and impersonal, he inadvertently caressed Calypso with a glance so achingly wistful that they both started in confusion.

"Give it a rest, May. Fourteen hours hoeing weeds in the sun is a picnic compared to line dancing," gasped Virginia, fanning her perspiring face with one languid hand. She smiled at Maybelleen and then her eyes strayed to Pete who was staring at Guadalupe. Virginia's relaxed body stiffened and her face hardened into sharp lines that thinned her mouth, narrowed her eyes and hollowed the flesh below her cheekbones. As the others followed her gaze, conversation sputtered to a halt.

Seemingly oblivious to the charms of the man who stood with dimple and cleft chin displayed to best advantage, the young Salvadoran briskly folded the tablecloth, picked up the loaded tray and, extinguishing the dining room light on her way out, vanished into the kitchen. Only then did Pete turn, surprised to find himself the center of attention. His expression was that of a small boy caught tormenting the cat and feigning wounded innocence.

Calypso and Jackson exchanged glances while Wheeler slipped an arm around Maybelleen's waist and shook his head slightly in wry amusement. Abruptly, Virginia jumped up and glared at her spouse.

"Time to go, Peachy," she snapped. Turning to Calypso and ignoring Pete, who was woefully studying his watch, she said, "It was great fun. I can't believe that you're such a good cook and so *thin*. Too bad Seth missed it all."

For a moment, as she rose to her feet, Calypso's face reflected pain and humiliation. Although she, Virginia and Maybelleen had skirted the subject, Calypso still hadn't voiced her suspicions to anyone, but her friend's choice of words and compassionate tone forced her to wonder if the others knew more about the situation than she did. Was she one of those women, pitied yet held in contempt, which was the last to know about her husband's philandering? Forcing a smile, Calypso replied, "Yes, it is."

Virginia turned to Maybelleen and gave her a quick hug. "It's a work-out, but line dancing's a lot more fun than hoeing weeds."

"That's a fact," added Jackson.

Maybelleen shimmied, clenched her fists in excitement, and drew an enthusiastic breath. "If we get really, really good we might even win this year's championship at Buttons and Bows." She slipped an arm around her husband's waist. "You don't know what you're missing, Wheeler, even if it's not tennis."

"Maybe one day I'll give it a try."

Virginia clamped one hand around Pete's wrist and began pulling him toward the door. "Come on, Romeo, the bus is leaving." Facing the darkened dining room, she called, "Front and center, Vince."

The kitchen door opened and, his uniform slightly askew, Vincent appeared. Sauntering into the living room, he turned and mouthed a kiss into the dark, simultaneously executing a surreptitious grind with his narrow hips. Amused and disbelieving, Calypso stared at the driver with raised eyebrows while Virginia muttered softly, "Oh, my God."

Dipping his head in a cocky salutation, Vince strolled to the entrance and stepped onto the porch. Almost immediately, guests clustered around the front door and, amidst a flurry of goodbyes, Maybelleen turned to Jackson in concern.

"I just hate to think of you driving back alone. Even though Virginia and I are double dating, I truly meant we'd love to give you a ride. We could've squeezed you in easy."

Her perfectly shaped brows drew upward in the center and there was a hint of moisture in the sky-blue eyes as Maybelleen placed a sympathetic hand on Jackson's forearm. His face crinkled in an affectionate smile and he hugged her reassuringly.

"Don't worry. I plan to visit a couple of clients out here in Riverside tomorrow so I booked into the Indian Springs Inn around the corner for tonight." Maybelleen visibly relaxed, her smile reappearing.

"I'm just so relieved you won't have that long drive all the way back to a dark, empty house by yourself." She gently squeezed his arm. "We're all so sorry that Starr missed her plane."

His face shadowed and Jackson shoved both hands into his pockets. Startled by Maybelleen's expression of sympathy, Calypso mentally coupled the two absent persons. Disgusted with her doubts and lack of trust, she tried, and failed, to recall those past moments of close intimacy that had comprised her life with Seth. In the awkward, momentary silence, a female voice belted out the first few bars of "Read My Mind."

"Here we go," piped Maybelleen, bouncing and shuffling onto the porch and down the front steps, trailed by the remainder of the group. Calypso leaned against the clapboard wall, her arms crossed against the cooler night air and pensively watching her guests. Reaching the street, waving and calling good-night, the two couples and Vince piled into the Bentley while Jackson unlocked his car, and then turned and moved slowly back toward the house.

"Can't I do something to help here?" he called. "Like clean up? Take the maid home? Whatever Seth normally does after a dinner party?"

Calypso opened her mouth to refuse and then changed her mind. She had no doubt that Seth's sudden emergency, presumably with a senator and two industrialists in Brasilia, was actually linked, if not to Starr, to the mysterious Norma Drefan. Ever since that terrible night when her snooping had uncovered the woman's name, Calypso found that she couldn't concentrate. She skimmed over her class preparations and presentations and gave minimal attention to both her consulting jobs and advisees while repeatedly trying to discover the identity of Seth's lover. Gradually, her spirits and confidence had evaporated, leaving her angry, hurt and resentful.

"You know," she said hesitantly, "I'd really appreciate it if you could stay until the maid finishes. Her husband should be here soon to drive her home, and I'd feel more comfortable with another person around. It's absurd but I've never given a dinner party all by myself before," she ended weakly, feeling a fool.

"I'd be glad to."

Briskly, Jackson covered the walkway with long strides, then climbed the steps and joined Calypso on the porch. Side by side they waved to the departing Bentley as it crept away from the curb, gathered speed and vanished behind a thick screen of bushes, tree trunks and low hanging branches. Inside the house, Calypso gestured toward the bar.

"Would you like a little cognac while Teresa finishes up in the kitchen? Or something else?"

He nodded toward the sofa. "Cognac is fine, but sit down and let me get it."

"Thanks, but I'll just see how the clean-up is progressing."

Calypso stepped quickly through the dining room and disappeared into the kitchen. When she returned, Jackson had replaced Reba McEntire with Vivaldi and was seated on the sofa with two brandy snifters on the coffee table before him. With the easy camaraderie of an old friend, she sighed and settled down at the opposite end of the couch, one arm bent and supporting her head as she twisted to face her guest and watched him splash liquor into the glasses.

"I'm sorry; it looks like she was entertaining Vince out there rather than taking care of her kitchen duties. Please don't feel you have to stay."

"I don't. It's my pleasure."

Smiling her thanks, she picked up a snifter. "Cheers!"

They sipped in unison, Calypso's thoughts straying to the absent Seth and then sliding to the other three couples in the partnership. All of them seemed to have tangled relationships at best, and none seemed particularly happy. Maybe it was just a national characteristic; before her marriage, she'd been too involved in academics and politics to pay much attention to the state of her peers' marriages. Her expectations, she supposed, were based on her own relatives, which had been loving and kind, humorous and noisy. Her extended family traveled in packs to birthday parties, restaurants and to her grandparent's weekend house in unfashionable Atibaia. Every Friday through Sunday, cousins, uncles, great aunts and distant relations spilled onto the wooded, hilly property where they swam, hiked, rode horses or swung in the hammocks while Calypso's father kept the adults supplied with *caipirinhas* and her grandmother oversaw the preparation of vast meals. Everyone talked constantly and there was a lot of laughter. Not that it bore the least resemblance to her marriage, nor to those of the other partners, but perhaps her memory was focused and selective.

In the kitchen, silver clinked into a drawer and Calypso thought of Pete leering suggestively at Teresa. Thoughtfully, she tapped one finger on the crystal, her forehead slightly creased.

"Why do you suppose they stay together?"

"Who?"

"Actually, I had your cousin Virginia and Pete in mind."

Jackson placed his snifter on the coffee table with elaborate care. "That's not difficult. Between us, Pete's a ninny, and Virginia is not quite ready to admit another marital failure."

"How many has she had?"

"Two, counting Pete. Her first husband, Ferguson Fremont, was a terrific guy. Still is, I suppose. They were both from old San Francisco families, perfectly suited and in love. Maybe they still are. When they met our Granny had just died, and Virginia, who had been her companion with no spare time to pursue a profession or even higher education, was alone and somewhat adrift. Granny was gracious enough to leave Virginia a substantial inheritance and a vast piece of property in north-central California."

He paused, absently studying his fingers. "Personally, I didn't mind Granny but then I didn't live with her year-round. She was a humorless tyrant that kept Virginia locked into rigid rules of good taste and decorum and crushed any signs of independence. If my cousin dresses oddly sometimes, it's because Granny never let her experiment with clothes. No matter what Virginia wore, you could count on Granny saying, 'That's horrible. Take it off.'"

How sad, Calypso thought, but it tied together some

puzzling pieces of information that Virginia had dropped from time to time. And it also explained her sometimes strange outfits and devotion to furs.

Jackson looked up and smiled. "Anyway, along came Ferguson who'd always wanted to be a farmer but bowed to family pressure and became a university professor instead. Political science, if you can imagine. After the wedding, they went to Italy and France on what everybody thought was a dream honeymoon." Leaning forward, he grasped the crystal snifter and held it to the light.

"And it wasn't?" she prompted.

"I'm sure they thought so, but it certainly looked like work to me. They visited wineries, tested soil, measured climactic conditions, examined grapes and picked every successful vintner's brain with an eye to growing grapes on Virginia's property."

Calypso watched as he swallowed a small amount of cognac and replaced the glass on the table.

"When they got back, Ferguson resigned from the university and they established Fremont Castle winery, trying to produce Chardonnay in an area that grew mostly cotton, strawberries, potatoes and melons. Everyone thought they were crazy; especially his family, who threatened to disown him. But it was a little pocket of land that was perfect for wine and, after ten years of hard work, they finally produced an award-winning white wine that became a gold mine: *Ferguson's Folly*."

Startled, she exclaimed, "That's Virginia's? It's famous." This part of the story didn't make any sense. A perfectly suited, happy couple with a wildly successful business and they divorced? She frowned. "So what happened to them?"

Jackson shrugged and shook his head. "I'm not sure. Virginia says she was bored with farm life and wanted to move back to the city, which Ferguson wouldn't do, but I think there's more to it. She was overweight and very unhappy with herself, as she had been all her life. And she's always been controlling and bossy with a very sharp tongue." Calypso smiled and nodded. Glancing at her, Jackson added hastily, "Don't misunderstand me. To my knowledge she never spoke to Ferguson the way she talks to Pete and Vince." He shrugged again. "But they'd been married for nearly twenty years and, although Ferguson adored and respected her, admired her intelligence and listened to her opinions, it didn't seem to be enough."

Listening, Calypso sipped the brandy.

After a moment, Jackson spoke again, his voice soft and tentative. "I think it was about control. She was testing Ferguson, trying to see whether he'd follow her or not. He didn't."

Tragic, Calypso thought as silence filled the room. The kitchen door opened and, with hushed footsteps, Guadalupe crossed the dining room. Pausing at the threshold of the living room, she cleared her throat.

"I go now, Missus."

"Your husband's here?"

She nodded. "I see you next week."

As the maid retreated, Calypso leaned forward. "It's very sad."

"Yes, it is. They both dug in stubbornly and Virginia got a divorce. Then she remade herself. Plastic surgery, fat farms, new wardrobe...the works. She emerged stunningly chic but all alone and still no job experience outside of farming. I suspect that she married Pete to make herself feel young and gorgeous and to thumb her nose at Ferguson out on the farm. For a while, I also thought she might have been angling for a seat on the Board of my company.

Calypso smiled broadly. "Whatever made you think that?"

"Because she's been at loose ends ever since she left the winery and Ferguson. I was wrong about that; all she wanted from me was a job for Pete. Of course when I took him on I had no idea of what a moron he actually is."

Calypso laughed softly. "I don't imagine you did." She

studied the brandy.

"Virginia's changed a lot since meeting you ladies. Maybe she's discovered that the secret of happiness isn't glamour and control."

Sudden tears stung Calypso's eyelids and she pressed the fingers of both hands tightly against the etched snifter.

"What is the secret?" Her soft voice quavered only slightly.

Confused by the dramatic change, Jackson frowned thoughtfully. "Of all people, I thought you had the answer to that."

Mutely, she shook her head, shielding her eyes with one hand as tears began to run down both cheeks. Moving close, Jackson slid one comforting arm around her shoulders, gently pried the crystal from her grasp and intertwined his thick fingers with her slender ones. He bent his head to hers.

"Whatever I said that was wrong, I'm sorry."

"It's not you." Her voice was cracked and husky.

"What, then? I thought the evening was great. Everybody had a terrific time. I know you miss Seth, but he'll be back in a couple of days..."

His kindness and genuine concern dissolved the last of her self-restraint. Calypso began to cry with muffled sobs while Jackson, totally baffled, pulled her close in a comforting embrace.

"You don't understand." The words were thick with tears.

"No, I don't."

"I think that Seth is having an affair with a woman named Norma. I found out that he's been supporting her for a long, long time."

For an instant Jackson was paralyzed, his body frozen in a mold around Calypso, and then he felt a tremendous urge to laugh.

"That's impossible," he assured her easily, reaching into his pocket for a handkerchief that he offered her. "I know

Seth almost as well as you do, and he'd never even look at another woman."

Calypso blotted her face and shook with a new spasm of tears.

"That's what I thought too, but I have absolute proof."

Jackson's light humor evaporated as he realized that this was not simply a touch of depression over Seth's absence.

"But he's the most open, honest man I know. Seth would never cheat on you." He paused. "What kind of proof?"

Her throat rasped with grief and her chest ached. "Bank statements hidden in his desk and a conversation I had with the bank president." She turned her face against Jackson's chest and, when she spoke, her words were strangled and indistinct. "I thought we were so happy and now I don't know what to do."

Jackson was stunned. He never would have suspected his closest friend of craftiness and certainly not deception of this magnitude. Automatically, he enclosed Calypso's slender, trembling form in a protective embrace and one hand moved soothingly up and down her backbone as he rubbed his chin against her forehead. In a painful flash, he remembered a time long, long ago when he and Starr had shared close, intimate moments of joy and anguish, when he had taken fierce pleasure in his ability to comfort, guide and provide for his family's needs. Now he was nothing more than a meal ticket, and a damned poor one at that. His arms tightened around Calypso and, as she raised her face to his, their lips unexpectedly met.

They gently caressed one another as they slowly stretched out on the sofa, neither willing to break away and retreat once more into an isolated world of lonely humiliation. Unhurriedly, almost unwillingly, they stripped clothes from bodies warm with desire, although not for each other, and stroked skin that longed for other flesh. With the expertise born of years of practice, they made love while tears of shame, regret and guilt blurred their vision and anesthetized their minds.

Later, Jackson rolled heavily to a sitting position and balanced precariously on the edge of the sofa, his hands covering his face. Calypso flung one forearm over her eyes, wishing desperately that she could reverse the clock and stand on the porch waving goodbye to her guests—all of them! What, she thought with self-loathing, have I done now? Her personal code of ethics and standards had earned her the respect of her family, friends and herself and now that was gone. Seth and she were on the same level, down in the mud, and it was a very dirty place to be.

"I'm so sorry."

"I've never been unfaithful before."

"Neither have I."

Jackson miserably combed the fingers of both hands through his beard.

"I didn't even use protection."

Calypso's mouth curved thinly. "Don't worry about that. Seth and I have been trying for the last two years to have a baby and nothing works."

She wanted him to leave and he wanted to go but neither knew how to bridge the awkward pause that grew between them. There was everything to say and no way to say it, so they focused on the frenetic sound of Vivaldi's violins.

With a deep, ragged sigh Jackson began to dress, his face flushed and knotted with concern while Calypso remained immobile on the sofa, her face still hidden. Loosely knotting his tie, Jackson squatted beside the sofa and gently moved Calypso's arm to one side, then held both her hands. Mortified, they stared silently at one another.

"Please go."

Slowly, Jackson stood and crossed the room to the front door. For a moment he vacillated, frowning at his reflection in the window a few inches away. Then, without a backward look, he opened the door and closed it softly behind him. On the sofa, Calypso fumbled for her discarded blouse and draped it over her face, then folded both arms over her naked chest and wished she were dead.

ELEVEN—Los Angeles

Followed by Seth and Jackson, Virginia led the way into her sitting room and waved the men toward a large sofa. Upholstered in crewel embroidery, the once-elegant piece was now distinctly in need of replacement and proved a startling blemish in the comfortable, but chicly furnished, room. Jackson eyed the sofa and the grim set of his mouth softened.

"Still hanging onto the old monstrosity, are we?" he grinned, easing himself onto the couch and affectionately patting a cushion. Unobtrusively, Seth seated himself in an armchair, straightened his tie and adjusted his cuff links.

Embarrassed, Virginia shrugged and sat down beside her cousin. "Well, you know..."

"I imagine I do. Ferguson didn't want to come to the city but you brought him anyway."

Embarrassed, Virginia felt her face flush.

"Dr. Freud, that is absolutely untrue," Virginia said huffily. "I just haven't been able to find another couch that I like."

Of course her cousin was dead right; she had brought the sofa from their house at the winery because it represented the happiest time in her life, and she had clung to it ever since for the same reason. She had only to look at it to see Ferguson, his head flung back as he chuckled softly, one arm stretched along the back of the cushions while papers and charts spilled onto the floor. How well she remembered kicking the papers away, settling down next to him and sinking into the curve of his arm while closing her eyes in sheer contentment. Beside her, Jackson rattled a sheaf of papers, then tapped them on the glass coffee table and Virginia was drawn back into the present. Glancing at her visitors, she felt a clench of foreboding. Jackson had given no reason for this call but had made it quite clear that he had to discuss an unpleasant matter of vital importance; now his expression was severe without any residual trace of humor.

"I'm sorry. Would you like some tea? A drink, ?" Virginia lifted a heavy Steuben bell and gave it a hefty shake. Almost instantly, Vince leapt into the room.

"Madam wishes?" he asked with a sweeping bow.

"This is not the time for theatrics," she told him "Gentlemen?"

"Nothing, thank you." Seth's voice was edgy and Virginia felt a nudge of apprehension.

"I believe you heard, Vince." she said.

Snapping his heels together, he gave the group a zippy salute with one forefinger, then turned and marched from the room. The silence was heavy and uncomfortable.

"I gather this is bad news," Virginia said. "Let's hear it."

"Pete seems to be stealing from the company."

For a moment, Virginia's breath was suspended and her muscles locked rigidly into place. Suddenly, an invisible band seemed to squeeze her head, she felt the blood drain from the top of her body and her eyes refused to focus.

Now vaguely aware of strong arms pushing her torso downward, Virginia's face hung between her knees while her mind refused to function. Gradually her equilibrium returned and, along with it, consciousness of her surroundings. Taking a deep breath, she straightened and found herself gazing into the worried eyes of her cousin who, crouched at her knees, had looped one supporting arm around her waist. Seth seemed to have vanished.

"I'm sorry, Virginia. I shouldn't have been so abrupt."

Virginia shook her head slightly, mortified by her display of weakness. Nervously, she fiddled with the single strand of flawless pearls that accented her ivory silk trouser suit and matching cowl-neck cashmere sweater.

"Neither Pete's activities nor my girlish swoon are your fault," she said. Her forehead crimped in a deep frown. "But I don't understand. There has to be a mistake. Not because Pete is so ethical and moral, but because he doesn't need to steal. His salary is more than generous, and we unfortunately live on my money."

The dining room door opened and Seth appeared carrying a tall glass of water.

"Blanca and I just had a minor fight. She thought a silver tray with crystal glasses, a pitcher of ice water, linen napkins and a plate of bon-bons was in order and could not *believe* I would carry this with my bare hand. I'll never be invited back."

Virginia raised her eyes to the ceiling and smiled wanly, dissolving the tension. Seth handed her the glass and watched as she drank half of it.

"Are you feeling better?" he asked.

Virginia nodded, placing the tumbler on the coffee table. "Fine," she lied.

The men resumed their seats and Jackson leaned forward, hands clasped between his knees, head bent. Virginia took a deep breath and rubbed her pearls between one thumb and forefinger as if for luck.

"You'd better tell me exactly what's going on," she said. "And I promise to control myself."

Seth reached into his briefcase and extracted two

papers.

"I double check all the company financials and these were part of last month's accounts. Here's a memo instructing the comptroller to pay Pete ten thousand dollars along with a cancelled check in that amount. The memo says that it is reimbursement of business expenses in Brazil, but those are either paid directly by the accountants or put on a corporate card. None of us personally pay for more than the odd business dinner, and Pete doesn't even do that." He paused, and then spoke again. "My initial is forged."

Leaning forward, he handed the papers to Virginia, who studied them and looked up, puzzled.

"This doesn't make sense. Have you talked to him?"

"Of course I did. He turned on the charm and said he thought we owed him that amount."

With a grimace of incredulity, Virginia returned the check and memo to Seth.

As Seth placed the papers back inside his briefcase, Jackson looked at his cousin with sympathy. He spoke slowly, choosing his words with precision.

"Virginia, you are one of the most important people in my life. We've been best friends since we were children. Every one of those summers could have been hell but, thanks to you, they were months of fun. For that I will always be grateful. And I like you enormously as an adult, but we can't keep Pete in the company. He's either guilty of embezzlement or so brainless that he'll eventually destroy us all through sheer stupidity. I'm sorry, but we just can't risk having him on board."

Abruptly, Virginia stood, adjusted her cowl collar and moved aimlessly around the room, touching various objects without looking either at them or her two visitors. Returning to her chair, she sat down and massaged her cheek bones as though exhausted.

"Have you told him yet?"

Jackson shook his head. "We wanted to break the news

to you first."

"Let me at least try to get the money back before he's canned."

Impatiently, Jackson brushed the air with one hand.

"The project is very close to getting funding and backing from both Brazil and the U.S. The four of us are booked on a flight to Washington tomorrow morning to speak with the Secretary of Commerce, and right afterward we're on a plane to Brasilia. I don't want him along."

"I understand, but Peachy is very predictable. He'll be more informative if threatened than if he's already lost his job." She dropped both hands in her lap and shrugged. "Of course, if you don't care about the money, then it doesn't matter."

Seth and Jackson's eyes met in silent agreement. They were desperate for cash, appearances to the contrary, and could ill afford to toss away ten thousand dollars.

"Okay, Virginia, do your stuff. But give me a call tonight. One way or the other, Pete's out before we get on that plane tomorrow morning."

All three stood and moved slowly toward the entryway. Jackson slipped an arm affectionately around Virginia's shoulders and gave her a squeeze.

"I wish there were some other solution."

"Don't worry, Jackson. You've been more than helpful."

For a long time after the men left Virginia remained motionless beside the door. She wondered whether Seth had confided in his wife, and if Calypso now regarded her with pity? At the thought, a small shudder shook her body and a flush of embarrassment colored her cheeks. Clearly, California Consultants could not afford to maintain their association with her husband, and it was growing ever more apparent that she couldn't either.

Late in the afternoon, Pete stepped into the entry hall and closed the front door behind him.

"Honey, I'm home," he warbled cheerfully. Moving into the living room, he nearly collided with Vince who carried an empty tray. As the men passed one another, Pete paused, one hand shot out and he pinched the driver's buttocks. Without turning, Vincent stopped and growled, "I've told you before: keep that shit up and I'll slice your hand off and feed it to those fish."

"You're such a tease."

At the far end of the room, Virginia turned away from the aquarium they had brought from San Francisco and looked at her husband with anger and distaste. She could vaguely remember finding him wildly handsome with a boyish charm; infantile was more like it.

"I need to talk to you," she snapped, waving Vincent out of the room and setting her martini glass down on a glass topped coffee table.

"You are my queen. Command me!"

Virginia flushed an unhealthy crimson. Feet planted slightly apart, she crossed her arms over her stomach, sighed and shook her head as though clearing her vision.

"I understand you've been stealing from the company." Her voice was controlled with just the slightest tremor.

Pete placed one hand dramatically over his heart. "*Moi*? Certainly not..."

"Don't lie to me, you idiot."

"I wouldn't think of it. I adore you, cherish you, worship at your feet."

Twisting slightly, he bestowed his most lustrous smile on Virginia, who picked up a sofa pillow and heaved it in his direction.

"I keep you in a lifestyle you would never otherwise know, you have a cushy, lucrative job thanks to my relationship with Jackson and now you repay us by stealing from the company."

Taking a quick sip from Virginia's martini, Pete turned sorrowful, brown eyes on his wife. His shoulders sagged helplessly.

"I've made sacrifices, too, you know. I hate working in an office wearing a suit and tie. I always wanted a job as a male model."

"So why didn't you pursue that lofty ambition?"

A tiny frown puckered his smooth, tanned forehead. "It's so much work, Ginny, even though models get to meet lots of girls. And boys."

Unreal, thought Virginia, staring at her handsome, youthful husband. Which of us needs a psychiatrist the most?

"We're talking about theft, you cretin. I want to know about the ten thousand dollars. If you don't tell me everything, then I promise I'll chuck you out with just what you brought to this marriage, which is almost nothing. And I'll phone Jackson to do the same, and then you'll never be bothered by a suit and tie again."

Pete's eyes widened in panic: "You wouldn't..."

"Try me!"

"If I tell the truth, can I keep everything?"

"You are a loathsome fool."

Her voice was steely and contemptuous. Pete decided the game was up.

"Wheeler and I are just trying to keep the company afloat until the Brazilian government pays the five million. We're sort of like bankers."

Virginia's eyes narrowed.

"Wheeler? What's he got to do with it?"

"He asked me to submit the memo and initial it for Seth, and when I got the check we opened special bank accounts, one for each of us."

This was far too complicated for Pete to invent. Virginia paced slowly to one side of the room and back to the center, knowing it was vital not to scare her husband into lies or silence. She studied her hands for a moment, trying to control her voice. Raising her eyes, she spoke quietly.

"I don't understand."

Encouraged by her apparent interest and sensitivity, Pete swaggered around the room. "Not many people understand what we do. It's very technical. We consultants are preparing specifications for a project—"

"The money," she interrupted. "Is it still in Wheeler's special account?"

"No, he spent it on company expenses plus about five thousand more, but it's okay. He and I write checks back and forth so no one knows his account is overdrawn."

Virginia could feel her heart beating in her throat.

"Let's see if I have this right: Wheeler sends you a bad check and you deposit it and, at the same time, write out a bad check to him."

Pete paused at the aquarium and looked at his reflection in the glass flexing first one bicep, then the other.

"Pretty clever, huh?"

Virginia's face again flushed with anger and both hands folded into fists.

"No, you moron, it's incredibly dimwitted. You and Wheeler are kiting checks, and that's a felony." Her voice was compressed into a choked whisper.

"Don't worry, Ginny," he assured her lightly. "Wheeler would never do anything illegal. Like he told me, in view of all I've done for the company, California Consultants owes me the ten thousand."

Pete stopped in front of the aquarium and now flexed his well-developed triceps, moving slightly to catch a better reflection in the glass. After a few moments of self-admiration, he turned and held out his arms to his wife.

"Don't be cranky. Let's kiss and make up," he murmured.

Tall, stunningly handsome in a Turnbull and Asser gold linen shirt and Armani trousers of a slightly deeper hue, Pete closed his eyes in anticipated ecstasy and moved toward Virginia, arms still outstretched. Halfway across the room, he tripped over a footstool and sprawled gracelessly onto the floor.

"I think I broke my leg," he whimpered.

With complete detachment, Virginia watched her spouse rolling dramatically on her rare Kazak carpet while wearing designer clothes bought with her money. In silence, she turned and strode down the hallway and into the bedroom, brushing past Vince who had obviously been eavesdropping. Pausing only to lock the door, she entered her dressing room, closed the door and picked up the phone with her private line. Viciously she pushed one of the buttons and waited while the programmed number rang.

"Bailey residence..."

"Hello, Starr; it's Virginia. I'm sorry to bother you, but may I speak to Jackson please? This is urgent."

"Just one minute."

"Jackson here..."

"You have a bigger problem with Pete than you realize."

"Bigger than theft?" He sounded both amused and skeptical.

"According to my husband, he and Wheeler are kiting checks."

For a time there was total silence on the line.

"Kiting checks is a *felony*."

"Yes."

There was a prolonged rattle of ice cubes before Jackson spoke again.

"Pete's invented some fairy story about Wheeler to save his skin."

"I don't think so," said Virginia. "My *beloved* is not bright enough to make this up. He thinks they're performing a clever service for the company, and he's convinced he's owed the ten thousand dollars, which seems to have vanished."

Again there was a lengthy pause before Jackson's voice, much lower in pitch, was heard again.

"I can't deal with something like this now. These meetings are absolutely crucial and cannot be rescheduled." The only sound was Jackson's breathing on the other end of the line. "I certainly can't get rid of either man without knowing the whole story." His voice lifted hopefully. "And there's always the possibility that Pete has it wrong."

"Peachy usually does."

Jackson sighed heavily.

"This will have to wait until we get back next week; there's no other way. I'll pass the information on to Seth and I'd be truly grateful if it could be kept between us, Virginia."

"Of course... Good luck on your trip."

His chuckle was harsh and humorless. "Thanks. See you when we get back."

After replacing the phone in its cradle, Virginia padded silently into the bathroom and studied the trees in the garden. Earlier blooms had turned into ripe pears and peaches that echoed the pale apricot tones of the bathroom. Her lips curved in a sad, ironic grimace. How appropriate of her to choose a color scheme that served as a constant reminder of her husband.

Thoughtfully, she tapped one nail against a tooth. Her marriage, which had been disintegrating steadily, had now collapsed and, even though she'd promised Jackson her silence, she needed to talk to someone. Retracing her steps into the dressing room, she picked up the phone and dialed Calypso's number.

TWELVE—The Amazon Basin

*T*he small plane rose on an abrupt updraft, tottered uncertainly and then plummeted to the bottom of a fifty foot air pocket. It shivered for a moment and then began a rolling, lurching, upward struggle.

"Look at that," breathed Pete in wonder.

"What?" Jackson's annoyance was intensified by both nausea and fear.

"This rain! Have you ever see anything like it?"

Jackson stared at Pete before shaking his head in disgust while Seth gripped the arms of his chair. Across the aisle, Wheeler covered his face with both hands, pressing his fingers to his forehead in an attempt to stop their trembling. The only person on board utterly unperturbed by the aerial violence to which they were being subjected, Pete pressed his nose against the window. The torrential downpour, hammering on the aircraft's metal shell, curtained the thick Plexiglas panes, shielding the four men from any glimpse of the jungle below.

Jackson hoped he wouldn't add to the misery of the

trip and disgrace himself by throwing up. He'd been on dreadful flights, ones that seemed, in retrospect, much worse than this and he'd never felt queasy. This entire venture, however, had been wrong from the outset and, despite their success in Washington, he had a feeling that the worst was yet to come.

"Is this the only plane you could find, Pete?" asked Wheeler, dropping his hands to his lap and knotting them together.

"It's a great charter company," he replied cheerfully, still mesmerized by the storm, "and a real bargain because Captain Lopez and the co-pilot came with it."

The other three passengers looked at the slim, dark-haired pilot in the immaculate uniform who appeared to be wrestling with the controls, and then Jackson shifted his attention back to Pete. After their flight from Miami had developed electrical problems and was diverted to Caracas, he'd asked Pete to make alternative travel arrangements while the other three phoned São Paulo, Brasilia and Los Angeles.

"Of course," Pete continued, "we're going to have to stop in Manaus for refueling, but that won't take long."

"Why didn't you delay a day?" asked Seth in a voice tight with trepidation.

"I couldn't do that; we have meetings tomorrow in Brasilia."

"Tell me something about this airline company, Pete." Seth's voice quavered and he felt hollow in the pit of his stomach.

"It's famous. Just like the Pony Express, the planes always get through."

Seth cupped his hands in prayer position over his nose and mouth, closed his eyes and took a deep, ragged breath. Was this simple bad luck or divine retribution, he wondered? For years he'd tried to make amends and thought he had almost succeeded, but God might be indicating a difference of opinion. Since meeting Calypso he'd been so happy, so truly content with his life, but maybe he wasn't destined to overcome the past.

In the cockpit, the radio crackled briefly and then lapsed into silence. As if on a puppeteer's string, the Cessna bobbled up and down before being flung into a brief, sideways spin. All the tales he'd heard about man-eating plants, piranhas, giant lizards and killer insects flashed through Seth's mind as he wondered if the pilot was familiar with the jungle.

"The airline company is owned by an influential Venezuelan farmer," Pete volunteered.

"I see." Wheeler's eyes darted fearfully toward the window and back again. His voice was barely under control. "And how many of these *jumbo jets* does he have in his fleet?"

"Two."

Seth shut his eyelids tightly as Jackson and Wheeler leaned forward in alarm.

"Two?"

"All the major airlines were canceled because of weather," Pete protested.

"That should tell you something," commented Wheeler sourly.

"The rain didn't look too bad to me when we took off." Pete again turned his attention to the window.

Wheeler lurched angrily forward, restrained only by his seat belt. "Shut up, you idiot," he snarled.

The aircraft gave a series of wrenching jerks and they heard the ominous thump of loose cargo in the tail section as they rose rapidly, and then abruptly dropped several hundred feet. Jackson gasped involuntarily and tried to breathe deeply and regularly.

"Now's the time to have a little faith," he said, trying to focus on the sermon he, Maybelleen and Wheeler had heard last Sunday at the Pasadena Methodist Church. That seemed like another life altogether.

"I have faith," Pete responded cheerfully. "I used to be

an altar boy in San Francisco."

"Well, that's just wonderful. You have an inside track," Wheeler seethed.

The Monsignor had loved Pete for his devotion, and the ladies of the church had adored him because he looked like an angel. His first taste of power through beauty was experienced in a cloud of incense with a choir accompaniment, but his faith, if it could be called that, waned when he discovered the difficulty of being a good Catholic while living an irresponsible and hedonistic life. Religion placed too many restrictions on his behavior, so he'd dispensed with it just as he had any other inconvenience.

"This reminds me of my first trip to Africa in the late sixties when we were doing a lot of surveillance there." Hoping to calm and distract his colleagues, Jackson listened to his own voice, amazed that it betrayed no trace of the fear and panic he was experiencing. "The plane had propellers that nearly always worked and, when we took off from Rome, the stewardess appeared wearing a parachute and asked us to raise our hands and tell her where we wanted to go."

The splash of appreciative laughter was overwhelmed by a crack of thunder.

"Who's meeting us, Pete?"

"I didn't have time to line up a plane and pilot *and* a driver but I guess Atilio Carvalho may send some of his henchmen."

Jackson flinched.

"Are those like molls and G-men, Pete?" asked Seth, temporarily forgetting his fright. "I mean, will we recognize the senator's staff because they're wearing slouch hats and raincoats in spite of the tropical heat?"

"Pete," explained Jackson with careful patience, "I want you to remember that we only do business with honest reputable firms and officials and they hire employees, not thugs or goons. Or henchmen."

Pete again pressed his forehead against the window. "Say, this is really a show."

There was a lessening of noise, a void more terrifying than the most piercing scream and, for a moment, Pete's three partners sat paralyzed. Jackson listened to the thunderous and monotonous roar of the rainstorm against the metal skin of the aircraft and felt, rather than saw, the blue-white flash of lightening that illuminated the world outside. In that instant, all four men realized that what they were not hearing was one of the engines, an absence of sound that emphasized the shriek of full power on the remaining one. The pilot and co-pilot muttered to one another in clipped Spanish, flipped switches and turned every knob on the overhead console. The plane began a controlled, but forced, gradual descent.

Pete studied his reflection in the window; his lips thinned as he practiced looking aristocratic and haughty. No one had commended him on locating a plane at short notice despite incredibly bad weather, just as they failed to praise his many other accomplishments. It was always pick and complain about every little thing. They'd be sorry when he handed in his notice, which he planned to do just as soon as Wheeler's promise was fulfilled and millions poured into the company so that he could stop writing bad checks. Oblivious of the failed engine or the aerial contortions that the plane was undergoing, Pete settled into a deep pout.

The rapid descent continued, accentuated by the violent buffeting of the storm. Both pilots worked frantically over the controls but there was no response from the engine, radar or radio. Suddenly, the second engine stopped, followed by a unified gasp from the men. Now the plane was increasing speed, gliding, rising briefly on the currents then twisting violently to rush earthward like a mechanical monster programmed for self-destruction. The pilot abandoned all efforts to restore power to the engines and devoted himself to guidance of the craft.

Jackson stared at the thick, green jungle, now clearly visible through the rain, with the same detachment that had enabled him to observe his business projects objectively and judge both his decisions and those of others. He could see the plane and its passengers racing toward unknown, and perhaps uninhabited, terrain, and he wondered whether California Consultants had been worth the sacrifice of his morals and ethics. If it had brought happiness to his family and restored the loving closeness that had evaporated so many years ago, he would have paid any price, but it had been for nothing. He was leaving a selfish, unhappy wife, two estranged grown children, and a bankrupt business as his legacy. He glanced at Seth, his thoughts flashing to Calypso. In the recent mess he'd made of his life, he'd even managed to betray his closest friend. No longer frightened, sick or concerned with earthly matters, Jackson closed his eyes. He'd failed in all that mattered.

The pilot, his white shirt drenched with sweat, peered intently downward, spotted what appeared to be a stream, and wrenched viciously at the yoke. Trees on both sides closed in, the tallest of them seeming to pluck at the powerless aircraft with long, wispy fingers.

"Time to pray," announced Seth grimly.

Pete thought that was a good idea and vainly tried to remember the "Our Father" and "Hail Mary" he'd earnestly recited countless times as an altar boy. After a short time, he gave up and absent-mindedly entreated God to bless and save him. The basic drawback was his refusal to believe that the plane was in actual danger. Of course he knew they were without power and was aware that they were skimming treetops, apparently following a creek some fifty or sixty feet below, but he had confidence in their pilot. After all, he and the airline had been highly recommended by a knock-out male flight attendant in Caracas who'd promised to have cocktails with him in São

Paulo.

Now he'd be a hero. Abandoning even the most casual attempt to communicate with God, Pete leaned back in his seat and focused on the fabulous story he would make out of this landing in the jungle. Maybe develop a limp to make it even more dramatic. Closing his eyes, he envisioned the crowds of men and women who would mob him, adoring and worshipful, anxious to comfort and caress the brave but suffering crash survivor.

The captain searched frantically for a clearing below. Suddenly, he was below the treetops, rushing forward just a few feet above a twisting thread of deep green water. He tilted the plane slightly to avoid branches on one side. A narrow strip of swampy vegetation edging the river abruptly widened, just ahead, into a small clearing. That's it, he thought.

He muttered to the co-pilot and nodded toward the narrow beach without removing his hands from the controls.

Behind him, Wheeler tried to remember the procedure for plane crashes on United or American but all he could recall were uniformed ladies, smiling impersonally in their lifejackets as they demonstrated the correct way of inflation. That wasn't really useful now since there were no lifejackets.

Suddenly, tree branches scraped the wings of the plane and the sight of brush, old rotting logs and hanging vines swept past the windows in a blur. Wheeler was consumed with a fury that vanquished fear. They were going to crash and die and all his planning and plotting would be for nothing. Months spent organizing his eventual takeover of the consultancy and monopoly of yet undiscovered alexandrite deposits, and now it was wasted. Nobody would win this one. His face mottled and breath ragged, Wheeler scarcely felt the belly of the plane splash through the river and touch tentatively on the wild, marshy embankment as he pounded one fist into the other palm.

A moment later, he released his safety belt, sprang to his feet and threw himself across the aisle where he awkwardly wrapped both hands around Pete's neck.

"It's your fault, you moron," he hissed, feeling himself slip to his knees, his hands suddenly clutching the air as the plane bounced and rolled sidewise. "You've killed us all!"

Several hours later the rain stopped. Moonlight shone brilliantly on exposed portions of the jungle while shadows were inky black; the air was disturbed by hints of invisible activity and the chattering of nocturnal animals. Overhead, the milky sky gleamed luminously with thousands of stars.

On the riverbank, the mangled Cessna sparkled and twinkled, its nose crushed against a tree, the tail ripped away and half submerged in the water. A wing lay, together with a wheel and one crumpled human body, several feet from the aircraft; papers and pieces of luggage were scattered over the ground.

Inside the aircraft it was very still, the silence broken only by the stirring of a man strapped into his seat and pinned against the port bulkhead. Grunting, he struggled with the seat belt, finally wrestling himself free only to drop a few inches to the floor of the Cessna. Jarred and groggy, Jackson lay still for a long time, then finally stumbled to his feet, attempting to get his bearings. Disoriented by shafts of moonlight that slashed the blackness of the plane's interior, he blinked rapidly to clear his vision, suddenly realizing that he was staring at the jagged edges of a gigantic hole in the fuselage. A wing was gone, and so was the tail. He turned his attention to the interior of the plane.

"No," he whispered, leaning against the bulkhead for support. In his ears, the noise of the surrounding jungle increased to a thunderous din and one glance at the menacing ebony shadows just beyond the clearing convinced him that he could never leave this shelter.

Gradually, he became aware of a rhythmic drip not far away and, swallowing a wave of cold fright, lurched uncertainly toward the cockpit. After three steps he halted, staring at the pilot and co-pilot who remained strapped in their seats. The pilot had been decapitated and his second in command was crushed. Struggling to control his panic, he smelled gas and suspected that the steady drip was fuel.

The full danger of his situation suddenly struck him. When the sun rose, bringing the tropical heat, the aircraft would steam and the bodies would rot. In this part of the world it would take very little time for decomposition to set in and even less for scavenging animals and birds of prey to appear in search of a meal. He forced himself to be calm, to stand quietly and take several deep breaths.

Unsteady, yet pushed by a growing sense of urgency, Jackson searched the cockpit for any useful articles. Within a short period of time he had scavenged a few maps, batteries, and a compass which he deposited in the pilot's empty duffle bag; the discovery of a flashlight brought a surge of hope. Clicking it on, he swung the beam of light in an arc, jolted and dismayed to see one of his partners still strapped into a seat that had been ripped from the frame of the plane and overturned. As he stumbled toward the man, he tripped over a fourth body wedged between the seats. Kneeling, he examined both corpses with increasing desperation, feeling for a pulse, searching for any sign of life and finally forcing himself to admit that both Seth and Wheeler were dead.

Numb with shock and propelled by terror, he operated on a primitive level of survival, his mind steeled both against the reality of dead bodies close at hand and the imagined threats awaiting him outside in the dark. Rising clumsily, he flashed the light around the interior of the craft, noticing a metal box adjacent to the captain's seat. With a tug of hope, Jackson moved forward, squatted next to the container and opened the lid.

"A survival kit," he whispered in something very close

to reverence. His hands slick with sweat, Jackson examined a thermal blanket, now a compact five inch square of aluminized plastic film, a first aid kit, life preserver, package of antibiotics, flare gun, signal mirror, insect repellent, a wicked looking knife and a wire saw. At the bottom of the box he discovered a small revolver with several rounds of ammunition.

For the first time since regaining consciousness, he felt that escape from the jungle might be possible. After double checking the wire saw, knife, compass, maps and other items, Jackson closed the box with a resounding click. Hoisting the kit, he rose to his feet and, averting his eyes from the pilots' bodies, located the radio and very gingerly twisted the dials. Fearful that any functioning instrument might spark an inferno, he was nonetheless dismayed to find that the unit was as lifeless as his colleagues. Jackson switched off the flashlight, hoisted the bag and kit and tottered out of the aircraft into the moonlight. For a moment he gazed in confused disbelief at the scene of destruction.

When he saw the body that had been flung far from the plane, he groaned in anguish. Stumbling across the clearing, he squatted awkwardly beside the twisted form and searched for a heartbeat or breath, then slowly sat back on his haunches and stared at Pete's remains. Death might have been a blessing. Certainly, no one that gravely wounded would have gotten out of here. It was entirely possible that he himself would die, and perhaps suffer a much more painful, hideous end than anything endured by his colleagues. Until this instant, he had treasured the hope that one of his companions had survived and now he was overwhelmed by the fact that he was utterly alone and miles from civilization. At fifty-five, Jackson was not only the oldest of the men, but physically and mentally unprepared for wilderness survival. On the other hand, he was the only one with experience in desolate wastelands, so there might be a sliver of hope.

Again, fear washed over him and he shivered in spite of the sultry, nocturnal heat. Warily, he stared at the blackness that fringed the circle of moonlight, imagining hundreds of unseen creatures. Not to mention the possibility of hostile Indians. He had to get out, but how?

With fumbling fingers he took the maps from the bag and studied them intently. The charts were excellent and there were several kinds, ranging from commercial road maps of Central America and Brazil to geological and topographical charts, but the storm had screened any possible landmarks from view and he was ignorant of the pilot's flight plan. Maybe the captain was off-course . Jackson was hopelessly lost.

Abandoning the maps, he stood and again scrutinized the clearing, jarred by the sight of his suitcase not far away. As he stared at the sturdy canvas and leather bag, he was gripped by the recollection of the many civilized airports he and the satchel had visited together. He shook off the memory, moved to the suitcase and rummaged through the contents, extracting the heavy boots he wore when visiting the Brazilian countryside, several pairs of socks, underpants and a windbreaker. Jackson put on the boots and jacket, then stuffed socks and underwear into his duffle bag. Hesitantly he lifted a box of candy intended as a present for the company secretary. No point in taking anything unnecessary, but it was the only food on board. He dropped it into the bag.

For a moment he stared at the papers and briefcases scattered over the ground, fighting an inclination to heap them together in one big bonfire. These were top secret memos spelling out the connections linking California Consultants, Globaltrac, Washington and Brasilia and clearly identifying the roles, legal and illegal, that every group and individual was playing in the current scheme. The discovery of these papers would demolish them all.

Then the absurdity of the situation struck him and, for the first time since leaving Washington, a smile curved

Jackson's lips. He was lost, perhaps forever, in terrain that was probably a rain forest and certainly unfriendly, where the elements alone would reduce everything but the plane to mud in a matter of days, and here he was worried about the press finding his papers. He wished that were possible. Right now, even years of jail time looked appealing.

After taking a deep breath, he walked toward the river, stopping at the edge. It was wider than it had appeared from the air, deep and dangerous but apparently without movement. Crouching, he stuck one tentative finger in the lukewarm water, surprised by the strong current just under the surface.

Perplexed, he massaged the skin under his eyes and then rubbed his forehead in frustration. So he knew the direction of the current. It meant nothing. In elementary school, he'd been taught that rivers always flowed toward the sea, but more recently he'd learned that at least one river in Brazil did not follow that pattern.

Sighing, he began to walk downstream along the embankment. Since he might not even be close to Brazil, he'd assume that this creek played by conventional rules and would eventually empty into the ocean, but how far was it and what lay between that body of water and this little clearing?

THIRTEEN—Claremont and Los Angeles

Oblique shadows cast by the late afternoon sun fluttered and swayed as a breeze gently rocked tree branches just outside Calypso's study window. Her back rigidly straight, both clenched fists supported her jaw as she stared at the patterns that swept back and forth across the hardwood floor and onto her paper-strewn desk. She gave no sign of hearing a tentative knock at the door, or a louder one a few moments later. Behind her, the door opened and Guadalupe stepped hesitantly inside, her scuffed, shapeless black loafers making no noise.

"Señora, it five-thirty; I go home now." She stepped closer to the unresponsive figure and spoke again. "I put lunch back in the fridge. You no eat nothing. You no eat, you get sick."

Lowering her hands to the desk, Calypso turned. Her pale, sad face softened as she watched the maid twist both sides of her apron. "I'm just not very hungry."

"With family, you eat. Make Mama and sisters happy."

"I'll eat later. I promise."

"Mr. Seth a good man. They find him."

"I hope so."

"I say special prayers."

Calypso smiled. "Thank you." After a moment, she spoke again. "I'll see you in the morning."

Guadalupe still didn't move and Calypso raised her fine, black brows in a wordless question.

"Why you mama and sisters not stay?" she asked.

"Because they have their own homes and families to take care of, just as you do." Her tone was now one of finality. "Have a good evening, and don't forget to do the silver in the morning."

"Yes, Señora. Good night."

The door closed softly. Calypso drew a deep breath and looked toward the open window, her attention caught by the ivory colored, hand-woven curtains she had brought from Brazil. They were very thin and, as they shifted gracefully in the breeze, she was reminded of the trip to choose them with her two sisters, one a doctor, the other an architect. The town of Carmo do Rio Claro, and the outlying area in the State of Minas Gerais, was filled with weavers; some belonged to co-ops and others operated independently. Only after two days of conversations with the weavers, comparison of fabrics and serious debate among themselves, had the sisters finally selected this particular cloth. It was such fun and Calypso was filled with uncertainties, wondering not for the first time if it hadn't been a mistake to move so far away from her family. She had mentioned her doubts to her father who dismissed it as bridal qualms, which it was not; she had never been entirely sure the decision to plant herself permanently thousands of miles from the family she adored was a wise one.

Two weeks ago, when it became clear that Seth's plane had vanished and no one seemed to know where to search, her sisters, parents, a favorite cousin and two aunts had all flown to Los Angeles, taken a series of taxis to Claremont and assumed command of Calypso's life. For her, it had been a wonderful fortnight, back to babyhood, when all the decisions had been made for her, including the one to take a two-week leave from classes. Meals had appeared, tears were wiped, and words of love, supportive encouragement and cheer—in Portuguese, which took her back to the comfort and security of her childhood—were spoken. The family urged Calypso to take a sabbatical and return with them to Brazil, and the temptation to do so was almost overpowering. However, she couldn't accept their main argument, that she could do nothing to help the search by staying in Claremont. Although she couldn't bear to tell them that Seth was probably leading a double life, she felt very strongly that, if she could just discover the truth about Norma Drefan, she might also find clues leading to the location of the plane. And she couldn't do that in Brazil.

Now her family was gone, back to their own lives and responsibilities, leaving an emptiness and loneliness that she couldn't seem to surmount and would never admit to others. Absently, Calypso rubbed one alexandrite earring between thumb and forefinger, her eyes straying to Seth's desk where the misery and unhappiness had started, the doubts and suspicion that had poisoned her marriage.

Abruptly, she stood up and walked quickly across the room, her step determined and her face equally resolute. The desk was locked, Seth had mysteriously disappeared and her life had unexpectedly spun radically out of control. It was time to take charge, open the drawer and smoke out her husband's secrets no matter what they were. And then she must phone Virginia and Maybelleen to see if they had uncovered any useful information.

The deep silence in Wheeler Webb's study was broken only by muffled sobs. Her head resting on the mahogany desk, Maybelleen's tears dripped onto a stack of papers that she had been attempting to sort before collapsing completely. Steve Stockley, his face twisted in sympathy, awkwardly massaged his daughter's neck with one hand and chain-smoked with the other while Maybelleen's mother perched uneasily on the leather couch, intermittently blowing her nose and indulging in cigarettes. Only Blossom, seated in a ladder-back chair in one corner, his legs and arms crossed, betrayed no hint of emotion.

"He was such a wonderful man, Daddy," Maybelleen whimpered, her words blurred and soft. "He worked so hard, was so smart, and gave me everything, prayed with me every night and now he's gone." She sobbed raggedly. "Wheeler always told me he'd protect and love me for three lifetimes, but we barely had a year together."

"Hold your horses May; we don't know what happened to the plane. Nobody does. He could come walking through that door anytime, so you can't give up till the fat lady sings."

Maybelleen lifted her head. "You think?" Her puffy face was streaked with mascara and her eyes red-rimmed; even the platinum curls seemed to have lost their bounce and shine.

"Sure as shooting. Search's still on; right, Babe?"

Steve turned toward his wife for confirmation. Two jet streams of smoke spurted from her nostrils as Maybelleen's mother nodded vigorously.

"All over the Amazon..." She crushed out her cigarette and honked into a paper tissue. "And that's a pretty big area."

"Bet'cher boots it is. Enormous..."

"But it's been so long since they disappeared."

"Not that long, May; it's only been two weeks and they got lost in one dandy storm. Hells bells, for all we know they may be on a tropical island having a whale of a time."

"Daddy, you swore!" Grief had been momentarily supplanted by teary indignation.

"I'm sorry; I just lost it for a minute. Sugar, you've got

to be strong and brave. Make Wheeler proud of you."

Blossom rolled his eyes and pressed his lips together as he tilted his chair against the wall. Punky sauntered across the floor, pausing to stretch elaborately before springing onto Maybelleen's lap. After giving himself a quick bath, he curled up and went to sleep. With one last, moist sniffle, Maybelleen straightened her shoulders.

"You're right, Daddy. I don't want him to come back and find a crybaby instead of the future airline mechanic that he promised to love and protect for three lifetimes."

"That's my girl."

Blossom closed his eyes.

Maybelleen suddenly slumped against the back of her chair, tears once again sliding down her cheeks.

"I want to be brave, but I just don't think I'm up to going through his things."

"I know it's hard, May, but this is important," he said sternly. "It's your duty to look for anything that would help the search team. Like a personal agenda or some of Wheeler's notes."

With a determined effort, Maybelleen straightened her spine.

"Daddy, you always have the right idea. I'll finish with these drawers and then we can have lunch. Maybe get Virginia and Calypso and go to the Vicolo West." Her face clouded and again there was a hint of tears. "Although, Virginia might find it really painful."

Blossom's chair thumped to the floor. He opened his eyes and stared at Maybelleen. "Why?"

"Because that's where we saw Pete and that strange lady having lunch a while ago. It would bring back so many old memories."

"And she'd be sad at the thought of his possible survival?."

"My stars, I can't believe you said something so unkind."

With pursed lips, Maybelleen pulled open the top right

desk drawer and began sifting through the cluttered contents. Alert to the possibility of a more comfortable bed, Punky awoke and leapt into the drawer, paws churning papers and bills into a chaotic heap onto which he settled. Briefly content, his claws rhythmically kneaded the jumble. A moment later he rose, an indignantly switching tail strewing paper, pencils, rubber bands, metal clips and plastic headed tacks over the desk and onto the carpet before he vaulted gracefully to the floor. Tail aloft, he made a disapproving and dignified exit from the room as tears once more gathered in Maybelleen's eyes.

"Even Punky's naughty today." Her breath quivered with suppressed sobs, as she bravely scooped out the remaining contents of the drawer. "I wish I didn't feel so *sad* all the time."

"Just let us help you." Blossom pulled his chair next to Maybelleen and began to gather and smooth papers, inspecting each page before placing it on a neat stack. Babe was already cleaning up the carpet.

"Many hands make light work, girlie," advised Steve. "We better get these tacks put away before they do someone an injury. Got anything there to put them in, like a cup or dish?"

Heartened by the assistance that she had earlier rejected, Maybelleen slowly shook her head, bedraggled curls managing a dispirited bobble. "I don't see anything. Wheeler was a little messy but he's entitled to a tiny fault. Only Jesus was perfect."

Blossom's face reflected nausea. Steve pulled out a second drawer and then a third, searching for any type of container.

"Babe," he grunted, scrabbling at the back of the bottom drawer with one hand, "why don't you go to the kitchen and get one of those plastic things you use for leftovers? Maybe a...hey wait, I've found something."

Bending down, he retrieved a small wooden box, intricately inlaid with thin strips of darker wood and ivory.

Babe abandoned the carpet and stared at the container.

"That is just beautiful," said Maybelleen.

"But not big enough to hold all the tacks."

"What's inside?"

When Steve raised the container to one ear and gave it a shake, a slow grin spread across his leathery face. "I hear something," he announced impishly.

"Come on, Daddy, don't tease."

After jiggling it one more time, Steve placed the box on the desk and, with a dramatic flourish, removed the lid. The interior was unlined and contained a single key.

"Mercy's sake, a key," exclaimed Maybelleen, leaning forward for a closer look. "But it's so funny-looking."

"Sure is," agreed her father.

"You know what that could be for, Steve?" asked Babe.

"Got me; Maybe a padlock?"

"Na..."

"Why isn't it with the rest of his keys?"

"Maybe it's for an old desk or a cupboard and he forgot he had it," offered Maybelleen with a return of confidence. "Or it could be a spare for one of his suitcases."

Shaking his head, Blossom picked up the key and turned it over several times.

"I don't think so. Suitcases have tiny keys and all my cupboards have skeletons." He smiled broadly at the pun, a grin that faded when no one else seemed to grasp his humor.

"Well, it must be important or he wouldn't have it in a box all by itself."

Gently tossing the key from one palm to the other, Blossom frowned thoughtfully. "That's true."

"Well, I'm calling Calypso and Virginia," announced Maybelleen. "They're both smart, and I bet they'll have some idea about this."

FOURTEEN—Claremont and Los Angeles

*F*lanked by Calypso and Maybelleen, Virginia tossed her lynx stole over one shoulder then turned to Maurice Finchley the bank manager who hovered just inside the door.

"You may go now, Maurice." Virginia's tone was curt and final.

For a moment the two faced one another in silent, expressionless antagonism then the man raised one eyebrow in resignation. "You know this is very irregular, Mrs. Morrissey. I'm only allowing it because we are all from San Francisco."

"And because California Consultants has their account here, which we all hope is sizeable. Don't worry, Maurice, this is our little secret."

Reluctantly, the banker eased out of the room and closed the door. Virginia dropped the stole and her calfskin handbag on the floor, turned and pulled the metal strong box closer.

"I don't think we should get our hopes up too high," warned Calypso. "We'll probably just find legal papers for California Consultants inside. Or it may be empty. They could have taken the contents with them."

"Very likely," said Virginia. "It's pathetic, but this seems to be the only clue we've got."

"You are so very, very smart," breathed Maybelleen in awe. "How did you know the key was for a strong box in a bank? And in this bank?"

"All bank vault keys look more or less alike," explained Virginia, "and, when you said your personal banking was at Pasadena Third National which has only one branch, one room and a tiny vault for the bank's own money, I knew it couldn't be that one. Logically, the key came from the bank where our delightful spouses have their business account, which is here, at The James Brothers Savings and Loan."

"You are absolutely the most intelligent person I know. And so are you, Calypso," Maybelleen amended hastily. She looked at the closed door and lowered her voice. "But Mr. Finchley said we shouldn't be in here. Is that true?"

Virginia waved one beautifully manicured hand dismissively. "Don't worry about it. Banks are bureaucratic."

Turning her head to hide a smile, Calypso studied the steel door. Her mind flashed back to Brazil, where the lack of a signature card for a safety deposit box would never be an obstacle if one could produce the key and claim professional friendship with the bank manager. Obviously, it wasn't much of an impediment here either, but bowing to the inevitable and breaking the rules in this country produced waves of guilt and fear rather than the pleasure of a conspiratorial triumph over a maze of rules and regulations. In Brazil this discovery of a way over or around a barrier was called a "*jeitinho*", a word with agreeable associations; here it was regarded as criminal activity.

149

Maybelleen peered anxiously through a pair of rose-tinted glasses with rhinestone-studded butterfly frames.

"But is this legal?" she persisted.

Calypso turned and watched Virginia place the box on a table.

"It must be since Maurice himself let us in."

Maybelleen allowed a giggle of relief to escape her glossy, lavender lips. "That's true. You were just amazing, reminding him of all those things in his past that he'd forgotten. You knew so much."

"Knowledge can be very useful. Now let's see what we've got."

Virginia opened the metal box and the women leaned forward, their heads touching.

"How peculiar..."

Except for a roll of purple felt, it was empty. The women exchanged puzzled glances, and then Virginia reached down and removed the small bundle.

"That's it?"

"I guess so."

Laying the parcel on the counter, Virginia carefully opened the fabric, straightening it into a square. She was stunned by the sight of a number of polished greenish-blue gemstones of varying size and cut in the center. Calypso plucked one and held it high, turning it from side to side in the florescent light.

"My stars," gasped Maybelleen. Eyes wide in shock, she pressed one hand to her throat. "Those look like alexandrites, Calypso."

"They certainly do."

Virginia stared wordlessly at the stones and slowly shook her head.

"And what a funny shape, all round on top," Maybelleen commented, leaning forward for a better look at the gemstone Calypso held.

"It's non-faceted and called a cabochon cut. Unlike this one."

Replacing the cabochon, she selected a square-cut stone and examined it at arm's length. Maybelleen took off her tinted glasses and squinted at the rock, clearly bewildered.

"I don't understand. What was Wheeler doing with these?"

Good question, thought Calypso. Wheeler just had the key. This was a company box, and Wheeler, Jackson and Seth all had access.

"Why do you think Pete isn't on the card?" asked Maybelleen.

Virginia's mouth twisted.

"Someone had the good sense not to give Peachy right of entry."

Slowly, Calypso replaced the alexandrite and shrugged wordlessly, then re-rolled the cloth and tied it up securely. For a moment, the three women gazed fixedly at one another.

Virginia turned to Maybelleen: "Did Wheeler say anything at all to you?"

Maybelleen slowly shook her head. "About this? Not a peep; but if these *had* been his, I bet he'd have made them into a beautiful necklace for my birthday or Christmas present. Wheeler's so full of surprises."

Virginia's eyebrows lifted and the hint of a wan smile tugged her mouth.

"Aren't they all," she commented wryly.

"It doesn't make sense, any of it," said Calypso thoughtfully. "Good alexandrites are more expensive than diamonds. These," she touched her earrings lightly, "were my grandmother's, her most treasured jewels. There must be a small fortune here," she said, lifting the rolled fabric, "but neither Wheeler nor the other partners had that kind of money, nor were they in the gemstone business. And why didn't we know anything about this?"

Calypso dropped the parcel into her handbag. Virginia's body immediately stiffened and her face reflected outrage.

"Wait a minute. Why are you taking those?"

"That's right; we're not thieves." Maybelleen stared at Calypso's purse and frowned disapprovingly.

Calypso gazed directly at Virginia. "We can't leave them here."

"Of course not, but why should *you* take them?"

"One of us has to." Calypso felt anger beginning to build in the pit of her stomach at the hint of a hidden agenda. Temporary possession of the stones was simply to get them out of the bank, not away from the other two.

"That's stealing," protested Maybelleen indignantly. Calypso and Virginia ignored her.

"Don't you trust me?" Calypso's voice was hard, her muscles vibrating with tension. Virginia paused before responding.

"Trust isn't the point. Since this seems to be company property, we should all agree on who has the alexandrites, and what we do with them. Starting with knowing how many there are."

Calypso relaxed. Of course, it made sense. Extracting the parcel, she unrolled it on the table and they counted the stones, then recounted twice. Once again, the three stared at one another.

"Fourteen. Right?"

"Incredible but correct." It was an overwhelming number. Calypso again rolled up the fabric and tied it very securely. "On second thought, maybe you should keep the stones since you have a safe and I don't."

"I'd be glad to but I think we should have these appraised at the Gemological Institute so we know what we've got," suggested Virginia as she replaced the strong box, turned the key and dropped it into the pocket of her olive green woolen suit.

"You mean we're stealing them after all?" asked Maybelleen, shocked.

Virginia's patience was at an end and she glared severely at her friend. "Technically, right now they belong to us, and we're moving them for security reasons. If anyone asks us, the box was empty."

"And we lie about it as well?"

"Maybelleen, the box is empty as of this moment. We're just shading the truth a little because these stones are clues, and the only ones we have, to where our husbands might possibly be."

"The Bible says it's wrong to deceive."

Virginia pressed her lips together in exasperation.

"Yes, I'm sure it does, but our spouses are the ones that seem to be experts in that area."

Maybelleen slipped on the tinted glasses and her thick, black lashes brushed the lenses. Virginia turned toward Calypso, the package still on the table.

"What do you think about an appraisal?"

"Good idea. Although I'm almost certain these are alexandrites, there's always the chance that they're fake."

Virginia tucked the package into an inside pocket of her handbag. "Let's pray they're real. It may be all that's left of the company."

Maybelleen clasped both hands behind her back and twirled across the polished, hardwood floor, broomstick skirt rippling high over her white cowboy boots, her gold and rose paisley vest flaring open over her lemon silk shirt. In the center of the living room she halted abruptly and beamed at Calypso.

"I just love your cozy, beautiful house; and I'll never forget that wonderful dinner when we line danced half the night."

A spark of pain, quickly banished, crossed Calypso's face, and her breath caught in her throat. Just as swiftly, realization of what she had said flashed in Maybelleen's eyes and she clasped her hands to her breastbone in apology.

"I'm so sorry. That was the last time we were all together. Well, most of us were here, and now the men have vanished. It's so sad, and there I was dancing and smiling."

Virginia placed a firm arm around Maybelleen's waist and guided her gently onto the sofa next to Calypso.

"Being unhappy isn't going to help anyone. Remember what Reverend Tom said at the Prayer Service."

Blinking against tears, Maybelleen absently stroked the upholstery fabric, her glistening lips curved in a sorrowful smile.

"That they lived courageously and bravely..."

Virginia's face reflected disbelief. "I was referring to the minister's advice that we get on with our lives," she said crisply.

Absently struggling to twist her tangle of curls into a bun, Calypso's voice held a trace of asperity. "That's what we're trying to do, Virginia," she said. "Please sit down and let's get started."

It reminded Calypso of her childhood and the difficulty her mother had experienced when the family went on an excursion. They could never seem to get out the door and into the car; one or more of the girls wasn't dressed, or there was an emotional crisis or the phone would ring. A bathroom call. A lost earring. Through it all, their mother urged and shepherded, supervised and maneuvered until they were finally on their way. How did she do it, Calypso wondered? Here we are, three adult women with an urgent problem, and we can't manage to seriously discuss the next steps we should take.

"Even though Starr has told us many times and in many ways that she has no interest in company business, ethically I think we should keep her informed," Calypso said in another attempt to bring the meeting to some kind of order.

"Absolutely," agreed Virginia, settling onto an overstuffed chair. "And I imagine we'll find her very interested when she learns the value of the gemstones."

"That's mean, Virginia. I'm sure you don't really think

those unkind words are true." Maybelleen's tone was tart.

"I am mean; and I do think my words are true."

The kitchen door opened and Guadalupe backed into the dining room carrying a large tray. Abandoning her hair, Calypso leaned forward and leafed briefly through an open, leather-bound notebook in an effort to stay out of the verbal crossfire while the maid arranged a variety of small sandwiches and cakes along with tea and coffee on the dining table.

Calypso's nerves were taut. She needed to talk about Seth's deception and her continuing anger, guilt and remorse, but there was no one in whom to confide. Not her family, who would never forgive either of them, and not Maybelleen or Virginia, neither of whom would understand. In spite of it all, Seth was her best friend, and she began and ended each day with a desperate prayer that he was safe so they could have another chance. To forgive and be happy again.

Guadalupe returned to the kitchen and, with an effort, Calypso erased the lines of strain from her face as she looked at her guests. The tremble in her voice was so slight that only she was aware of it.

"Thanks so much for taking care of the appraisal. Sorry I couldn't be there, but I can't miss any more classes."

Virginia waved one manicured hand dismissively.

"No problem at all, although I had to ask Vince to go to the car for his own bizarre idea of quiet time."

Maybelleen tossed her curls over one shoulder.

"He was only peeking in through the window..."

"More like leering at the jewelry on display and looking like a very threatening East L.A. thug."

"But it was as plain as the nose on your face that he was joking. And Mr. Perkins actually wanted to call the police. That man has no sense of humor even if he *is* very smart."

"Mr. Perkins is a gemstone appraiser, and a very good one. His job description doesn't include gallows wit and miming with members of the underworld."

Calypso shuffled through the papers, selected one and began to read.

"According to the appraisal, they're not fakes. Here's the appraisal: the stones are natural alexandrites of varying size, fine quality. Two of them are extra fine and worth nine thousand dollars a carat, wholesale. The biggest ones are valued at ninety thousand dollars and up, and the others are around fifty to sixty thousand." She looked up and smiled faintly. "It makes my earrings look puny. Grandmother would be distressed."

"Isn't it amazing?" breathed Maybelleen, her blue eyes wide. "Mr. Perkins said that not even emeralds, rubies and sapphires are worth that much."

"We have a minor fortune here. The question, of course, is why we have it at all." Calypso looked up, her glance moving from Virginia to Maybelleen. "Did Mr. Perkins say anything else about the stones?"

"Oh, yes," Maybelleen answered enthusiastically. "He told us that alexandrites were first discovered in Sri Lanka and in Russia, but now the only working mines are in Brazil. I thought he meant the Amazon, but he said Minas Gerais, and that's where our husbands have spent a lot of time. Isn't that the most incredible coincidence?"

"You could say that," commented Virginia wryly. "Another interesting item: he also told us that, unless the buyer was incredibly wealthy, the stones were almost certainly acquired at one of the mines."

Calypso frowned. "I called São Paulo and spoke cautiously to the company secretary. She knows nothing about any California Consultant business other than telecom and doesn't seem aware of those visits to Minas." She looked at each of them in turn. "I don't know where that leaves us."

Virginia smoothed her linen skirt and shifted on the chair. When she spoke, her voice was tense and thin.

"I don't know if this fits in or not, but you ladies

should be aware that Seth and Jackson paid me a visit just before they made that final trip and told me that Pete had stolen money from the company and was going to be fired, probably that evening. When my devoted spouse got home I asked him to explain, and he cheerfully boasted that he and Wheeler were kiting checks, which is a felony and much worse than simple theft." Maybelleen clapped one hand to a mouth gleaming with crimson lip gloss that matched her nails.

"Wheeler wouldn't do anything criminal." Her voice quavered slightly.

"I think he probably did," Virginia said. "When I told Jackson about the checks, he refused to take action until after the trip so he could give it his full attention and be absolutely fair." Virginia twisted one pearl earring. "For me, it was the very last straw. I marched to the phone and called my attorney, asking him to file for divorce."

Maybelleen flung both hands wide in despair.

"Virginia, the Bible says let no man put asunder what God has joined together."

"Let's not involve God."

Theft and check kiting? These were colossal, devastating events, and yet Seth hadn't mentioned anything about them. It just showed how far apart they had drifted. Calypso's frown deepened and she felt suddenly empty. A year ago, Seth related every minute detail of his business and they spent hours discussing possible solutions to any difficulty, large or small. Maybelleen's voice pulled her back into the present.

"But Virginia, aren't you going to stand by your man? They need us."

Virginia pressed one palm against her forehead and briefly closed her eyes before turning to Maybelleen. Harsh afternoon sunlight slashed through the living room, piercing a thick screen of leaves and branches just outside the window and Calypso thought Virginia suddenly looked older. The light shifted and she was once again a chic thin woman of indeterminate age.

"Maybelleen, we don't know where they are or what they need." Her voice was kind. "I've spent years standing by Pete, who clearly didn't deserve anything other than a sharp kick in the butt, and now I'm going to think about how to get myself untangled. Mentally, emotionally and matrimonially."

Incredibly tired, Calypso stood, indicating that the others should follow her example.

"Ladies, let's have some tea and cakes and then get down to business. We have to work out a plan of action, starting at zero."

"Not exactly," said Virginia, rising to her feet. "We could begin with a couple of million dollars."

FIFTEEN—Los Angeles

*M*aybelleen planted her arms firmly on the table and leaned forward, her eyes fixed earnestly on Blossom's. The postal worker's attention strayed very briefly to a passing waiter, and then he tilted his chair back on two legs and gazed at his companion. The Buttons and Bows' large, revolving, mirrored ball overhead reflected shafts of light that bounced off Maybelleen's platinum ringlets while the sawdust-covered floor shook and rattled as dozens of feet stomped to the beat of "I've been Livin' on the Wrong Side of Memphis."

"Life was just so perfect, and now it's one big horrible mess," Maybelleen piped plaintively over Trisha Yearwood's warbled lyrics. "Wheeler's missing and falsely accused of bad deeds and we may be running out of money. The only good thing is airline mechanic's school."

Blossom smoothed his long, silvery pony-tail, the clatter of his thin, sterling wrist bangles severely muted by Trisha's song-fest. Allowing his chair to thump down on all four legs, he hunched forward, gazing reflectively at

159

Maybelleen. After a moment, he straightened, picked his black Stetson off the table and slowly fanned himself.

"Life's a roller-coaster, May, and right now you're on the down swing."

"Down swing? It gets lower?" Her full lower lip protruded slightly in an unhappy pout.

"It could, Ducky. I warned you from the beginning; you married a major phony. Changing the subject, where are the alexandrites now?"

"I can't tell you." Puzzled, Blossom frowned slightly. "I mean, we promised not to tell anyone. Not even our best friends, although Virginia, Starr and Calypso *are* best friends, and I don't think they have others." She reached across the table for Blossom's free hand. "I hope you're not mad because I have a secret. I wasn't even supposed to say this much."

"Of course I'm not mad." His baritone sliced through Trisha's final notes and the thunder of cheers and whistles that followed. "Just make sure the gems are in a safe place." He tossed his hat back onto the scarred table and took her hands between his. "And don't sit around waiting for Wheeler to turn up. If school isn't enough to keep you busy, work part-time as a truck and auto doctor." After a moment, Maybelleen flashed him a brilliant smile, her perfect teeth startlingly white against vermillion lipstick. Freeing her hands, she shimmied briefly.

"You're right. Time to stop feeling sorry for myself. Life's one big disaster, but at least we have a plan."

"Who are *we*?"

"Calypso, Virginia, Starr and me, silly. And if you get me another ice tea, I'll tell you about it."

Blossom slicked back his pony tail and crooked one index finger to signal a nearby waiter who promptly wheeled about, loaded tray balanced overhead, and stopped beside their table. The two exchanged a long, meaningful look and Blossom's lips curved in a sensuous smile.

"May I help you?"

"You certainly may, sweetheart. Bring Mrs. Webb another ice tea with plenty of sugar, and I'll have you."

"Blossom!" Maybelleen was scandalized. "I can't believe you said that."

"And I'll have a G and T chaser," he added, with another suggestive stare. As the waiter scurried away, Blossom tilted his head and smiled at Maybelleen. "You've got to lighten up."

"Lighten up? I declare, Blossom, you can't go around saying those things. It's embarrassing."

"Excuse me." The stranger's voice was melodious, slightly hoarse and startled both of them.

Two platinum heads swiveled toward the woman who had suddenly appeared beside the table and was looking directly at Maybelleen. Wearing a black and white striped silk blouse under a black suit with a long skirt and long jacket, she was very chic and totally out of place in the Buttons and Bows. Small gold and diamond ear studs emphasized the sculpted planes of her face and set off the cap of black hair that was streaked with silver strands. Blossom stood and tucked his plaid shirt firmly into skin tight, stone-washed jeans; Maybelleen stared wordlessly and wide-eyed at the elegant stranger.

"Excuse me, but the bartender identified you as Mrs. Webb."

Her spine rigid, Maybelleen self-consciously adjusted one large, rhinestone earring shaped like the state of Texas. "Yes, I am."

"I'm so glad I finally found you," said the other woman in obvious relief. "I do apologize for intruding like this, but I'm Rebecca Bauer."

Stretching out her arm, the woman shook Maybelleen's hand, her eyes narrowing slightly when she detected no reaction to her name. Turning to Blossom, she offered her hand and asked, "Are you...siblings?"

With a tinkle of delighted laughter, Maybelleen relaxed

and smiled.

"This is my best friend, Blossom Strong. Would you like to sit down?"

"Thank you."

As she settled onto the wooden chair opposite Maybelleen, the newcomer gave a cursory glance around the Buttons and Bows and commented archly, "It's very noisy here, isn't it? And active."

"Yes, we love it."

"That's what I understand. Calypso Laskar told me that you're here on most Monday, Wednesday and Friday evenings."

Maybelleen's face was illuminated by another smile and her curls seemed to shimmer with extra brilliance.

"You're a friend of Calypso's?" Obviously, this gave the stranger great credibility.

Rebecca's fingers tightened on her smooth, calfskin handbag and her face hardened almost imperceptibly. Blossom eased down onto his chair and leaned forward on his elbows, closely observing the women.

"No, I'm not. Doesn't my name mean anything to you?" Her opaque, gray eyes seemed to flatten as she stared intently at Maybelleen. Slowly, the latter shook her head, the smile vanishing as she frowned thoughtfully.

"Are you a member of my church? I just joined Bible Study and I don't know everyone there yet."

A muscular spasm curled the edges of Rebecca's lips and her finely plucked eyebrows lifted, clearly signifying contained amusement.

"I'm Wheeler's second wife," she explained.

"Second wife?" Maybelleen whispered hollowly. Blossom's eyes flashed.

"It's a long story, but I've been trying to track him down for months. I only found out about California Consultants when I ran into Seth Laskar, who used to be one of my clients." Seemingly unaware that Maybelleen's eyes were wide with shock, and her pale skin blanched to the hue of skimmed milk, Rebecca's lips thinned. "We had a friendly, professional relationship in the past, but Seth seemed hostile when he told me he'd hired *your husband*. I cannot imagine what story Wheeler fed him, but it apparently wasn't a pretty one."

"Second wife?" Maybelleen breathed.

Rebecca's voice was cold as tile. "I tried calling his office several times but he was never there, so I used a little ruse to get Calypso's office number."

"You mean a trick?" Maybelleen asked tersely, both hands now pressed to her throat. Blossom slid a supportive arm around her shoulders as John Michael Montgomery blared his plea to *be my baby tonight* and the Buttons and Bows patrons responded with strident yells, screams and a stampede to the wooden dais where they energetically kicked and stamped a noisy Slap Leather. Rebecca's slate-gray eyes flicked over the scene, her expression signifying intense distaste. Primly, she straightened in the flimsy wooden chair as though disassociating herself from her surroundings.

"A harmless one; I told the secretary we were old school chums."

Color flooded Maybelleen's face, and then faded in patches as she drew in short, shallow gulps of air.

"You fibbed. And anyway, I'm Wheeler's first and only wife."

Rebecca's chin lifted and her eyes glinted with sardonic amusement.

"You're either joking or are vastly misinformed. His first wife was Patsy Jo Adams, a Vegas show girl he left with huge debts and no resources in Montana when he skipped out for L.A."

"I'm his *third* wife?"

"And to make a long, tragic and infuriating story short, he sold me a big bill of goods, becoming my business partner and vice president in Beverly Hills Travel. Have you heard of it?"

In unison, Maybelleen and Blossom negatively wagged their heads. Maybelleen was pale and dazed.

"Before Wheeler ruined my life, it was California's busiest and most successful agency. Seth was a client, and that's how he met Wheeler. Anyway, Wheeler and I got married, after which my beloved spouse cashed in a stock portfolio we held jointly and then disappeared. Of course, the securities were all mine originally."

She paused to flag down a waiter. While she ordered a Chivas and soda, both Maybelleen and Blossom remained frozen in place, their eyes fixed on the woman as though observing an exotic form of amoeba. A frosty smile momentarily flicked across Rebecca's patrician features.

"And that's not all: when I filed for divorce, I found that he was still married to Patsy Jo. In addition to everything else, Wheeler's a bigamist."

With a high-pitched squeal that momentarily stunned the entire room, Maybelleen jumped to her feet. Both arms were rigid at her sides, her fists clenched, and the cords in her soft neck knotted.

"That can't be true!" Her words soared shrilly overhead. Concerned waiters began to gather in small knots, and patrons at nearby tables turned to look and listen. Blossom leapt up to stand protectively next to his best friend. "Don't say those nasty things, especially when Wheeler's not here to defend himself. He's wonderful, and we do everything together: go to church, ride motorcycles... And he's so smart... He's got his own secretary, and a college degree in geology from the University of Nevada."

"No, he doesn't. Patsy and I both heard that one, so I checked up and he has a community college AA in geology. And he's taken some specialized gemstone classes."

After a stunned pause, Maybelleen ferociously stamped one high heeled cowboy boot on the carpet of sawdust. "You're making this up, and it's giving me a terrible headache."

"May, it could be true," cautioned Blossom. "I always told you that Wheeler was one bad dude."

"You just don't like him," Maybelleen snapped.

"That's a fact, girlfriend. He's never been number one on my hit parade."

Rebecca stood and leaned over the table. Tall, elegant and angry, her steely voice undercut John Michael Montgomery's nagging lyrics.

"He's a rotten, lying piece of trash, if you really want the truth. Everything he says and does is a fake or a lie or part of a scheme. If I had all year I couldn't tell you half the things he's done to Patsy Jo and to me, but here's a sample: he promised me he'd pay back the value of my stocks, and guess what he did to make it look good? From time to time he'd send a check, but it was always a bad one or forged or on an account that was opened and closed on the same day. And then, when I finally rooted out an unlisted telephone number for him, which was almost immediately changed, he'd weep and blame the bank or the post office or his accountant and vow to replace the check, which he wouldn't do until months later when he'd put on a repeat performance."

Although Rebecca's voice maintained the same pitch, it seemed to grow in volume and cold intensity. Without warning, she slammed her designer shoulder bag onto the scuffed wooden table for emphasis. "I am sick of it. Do you hear me?"

Momentarily forgetting her own grief and pain, Maybelleen stared at the woman. Trickles of perspiration painting stripes on artfully applied layers of makeup, blush and powder, Rebecca suddenly placed both hands on the table and deliberately bent forward until her face was scant inches from Maybelleen's. "This may be an amusing game for others, but I'm not playing Hide-and-Seek with Wheeler anymore. Where is he?"

Two bouncers dressed as old-time card sharks trotted

toward the scene, their husky bodies urgently carving a ragged path through the mob. Alarmed by the unexpected attack, Maybelleen jumped backward and then, energized by Blossom's reassuring hand on one shoulder, stepped forward. Leaning over the table until her nose nearly touched Rebecca's, she glared at the other woman.

"I haven't any idea."

For the first time, Rebecca seemed confused: "You don't know?"

Maybelleen stood very straight, put both fists on her hips and cocked her head to one side. "I can see that you don't follow the news or you'd know that Wheeler and his partners were in a plane going to São Paulo that disappeared in a storm. That was weeks ago, and there's not a trace of them anywhere. We even had a special Prayer Service at the Methodist Church that Jackson and I attend in Pasadena and I spoke." Suddenly, her full lower lip trembled and she squeezed one of Blossom's hands in both of hers as she blinked against the threat of tears. "The church was packed and everyone was crying and there were so many flowers..."

"What?" Red-faced and trembling with anger, Rebecca hissed, "You mean to tell me he's disappeared again? Maybe faked his own death?"

Stunned, Maybelleen opened her mouth but no words came out.

"Offhand I'd guess this is another scam and those guys are lolling on the beach in the Caymans counting their cash. But I promise you one thing," Rebecca snapped, "if that double-crossing, cheating fraud turns up alive, then I will kill him myself!"

Pivoting, she scooped up her shoulder bag, pushed past the bouncers and strode to the door. Maybelleen looked at Blossom as the spectators gradually returned to work, drink and line dancing.

"Could it be true?"

"Which part?"

"That I'm his third wife?"
"May, I think there's more than a slight possibility."

SIXTEEN—The Amazon Basin

*H*e was going to die, that was certain. In fact, he didn't know how he'd survived the plane crash, nor did he understand what had kept him going through the jungle these past days...or weeks...or months. Long ago, Jackson had lost track of time as the nightmare lengthened and blurred into rhythmic repetitions of days and nights, each one bringing new threats.

The first day or two, when hope was fresh and he expected to see a cluster of *palafitas*, or shacks on stilts, and at least one canoe around every river bend, he'd subsisted on that box of candy, steadfastly refusing to eat the strange vegetation that grew along the riverbank. But then, when the sweets were gone and he'd begun to starve in earnest, he'd devoured anything that might be edible. Just as well die from food poisoning as from snake-bite or a wild animal attack or maybe even a lethal dart from an Indian blow-gun.

Not that he'd seen evidence of any humans, or large animals either, but he felt them surrounding him, just as he'd sensed they were lurking outside the circle of moonlight on the night of the crash. Waiting, stalking, taking their time and knowing that he was bound to lose at some point, they waited to pounce, and the victim's identity wouldn't matter.

Jackson's thoughts turned to his past life and the choices he'd made; most of them appeared, at this point, to be the wrong ones. When he'd met Starr she was nineteen, glamorous, beautiful and attending community college; he'd been dazzled blind. And had stayed that way for many years, he reflected bitterly, glowering at the sluggishly moving river. It was his own fault for pampering her, trying to make himself into the kind of man she'd admire. Even his children were strangers and probably always had been; he was so busy trying to make Starr proud of him that he'd never focused on Sophia and Lorenzo. So preoccupied with his business and status that he failed to notice that his marriage had no substance at all and his connection with Starr stretched only as far as what he could materially provide.

He paused, ears attuned to a sudden, if faint, rustling in the dense canopy overhead. It stopped after a few moments then began again with a fraction less caution. Pressing his motionless body against the twisted trunk of a tree, his eyes probed the constant gloom of the thick rain forest, one hand clutching the metal box. Since the beginning of the ordeal, his senses had sharpened and his nerves tightened until he now seemed to operate on permanent tension and anxiety. The situation was far too dangerous to allow the luxury of deep sleep either day or night, although once it grew dark he forced himself to rest and nap, either in the thick branches of a tree or in some form of ground shelter. He'd discovered very quickly that far too many of these animals were nocturnal. The jungle teemed with activity at night, a fact he'd begun to discover when he stumbled over an armadillo.

Although an armadillo is harmless, the encounter had

frightened him into a state of near paralysis. For two days and nights he'd remained in a tree watching a procession of animals and snakes on the prowl below. Not until he witnessed a vicious battle between a creature resembling an oversized guinea pig and an ugly, brownish-black spotted snake did he comprehend the primitive level of existence on this riverbank. He had to move forward again. It was very clear that otherwise he'd soon be dead.

In addition to dining on unidentified leaves that had once proved to be excruciatingly bitter and, on another occasion, were either nettles or a close first cousin, Jackson caught fish. Raw fish, sliced open while still twitching and gobbled down in huge chunks had helped to keep him alive. At first, he'd been timid about lunging into the water and reluctant to spend the necessary time crouched in a motionless, semi-submerged position, lulling the fish into a feeling of security before delivering a sharp blow to the head. For one thing, he'd be one tasty bite for an alligator. In addition, he'd heard that vast schools of piranhas, capable of stripping the flesh from a man's body in seconds, infested the rivers of South America along with a tiny species of fish that entered any bodily orifice and had to be surgically removed.

Well, he couldn't worry about any of that. The river had become his friend, the only possible road out of this wilderness. He bathed very quickly in the water while watching carefully for rapid currents or sudden deep drops that might indicate a downward undertow; he washed his ragged clothes in the river and drank from it. Occasionally he wondered if he might not be quaffing typhoid fever, but it wasn't a major fear. Of far greater concern were the insects, carnivorous animals and brilliantly colored, highly poisonous frogs that he recognized from the zoo at home. Just a few drops of venom on the skin from these tiny amphibians could kill a man; this was the substance Indians used on their spears, arrows and darts. Everything was a danger, including razor-sharp plants, since the gravest threat was the possibility of a non-healing cut or bite.

Jackson sagged against the tree.

"God", he whispered, "if I live, I promise I'll go to church every Sunday, no matter what. And I'll get out of the surveillance business and work for the good of other people. Try to make up for my shady dealings in the past by really helping those that can't help themselves." He paused, and then spoke again: "And please help me to forgive myself for that night with Calypso."

Lately, Jackson had begun talking to God on a very personal, conversational level, as though they were in this together and would emerge side by side. Only once, when he watched a grotesque reptile that seemed to have a head at each end of its scaly body slide down a tree and undulate into the undergrowth, did he doubt celestial support and his ultimate rescue. However, this temporary lack of faith was quickly subdued. If he gave up today, either on God or himself, he'd be dead tomorrow.

Still flattened against the tree trunk, he lifted his eyes and saw the source of the rustling overhead. A fat boa constrictor inched lazily through the foliage, scattering a band of chattering sagui monkeys that swung through the treetops and foraged in the tangle of vines on the riverbank. In something close to panic, Jackson leapt forward, colliding with dangling roots that stretched toward the swampy riverbank, stumbling over hidden rocks and slipping on rotting vegetation. Boas might not be the swiftest reptiles in the world, but they were extremely dangerous. His São Paulo secretary had told him that two pigs had been strangled and eaten by a boa constrictor on her brother's farm in the State of Tocatins. It was a tale burned into Jackson's mind.

Its midnight blue wings extended to show spectacular flame spots outlined in black and circled in gold, a sun bittern swooped down from the treetops and plopped into the shallow water to fish for dinner. Panting from exertion,

Jackson slowed and then stopped in confusion. Only at sundown did these birds leave their nests, so it must be later than he had imagined. That was bad. He tried to make definite progress downstream every day, looking for changes in the topography or geological alterations, but so far there was nothing but the same jungle, same animals and birds. And today he'd been so immersed in evaluating his past life and praying for forgiveness and survival that he hadn't kept a sharp lookout.

Frowning, he teetered on the riverbank and scanned the water in all directions, wishing fervently for the sight of a floating Coke bottle or crumpled gum wrapper— anything to indicate that civilization was somewhere in the vicinity. "Please, God, let me see some sign of humanity," he begged aloud, scrutinizing the river again and hoping for a miracle. Nothing: no evidence of humans nor any hint that he would ever reach civilization. Briefly Jackson wondered if he might be traveling in a circle, but quickly stifled the thought. It was as dangerous to contemplate such a disastrous mistake as to give up entirely.

With great effort he moved downstream, knowing he should take advantage of the last rays of sunlight. Today he'd felt oddly unwell, dizzy and slightly feverish, with a dryness in his mouth that fell just short of thirst and a weakness that went beyond his customary sleepless fatigue. Severely tempted to dip into the antibiotics, he was restrained by an uneasy premonition of future danger, or perhaps it was simply excessive caution. Stoically, he gripped the box and tried not to think of the medication inside.

Plodding downstream, the reflection of the sinking sun upon the river temporarily blinded him; when his vision cleared, Jackson saw Calypso a few feet ahead. Her long, loose hair was a jumble of tangled curls, alexandrites dangled from her ears and matching stones encircled one wrist. She smiled and beckoned him forward, her swaying body encased in a shimmering, gold-toned gown. Jackson felt his breath catch and, when he tried to call out to her, his voice was but a croak. Still smiling, Calypso beckoned again, moving backward behind tangled trees and brush.

His heart thumping erratically, Jackson started forward, only to find the path blocked by the same vegetation that had proven no obstacle to Calypso. Where had she gone, he wondered, and how? And why wasn't he surprised to see her? He was missing something, he thought, some important fact, but his mind felt sluggish and unable to grapple with the problem. Shifting his eyes toward the ground, he felt the tightness in his chest loosen; he certainly couldn't go over or around the blockage but there was a way to follow Seth's widow.

Dropping to hands and knees, Jackson crawled under the thick mass of intertwined vines, stood and stopped short. Instead of seeing Calypso's luminous form, he was looking at the body of a swamp deer crumpled over a mossy log, its neck twisted grotesquely, the double forked antlers digging into the marshy riverbank. Although Jackson had frequently seen small groups of these animals feeding on aquatic plants and reeds during the night, he'd never caught sight of one during daylight hours. Automatically, he leaned down and touched the body, recoiling in fright. It was warm; the animal hadn't been dead for long.

Shakily, he walked around the deer, peering at every side of the hairy brown corpse. At the far side he stopped, stunned and unwilling to believe his eyes, then forced himself to bend down for a closer look. Protruding from the deer's throat was the shaft of an arrow.

Mentally reeling, he straightened, trying to control the panic that coursed through his body in waves. Intent only on escape, Jackson whirled and clawed frantically at a tangle of brush obstructing the riverbank. Plunging forward, he dove toward a half-suspended log.

Aware that the volume of jungle chattering had increased to a din, indicating disruption of the normal jungle routine and the presence of danger, he rolled under the log, dragging the metal box behind him. Stretched full length on the damp, swampy ground, he quietly opened the box and rummaged about until he found the pistol and ammunition. He examined the weapon, tested, and then loaded it, tucking additional bullets into his jacket pocket. Muscles taut, he peered into the deepening gloom. Overhead, Screamers dipped and soared, shrieking out a primitive warning, while the boa continued to inch imperturbably along a tree branch.

SEVENTEEN—Claremont

Chin propped on the heel of one hand, Calypso twiddled a red pen between two fingers of her right hand while scanning the first page of a student paper. She paused, then began to reread with great care and enthusiasm, glancing at the author's name. Betsy Bettencourt. The undergraduate course, Brazilian Women's Fiction in the 20th Century, was a very difficult prerequisite in several disciplines and the assignment, to compare and contrast the writings of Rachel de Queiroz and Lydia Fagundes Telles, had brought her a record number of mediocre essays.

Ms. Bettencourt, however, had honed in on the fact that, while the two novelists were concerned with very different social classes and problems, the writings of both clearly reflected the politics of the time. Which meant that this student had actually read some stories written by Queiroz and Telles and analyzed them. Calypso was joyous. Maybe the readings had even been in Portuguese, if Betsy B. was ambitious and enthusiastic enough. A cloud drifted across her mind and her excitement ebbed. Of course, if she was sufficiently bright and fairly resourceful, Ms. B could have boned up on cheat notes and abstracts with the same results.

At her elbow, the phone rang. Aroused from her reflections, Calypso frowned accusingly at the instrument, and then peered around the side of the desk to stare at the jack. She could have sworn she'd unplugged it but apparently had not. That was not bright. The ringing continued. Tensely she swept the receiver from its cradle and clamped it to one ear, tapping Betsy's stellar paper with the red pen. Once interrupted, she could never recapture the total concentration that allowed her to skim through countless papers in a short period of time.

"Dr. Laskar..." She hoped her voice conveyed nastiness.

"Good afternoon, Doctor. This is Mike Cardona. I work for the State of California in the downtown Los Angeles Welfare office."

"Yes?" Wariness replaced hostility.

"You're married to Seth Laskar? Seth L. Laskar?"

For a moment her voice failed, then erupted hoarsely: "Yes, I am."

"We have a bit of a problem here. It seems that your husband has applied for welfare, but state and federal records show that he's currently an executive employed by California Consultants based in Los Angeles, and has never been out of work. He claims he's not married and has no home, but records disprove this as well. We're wondering if you could shed some light on this situation."

Sunlight slashed between the venetian blinds in the study and momentarily blinded Calypso as she stared, unseeing, at the superb essay. Slowly she pushed away from the desk, clutching the telephone with stiff, white fingers.

"Seth's there?" she whispered, closing her eyes. Sweat broke out on her forehead and began to trickle down both temples then run down her neck onto her chest. She stood and moved to lean against the wall.

"Well, not at the moment. He was here for quite a long time, but we couldn't make much sense of the claim so we gave him a return appointment for tomorrow afternoon."

Calypso's face was very hot and her breath uneven.

"You let him go? Just let him walk out?"

The voice on the line was tinged with antagonism. "Is there some reason that he should have been detained?"

"Did you actually see him? Talk to him yourself?"

"Yes..." Now he was definitely unfriendly.

"We've been looking for Seth and his partners for weeks. They were in a chartered plane going to South America and vanished in a storm. We assumed that the plane had crashed, and no one's seen or heard from any of them, and now..." As Calypso began to hyperventilate, short gasps replaced words.

"Doctor, calm down. Take deep breaths."

Obediently, she sank onto the hardwood floor and filled her lungs with air. The room seemed to tip around her. She closed her eyes but it was worse than the giddiness she'd experiences after she'd had too much punch at her cousin Dorotéia's wedding. Mr. Cardona's voice swirled thickly into an ear.

"Dr. Laskar, shall I send help? Doctor, please respond."

With an effort, she opened her eyes and leaned forward until her forehead touched the floor. "Yes, I'm here."

"Do you need assistance?"

"I don't think so." Unsteadily, she rose to her feet and grasped a carafe on the desk. She poured a glass of water, drank and lowered herself unsteadily onto her desk chair. "Do you know where Seth's gone?" she mumbled.

"Back to the shelter where he's staying, I imagine."

"Give me the address and I'll go there now."

"Not a good idea. Due to the circumstances, I need to be present when you meet."

"Then we could go together."

"I doubt that would be permitted, but I'd like the three

of us to meet here at the office tomorrow."

How could she wait until tomorrow, knowing that Seth was alive? "What time?"

"His appointment is for one o'clock."

"I guess that will have to do. Mr. Cardona, how did he look?"

"Clean, neatly dressed, but tired, confused."

"Did he say how he got here?

"He claims to have been living on the streets in L.A. for years."

Tears began to run down Calypso's face and drip onto the homework assignments. "He must have amnesia."

"That's the most likely explanation."

She wanted to jump and scream, run in a circle and pound the wall, kick the pile of pitiful homework essays into the yard and stamp on them, anything but stand here speaking in nicely modulated tones to a faceless man that had just spent most of the day with Seth. Her chest contracted in a sudden spasm and she once again began to breathe deeply and noisily.

"Are you sure you don't need help, Doctor?"

Did she need help? Right now she needed a respirator to breathe, a crane to hold her up and a pacemaker. Her nerves were tightly coiled, her face aflame, but the help she longed for would only come from Seth. She needed to tell him that in the weeks when he was lost, possibly dead, she'd discovered that she loved him profoundly in spite of everything. That she was sorry for spying on his personal papers, suspecting him without any kind of dialog or discussion and effectively poisoning their relationship. Nothing was quite right without him. Nothing ever would be.

And her own lapse? As always, Calypso was assailed by guilt and shame. How could she have done such a thing? She could never admit her disloyalty to Seth and risk losing the respect, trust and love that she now enjoyed. She could forgive him but she wasn't able to absolve herself and wasn't certain Seth would forgive her either. It was a heavy price to pay for one night of anger and loneliness.

"Doctor Laskar?"

"Yes, Mr. Cardona, I'm quite all right. I'll be there tomorrow at one. And thank you for the wonderful news."

Calypso put the receiver into the cradle but didn't remove her hand. For a few moments she stared at the leaves brushing against the windows, creating the intricate patterns of sun and shade on the office floor that she usually found delightful. She pressed one of the automatic dial buttons and clamped the receiver to her ear, supporting her forehead with her free hand.

"Hello, Virginia? You aren't going to believe this, but a man from the Welfare office just phoned. They've found Seth."

Wearing dark, tailored business suits, designer scarves and a minimum of gold jewelry, Virginia and Calypso strode briskly past the long line of men and women waiting silently outside the Welfare office. The crowd was faintly shabby, nearly clean and exuded an air of despair. Not one pair of eyes appeared to focus upon the women, but both Virginia and Calypso were acutely aware that they were under intense scrutiny.

Maybelleen, in the lavender outfit she had worn to the bank and the one she considered most professional, trailed behind her friends, azure eyes swiveling from side to side and her face knotted with anguish. At the open doorway, the two women paused and Virginia turned, motioning impatiently to Maybelleen.

"We're already five minutes late."

"This is terrible," Maybelleen stage-whispered, fanning her flushed face with one hand and breaking into a fast trot. "These people are so *sad*."

Every head turned and all eyes fastened onto Maybelleen.

"And did you see all the homeless folks outside?" she

insisted, her high, clear voice returning to normal as she caught up with the other two.

"Of course I did."

"We have to help them."

"Not right now, Maybelleen." Calypso was very pale and patted her throat with nervous fingers.

Virginia grasped Maybelleen's elbow and propelled her into a large room filled with rows of wooden chairs, all of them occupied. The walls, obviously painted many years ago, were a dingy industrial ocher, scarred on the lower portion by gouges and scuff marks. Foot-high plywood dividers partitioned a counter running the length of the room into small cubicles, each of which was manned by an employee. Weak, gray natural light, filtered through a heavy film of smoke residue or dust that coated a wall of barred windows, was augmented by the harsh glare of intermittently blinking florescent ceiling fixtures. An unpleasant odor, reminiscent of soiled baby diapers and rancid fat, stopped the trio just over the threshold; Maybelleen again fanned her face and Virginia briefly held her breath.

After a slight hesitation, Calypso led her friends toward one of the cubicles where a middle-aged woman with graying hair in an unkempt bun waved papers and issued lofty pronouncements at a young man with dreadlocks and a backpack. A dingy, plastic desk plaque with scratched black letters informed them that the employee's name was Selma McGraw and she was a clerk grade I-B. As the trio approached, they felt a wave of hostility fill the room and an anonymous female voice called from the rear, "Wait your turn like everybody else."

Maybelleen swiveled and scrutinized the crowd, her nose wrinkled against the rankness of the room.

"Don't pay any attention," Virginia advised, draping the lower part of her face with a lace handkerchief.

Calypso stepped to the counter and met Selma McGraw's unblinking and unfriendly gaze.

"Take a number and wait till it's called," snapped the clerk, busily rearranging a stack of official papers. Beside her, the young man played tic-tac-toe with himself on one of the forms.

"We have an appointment," stated Calypso coldly.

"So do all these people, and about three hundred others that didn't show up. Get a number and line up outside."

Normally patient even with the most difficult students, Calypso felt her body tingle disagreeably and her temperature rise as she studied the sulky face on the other side of the counter. Stress and tension of the past few weeks, combined with the added strain of her classes and the attempt to maintain a normal facade, pressed down like a physical weight and her self-control began to crumble. Seth was somewhere in this building and she planned to see him now. Leaning far over the countertop, Calypso spoke in a low, even tone.

"Listen, my friend, my name is Calypso Laskar, and I'm not taking a number, and I'm not waiting. We have an appointment with Mike Cardona at one o'clock, and I want you to let him know we are here. Immediately!"

On her right, dreadlocks belled out in a half circle as the boy abandoned the thrill of tic-tac-toe and swung his head to stare at Calypso. A smile curved his lips. "Way to go," he whispered approvingly. "Tell sour puss where to get off."

The clerk jumped up and stepped backward.

"Mr. Cardona?"

"I assume you know him." Calypso's edged voice rose a half tone and her body tilted forward as though about to spring over the counter.

Turning, the clerk shuffled toward a closed door to the left. A pair of black eyes sparkling with amusement appeared over the partition.

"Mr. Cardona's our boss," advised a soft voice before the head vanished.

Piqued by their arrogant reception, Maybelleen poked her head around the plywood divider and stared at the informant.

"Well, I think it's just pitiful that Miss McGraw couldn't be polite until she knew we'd come to see the boss. Good manners are *free*, you know."

Stamping one lavender stiletto heel in angry emphasis, Maybelleen pivoted slowly to include the entire room in her scowl of disapproval. Her high voice, further thinned by indignation, had reached, and silenced, the crowd. With a final toss of platinum curls, she lifted her chin and turned to face the cubicle just as the door on the left opened and Selma McGraw emerged, followed by a tall man of about forty.

With straight, black hair slicked into a long pony tail that emphasized the angular planes of his bronze face, the man wore jeans and a blue open-neck shirt with rolled up sleeves. A gold stud sparkled in one ear lobe. Glancing at the women, he smiled impersonally, lifted a section of the counter and motioned them forward.

Irritation was replaced by effervescent delight and Maybelleen's eyes sparkled. "He looks just like Blossom."

"Blossom's not Mexican," commented Virginia dryly as they moved forward. Maybelleen tilted her head and studied the man reflectively. "You think maybe he's Spanish? I didn't notice that. I was just looking at his clothes and hair and thinking he has such a very kind face."

Virginia sighed. "I have to admit he does resemble Blossom in a way. Whatever's happening to the Civil Service?"

Calypso stopped at the counter.

"Mr. Cardona?"

"That's right." His dark brown eyes flicked a quizzical glance toward Maybelleen and Virginia, and then returned to Calypso. "And you are?"

"Doctor Laskar. I've brought two close friends along

for moral support. Their husbands were also on Seth's plane." He hesitated and Calypso spoke again, very quickly, crossing the fingers on both hands against the white lie she was about to tell. "I mentioned them over the phone yesterday."

His finely arched eyebrows lifted fractionally before he shrugged and gestured for all three to move inside the barrier.

"Okay. It's irregular, but this whole thing is weird." Although he had closed the office door, Mr. Cardona's moderate voice dropped to a nearly inaudible whisper and he hunched forward conspiratorially. Calypso's breath caught. Something was terribly wrong. "Fortunately, Mr. Laskar came back today. They don't always do that when they've been on the streets for a long time."

Calypso spasmodically clenched and unclenched both fists and struggled to speak. Her throat was thick and taut, her breath irregular.

"He might have been in the jungle or the mountains for a while, but he can't have been on the streets for long."

A disembodied male voice bellowed over the public address system, summoning number eighty-nine to one of the cubicles and a wave of dissatisfied grumbling swept through the waiting room. Mr. Cardona murmured, "That's just it. We've got a mystery here. Although the records show that your husband is a successful businessman and professor, Seth claims he's been living on the streets for years. Both stories check out. He's originally from Daly City, up by San Francisco, and went to Vietnam when he was eighteen. About six months later he disappeared and was presumed dead, but at some point he made his way back to California. He's been drifting up and down the state ever since, in one shelter after another, with a serious drug problem."

Calypso felt her world tilt. Daly City? The bank that issued payments to Norma Drefan was in Daly City.

"That's impossible. Seth wasn't in Vietnam, and he's

from Montana. We've been married for over two years. I live with him in Claremont where he teaches and where he got an MBA eleven years ago, so there is no way he could have been a street person. You have someone else in there."

"That's right," chimed Maybelleen. "Seth's a famous person and one of my nicest friends. He would never, ever use drugs."

Slowly Cardona shook his head.

"There's no mistake about the identity. We've checked this guy's fingerprints and it's Seth Laskar. He's in a local shelter, attends AA and NA meetings regularly and seems to finally be serious about rehabilitating himself. The shelter director was the one that sent him to us since, as a street person and vet, he's entitled to assistance. But not, of course, if he's part owner of a successful company and a university professor."

Virginia stared narrowly at Mike Cardona, wondering whether Seth might not have lived a double life. It made no sense.

"Maybe there are two Seth Laskars?" Calypso suggested.

The man shook his head. "Impossible. When the records showed that Mr. Laskar was actually a businessman, the first thing we looked for was a duplicate name. We checked Social Security, the armed services, FBI, you name it, but we're pretty certain the only Seth Leib Laskar is sitting in my office."

Puzzled, Calypso tilted her head and frowned.

"Seth never used his middle name but I somehow thought the initial stood for Leigh."

"No. It's Leib."

"Probably the reason he never used it," offered Virginia tartly.

Suddenly, Calypso pushed past Mike Cardona and strode toward the closed door. With her hand clenching the knob she stopped, aware of the heavy pounding of her heart and the sweatiness of her palm. Gently, Mike Cardona pried her fingers from the knob and pushed the door open.

"Shall we go in?" he invited. Woodenly, Calypso, trailed by Maybelleen, Virginia and Cardona, stepped into the office.

Blood drained from Calypso's face and her body was cold; she cupped both hands over her mouth. Nothing broke the perfect silence of the airless room until Mike Cardona closed the door and stepped behind a utilitarian wooden desk, heaped with papers, bearing the scars of many years. With both fists resting on the desktop, he leaned forward and scrutinized the women intently.

"My stars," breathed Maybelleen.

About Seth's age, a man in a straight-back wooden chair beside the desk impassively returned the fixed stares of the three women. Slender, wearing chinos and a yellow polo shirt, he had pouches of fatigue under both eyes and appeared to be of Middle Eastern ancestry.

Carefully, Calypso moved her hands into prayer position with the finger tips under her chin as she continued to gaze at the stranger.

"That's not my husband." Her voice was no more than a whisper. "You've made a mistake." Suddenly, she fumbled in her bag and, with unsure fingers, extracted a photograph from her wallet. "*This* is my husband, Seth Laskar."

Glancing at the picture, Mike Cardona slowly shook his head. "I'm sorry. The man in the photograph may be your husband, but the man in front of you is Seth Laskar."

Staring at the stranger, Calypso dropped the photo back into her handbag.

Her eyes huge and her face frozen, Calypso felt her legs sag as she swiveled slightly toward Mike Cardona. "Mr. Cardona, if this is the real Seth L. Laskar, then whom did I marry?"

EIGHTEEN—Claremont

*E*ven before the nurse summoned her from the doorway, Calypso knew the answer and had known it for quite some time. Staring fixedly at a magazine on her lap, she was oblivious to the quiet conversation and occasional chuckles of other women seated in upholstered chairs nearby. It was a self-consciously cheerful room, with Chagall and Miro prints on the sunny yellow walls, linen vertical blinds screening large windows and bamboo table lamps casting an indirect, pleasant glow. Despite the comfortably reassuring atmosphere, Calypso was worried and depressed.

"Dr. Laskar, please come in."

Silence spread throughout the room as appraising eyes fastened on the small-boned woman with a tangle of long, wild hair who slowly stood and hoisted her shoulder bag. Stunning and professional in her pink linen dress and rose colored blazer, Calypso moved rigidly toward the smiling nurse.

"How are we today?"

I'm not sure, Calypso thought, as she was led down the hall and into the familiar office of Dr. Phillip Callahan. Tall and chubby in an immaculate, white lab-coat and traditional Harvard tie, his eyes magnified by very thick lenses, the physician was already striding around his desk with one hand outstretched as Calypso entered the room.

"Well, Dr. Laskar," he enthused, pumping her hand vigorously, then motioning to a chair facing his desk, "this is quite an occasion."

Numbly, she sank onto the pseudo-leather cushion and watched as he resumed his seat on the other side of the desk. Hands clasped together in a loose knot on the clean, brown leather-bound blotter, Dr. Callahan leaned forward and bestowed a wide, happy grin on his patient. A moment passed, then another, and his euphoria faded a bit.

"Don't you want to know?"

"I think I have an idea."

"Then I'll confirm. You are going to be a mother."

Calypso exhaled slowly and slumped against the back of her chair, staring at the doctor before closing her eyes.

"Success at last," he said uncertainly. "Isn't this terrific?"

She took a deep breath. "I'm not sure."

"I'm sorry, I don't understand." In the heavy silence, the sound of a lawnmower outside was intense and jarring. The comfortable, teddy-bear facade faded as Dr. Callahan tilted back in his swivel chair. "What about all the tests you and Seth have been through, not to mention the surgical correction of your tipped uterus?" He paused, baffled by her attitude and silence. "And I clearly recall a discussion not too long ago concerning possible artificial insemination using sperm from a bank, since Seth's count is so low."

Only her eyelids moved as she opened them and focused on Dr. Callahan. "How far along am I?"

"Nine weeks."

Nine weeks ago she'd been unfaithful to Seth for the

first and only time. For the past month, she had blamed her constant fatigue, nausea and craving for avocado on stress, denying her growing suspicion that tension wasn't the cause of her unpleasant physical changes.

"Did you know that Seth was on an airplane lost somewhere in South America nearly four weeks ago?" Her voice was a whisper in the quiet room.

The doctor's mouth opened then closed. Clearly stunned, first by Calypso's reaction to his good news and then by this unexpected and appalling information, it was a moment before the physician responded.

"I'm sorry," he repeated. "I had no idea. I do recall reading something about a plane crash â€" a charter flight, I think it was, on a flaky airline â€" but I just skimmed it one morning." Picking up a pen, he turned it absently between his fingers. "Have they located the plane? Or any survivors?"

"No. There was a prolonged search covering a lot of territory but no flight plan was filed and the pilot might have lost his way, so they really were hunting blind." Calypso clasped her hands in her lap and slid back in the chair.

Dr. Callahan removed his glasses and methodically polished them on a paper tissue hastily taken from a box on the desk.

"I did wonder why you waited so long to confirm your pregnancy." Myopically, he looked in her direction while buffing the lenses. "I'm profoundly shocked and hardly need to tell you how sorry I am. They haven't found anything?"

"No trace of the plane, cargo, passengers...nothing." Calypso's voice thickened and she was again caught in the vortex of despair, guilt and grief that had intensified since she first suspected pregnancy. With an effort, feeling tears prickle her eyelids, she continued: "I was so eager to have a child, and normally this would be a day to celebrate, but I never planned on single parenthood. With Seth gone, I'm entirely alone in this country."

Calypso despised herself. Of course she was alone in America but, under ordinary circumstances, that would be a minor problem. Like most Brazilians, Calypso thought that a family was only complete with children and she looked forward with boundless enthusiasm to a future in which the joys, love and closeness of her happy childhood could be replicated. Seth, on the other hand, had been oddly ambivalent, even slightly antagonistic toward the idea of parenthood. Although he clearly didn't understand or share his wife's adoration of babies, he nonetheless sympathized with Calypso's disappointment when, each month, she found that, despite all their efforts, she was still denied motherhood.

Now, the news that should have brought elation and euphoria induced fear and doubt. Not only was she uncertain regarding the paternity of the baby, she had no idea of Seth's real identity. It wasn't exactly what she'd envisioned in her desperate prayers for pregnancy.

Dr. Callahan held his glasses up to the light, and then put them on again, making careful adjustments over both ears.

"Is there a continuing search?"

Frowning thoughtfully at a bronze mother and child on a marble pedestal, Calypso replied softly, "No."

Intently, the doctor studied his patient.

"That changes the picture somewhat."

"Yes."

"I suppose termination could be considered under the circumstances. I don't recommend it after your difficulty conceiving *and* the fact that Mr. Laskar may be found alive and well, but it is a possibility. A great deal probably depends on your financial situation. Having a child is neither easy nor cheap, especially on one's own." After a short pause he added, "In the event that you do remain alone..."

His words jolted Calypso, forcing her to acknowledge

the fact that Seth might never be found, leaving her in an emotional and legal limbo. It was equally possible that one day his body would be discovered or, on the other hand, he would turn up alive. It was the worst possible situation and certainly didn't provide much guidance when it came to decision-making on any level.

California Consultants had left a paper quagmire as a legacy. The more the wives investigated, sorting through company documents in Jackson's coach house office, the more confused they became. Tentatively, the women concluded that their husbands were certainly involved in Brazilian telecommunications, but their major business interest was some other activity, cleverly concealed along with any cash that might have accrued. Bank records showed occasional modest deposits and almost immediate withdrawals. Company accountants were as baffled as the women by lack of corporate resources since there had been an abundance of cash in the months before the accident.

After making numerous phone calls to banks, accountants and California Consultant employees in São Paulo, Calypso had discovered that even less was known in South America about their husbands' activities. The only clue seemed to be the alexandrites, adding to the puzzle rather than offering a solution. How fortunate, Calypso often thought, that all the wives were financially independent; even Maybelleen had gone back to work as an auto mechanic.

Clasping her hands loosely on the desk top, Calypso studied her short, flawless nails with their opaque half-moons. From early adolescence, virtually all Brazilian women regardless of social standing had weekly, professional manicures, and it was a routine Calypso maintained in her adopted country. Now she slowly turned her fingertips, observing the transparent, sparkling lacquer, while pondering her choices.

There weren't too many. Have the baby or don't, and

that decision didn't depend on her finances, which would certainly be adequate. She had always felt deeply sorry for single parents who were forced to deal with problems and difficulties alone but, even if her husband proved to be alive and the father of her child, which was an unknown factor, she didn't know his true identity. Everything pointed strongly toward termination, and yet she balked at the idea.

Her religion did not condone it, of course, but she was a progressive, pro-choice advocate who had marched in more than one demonstration to keep Wade vs. Roe on the books and the abortion clinics open. The path should be very clear, and yet her mind stubbornly focused on the tales of women who were unable to conceive following an abortion, as well as those who were clinically depressed and suicidal afterward. She was uncomfortable with the idea when applied to herself. In addition, at the back of her mind was the suspicion that this might be her only opportunity to become a parent.

Lifting her eyes, she watched Dr. Callahan doodle aimlessly on a scrap of paper and realized that his customary air of professional authority was gone. He seemed perplexed and at a loss for words. At last, the doctor tucked his pen into a crystal bowl crammed with writing devices, interlaced his fingers and propped his chin on them.

"I personally think termination would be a mistake that you might deeply regret later on. If Seth isn't found, this may be your best and most treasured memory of him."

Or of Jackson...

"However, the decision is up to you."

"I know," she said.

The obstetrician stood up and so did she.

"I need to warn you, there isn't much time. If we're going to terminate with safety, it has to be very soon."

"Yes, I understand."

He crossed the room, opened the door and waited

while Calypso walked slowly in his direction. Pausing in front of the bronze mother and child, she gathered her frizzy hair at the nape of her neck and twisted it into a loose bun that sprang free the instant it was released. After studying the sculpture for a very long time, she faced the doctor and involuntarily sucked in her stomach, aware of how uncomfortably tight her waistband had become.

"I need a little time to think."

"Of course. But not too long."

"I'll phone next week to either schedule the operation or make an appointment for a pre-natal visit. And thank you."

NINETEEN—The Amazon Basin

*J*ackson was exhausted. He longed to stretch out beside the river, close his eyes and know that he wouldn't have to leap up in fifteen minutes, or two hours, or three seconds to ward off a red ant attack or run from two mating alligators thrashing their way along the water's edge or back away from a gigantic lizard that looked just like a prehistoric, scaled-down dinosaur and might well be dangerous or poisonous. He still flinched at the sudden shrill screams, chattering and yelps of hidden birds and animals in the jungle, his nerves constantly torn and frayed by the unexpected and unusual sounds.

Sometimes, particularly when sheets of rain sliced through the hot, still air and the smell of rot and decay hung like a heavy blanket in the humidity, he felt oddly lightheaded and numb, as though he were already dead and touring the outer fringes of hell. At those times, Calypso floated just beyond reach, usually wrapped in thin, gold gauze that bore her up, over the treetops and out of sight. Occasionally, Starr appeared, elegantly dressed and with a

193

cell phone pressed to one ear, and scolded him for his financial ineptitude before she vanished through the tangle of vines. Once or twice his children peeped around tree trunks to complain about his lack of attention when they were children, and one time Wheeler danced just out of reach, laughing as he tossed one hundred dollar bills into the air.

More than once, Jackson wondered if he might not be losing his grip on reality; it was a terrifying thought, one that always returned his mind to a sharp awareness of his fragile and vulnerable hold on life and the need to keep his dulled wits and failing body on alert at all times. The alternative was to surrender to the Indians, whom he was certain were stalking him in a cat and mouse game, or to one of the carnivorous plants he'd seen devour small amphibians, or to the poisonous reptiles that appeared frequently on the riverbank. But then again, had he imagined the arrow and had the plants been as ethereal as the visits of Calypso and his wife?

Crouching under a tangle of vines, the metal box close at hand, Jackson let his eyes close, felt his head roll and then drop heavily onto a moss covered tree trunk. Minutes or maybe hours later, he jerked into full consciousness. The jungle was a pattern of greens and blacks in the muted touch of earliest dawn and he automatically shrank and drew silently into a compact ball under the protective cover of undergrowth. Tense and watchful, he heard the warning shriek of the boatbills and the frenetic chattering of hidden marmosets, then the nearby crash and splash of an invisible body in the water, accompanied by noisy snorting and groaning. Almost immediately, he relaxed, identifying the raucous sounds as normal grazing of the manatee, a huge, harmless and rather pathetic aquatic mammal that spent nights devouring aquatic plants and grasses at the river's edge and disappeared into the water at the first hint of day. Once, days or possibly weeks ago, he was badly frightened when the beast's early morning snorting and stamping had ended in a chilling scream followed by silence. Much later that morning, Jackson had crept downstream and discovered a huge pool of blood, together with two broken arrow shafts, the arrowheads reclaimed. In retrospect, he wondered whether the slender sticks might not be thick bark or branches sloughed off by one of the taller trees.

He stood, and then abruptly sat down again feeling dizzy and unsteady. His body was thin to the point of emaciation, despite a fairly steady diet of raw fish, roots and grasses, and recently he'd begun to feel wobbly at the slightest exertion. As he did every morning, he scanned the clear sky and glanced at the river, searching for the slightest sign of civilization and, as always, found nothing new. No oil slicks, jet trails or candy wrappers marred the panorama. How he hated pure, unadulterated nature.

Grasping the metal box, he was about to stand again when a form shot by overhead and he heard a sharp cry directly in front of him. For a moment he was unable to breathe, as he listened to the snarls and screams of a vicious struggle a few yards away. Stealthily, pausing only to extract his gun from one pocket and hold it loosely in his right hand, he backed away from the reeds and thick vegetation that swayed and snapped under the weight of rolling, fighting bodies. He was surrounded by a cacophony of chattering, frightened squeals and cries as the jungle awoke and signaled danger.

Underbrush bordering the river quivered, then fell, mowed down in battle, allowing Jackson a clear view of a spotted jaguar and its dying prey, a capivara. He had been introduced to the world's largest rodent years ago at the zoo; in his jungle wanderings, the man had come to regard this placid herbivore as a shy, fat friend that wanted only to be left alone.

Chilled by the sight of the triumphant jaguar, he saw that the gentle capivara had used its long, sharp teeth to slash the jungle's most feared predator on one leg. That was bad. Very bad, since any wound would quickly fester in the moist, hot jungle atmosphere and a sick jaguar was a greater threat than one simply driven by hunger. He watched as the cat sank its fangs into the rodent's neck and ripped off a huge chunk of fat and flesh, swallowed voraciously and again tore at the chest and throat of its still twitching victim.

Prodded by the knowledge that the jaguar would soon be sated and then provoked by pain to further attacks, Jackson looked desperately for a nearby hiding place. Of course, nothing was really inaccessible to the feline; it could climb and swim with ease, was noiseless and perfectly camouflaged, but it was suicide to simply stand in the open. With something close to panic he listened to the throaty growls of the animal as it gashed and shredded the luckless capivara, barely swallowing huge chunks of flesh before slashing again at the mutilated carcass.

To the right was a hollow tree. Not unusual in this jungle where everything grew rapidly to glorious, brilliant double size and then died just as fast. Life expectancy here was very short, and that included the trees that decayed in an upright position and then tottered over, pulled to the ground by a combination of overpowering vines and gravity. Briefly, his mind wandered back to those two arrow shafts, then focused on the current crisis. Occasionally he'd sheltered in hollow trees but he avoided them, if possible, because a multitude of unpleasant surprises, including tarantulas and bats, tended to congregate inside. More importantly, a hollow tree was a dead end with no way out should natives decide on an attack. At the moment, though, he was more afraid of the cat than he was of unseen dangers.

Very carefully, stooping low, Jackson eased to one side while training his eyes on the feeding animal. In an emergency he could always shoot the jaguar but ammunition was limited and preservation of anything that might be needed in the future was essential. Inching backward, he flattened himself against the tree, remaining motionless for a few breathless seconds when the feline paused, lifted its head and sniffed the air. As the cat returned to its meal, Jackson stuffed the gun into his pocket and squeezed through the tree's narrow opening.

Almost immediately he was stunned by a shriek that reverberated through the inky blackness, nearly piercing his eardrums. As he rocked forward, he felt a sharp, searing pain in his right shoulder followed by the brush of a feathered body against his head. Automatically, he dropped the metal box and struck out with his right hand while the left dug into his pocket for the wire saw.

The screams increased in frequency and volume and he was struck again, this time on the left elbow. His entire body shook with pain, yet he was galvanized into action by the realization that he was being attacked and unless he struck out against his enemy, he might die right now in this tar-black hollow tree trunk.

Grasping one looped end of the wire saw in each hand, he lashed out, striking the creature with the knuckles of his left hand. Frantically, Jackson chopped at the air with the taut wire, grazing the winged creature that screeched with fury and swooped down again. Forgetting his pain and fatigue and even the jaguar just outside, Jackson concentrated only on the need to outwit his opponent here in the churning, swirling blackness. He tried to gauge the rhythm of the attacks, tuning his ears to undercurrents beneath the raucous shrieks, hoping to find some pattern that would warn him of the next sharp blow while his arms pumped overhead with the wire, whipping the damp, fetid air, striking either the attacker or the sides of the tree and catching nothing.

He was winded and exhausted. Nothing in his past surveillance work, and those grueling desert and arid mountain trips, had prepared him for this interminable jungle ordeal. Jackson knew his age was a handicap and suddenly felt dizzy and disoriented. The deafening cries seemed to recede and he heard a dull ringing in his ears, overlaid with the rasp of his own hoarse gasps. He was never going to get out of this alive.

Suddenly the wire caught on the slippery, attacking form and he heard a sharp scream inches from one ear. Fatigue evaporated and he was again, if only for a few seconds, young, agile, quick-witted and cunning. He threw the other arm in a wide circle, trapping the creature in a coil of wire, and then snapped the handles of the saw with all his strength. There was an immediate silence and in the unexpected hush, the crunch of bone and spurt of blood were clearly heard as the wire sliced through his assailant.

Clutching the inert bundle, he lurched into the open, oblivious to natives, snakes, jaguars, poisonous frogs and all other dangers in his anxiety to escape from the tree. For a moment he studied the lifeless heap of brilliant red, yellow and blue feathers in his hands. A macaw, he thought dully, and this was its nest. One of those beautiful birds that sometimes clung to the cliffs bordering the riverbank, feeding on whatever minerals and insects could be found in the rock. He'd seen them in pet shops at home, sitting on perches with their wings clipped and a price tag that could buy a new car. A large, "Do Not Touch: This Bird Bites", sign was always posted but only now did he fully appreciate the meagerness of that warning.

With an effort, he flung the wad of flesh and feathers into the nearby undergrowth, hearing an immediate rustle and growl. Something was already having his parrot for dinner. That was life in the jungle—either having a meal or stalking one or figuring out how to avoid being one.

Cautiously, he looked around for the jaguar and was relieved that the animal had finished eating and gone, yet worried that the cat might be lurking in the vicinity. Stuffing the wire saw back into his pocket, he ducked back into the tree where he retrieved the metal box then stumbled unsteadily to the riverbank and slumped to his knees. Now that the adrenalin had receded, his body burned with pain and it was with gentle, cautious fingers that he lifted the shredded and bloody shirt from his shoulders and peeled it from his gaunt arms. Bending low to the water, he stared at his wounds in the silvery early morning reflection. A small bit of flesh had been torn from his left shoulder and scratches and bites appeared lower on his arm. Blood was everywhere, in his matted beard, long, straggly hair and smeared over his thin, bare chest, but whether it was his or that of the parrot wasn't clear.

Cupping his hands, Jackson dipped them into the water and quickly washed, gritting his teeth as the cold liquid touched his open wounds, knowing he had very little time before the scent of blood attracted leeches, worms and carnivorous fish and animals. A thorough cleaning was essential to eradicate the smell of death and injury or he would be a target for every hungry creature in the jungle.

Using the water as a mirror, he drenched the injuries with rubbing alcohol, willing himself to calm consciousness as the disinfectant sent cold flames of pain through his body, raising gooseflesh on his arms and legs. Carefully capping the bottle, he extracted sterile gauze and waterproof surgical tape and bandaged the wounds, then slipped on the jacket that, until now, had been tied around his waist. It would be hotter than hell, he reflected bleakly, but it was protection. Ripping open the box of antibiotics, he swallowed two capsules, hoping that they weren't totally out of date.

Closing the metal box, he sat back on his heels and stared at the river in resignation. Time was running out. He'd always known that survival was problematic, but as a wounded man his chances dropped dramatically. Healing without extensive drugs or knowledge of native medical treatments was impossible in this steamy, hot climate, and it wouldn't be long before either gangrene set in or maggots encroached or maybe some tropical disease that he'd picked up from the bird would get to work. He was saving one bullet: no way would he die here of some agonizing disease or be eaten alive by parasites or natives or animals.

Suddenly, he focused intently on the stream to which he had earlier given only a brief, cursory glance. The current had become more rapid, and lifting his eyes to the far embankment he was astonished at the width of the waterway. No longer a meandering brook cutting a haphazard swath through the tangle of rotting trees and impenetrable undergrowth, it had straightened and become a real river flowing toward the sea. It was the first sign of change and dispelled Jackson's growing suspicion that perhaps he had been wandering alongside one of the many tributaries that looped, crossed and joined other small streams for hundreds of miles before feeding into larger bodies of water.

With muted excitement and a sense of hope, he stood, wincing as pains from his shoulder shot through his body. Pausing only for a moment, he hoisted the metal box and began to thread his way along the riverbank. He hadn't much time but there was a tiny chance he'd make it. Depending, of course, on what lay ahead.

TWENTY—LOS ANGELES

Side by side, Calypso and Virginia bent over their handlebars and peddled down the Venice Beach bike path. Sun shimmered on their oiled, sweaty skin and florescent spandex exercise outfits and glittered on the whirling spokes of their rented bikes.

"Want to ride out to the end?" asked Virginia.

"Clear to Redondo? Hardly. Do you?"

Virginia chuckled. "I hate any form of exercise, but this is moderately more fun than working out or lifting weights."

A man wearing a print sarong skirt tore past on roller blades, followed more slowly by two very senior citizens with stringy calves who skated expertly through and around the numerous cyclers and skaters. On the crowded boardwalk, pedestrians loitered beside stands offering tee-shirts, dark glasses, bead jewelry, incense and tie-dyed garments for sale. A sizeable audience stared at an inept female dancer who, with raised arms, transparent clothes and no underwear, drifted around a collection of guitar and bongo players on the strip of grass that separated bike path and boardwalk.

"Isn't it amazing how many people are at the beach on a Friday," commented Calypso, glancing at the long stretch of sand. In spite of its enormity, the beach was crowded with couples, families and singles, all seemingly well supplied with blankets, radios, food hampers, towels, toys and surf boards. Near the sea, Frisbees were chased and footballs tossed while children built sand castles or dug for sand crabs, unfazed by sun, heat and salty air.

"It gives new meaning to the term 'long weekend'," agreed Virginia. "Are Brazilian beaches like this?"

Smiling, Calypso shook her head. "Some. Not all. We have three thousand miles of beaches and a lot of them are completely deserted, with clear water, clean sand and palm trees."

For a moment she felt tears prickle her eyelids as she remembered holidays spent at her Aunt Alaíde's small vacation house in the village of Boiçucanga. With no paved streets and the most haphazard of water, electrical and garbage collection services, the hamlet was separated from the beach by a two-lane coastal road. Every day had been a wonderful adventure as she and her sisters romped and played on the sparsely populated Boiçucanga beach or those of nearby Maresias, Camburi and Ponta da Baleia. They swam with schools of multi-colored fish in quiet coves, jumped waves on the straighter shores, watched the fishermen with their lines and nets and sailed up and down the seashore in Uncle Herminio's boat. Calypso was pinched by a wave of homesickness even though she knew her childhood memory was no longer a reality; now, the beaches were packed, high rises lined the coastal road which was paved and jammed with vehicles from Thursday night until Monday morning, and there was still an inadequate infrastructure to cope with the huge influx of holiday visitors.

"Unfortunately, near the big cities the beaches are

crowded but not with bicyclers and skaters. Brazilians love bodies, adore showing off physiques in the tiniest bikinis, so most of the activity is just sauntering up and down the beach looking flirtatious. Or taking a sunbath or drinking a coco gelado and eating fried shrimp at a beach stand. It's very *tranquilo*, low speed."

"I think it's a pity that we didn't get to a beach while we were in São Paulo."

"Yes, it is. Maybe someday I can show you one of the islands, Ilha Grande or Ilha Bela, where they have fewer people." She was suddenly terribly tired. "Could we stop for a water break?"

"Good idea."

Slowly, the women glided toward a pair of palm trees sprouting from the narrow grass strip on their left, coasted onto the ground cover and stopped in the meager patch of shade provided by palm fronds. Straddling the bikes, they gulped thirstily from plastic water bottles then mopped their steaming faces and necks. Grinning, Virginia lifted her container and poured the remainder over the top of her head, her smile fading as she noticed Calypso's fatigued expression.

The Tin Man, as he was known locally, whipped by in reverse, sunlight flashing on his silver roller blades, helmet, toga, leggings and gloves. He leapt in the air, twisted and landed gracefully on one foot, and then executed a perfect cartwheel and sped down the path with one leg extended behind his body.

"What a show off," Virginia said. After a pause she added wistfully, "I wish I could do that."

Calypso tucked her water bottle in the bike pouch and removed her square-cut, designer dark glasses. Bending her arms, she leaned forward, resting on the handlebars of her bike.

"There's something I have to tell you," she began.
"What?"
After a pause, Calypso took a deep, ragged breath and

whispered, "I'm pregnant."

Virginia felt a sharp stab of jealousy. Initially, she and Ferguson had wanted children, not desperately, but as a completion of their happiness and unity as a couple. It hadn't happened, even though all the tests showed that there was nothing amiss with either of them. From time to time they'd discussed adoption but it was so complicated that it seemed wiser to adopt through one of the South American countries. That wasn't an easy route either, and gradually the subject was dropped. She hadn't thought of children in relation to herself for years, so why, she wondered irritably, was she upset over Calypso's news?

Palm fronds clattered dryly in the sudden silence between the two friends. Skaters whipped past, the scrape of their roller blades on asphalt nearly blocking the rhythmic rumble of the surf and cries of low-flying gulls, and yet neither woman spoke. Finally, after a quick, involuntary glance at Calypso's stomach, Virginia broke the hollow stillness.

"I really don't know what to say. Congratulations, of course. I know you want a family, but it is rotten timing."

"To say the least."

"How do you feel about this?"

Calypso sighed and stared at a group of children playing in the sand.

How did she feel? Confused and conflicted, as though any decision would be the wrong one. Time was not her friend, and Calypso's days were a blur of unresolved tension, her mind constantly skittering from the question of an abortion to single motherhood to motherhood with a partner whose identity she didn't know. There was no right answer and the more she probed the limited possibilities, the more uncertain she was about the best path to choose.

"I don't know since I don't know who Seth really is," she answered truthfully, her mind veering from Jackson's possible role in this scenario. "Dr. Callahan said that if I want to terminate, then it has to be soon, but I simply can't bring myself to do that. For a number of reasons..."

After an awkward pause, Virginia asked, "Should you be bicycling?"

Calypso smiled. Straightening, she pulled the rubber band from her pony- tail and firmly twisted the mop of flyaway hair before securing it again.

"I'm pregnant, not an invalid. I bike around Claremont all the time." She glanced down at her thickening waist. "Although, I won't be able to wear this spandex outfit for much longer..."

Absently, Virginia eyed her friend's yellow, green and blue ensemble, the colors of the Brazilian flag that had been specially ordered from a manufacturer in São Paulo. Slowly, she turned to face the sea, pale blue in the far distance where it disappeared into the sky. Close to shore, the water was deep green, lifting periodically in huge, frothy white waves that sent surfers skimming diagonally across the curling water in a graceful dance.

"Why don't we go back to the condo, shower and change and look over all the business information we have, and then reward ourselves with a terrific lunch?" she said. "I keep thinking we must have missed something. So far all we know is that there's some life insurance but, until we know the men are really gone...or wait seven years, it can't be collected. We have a fortune in alexandrites that we can't sell because we don't own them, and haven't a clue as to who does. And that's about it."

The front doorbell chimed and, in Virginia's study, the two women exchanged quizzical glances before silently sliding the sheaf of papers they had been studying into a leather folder. Standing, Virginia adjusted a heavy gold necklace, brushed at a wrinkle in her black linen trousers and said, "I'm not expecting anyone."

"Hey, Toots, you got a visitor". Vince's voice hissed dramatically through the space surrounding the fish tank, his face wavering behind colorful aquatic bodies that darted through the water. Striding to the oscillating image, Virginia placed her own nose close to the glass.

"I am not amused. Who is it?"

"It's a she, and you're going to be surprised." Her driver's grin broadened and his black brows wiggled briefly before he abruptly vanished.

Virginia glanced at Calypso, who had now risen and was reaching for her handbag.

"Don't go. I'll deal with whomever it is and then it's lunch time."

Just outside in the hallway, Vince's voice growled a summons. "Your guest awaits, Toots."

Heels sinking into the thick carpet, Virginia crossed the room, opened the door and frowned at her employee.

"While I am entertaining my visitor I want you to get out the Yellow Pages and find a finishing school—one that accepts men and teaches elocution and manners."

"You want I should apply to teach electrocution? I'm too busy."

"Perhaps it would be useful for you to wash the car and help Blanca with the windows."

Virginia, followed by Calypso, strode past Vincent and moved into the living room where a woman, her blond hair in a prim bun, was now observing the fish. Tanned and freckled, wearing an elegant navy blue trouser suit with a one button jacket, the visitor turned to face her hostess. In mid-step, both Virginia and Calypso halted, muscles paralyzed, smiles congealed. Virginia recognized the extraordinarily pretty woman that she, Calypso and Maybelleen had seen lunching with Pete at the Viccolo West months ago. Calypso's mind instantly flashed back to the accident they had witnessed in Hollywood.

Recovering quickly, Virginia moved forward, her smile fading as their hands met in a weak handshake.

"Mrs. Morrissey? I'm Sally Jacobson from the DEA. I do hope this isn't an inconvenient time for you." She looked meaningfully at Calypso. "What I have to tell you is very private."

The DEA, thought Virginia? Trust Peachy to have a problem with the government.

"This is Dr. Laskar, one of my closest friends and the wife of one of the men on the plane. I want her present." Virginia's voice was firm and her tone discouraged any discussion.

Calypso's intuitive judgments were usually accurate and she immediately distrusted this woman even though the visitor was chic, well groomed, articulate and friendly. Mentally, she recalled the car of hoodlums that had swerved into the intersection and deliberately struck Ms. Jacobson's car. Lunch with Pete and now an uninvited visit to Virginia? Calypso felt an unaccustomed surge of hostility that she put down to her current physical and mental state; she and Sally Jacobson exchanged wary, cool glances and then the latter switched her attention to Virginia.

"This is very urgent. May I sit down? It won't take long."

Virginia nodded, hoping it was an opportunity to actually discover what Pete had really been doing. "Certainly."

The women perched uneasily on the edges of their chairs.

"I was working very closely with Pete on a terribly sensitive project. Since the plane and all the passengers seem to have vanished, I need your help," Sally explained.

"And I need to see some ID."

"Of course."

Watching Ms. Jacobson fish about in her navy blue Fendi bag, Virginia wondered about the pay scale for civil servants these days. Maybe Blossom should switch agencies and be a spook for a while.

"Here we are." Opening a small leather card case, Sally extracted a laminated ID card which she held up for display. Virginia reached for the document and, for a moment, the two women played gentle tug-of-war until the lady of the house gave a definitive wrench that plucked the card from her guest's grasp. The ID seemed, to Virginia's untrained eye, to be authentic, but of course one never knew. Opening the drawer of a scrolled and gilded end table, she pulled out a pad and pencil and began to copy the information on the card, wishing she could duplicate it on the FAX machine in the next room.

"Is that necessary?"

"Yes. My husband, with luck late husband, was an idiot, but I'm not."

Glancing up from the pad, Virginia caught an odd look, quickly expunged, on Sally's face. Perhaps the agent had expected a deeply grieving dimwit, she thought. Closing the pad and pencil in the drawer, Virginia passed the card to Calypso, who scrutinized it while wondering about this woman's real identity. Calypso returned the card to their guest , folded her hands together in her lap and, with Virginia, stared levelly at Sally.

"Now, what can I do for you?" asked Virginia.

"Let me emphasize the importance and delicacy of this operation," she began, staring frostily at Calypso for a moment. "None of the other partners knew of Pete's very crucial role in our organization."

Virginia didn't doubt that for one minute. Sally's attention swung back to her hostess.

"Very briefly, Pete had agreed to set up a ten-second lag in the telecom system his company was installing so that everything could be routed through DEA headquarters. That way we could track any suspicious movements in the Amazon and also find out what the Brazilians are up to. And edit information. At the time of the crash, the preliminary system was up and only waiting for permission from Brasilia to operate." She leaned forward confidentially, her voice dropping and her eyes wide. "Undoubtedly, another firm will now take over, but we need to know whether Pete was successful in installing the lag."

Virginia and Calypso exchanged quick, baffled glances.

"My husband never discussed his work with me, Ms. Jacobson."

"Please call me Sally," she invited warmly. "I'm sure he was very closemouthed. Mr. Morrissey's concern for the security of his country is nothing short of heroic." Virginia and Calypso both heard a distinct snicker from the hallway; the latter struggled to suppress a smile while Virginia pressed her lips grimly together. "However, if you run across anything in his records or papers that might give us a clue one way or the other, would you call me?"

"The number on the card is your office?"

"My direct line, yes."

That, thought Virginia, could mean anything. Her spirits soared. At least now there was something tangible, a tiny clue that could be followed. She picked up a small brass bell, rang it and, before the chimes faded, Vincent popped in from the hallway.

"My, that was quick footwork," commented Virginia tartly.

"In the 'hood' my name's Speedy."

"I'm sure it is. Please escort Ms. Jacobson to the front door."

The women stood and shook hands, exchanging insincere smiles and farewells. After the driver had followed Sally from the room, Calypso spoke.

"You said you saw Ms. Jacobson having lunch with Pete?

"That's right," Virginia replied with a pensive frown. "Some time before the airplane accident Maybelleen and I were lunching at Viccolo West and we spotted Pete there with that woman, although neither of them saw us. But I just realized that Vincent wasn't present in the restaurant that day and yet he obviously recognized the woman."

"And so did I."

Virginia stared at her friend: "You did?"

"Remember the little car crash in Hollywood when those thugs that Vince seemed to know deliberately ran their car into another one at the intersection? I think we were on our way to Maybelleen's, although I don't remember much other than the incident. Sally was the woman that jumped out of the damaged car."

Virginia's eyebrows lifted and her lips parted in a faint smile. "Of course..."

Calypso couldn't miss the biting venom in Virginia's voice, but Vince's sudden appearance spared her the necessity of a reply.

"Vincent, I have a question."

"Speak, Mrs. M. My brain is your brain, as my mama used to say."

"How do you know Sally Jacobson?"

His smooth, olive face reflected genuine surprise. "Same way you do."

"And how is that?"

A slow grin curved his lips. Reaching into his breast pocket, Vincent extracted a pack of cigarettes and shook one out.

"Remember when I took you to meet Mrs. Webb for the first time?"

"Yes, of course."

He scratched a match on one thumbnail, lit the cigarette and blew three perfect smoke rings.

"And on the way back we took a spin through Hollywood where we saw a little car accident."

"Ah, yes. Sally's car was deliberately hit by those sleazy jailhouse friends of yours right after you waved some gang signals back and forth."

"We were talking with signs, like deaf people do."

Virginia closed her eyes to signify disbelief, then opened them and stared at her chauffeur. "Is that the only time you've seen her?"

Vincent's faults were almost countless but his loyalty

was absolute, and so was his honesty. "I saw her today."

"I know that," Virginia responded impatiently. "She says she's a DEA agent who recruited Pete."

In the process of inhaling deeply, Vince began to snort with laughter, and then to cough painfully. His body bent double for a few moments as he choked and gasped, tears leaking from his eyes. After regaining control of himself he straightened, pulled mirrored sun glasses from one pocket and put them on.

"If she's DEA, then I'm Bertie Einstein."

"Your gangster compatriots that crashed her car apparently knew her."

"Seems that way."

"Do you think if I offered a little bonus they might remember something? Like who Sally is and what she does?"

"For the right price they might."

"For a nickel you'd all kill your own mothers."

"For this dude it'd have to be at least a quarter."

"What a relief to hear it. Just have a little chat with your fellow felons and mention a generous offer in exchange for information. We may need to neutralize Sally's activities."

"You mean a sanction?"

"I do not understand the jargon of the underworld and I don't need to expand my education in that direction, but if the term indicates permanent retirement for the lady, that is not what I had in mind. I just don't want her popping up here and there and causing trouble." Virginia paused and frowned at Vince. "Take off those glasses. If you're going to imitate Ray Charles, you'll have to learn to sing."

"I sing pretty good after a few tequilas." Vincent removed the glasses and slipped them into his pocket.

"Thank you. How about Pete? Could he have had his own agenda?"

"You mean an independent thought?"

"You could put it that way..."

"Not a chance."

She looked at her watch. "Why don't you make some phone calls to your friends? Dr. Laskar and I will go to lunch in half an hour, and then you might take me to check up on Maybelleen."

"You mean Mrs. Webb?"

"Yes; of the thousands of Maybelleens I know, I'm referring to Mrs. Webb."

After blowing another perfect smoke ring, Vince saluted smartly and then shuffled from the room in what could only be described as an East L.A. samba with strong African overtones. Calypso quickly bent to search in her handbag, hiding a broad smile while Virginia, not amused, glared at her employee's retreating back.

After lunch on the terrace of Chez Lucille, Calypso drove back to Claremont and Virginia directed her driver toward Maybelleen's house.

"Go through the hills, Vince. It's much more scenic."

"That's the long way," he commented, swinging the car left on Sunset, then right. The Bentley slowly climbed a steep, winding road. "I think this is close to where Charles Manson wasted all those hairdresser cats."

"I'm a little worried."

"Why? Charlie's still doing time as far as I know."

"This has nothing to do with Manson's achievements. I don't understand the connection between Sneaky Pete and his sidekick Sally."

At the top of the hill, Vincent turned west on Mulholland Drive. The road twisted and dipped, flanked by large, sprawling homes set well back from the street and nearly obscured by a profusion of thickly tangled trees and shrubs. Accompanied by romping dogs, a number of horses grazed on hilly pastures that were well defined by wooden fences. Panoramas of Hollywood and downtown Los Angeles on the left and the San Fernando Valley and the nearby mountains on the right were occasionally visible through the screen of heavy foliage.

Brown eyes hidden behind his mirrored sun-glasses, Vince observed his employer in the rearview mirror.

"Fear not, Mrs. M. I called in a marker and found out some stuff about Sally. It was a freebie, so do I get the bonus?"

"That was quick. We only spoke three hours ago." Gleefully, Virginia tossed her fox stole over one shoulder then stroked the dead creature's head affectionately. "You shall receive your reward."

"Not in heaven, sweetheart. I want it in the bank account."

"What did your unsavory associates tell you?"

"What about the money?"

"I am astonished that you'd put the bite on me when our relationship is based on mutual trust. In case you've forgotten, you'd be languishing in Soledad or Vacaville if it weren't for me."

The pair rode in silence for several minutes.

"Alright." Virginia lifted both hands in defeat. "You'll get a cash bonus with your next salary."

Removing his sun-glasses, Vince trained dark brown eyes on her in the mirror.

"And keep your eyes on the road. I want to live to hear this."

"Your wish is always my command." Once again he hid his eyes behind mirrored lenses. "The driver of the car that day was named Armando. He told me that this Sally chick works with some jewel smugglers over in Gardena."

"In *Gardena*? What kind of jewels, rhinestones and sequins?"

"Gardena's where they operate: their HQ, so to speak. They're also fences. You know, like when there's a big jewel robbery they take hot items down to Mexico before the police even file the report, then they carry the merchandise across Mexico, up through Arizona to

Nevada and Oregon, and then back here again. Pretty slick, but their big thing has been illegal gold and jewels. They've been dealing in the gold district downtown but now they're trying to move into Beverly Hills, and that's Rolly Denton's turf. So Fat R hired Armando to deliver some warnings."

"So your chum Armando was at work that day?"

"That's right."

Virginia's eyes squeezed shut in fury and her lips twisted into a thin, crooked line. Wadding her hands into fists, she ground them savagely into the leather seat. Her eyes flashed open and she stared at Vince's sun glasses.

"I can't believe that even Peachy could be so stupid as to think he was becoming a national super hero by collaborating with the DEA when he was actually involved with a bunch of gangsters ."

"Believe it."

"He's a perfect moron."

"Surprises you, does it?"

"Not really..."

For a few moments, silence filled the Bentley as they traversed the winding road. A breeze had cleared the air of smog, and in the distance Virginia could see the flat, metallic sheen of sunlight on the Pacific Ocean. Vincent frowned slightly.

"Toots?"

"What?"

"So we know this is a slick chick who smuggles diamonds and emeralds and now probably sees a chance to latch onto some alexandrites, but why is she screwing around with ten second lags and a jackass like Sneaky Pete?"

Virginia continued to stare at the misty horizon where deep green water and sapphire sky had blanched into pearly uniformity. Vincent had just put her thoughts into words.

TWENTY-ONE—LOS ANGELES

Calypso pressed the bell beside Maybelleen's double front doors, closed her eyes and lifted her face to the sun, then stepped into the shade of an enormous fig tree. It was unusually hot and damp for Los Angeles, even here close to the beach, and she felt a sudden loneliness and yearning for the familiarity of home and loved ones. Opening her eyes, she frowned sternly at the doors. In fact, she reminded herself, she was lucky that her devoted and doting family knew nothing about the mess she'd made of her life.

Maybelleen opened the door wearing work overalls. Instead of her usual enthusiastic greeting, she offered her guest a grim smile, putting Calypso immediately on her guard.

"Maybelleen, is something wrong?"

"If you'd ask me, I'd certainly say so, but it has nothing to do with you. Please come right in. Virginia's here, and I hope you don't mind, but I invited Blossom as well. Mommy and Daddy are coming over later, and Mommy wants me to go to church and pray for the men, but I'm so mad at Wheeler I'd kill him if he weren't already dead."

Alarmed, Calypso frowned at her hostess before Maybelleen slammed the heavy door shut and they moved into the lush garden.

"What's this all about?"

Maybelleen's boots slapped an angry tattoo on the flagstone path as they crossed a knoll of Korean grass. "I thought Wheeler was the most wonderful man in the world, but now I know that what he mostly told me were lies. Besides everything else, I found out that Patsy Jo Adams has to cover a string of his rubber checks in Montana, as well as unpaid taxes for two years. And he stole poor Rebecca Bauer's stocks and left her with a big American Express bill. Can you believe it?"

Calypso was puzzled as well as worried. "Who's Patsy Jo? I remember her name came up months ago in São Paulo, but no one seemed to know who she was, including Wheeler."

"She and Rebecca were his first two wives, each of whom he forgot to mention to me. I guess I'm lucky he didn't leave me any debts, and I do have a good job as an auto mechanic. Mommy says we should read the Bible and turn the other cheek, but Daddy says that Wheeler had better be dead if he knows what's good for him. That is so unkind. But you know what? Daddy's right."

Vaguely aware of Virginia and Blossom watching from the far end of the terrace, they stopped and faced one another. Calypso had never seen Maybelleen angry but her friend's blue eyes sparked dangerously, her pale skin was flushed and her breath came in audible snorts. Accustomed to soothing her hostess's tears and grief with words of comfort, Calypso floundered in the face of this transformation. Off-balance, she picked her way carefully, speaking slowly and hoping she could bring calm to this unexpected situation.

"Maybelleen," she said gently, "they may all be crooks.

We know for a fact that Wheeler and Pete were kiting checks and stealing from the company. I have no idea who or what Seth really is, and remember I trusted him too." She paused thoughtfully. "Jackson is a blank. I suppose it's possible that the head of a company could hire only thieves and swindlers and know nothing about it, but that's just not likely."

"But I *believed* Wheeler. I had faith in my husband, just like wives are supposed to, and all he did was sneak and lie." Maybelleen's buxom figure trembled with rage as she clenched and unclenched fists that were only slightly tinged with axel grease. "He took advantage of me; and he's a bad person." Maybelleen glowered angrily at the trees.

Slipping an arm around her friend's shoulders, Calypso gave her a little shake. "It seems that they all, with the possible exception of Jackson, took advantage of us, and now we have to get on with our lives. Unless they turn up, we'll probably never know all the answers."

Hoping to change the subject, she glanced at the banks of flowers and shrubs that surrounded the Korean grass and flagstone path and encircled the distant swimming pool. With relief, she noticed a stone arch on one side and said, "That's lovely. Is it new?"

Moving across the garden, the women stepped under the crescent and into a small, shady alcove with an intricately patterned, gravel ground cover, a stone fountain and a shallow small fish pond. Except for gently splashing water, the silence was profound and very soothing.

"Pretty new," answered Maybelleen, visibly calmer. "It's a Japanese garden."

"It's so peaceful."

"Blossom's friend Suki, at the post office, designed it, and Blossom, Daddy and Suki made it. It's for meditating, but I don't know how to do that, so I rake the gravel every day and sometimes study here for my airline mechanics test."

Suddenly, Punky, customarily placid and calm, streaked under the archway, scattering a shower of small rocks and stones, slid to a stop beside the pond and jabbed the water with one paw. Extracting it after a moment, he examined his pads with apparent disappointment. Body tense, he studied the pool then lunged again, lost his balance and, with a splash, toppled in with the carp.

"Punky!" Maybelleen's reedy voice was fearful as she dashed across the smooth pebbles and knelt to rescue the cat. "Naughty, naughty boy! Stay away from those fish!"

Back on solid ground, the sodden feline gave a shrill yowl, shook himself briefly, then sped back into the garden and disappeared. Rapidly fanning her face with one hand, Maybelleen stood.

"That's so frightening. Punky can't swim." Calypso was happy to notice that Wheeler, along with Maybelleen's rage, was forgotten in the current crisis.

"All animals can swim if they have to."

Arms again linked, they moved into the garden toward the far terrace where Virginia and Blossom lounged in recliners.

"You think? Animals do drown."

"It happens when they're exhausted in flood conditions or the ocean or a lake, but not in a small fish pond."

Blossom and Virginia stood, kissed Calypso on both cheeks, then Virginia slumped back in the chaise lounge as Calypso and Blossom seated themselves on director chairs.

"Where's Starr?"

"Working, I suppose. Basically, she's still not at all interested."

At a round, mosaic table nearby, Maybelleen poured glasses of iced tea, placed them on a tray along with slices of lemon and a bowl of sugar cubes and offered the tray to each guest.

"This is the way they do it in Brazil," she announced, without a trace of her recent anger.

Puzzled, Virginia frowned. "Do what?"

"Serve things. Always on a tray, never with the hands; that is considered to be rude."

"That's exactly right; that's how we do it," Calypso agreed.

Turning, Maybelleen placed a plate of cookies on the empty tray and passed it. "I made this pecan and cashew shortbread today. Punky and Daddy love it."

Calypso selected a small, sweet square and gave her friend an affectionate smile. "Thank you for agreeing to meet with me." She looked at Maybelleen. "And especially thank *you* for offering your house and taking time off from work. I hated asking you to come all the way to Claremont just so I could share some new information with you."

Blossom placed his iced tea carefully on a small table, smoothed his platinum pony tail with both hands and crossed one leather-encased leg over the other. Silver bangles clinked noisily as he interlaced his fingers and rested them on one knee.

"No problem at all," he boomed, "but I have to leave in about half an hour. Suki and Rayjean both called in sick, so we're shorthanded at work."

"Poor Blossom," breathed Maybelleen, sliding into the adjacent chair and patting his hands sympathetically. "All that responsibility."

Calypso inhaled deeply, and then spoke.

"First, about our trip to Minas Gerais next week. I've decided we must take Vince with us."

All three stared at her in consternation. As a result of her persistent telephone enquiries to Brazil, Calypso had discovered that the missing men traveled frequently to a mine in a remote region of Minas Gerais, although no one seemed to know why. Since it was their only clue to both the source of the alexandrites and the possible fate of their husbands, the three women planned to visit the mine and probe for additional facts.

"Why should we take him?" asked Virginia.

"The trip will be long and much more uncomfortable

and dangerous than we first thought. We have our flights booked to Belo Horizonte, the state capital, but there's another ten or eleven hours over unpaved roads that are little better than trails. You have no idea how bad Brazilian roads can be, and our choice is between infrequent bus service and a rented four-wheel drive. I vote for the car, but not with just three women."

Planting both elbows on the arms of his chair, Blossom's hands became a steeple supporting his chin. Maybelleen's glistening lips formed an 'O'.

"Why is it dangerous?" she asked.

"If the car breaks down, no one's going to come to fix it. There is no AAA, no road service and the rental company may or may not send someone, but even if they do, it won't be in a timely manner. In the interior of the country, travel is mostly by horse, horse and cart, ancient truck or bus."

"I'm a mechanic; I can repair any car," Maybeleen said definitively.

"Of course you can, and you may have to, but road robberies are common, and a nice car with three women in it is a target."

After a moment of silence, Maybelleen spoke again: "Well, then let's take a bus."

"She already said they were infrequent," commented Virginia tartly.

"And that would be all right going to the mine, but we couldn't leave until another bus came along, which would be disastrous. Brazilian mines are primitive, and miners are lawless. We need Vince for protection and to navigate the roads."

"I didn't notice anything like that when we were in Brazil. Did you, Blossom?" persisted Maybelleen.

"No, but we were in São Paulo, the third largest city in the world."

"We can't go without Vince," announced Calypso firmly.

Slowly, Virginia nodded agreement. "It sounds like the only way." Her voice hardened. "He'll be absolutely impossible, swaggering around, talking about all the luscious ladies that fell at his feet; I can't stand it." Her face contorted as though she had just bitten into an unripe persimmon.

Calypso smiled. "He won't have time on this trip to dally with women. And we´ve got to get back right away. At least I do, in order to follow a lead that´s turned up."

Radiating sudden hope, all three stared at her.

"A lead?" Virginia prompted.

"That's the second reason I wanted this meeting. Last week I went through all the papers at home one more time and came across two business letters to Seth from someone named Ralph Russo, one dated about six months ago and another a year ago last July. I don't know how I missed them before. Both said that Bonny King had been receiving her regular payments and that they were spent as directed."

"Who's Bonny King?" asked Maybelleen, her eyes wide.

"I haven't any idea, but Mr. Russo is a private detective."

"Golly," breathed the hostess.

"Detective?" rumbled Blossom.

"So I hired another investigator to see what this is all about and he gave me some information about Mrs. King that I need to follow up. At the very least, I'm hoping to find out who my husband actually is." And, she added silently, what place Norma Drefan and Bonny King have, or had, in his life.

"This may be the missing piece we've been looking for," murmured Virginia.

Pondering this unexpected news, Calypso's companions sat in silent reflection, the serenity of Maybelleen's garden and roofed terrace scarcely noticed. Banana trees, hardy but barren, arched over the far end of the swimming pool deck, their leaves brushing together and echoing the whisper of a tiny stream that burbled down the slope under the trees to feed the fountain and coy pond in the Japanese garden. A thick tangle of bougainvillea vines, heavy with magenta and rose flowers, hung from the tiled veranda roof shading an empty hammock that Maybelleen had brought back from Brazil. Speaking briskly, Calypso broke the hush.

"I've taken the liberty of buying a ticket for Vince and I've reserved a car in Belo. I've also located a decent pousada in Teófilo Otoni, a small town on the way to the mine, where we can spend the night on the way there and back and get a passable meal."

"Wow," breathed Maybelleen. "You've really thought of everything." She turned to Blossom. "I wish you'd come with us."

Calypso chuckled and Blossom grinned broadly. "Well, the idea of a long, dangerous, uncomfortable trip *is* tempting, but fortunately I don't have any vacation time or personal days left."

Virginia turned to Calypso. "Should you be making this trip at all? In your condition, I mean."

Calypso sobered instantly. Wondering the same thing, she had asked Dr. Callahan's advice. While he strongly suggested she abandon any thoughts of such a venture, she had made up her mind to go. Almost immediately, she doubted the wisdom of her decision but she was essential as a translator; two gringos and Vince would be useless in the interior of Brazil, and this was one trail that they must follow.

"I think so," she said with more confidence than she felt.

"I don't like the idea at all," said Virginia. "And when we get back we'll have to discuss your living arrangements."

"What about them?"

"You can't stay all by yourself way out in Claremont."

Calypso smiled.

"I certainly can. Far away Claremont is part of Greater L.A., and I have modern conveniences in case of an emergency. Like a telephone. As I told you before, I don't have a terminal illness."

Now dry, Punky padded onto the veranda and sprang into Maybelleen's lap where he proceeded to wash his face.

"Well, it's your life, but I think someone should be with you."

"I have Teresa," Calypso protested.

"Oh, maids," Virginia snorted, flapping one hand in disgust. "Yours is only part time and none of them notices a thing except their salaries."

Calypso looked at the other three and her heart twisted, both with love for these three dear friends who were genuinely worried about her well-being, and with sorrow for the chaos she had created. Reaching over, she took Virginia's hand and squeezed it affectionately.

"All right, we'll talk about it later, but right now the most pressing concern is our trip to the mine and what we can find out from Mr. Ernesto."

"Who's Mr. Ernesto?"

"I was told he's the supervisor there." She paused, her forehead furrowed. "And the minute I get back I must see about Bonny King."

TWENTY-TWO—The Amazon Basin

*J*ackson lay panting on the riverbank, his eyes unable to focus properly, his shoulder and entire left side throbbing in pain. Weakly, he moved his right hand along the mud and sand, feeling for the metal box that he'd dragged through the jungle for days, weeks, or maybe even months. Time, since his battle with the parrot, had blurred into a hopeless and dizzying pattern of days and nights, blinding light and inky blackness punctuated by the raucous and frightening sounds that he now no longer noticed. Onward he had plodded, sometimes crawling, following the river that was noticeably wider and changing dramatically.

Not long ago, he'd found himself poised on the edge of a precipice, the placid body of water disappearing into a steep gorge that mandated a detour into the jungle and down a cliff. It had taken two periods of darkness before he joined the waterway again, and during that time he'd been as keenly alert and tensely attentive to sounds and directions as he had been just after the plane crash. All too aware of the consequences should he wander away from the river, his relief, when he finally saw white moonlight glittering on water, was so great that he felt physically ill.

Now he was sick again, but this time it was the spreading infection from wounds refusing to heal despite the antibiotics he had consumed until they were gone. Behind him, the river bubbled in rocky rapids that had necessitated a steep descent over massive, slippery boulders; with great care he had floundered and skidded from one rock to another, aware that a single slip could mean a broken ankle or a foot trapped between stones. After the waterway smoothed again into a glassy expanse, he sloshed ankle-deep through stagnant ponds of green water mixed with mud and decomposed vegetation that left him with steaming boots and trousers. He should have removed his clothes and allowed them to dry but he simply hadn't the strength. What difference does it make, he thought, if I die with unhealed lesions on my feet and an infected arm, when the whole body's going to decay and fall apart very soon anyhow?

Limply, he patted his right trouser pocket and, reassured that he hadn't lost the gun and remaining bullets, pulled the metal box closer and shut his eyes. He should try to catch a fish or hunt some kind of vegetable for a meal. He couldn't remember when he'd eaten last, having long ago passed the point of hunger. Sternly, he now reminded himself that starvation would be the ignominious end if he didn't try to scavenge food.

Turning his head toward a sudden faint breeze, he watched Starr, chicly dressed in her yellow trouser suit and matching hat, float from a cloud of mist and sail toward him. Stopping a few feet away, she frowned severely and bent over him.

"If you'd had your priorities straight and thought of me first, this would never have happened." It was strange, he thought lazily; she didn't actually speak aloud and yet he knew just what she was saying. "Since you didn't share your money with me, I won't share food with you." A bunch of grapes appeared in one of her hands; with delicate, bejeweled fingers, she slipped a single grape into her mouth, and then tossed the remainder over her shoulder. A nasty smile curved her lips. "This is the gift I have for you." Inhaling deeply, her mouth formed a round circle and her cheeks ballooned as she exhaled a shower of icicles that enveloped her husband, rocking him gently on the sandbank for a few minutes before clearing. Odd, he thought without great curiosity, the blast of wintry air had been tropically hot; he felt feverish and disoriented. Blinking to clear his vision, he saw that Starr had vanished.

He dozed, feet swelling inside the wet leather, his fist weakly clutching the handle of the metal box. Abruptly, he jerked to full attention, his mind sharp and very clear. Adrenalin flooded his gaunt body and he snapped to a sitting position, scanning the cloudless, milk-blue sky. He heard an airplane. It was the first mechanical noise since the crash and intruded on the routine jungle din like the crack of his gun on those rare occasions when he'd been forced to use it. Within seconds, the wilderness pulsated with the scurrying, scampering, slithering and flying of alarmed birds and animals.

Carefully, he scrutinized the empty sky while the sound grew more distinct. Removing his dark glasses, he dipped them in the water, cleaned them hastily on his ragged trousers, and replaced them. The plane must be just out of sight, hidden by thick shrubbery or an overhanging tree, ready to either fade into the distance or turn back and flash into sight.

Opening the metal box, he rummaged hastily through the contents, looking skyward every few seconds. He shook the box, then lifted the carefully folded thermal blanket and sighed with relief as he spotted the signal mirror and, just underneath, the flare gun. Shoving the latter into his jacket pocket, he grasped the mirror and struggled to a standing position. Unmindful of poison frogs, eels, crocodiles, man-eating fish or parasitic creatures that infested the river, he waded into the water. His boots filled and his trousers soaked to hip level as he pushed further into mid-stream, the mirror held tightly in his right hand.

At a moderately low altitude, the two-engine plane appeared, lazily swinging from one side of the river to the other, its polished, silver wings reflecting the mid-day glare. Not a hydroplane, he noticed, which eliminated any possibility of immediate rescue. Squinting dizzily at the aircraft, he saw Calypso wrapped in a froth of bronze gauze. She was seated on one wing, holding a glass of champagne in one hand and a book, which she was reading, in the other. Starr stood on the other wing. She now wore a pale green gabardine coat and matching skirt and was accompanied by a number of her elegantly dressed clients. Starr stared down at her husband and pointed directly at him. As her entourage burst into strident laughter, she spat another volley of icicles that spread into an opaque cloud and then vanished before touching the ground. When his vision cleared, Jackson saw that the women were gone.

Trembling, he lifted the signal mirror, his thumb through the center hole, and flashed it rapidly in the sun. Somewhere from the recesses of his now sluggish brain sprang the Morse code that he'd learned as a boy. He tried to spell out an S.O.S., hoping he had sufficient control over the mirror to do the job properly.

The plane turned away and Jackson tried desperately to raise his crippled left arm in a wave, his working arm continuing to catch the sun's rays in what he hoped was a message. Abruptly, the plane arced and returned, looping languidly just overhead before sweeping toward the opposite river bank.

"Stop! Don't leave!" he whispered hoarsely, flailing the mirror weakly in an up and down pattern, code abandoned.

Once again the plane doubled back and circled briefly

but, as Jackson uttered a feeble cry of joy, it moved downstream. His arm fell heavily, and as he stared at the receding aircraft in hopeless disbelief his muddled mind suddenly realized that he should have used the flare gun first. Dropping the mirror, he struggled to extricate the gun from his jacket pocket, pointed it upward and fired. The shell exploded just over the center of the river, a high puff of white smoke that immediately began to drift earthward in feathery filaments. Jackson fired again and then a third time before slowly lowering his arm, the gun dangling uselessly from one finger. The plane diminished to a tiny, glittering speck and then vanished in the distance.

Slowly, he splashed back to land, his head hanging heavily, and his shoulders sagging in defeat. Crouching on the sandy embankment, he methodically replaced his precious supplies in the box, taking care to dry each article before stowing it away and closing the lid.

For a moment he squatted on his haunches, staring at the hot, blue-white sky, listening with dying hope for the sound of a returning airplane. If there was only a pilot, the flares and signals could easily have been missed, and even with a passenger chances were not good that his messages had been seen or identified. Realizing that he probably had not been spotted, he rolled onto his side and began to cry.

Gradually, his sobs became painful gasps for air as he curled up on one side, his matted hair in a pool of mud. He had no strength for travel, his mind was confused and his body ravaged by starvation and injury. It was unlikely that another plane would appear for many days or weeks, if ever, and he might be hundreds of miles from civilization. It was strange, he mused fuzzily, in the old days when he'd thought of death he'd hoped to leave this world as a very old man, the victim of a painless heart attack or pneumonia. Not at this age and certainly not in this way.

For several moments he lay in the wet, rotting marsh, defeated and beaten, before grimly struggling to his knees.

"I'm not dead yet," he whispered grimly, "and I won't give in until I am."

Lurching to his feet, he stood swaying, dizzy and off balance, then bent to pick up the metal box. It's so heavy, he thought, gazing downstream toward the horizon. With faltering steps, he picked his way over the roots and fallen foliage, his swollen feet throbbing inside the battered boots, his head light and bobbing upon thin, infected shoulders. And just before him, her figure almost translucent, floated Starr, her finger pointing derisively at her husband, her mocking laughter shrill enough to drown the sounds of the jungle.

TWENTY-THREE—The State of Minas Gerais, Brazil

*T*he rented Land Rover rolled slowly over a deeply rutted dirt track, pitching from side to side as Vincent maneuvered around the boulders and craters littering the road. He was a happy, high-spirited driver and now serenaded his passengers with a rendition of "Adios Mariquita Linda", greatly annoying Virginia who was seated beside him.

"Do you have to warble that sappy song?" she grumbled.

"Sappy? This is a tender, heart rending parting of two lovers," he answered, breaking into a falsetto for the female portion of the duet.

In the back seat, Calypso bent her head to hide a smile and Maybelleen leaned forward to pat Vincent on the shoulder.

"I think you have a lovely voice," she declared stoutly. In appreciation, Vince's voice soared into the stratosphere.

In a demonstration of despair, Virginia banged her

head softly against the passenger window, then relaxed against the head rest and shut her eyes. It had been two days since they left Belo Horizonte on a sparsely traveled, two-lane motorway thinly paved with a cracked and broken layer of asphalt. A few hours ago, Vince had reached this unmarked dirt trail that would, they hoped, lead them to the mine where the men had spent a great deal of time.

Although Brazil is a country with some of the world's most spectacular natural beauty, much of the State of Minas Gerais had been blessed with a wealth of mineral riches and deprived of visual splendor. For miles, the landscape was comprised of scrub-covered hills and occasional streams bordered by thin rows of spindly trees. Calypso stared out the window at the sky, its aquamarine color intensified by a sharp contrast with the brown hills, and wondered why she felt so content in such an isolated and drab corner of the earth.

"Are you all right?" Maybelleen asked, her forehead furrowed with concern. "You don't feel sick or anything?"

"I'm fine. I have to admit I really hadn't expected to feel *quite* this wonderful physically," she answered with a smile.

"It's probably because you're back in your home country. Daddy says that's the best medicine."

"I'm sorry this part of the countryside isn't more beautiful."

"I think it's exotic and exciting ," replied Maybelleen, turning to look at the rocky hills. "I can't believe Starr wasn't interested in coming along."

"Starr is only interested in herself and a guaranteed pot of gold at the end of her own personal rainbow," said Virginia acidly.

Maybelleen sucked in her breath: "That is such an unkind thing to say."

"But true."

"We haven't seen her for ages," commented Calypso.

"She might have a boyfriend."

"Meow," said Vince, immediately resuming his serenade.

"She's probably very busy working all the time. Like me," said Maybelleen with finality.

The car lurched violently to the right as one front wheel dipped into a hole. The Mexican song-fest ceased abruptly as Vincent braked, wrestled with the steering wheel and, with a minimal scraping of the oil pan, guided the vehicle up onto a rocky ledge and crept ahead. Virginia twisted toward the back and bestowed an amused glance on Maybelleen. "You're very loyal," she commented.

"Thank you. I even thought it was kind of fun when the water was turned off during my shower this morning and that nice hotel owner found bottled mineral water for me to rinse."

Virginia laughed. "Yes, that was an interesting place all right."

"And the home theater," Maybelleen interjected. "Gollee, watching the Formula I on that huge screen while we ate just about made me seasick."

"That video was three years old. I wonder how many times he's shown it."

"Poor man," said Maybelleen. "I bet he'd like to see a real Formula I and meet some mechanics."

"He's met you."

Maybelleen grinned, her eyes sparkling. "That's true."

A smattering of one-room brick shacks appeared on the right.

"Civilization," said Maybelleen.

"I wouldn't say that," remarked Virginia tartly.

Vincent edged slowly around a large crater. A collection of muddy, unshaved men wearing ragged shorts, torn tee-shirts and plastic flip-flops clustered around a rickety stand a few feet away. Obviously a bar, the shelves on its single brick wall held unlabeled bottles partially filled with clear yellow sugar-cane alcohol. Wooden poles supported both the shack's corrugated roof and a flimsy plywood counter piled with an assortment of plastic tumblers. As the car teetered precariously on the rim of the pit, then lurched over two sharp boulders, most of the men drifted toward the vehicle and, glasses in hand, peered curiously at the strangers.

Vincent braked sharply as one of the group wandered into the road. At almost the same moment a bronzed man, ripped shirt knotted at his stomach and head protected by a shapeless, frayed straw hat, peered into the passenger side of the automobile with dull brown eyes. Although he was young, probably no more than eighteen, his face was hard, his lips bent down at the corners. Vincent turned to a man hovering next to his open window and spoke in loud, authoritative Spanish.

"Is this the road to the mine?"

The reply was grunted and unintelligible.

Calypso leaned forward and repeated the question in Portuguese. The man nodded.

"How far is it?" Vince persisted, and again Calypso translated.

"*Um pouco longe*," he answered.

The young man with the frayed hat glanced at the car's occupants and then focused on a basket of fruit, mineral water, wine, bread and cheese on the floor. Digging in a pocket, he produced a small stone, offered it on one grubby, mud-caked palm and pointed silently to the basket.

"Give him the food," ordered Vince tersely, staring at Maybelleen in the rear view mirror.

After plucking the pebble from the man's hand, Maybelleen lifted the container and offered it to the intruder. Grabbing the handle, he wrestled his booty out through the open window and triumphantly displayed it to the others. Ignoring the grubby men that stumbled back and forth across the trail, Vincent accelerated, generating a spray of pebbles on both sides and another rasp as the oil pan scraped against the road.

"That poor man," exclaimed Maybelleen. "Do you think he's a deaf-mute?" Without waiting for an answer, she held the stone up to the light and examined it carefully. "This might be an alexandrite."

Virginia again twisted toward the back seat and addressed Calypso. "What did he say to you?"

"I asked him how far it was to the mine and he said that it's a little far—which could mean almost anything."

"Terrific."

"Who *were* those men?" asked Maybelleen.

"Miners." Maybelleen's eyes briefly met Vince's in the rear view mirror.

"And that's exactly why I said we had to have a man with us," said Calypso firmly. "Most of them have nothing, and that includes money, education and manners. They're gamblers, hoping for one big find. Most of them never get anything."

Maybelleen shook her head. "No wonder he wanted food."

Virginia stared pointedly at Calypso. "Are you *sure* you're all right and not just being brave?"

Calypso lifted her eyebrows and shrugged. "I'm just fine. Anyway, I'm not very good at bravery."

"That's not true," said Maybelleen. "I think we're all pretty good at that."

"You've got my vote," volunteered Vince. Stunned, all three women stared at the driver who bent slightly over the wheel. Maybelleen was the first to recover.

"Why thank you. That's just about the nicest thing you've ever said."

"And that should give us pause for thought," added Virginia sourly.

Vincent coaxed the car up a small hill and then braked sharply. Directly ahead, a narrow area had been divided into a patchwork of square pits, some sixteen feet deep but most fairly shallow. Hundreds, perhaps thousands, of men, their bodies coated with mud and steaming in the oppressive heat, their heads protected by tattered straw hats or ragged baseball caps, gouged out the craters or washed gravel in a nearby stream using large, round screens. Several men wrestled with pumps, removing water that collected in the pits.

"My word, could this be it?" whispered Maybelleen, leaning forward over Vincent's shoulder. "I was expecting a big hole in the ground."

"I think we're here," announced Virginia, as several miners moved toward the car. Switching off the engine, Vincent got out, stretched elaborately and approached the nearest man.

"Senhor Ernesto," he demanded gruffly.

Wordlessly, the miners turned and retreated, some glancing back at the car before exchanging a few words and a chuckle. One by one the swarm of men digging, panning or operating the pumps stopped work and stared at the Land Rover. Moving to the front of the vehicle, Vincent slouched against the hood and folded his arms over his chest. His tattoos and the muscles in his arms and shoulders were clearly visible as he stared straight ahead through mirrored sun glasses.

Calypso got out of the car and moved toward the driver. In Los Angeles, she thought, he was just another one of the many Latinos, but here he was clearly not Brazilian with their distinctive mix of oriental, Indian, European and Black blood. Like the majority of her countrymen, he was short, but there the similarity ended. Stocky, meticulously dressed in a guyabera shirt and chinos, his straight, very black hair had been slicked back from a coffee-toned face that would have been handsome had it not been for crooked teeth. To compensate for this perceived defect, he sometimes, as now, sported a very thin mustache and a goatee, which made him vaguely resemble Montezuma with sparse facial hair. Calypso was swept with affection for this cocky, irreverent product of the streets whose loyalty and intelligence none of them had ever doubted.

As Calypso joined Vince, a tall, pot-bellied man wearing clean jeans, a tee-shirt and a baseball cap picked his way around the pits and climbed uphill toward the Land Rover. As he approached, the man removed his dark glasses and headgear, patted his face and thinning, reddish hair with a crumpled handkerchief, and then jammed the cap and glasses back in place. All four visitors were startled by a glimpse of green-gray eyes and a pale, freckled forehead that contrasted strongly with his deeply tanned neck and arms. He glanced at Calypso and then stopped in front of Vincent, who straightened and hooked both thumbs into the back pockets of his chinos. The two men eyed one another warily.

"Senhor Ernesto?" asked Vincent.

"Eu sou Ernesto Parsons."

The man's accent was heavy and unmistakably American.

Vincent's relief was visible. "I'm Vince Soto."

"Call me Ernie." They pumped hands vigorously, as though old war buddies. "And this is Calypso Laskar. She's Brazilian and came as our translator."

And who didn't really need to be on this trip, she thought as she shook Ernie's hand. In Brazil, surnames are not routinely used; even official alphabetized lists are by first names, and it had never occurred to her that the supervisor named Ernesto could be a native English speaker.

Ernie walked to the vehicle and looked first at Virginia and then at Maybelleen. "Ladies," he said, "you'd better get out of the truck before you bake." He waved one hand vaguely toward the miners who were gradually returning to their tasks. "Don't mind them. Outside of drinking, stealing and killing each other, the men lack entertainment, and since we almost never have female visitors, they just had to gawk a bit."

Gallantly, he opened the doors and helped them out.

Removing his sunglasses again, Ernie looked questioningly from one to the other. "I'm sorry I can't offer you a comfortable place to sit, but it's strictly rough and tumble out here. Now, what can I do you for?"

The three women looked quizzically at one another.

"You tell him, Virginia," urged Maybelleen.

Warily, Virginia's eyes flicked toward the miners as she related the particulars concerning their husbands' disappearance, the failure of search teams to locate the plane and the discovery of alexandrites at the bank vault. "We're here because Calypso learned that the men spent a lot of time at the mine with a supervisor named Mr. Ernesto. And it's our only clue so far."

She paused, her forehead creased, one hand shading her eyes against the merciless sun. Ernie extracted a clean, folded handkerchief from his back pocket, snapped it open and tucked one edge under his cap. White chambray fanned out in a short cape that shielded his neck from the searing sunlight in a fashion statement reminiscent of Lawrence of Arabia. His eyes watchful behind mirrored glasses, Vince stepped in front of the group and faced the mine, planting his legs aggressively and folding his muscular arms across his chest.

"They were here in the *area* a good bit of the time," Ernie said, "checking out sites for a telecom system they planned to install, but as far as I know, they never came to the mine. And your information source is dead wrong on another count. I'm a gemstone dealer, not a supervisor. I come up here from time to time to buy stones and check out the various mines. It's really just by chance I happen to be here today."

"Could there be another Senhor Ernesto here? A supervisor?"

"Never heard of one; the supervisor here is Ubiracyr."

"But the alexandrites we found..." Virginia's unfinished question dangled in the scorching heat.

"They bought one or two very small stones from me,

but in São Paulo, not here."

Vincent and the women studied Ernie for any sign of mendacity or deceit. With an open, sunburned face and relaxed body, he was the picture of honesty.

"I'm sorry about your wild-goose chase, but someone connected the fact that I'm American and up here a good deal of the time with your American husbands coming to the same general area and reached the wrong conclusion."

"But couldn't the men have bought stones from someone else up here?" insisted Maybelleen, opening her hand to display the small rock she had received earlier.

"Anything's possible." Ernie plucked the rock from Maybelleen's palm. "What have we here?"

"Is this an alexandrite?"

Ernie examined it closely, held it to the light, then shook his head and gave it back. "I don't think so. Industrial quality maybe, but nothing more. Where'd you get it?"

"From a man by the bar; I traded it for food and wine."

Ernie's face crinkled with humor and then he guffawed loudly.

"In that case, it might be. No matter how carefully they're watched, these guys always manage to steal some of the stones."

"Watched?" asked Maybelleen. "By whom?"

Ernie turned and pointed toward the nearby hills. "See those fellows up there? Standing under the scrub?"

Squinting intently against the sun, all three were startled by the sight of motionless, armed figures nearly concealed by the thick, tangled undergrowth, rock shelving, and small trees that rimmed the mine.

"It's like a prison." Maybelleen's eyes flashed.

"No, little lady, most of those are police, and believe me, they're necessary. This is one of the most violent mines in the state, maybe in the country." Maybelleen's lips formed the letter O. "There've been fights, shootings, robberies, riots involving two thousand men or more, and burnings right here. Food's always a problem, and sanitation doesn't exist. The mine's been closed three times. Trust me, without the police, it's lawless; and even with them, it's barely controlled."

The women stared again at the ridge of scrub-covered rock seeing, or imagining they saw, dozens of policemen while Vince continued to scrutinize the miners.

"Not all the fellas with guns are cops," Ernie admitted. "A good number are private security guards hired to keep theft at a minimum and see that the property owner gets his ten percent of the profits."

Three baffled faces swiveled toward Ernie.

"Just ten percent?" asked Calypso.

"It doesn't seem very fair," said Maybelleen.

Ernie extracted his crumpled handkerchief and mopped his face and throat. "Brazilian laws aren't like those in the States. Here, mining rights belong to the government. Any individual or company can apply for a license to mine," he waved vaguely toward the miners, "and all these guys have one, but the property owner is rarely one of the miners. His cut is ten percent of the profits, but it's almost impossible for him to know the actual take without having an observer on the spot."

"I can't believe anyone would cheat the owner out of such a small amount." said Maybelleen indignantly.

Ernie chuckled and rubbed one ear as though for luck. "It's not always small, and this business is full of master crooks. The guards are fairly well paid, but a lot of stones still go out in pockets. And it's not just miners. Supervisors will never swindle me or other dealers they know, but when it comes to strangers they're regular magicians. Buyers can watch carefully while a stone is weighed and wrapped, and yet back home they find it's been switched with one much lighter, poorer quality and sometimes not even an alexandrite."

"Cheaters never prosper," declared Maybelleen firmly.

"They do here."

"How do you stand this heat?" Virginia exclaimed as trickles of perspiration ran down both temples and dripped from her chin. She wheeled about, opened the driver's door and, reaching between the seats, extracted a bottle of mineral water. Popping the plastic cap, she took a large swig and passed it to the other two women. Virginia turned toward Ernie.

"Mr. Parsons, thanks for your help. We'd better be going." She looked inquiringly at the other two women: "Anything else, ladies?"

Maybelleen and Calypso hesitated, disappointed at the failure of their trip.

"Dude hasn't told you nothing," Vince muttered, surveying the miners.

Virginia scowled at her driver and turned again to Ernie. "Can you think of anything—even a rumor—that might be useful? Where the men stayed up here, or how they accumulated those alexandrites?"

Slowly he shook his head. "As far as I know, they were roaming around hunting telecom sites, and I can't even guess at the stones."

Virginia scrabbled in her large handbag, drew out a small leather case and extracted a card that she offered to Ernie. "Here's my address and email address just in case you hear something or remember any information that might be helpful. Is there some way we can contact you if we need to do so?"

Ernie fished out an assortment of cards and papers from his breast pocket, sorted through them and handed a card to Virginia.

"Sorry it's so grubby, but the guys up here don't seem to mind."

"Nor do we," she said graciously. "Thank you again."

They all shook hands with Ernie, then resumed their places in the Land Rover. As Vincent reversed the vehicle, the gemstone dealer waved, then turned and retreated toward the mine, his head bent, the handkerchief pasted damply to his neck and shoulders.

"We know less than when we began," said Virginia.

"Sweets, that's what I told you back there," commented Vincent.

Slowly Calypso shook her head. "That's not true. We now know that they really came up here to look at property, although why in this area is a mystery."

"Which still isn't any indication of what happened to them, or where the gemstones fit in..."

A subdued, disappointed group boarded the plane for Los Angeles three days later, each one certain that they had reached the end of the trail only to find that it was a blind alley.

TWENTY-FOUR—Daly City, California

Calypso walked slowly down the wide gravel path, carefully studying the trailers squeezed together on both sides of the road. She was surprised to discover that these were semi-permanent homes, many boasting low picket fences, canvas awnings that stretched protectively over small patches of grass, and well-tended gardens adorned with plaster ducks, gnomes and saints. Although great efforts had been made by a scattering of trees and homey street signs to create a community atmosphere, Calypso felt tense and uncomfortable and wished, not for the first time, that she had accepted Virginia's offer to accompany her on this excursion. Her choice of clothing, a black linen trouser suit and white silk tank top, smartly casual in Claremont and Los Angeles, was as unusual in the trailer park as a tuxedo at a swim meet and now served to further tighten her nerves. She had never imagined a neighborhood like this in which she was clearly an interloper, her progress visually tracked by suspicious, silent residents.

When the private investigator reported that Bonny King and her husband Wayne lived with Norma Drefan in this trailer court, Calypso's first reaction was disbelief. Seth wouldn't even know someone on this socio-economic level, let alone become so involved that he was secretly sending support money. It just didn't fit. But again, who was the Seth she'd married? Certainly not the one she'd confronted in Mike Cardona's office.

Two hefty, middle-aged women wearing polyester pants and baggy shirts chatted and watered flowers in their tiny gardens but fell silent as Calypso approached. Initially intimidated by the hostility her presence generated, Calypso now felt her temper rise. Stopping in front of the pair, she returned their unfriendly gaze.

"Excuse me. I understand that Bonny King lives in this complex on Rainbow Way. Could you please tell me where that is?"

Pushing back several wayward strands of gray hair, one woman conveyed her disapproval and waved vaguely toward the right. "Next corner. Bonny's name is on the mailbox."

Nodding her thanks, Calypso continued forward, thinking that she was searching for information and needed to digest and assess any discoveries before telling others. What rubbish. There was virtually nothing Virginia, Maybelleen and, probably, Blossom and Vincent didn't already know.

She passed a pergola completely concealed by the intertwined and trailing branches of a flowering wisteria that it supported and then a small sandbox and plastic swing set. At the corner, a street sign told her that this was Rainbow Way. Almost at her elbow, an old fashioned, rusty mailbox bore the hand-lettered word "King" on the side. Slowly, she raised her coffee colored eyes.

Although the trailer itself was well painted and in good repair, a discolored beach umbrella had been jammed into the earth to shade an old rocker not far from the front door. Unlike its neighbors, the plot of ground fronting this structure was bare, hard-packed earth; not a flower, shrub or tree graced the premises.

Calypso pushed the gate open and, aware of her pounding heart and sudden anxiety, approached the dwelling. A striped awning protected the front doorway from direct sunlight, and as she moved nearer, Calypso noticed that the door was ajar. Looking vainly for a bell, she heard the sound of a televised game show inside, although it was difficult to see anything through the dusty screen.

"Hello," she called, sounding more courageous than she felt.

After a minute, Calypso clapped her hands as though applauding, the Brazilian way of knocking at a gate or door that has no buzzer. Choked by a rising feeling of foreboding, she clapped again and then turned to leave.

"Yes?"

Squinting against the sun, Calypso was startled by the sight of a figure standing just inside the screen door. Struggling to breathe normally and calm the pulse that raced through her body, she said, "I'm looking for Bonny King." Her voice was thin and strangled, and for the first time in years she was acutely aware of her foreign accent.

"Who's looking?"

The woman moved closer to the screen and Calypso saw that she was thin, her arms crossed against her chest in a gesture of antagonism.

"I'm Calypso Laskar."

There was no reaction.

"Seth Laskar's wife."

Silence.

"Seth was in a plane crash not too long ago and no one's found any trace of the plane or passengers. I need some information and was told that Bonny King could probably help me." Calypso fumbled for her wallet and extracted a photograph of her and Seth taken the previous

Christmas. "Look, here's a picture of my husband."

Calypso extended the photograph. The woman opened the screen door and slid her hand out, allowing Calypso her first clear view of the trailer's occupant. Wearing a faded print house dress that buttoned down the front, her gray hair was wound around large rollers and skimpily covered by a chartreuse nylon scarf. Weathered skin indicated a lack of pampering and a hard-scrabble life but it was her face that stopped Calypso's heart and breath for a moment. In spite of the suspicious, unfriendly expression and the pitiless, brown eyes, the woman strongly resembled Seth.

The screen door banged shut. As she studied the photo, the woman was joined by a balding man in overalls and a work shirt who scrutinized it carefully. A moment later, another woman squeezed between the two.

"I need to know if you are Bonny King," Calypso persisted.

Without looking up, she nodded.

Then the man with her surely must be Wayne King, and the other woman Norma Drefan. Calypso pressed both fists together in an unconscious gesture of combined prayer and agitation, and stared at the trio. Jabbing at the photo with one finger, Bonny turned to her husband. "Wayne, this looks a mite like Chester. Or Duke."

"Who are Chester and Duke?" asked Calypso grinding her palms together.

"My brothers." Bonny looked through the screen as Wayne slipped the photograph to Calypso.

Leaning forward, Calypso struggled to conceal her eagerness. "Do you think I could meet them?"

The frosty silence lengthened and the second woman stepped backward, fading from view. Finally, Bonny spoke, her voice harsh.

"Reckon not. Duke's a priest in Mexico, and Chester's in San Quentin again."

Calypso was physically drained. "And those are your

only siblings?"

Bonny coughed a wet, mucinous laugh. "That's a hot one. I got three more brothers, but we ain't heard from Ralph in a coon's age, not since he high-tailed it to Oregon. Been twenty years since Earle stole money from Brinks and disappeared, and Junior's dead." She paused. "And I have two sisters; Sharon and Norma."

Norma? Calypso felt goose-bumps on her arms.

Unexpectedly, Bonny spoke again.

"None of 'em around but somebody sends money every month to take care of Norma." She dipped her head, indicating the other female. "She never been quite right in the head, but only the boys would give a good goddamn."

Calypso stared through the mesh, her spine rigid.

"When was the last time you saw one of them? Or talked on the phone?" she asked trying to keep the hope from her voice.

"Don't recall. Years. Every month I meet the manager at Golden State National and we trade receipts for cash. Sometimes he asks questions or tells me how to spend the money." Suddenly, her jaw tightened and Bonny frowned. "What'd you say your name was?"

"Laskar. Dr. Laskar. My husband is Seth."

"That's what I thought. Seth Laskar," she mused, turning to her husband. "Remember him, Wayne? He was that friend of Duke's. A big football star at Daly City High that went to San Jose State on an athletic scholarship. Younger than us but real famous around here."

Wayne ducked his head in agreement.

Bonny swiveled to face Calypso. "He would have been in the football Hall of Fame if he wasn't drafted to Vietnam." She paused, scowling fixedly at Calypso. "Never came back. I don't know who you are, lady, but that ain't Seth in the picture, and you ain't Seth's wife." Bonny and Wayne disappeared from view and the door banged shut.

For several moments, Calypso remained immobile, stunned by her success. Although meager, the information

Bonny had grudgingly shared exceeded Calypso's hopes. This journey had begun as a desperate, wild goose chase, undertaken only because there were no other paths to follow or leads to pursue. Now she had confirmed Bonny, Wayne and Norma's relationship and was certain that she herself was married to one of the brothers who were supporting not a lover or ex-wife, but a handicapped sister.

Ecstatic, Calypso spread her arms, lifted her head to the sky and pirouetted on light feet. Suddenly she blanched, her arms fell and the dance came to an abrupt halt. Her husband hadn't been having a torrid love affair but supporting a sister and she, Calypso, had seriously damaged, possibly destroyed, their relationship through her suspicions.

Her eyes narrowed as she drifted slowly toward the street. Since the money was being paid to a sibling, why hadn't her husband told her about it? Why would this generosity be a secret? Frowning thoughtfully, she stopped and stared at the rusty mailbox marking the King trailer. She might be married to a Drefan brother, but which one? None sounded remotely like the Seth she knew and loved. Head lowered in thought, she turned and slowly walked toward the exit. If one of the Drefans was her husband, why had he taken another man's identity? Calypso had the uncomfortable feeling that, if and when she discovered the truth, she might wish she'd left well enough alone.

TWENTY-FIVE—Baja California, Mexico

Nervously, Virginia flapped a fox stole paw in front of her face as though it were a fan. Acutely aware of Vincent's scrutiny in the rear view mirror, she kept her eyes, shielded by dark glasses, trained on the countryside, a drive that she previously found interminable. Today it was flashing past at incredible speed.

Even though Calypso and Maybelleen had encouraged her to meet with Ferguson and discuss his business proposition, Virginia had postponed making this appointment for months. The couple hadn't met with one another since their divorce nine years ago and she felt edgy and insecure, unaware of Fergie's current marital status or possible involvement with another woman. Or of his attitude toward her. Perhaps he'd been so shattered by their separation that even friendship would be impossible to resurrect. Worse, he might pity her and be very, very kind. Patronizing. Although their infrequent telephone conversations were impersonal, friendly and never strayed beyond the subject of business, just the sound of her ex-husband's voice brought a flock of butterflies to her stomach.

"Doin' okay back there, Boss Lady?"

"Couldn't be better."

"That's a lie."

Virginia pressed her lips together and continued to stare through the window. After leaving the distended and diffuse borders of Greater Los Angeles, the multi-lane black freeway ran for miles between endless bare, yellow-brown hills on the left and the restless sea on the right. The appearance of San Onofre Nuclear Power Station with its more or less permanent crew of demonstrators was a welcome break, as were the clusters of buildings heralding the approach of San Clemente, famed retreat for ex-President Nixon after his dethronement. A scattering of beach villages gradually increased, multiplied and grew into the picturesque sprawl of San Diego and finally they passed American and then Mexican Immigration. Vincent smartly saluted the latter flag.

"Not a good idea, Vince."

"We're in my ancestors' native land."

"Probably your country of origin as well."

"Want to see my birth certificate?"

"No, but I'd like to know where you bought it."

"Downtown L.A. on Broadway and Grand but you can get better ones at the Xerox Mexicano on MacArthur Park if Reuben's not in jail or too stoned. If you got more cash, the best are in a house on Silverado just off—"

"I don't want a dissertation on phony I.D.s."

"You asked."

"And I thank you."

With vivid clarity, Virginia remembered the conversation that had convinced her that this would be a trip wisely taken.

"For pity's sake, just go. When we're not talking about alexandrites or Norma Drefan, you're bringing up

Ferguson and his grapes. So stop dilly-dallying and set up a meeting." Maybelleen sounded cross.

Both Calypso and Virginia had stared at her.

"Is something wrong?" asked Calypso in concern. "You're usually so sunny. And neutral."

"Well," admitted Maybelleen, "I've gotten lots older and more impatient in the last few months. And Virginia is just wasting her time, mooning around over what might or might not be true."

"Mooning? *Mooning?* I'll thank you to—"

"Come to think of it, you haven't been singing any hymns lately," swiftly interjected Calypso, her eyes focused on Maybelleen.

"I sing them in my head," Maybelleen announced loftily. The other two women smiled.

"For what it's worth, Virginia, I agree that you should go talk to Ferguson and see what he has to offer," said Calypso. "It's not like you're too busy. Right now both you and I are at loose ends, so this is the ideal time to meet him and see what you think."

And what excuse could she find to that? Resolutely, Virginia stared at the urban misery through which they were driving. Several years ago, in a desperate attempt to attract North American shopping and leisure money, seedy, desolate central Tijuana had been rejuvenated and the area now offered an excellent museum, many good hotels, restaurants and night clubs, a refurbished Jai-Alai Palace and elegant shops where the imported merchandise was nearly always genuine. Americans day-tripped and sometimes stayed the weekend in downtown T.J., where they gambled on the dogs, saw bull-fights, bought what they hoped was real Luis Vuitton at half the price and binged on Margaritas and burritos in four-star hotels.

This, however, was not downtown T.J. Unmarked, badly paved roads traversed the dusty outskirts of the city and wound around hills where an endless jumble of decrepit shacks replaced any trace of vegetation. Ragged, barefoot children of all ages, accompanied by scruffy, starving dogs, were everywhere, either playing in sandy dirt or hauling smaller siblings on their own bony backs. Oblivious to their surroundings, women rendered shapeless through too many pregnancies and a lifetime of work plodded stoically forward with gigantic hand-woven baskets or plastic-wrapped bundles balanced securely on their heads.

Business, occurring mainly in small huts with hollow interiors and no front walls, focused on the automobile. Some of these shacks were repair shops, others offered rusted, broken and bent parts for sale and even more harbored men who busily dismantled the almost unidentifiable remains of motor vehicles. Used tires were everywhere, heaps and stacks of them; and from time to time one could see cars being painted in between the seedy, one-story buildings.

"Everyone in Tijuana must have a car," remarked Virginia idly.

They passed a large woman selling tacos on a corner and a boy offering juices from a variety of pitchers. A small group of men, battered straw sombreros pulled low, slouched against the cracked facade of a bar.

"Get real, Toots. Gringos come here to have odometers turned back or dents hammered out or a cheap paint job before they sell their cars up North. And the local dudes that run drugs and people across the border need new plates, paint jobs...all kinds of changes on a regular basis."

"Amazing."

"Not really. It's work. Which road you want I should take? The old one?"

"Whichever goes closest to the beach."

"Hokey-doke."

Leaving Tijuana behind, it was a different world. A gently foaming, grass-green sea broke on fine sand that rose gradually to rolling dunes and, further inland, dry, parched hills. It was a peaceful scene, isolated and deserted with only an occasional shack to mar the solitude.

"Spooky out here," Vincent said.

"Looks perfect to me."

"Remember that most of the bandits and thieves in Mexico hole up in Baja from time to time. Mean dudes. Nobody messes with them; not the police, not Uncle Sammy's macho green berets, nobody."

"I'm told they're all up in the hills."

"Right on, Sugarplum, and so are the coyotes and foxes, and they all come into town sometimes. Think about that if you and Fergie do the winery bit here."

Vincent removed his mirrored glasses and stared at her in the rear-view mirror with his deep brown eyes.

"Security doesn't seem to be a big issue in Cabo," she countered irritably. This was not the time to throw water on Ferguson's project.

"Cabo? Who's talking Cabo?"

Before Loreto, La Paz, and Cabo San Lucas at the tip of Baja were restructured as some of the most expensive resorts in the world, the entire peninsula had been a collection of fishing villages, attracting mostly fishermen, surfers and recluses. Nature lovers, loners and the determinedly unconventional straggled in by small boats, motorcycles or ancient motor vehicles to pitch their tents or sleep on the beach. And some still did, but the vast majority of vacationers now arrived at the three luxury resorts by air, usually private plane or helicopter, and always dressed in designer togs.

"There's about seven hundred miles of nothing but criminals hiding out in the bushes between here and Cabo. I just got your safety in mind, Toots."

Virginia met his eyes in the mirror and smiled affectionately. She knew that was absolutely true.

A loose jumble of houses and buildings in various stages of disrepair and disintegration were reminders that the peninsula was civilization on a third world scale. They also indicated an end to the journey and Virginia felt her head and throat suddenly contract and throb with tension. Nervously rubbing her collarbone with two fingers, she coughed twice before speaking.

"There's the hotel, Vince. *Mi Casita.*"

Vincent flipped the wheel, then braked, and the car began a slow, circular skid on a gravel courtyard, raising a massive column of dust before coming to a stop. Directly in front of them, floating on pristine sand dunes, was a rambling structure completely covered with brilliant orange, magenta and red bougainvillea blooms and decorated with elaborate borders of intricately painted tiles. As the air began to clear, they saw a handsome man in his late fifties or early sixties clad in a blue linen shirt, chinos and sandals step from the shade of the veranda and move toward the car. Holding a handkerchief over his nose, he ineffectively fanned the clouds of dust with his free hand, his head bent as though against a strong wind.

"Ferguson," Virginia cried joyously, wrenching the car door open. Anxiety and apprehension instantly evaporated as she stepped from the car, and then raced to meet her former husband. Ferguson pulled her close in a hug so familiar that the divorce and subsequent unhappy years seemed never to have happened. Virginia closed her eyes and was once again half of a working and playing partnership, part of a happy couple that functioned on all levels. Or had done so before she destroyed it.

Reluctantly, she stepped away. Ferguson scrutinized her with kind yet shrewd eyes and then smiled. "You look wonderful. Somehow I thought you'd be more...I don't know. More Beverly Hills."

"I am occasionally."

The last time he saw her she was a balloon with frizzled hair wearing "Big is Beautiful" plaid shirts and farmer Jones dungarees and he was wild about her. Virginia didn't want to replicate that appearance but she didn't want to scare him off either and, after days of indecision, had chosen beige linen trousers and a brown and tan silk blouse with a geometric design for this reunion. Wisely, she left her beloved red fox stole, a blatant example of her questionable sense of style and taste, in the car.

Ferguson put an arm around her shoulders and began guiding her toward the veranda.

"I like you this way. A little on the thin side but otherwise you're perfect."

She glowed with a happiness that had been missing for years. Moving across the front veranda, they stepped into the cooler, darkened interior of the hotel where they stopped and looked at one another again.

"You seem...older," commented Virginia, "and successful."

"We're both older."

Suddenly, Virginia's elation was eclipsed by heartache for the two of them, not as they were here and now, somewhere between the villages of Prima Tapia and El Sauzal, but for the pair of lonely misfits that had fallen in love and undertaken the impossible in the wilderness of north-central California. She stared at her former husband, his body tanned and fit by the rigors of an arduous life, his handsome face now furrowed and weather-beaten but as kindly and pleasant as it had been when they'd first met. There was no doubt about it; Ferguson was the only man she had ever loved, and she'd willfully tossed that happiness away. Heated anger at her own mulish, destructive thoughtlessness flamed for a second, and then was forcibly extinguished.

"The property I'm thinking about isn't too far away but, if we decide to establish another winery, we have a lot of things to consider and investigate. This may take a couple of days."

"I thought as much, so I brought an overnight bag," she said.

"I've registered for both of us," he said.

"In the same room?" she asked lightly. With an

enormous effort, Virginia maintained what she hoped was a bland expression while her breathing became more shallow and her pulse more rapid.

"No." He began to chuckle. "I see you haven't lost your sense of humor."

Virginia forced herself to cackle along, both disappointed and reassured by his answer. Of course they would have separate rooms. She might be married to a dead man, but Ferguson was forever moral, unwilling to lose the scruples and high principles that had been his guides throughout life.

"Let's go out onto the terrace and have a drink," he suggested as merriment faded.

"Vincent," she called. Her driver materialized, shuffling, bending and clapping to a Salsa beat audible through the earplugs connected to his Walkman.

"Ferguson, meet my driver Vince. And Vince, this is Mr. Fremont." Still shuffling, Vince nodded a greeting and saluted with one forefinger while Ferguson dipped his head in acknowledgement. "Since I don't see any bellboys, why don't you take in the bags," Virginia ordered, "then find the bar and order two Margaritas. We'll be out on the patio."

Raising both hands over his head, he clapped twice, stamping hard and jerking his pelvis convulsively before executing a low bow in front of Virginia. "Sho 'nuff, sweet stuff, but they'll make you fat."

"Some domestics use their leisure time to improve their skills and minds. They earn university degrees or take up Japanese brush painting. It's very obvious your talents and interests lie in more physical accomplishments."

"So right, Snow White."

Pelvis again grinding, knees bent and rubbery, Vincent's feet slid swiftly over the broken tiles as he danced around a potted palm tree.

Turning, she nearly collided with Ferguson who, eyebrows quizzically raised, hands in pockets, had watched the exchange with amusement.

"Your chauffeur doesn't seem like the usual domestic servant."

Virginia felt the heat rise to her face. "He's not, really. He's very intelligent and completely loyal and we enjoy one another's bizarre company," she confessed, wondering why she'd never realized this before. "We can be completely truthful with one another. I guess you could say we're pals."

Ferguson tilted his head and stared at his former wife with an expression that could be either compassion or pity. "That's important. You never had friends before. Aside from Jackson, of course."

"And you." Embarrassed, Virginia looked down at the red tile floor. "One of the many things Grandmother didn't teach me was how to make or be a friend." Looking up, she flashed Ferguson a quick smile. "Now I have Jackson—if we can ever find him—Vincent, Calypso and Maybelleen. We women have become very close since the plane was lost."

"Good." He paused and nodded thoughtfully. "Why don't we sit down?"

Virginia followed Ferguson onto the lanai. The patio's palm leaf roof needed replacement and the large, red floor tiles, broken and uneven, disappeared into the sand, but the view of the green-blue sea was both peaceful and spectacular. A slight breeze blew inland from the deserted beach, rattling the dry palm fronds and cooling the air. Occasionally, the sharp, lonely cry of a seagull punctuated the rhythmic rumble of the breakers, underscoring the tranquility of the scene.

For a moment, Virginia was pinched by regrets. If she hadn't been so stubborn and witless years ago, they would be arm in arm, breathing the salt spray, savoring the fact that there were no other humans in sight, delighting in the presence of one another and the shared joy, pain and love that had accumulated through their lifetime together.

Instead, they were about to work out a business deal, very reminiscent of their successful vineyard venture in California, each one carefully exploring and avoiding the hopes, dreams and emotions of the other. They had become friendly strangers.

Brightly, she smiled at her ex-husband and gestured to the unsightly but serviceable wooden table and chairs near the edge of the patio.

"I guess we should get down to business. Since we´re talking seriously about establishing a vineyard here, I want to take a look at what you´ve done with the California winery, maybe cannibalize some of those ideas."

"Sure. Come up anytime."

"I hope you brought the papers for this one with you."

Ferguson eased into one of the chairs. "You bet, but I thought we should just talk about what's involved first."

"Perfect." She curved her lips into an easy smile. "Since you're sure about the paper work, you must have gotten a lot more systematic or have a wife who's very efficient and organized."

After stealing a quick glance at his left hand, Virginia composed her face into an expression of impersonal affability and anxiously waited for Ferguson's reply. No ring, but he hadn't worn one when they were married, nor did most of the men she knew. Now she was about to find out if he was unattached or not, information which she might not want to hear.

TWENTY-SIX—The Amazon Basin

*J*ackson lay quietly with the back of his head resting in the water and one boot clutched in his limp left hand. After cutting it from his swollen and infected foot, he couldn't stand up. No matter how hard he tried, first swaying on both knees, then attempting to haul himself upright with the help of the trailing vines at hand, his legs were like two rubber sticks that bent under the weight of his gaunt body. Gasping for air, he clutched the undergrowth, twining his rough and calloused hands into the ropey vegetation while straightening first one knee and then the other before falling backward onto the river bank.

Familiar jungle shrieks, splashes and faint ground rustling now were frighteningly magnified. He was being closely watched, encircled, and trapped by his physical weakness, with the eternally hungry animals and birds of prey waiting to make the final kill.

Gradually, he became aware of an acute change in the atmosphere. At first it was only a faint pulsing of the marsh underneath his body and then a disturbance of the water accompanied by a growing rhythmic clatter. As the din increased, hurting his ears and rattling his nerves, there was a surge in jungle activity, indicating the presence of a threatening alien element.

Screamers streaked overhead and monkeys, in hysterical frenzy, leapt through the overhead branches, chattering in high, panicked voices to one another, alerting the other jungle creatures. He should move, Jackson thought lethargically. Take cover under a bush or inside a hollow log until the noisy intruder could be identified, but his muscles refused to respond.

The gun, he thought in despair, remembering that he'd stowed his weapon temporarily in the metal box when he removed bandages for his foot. Weakly, he moved his right hand about in the mud, searching for the box he'd abandoned while struggling to stand. It was somewhere out of sight and out of reach. Gone. . Even if he located the box and extricated the gun, he almost certainly wouldn't have the strength to use it.

The noise increased to a roaring crescendo, then cut to a low rumble, creating a sudden, hollow vacuum as disturbing as the racket it replaced. Soft waves lapped against Jackson's face and he realized he was floating on his back in San Francisco Bay just off Larkspur. He shivered in the icy water and then smiled at the sound of Calypso's voice.

"Don't just lie there, lazybones," she urged. "Put the skis back on and try again."

The glare of reflected sun was blinding; he had lost his dark glasses and now found it almost impossible to focus past the slender reeds that grew just before his eyes. He must be very near the shore, he thought, wondering hazily where his skis might have drifted and why he was having such trouble with his backstroke.

A dark shape slid into his sphere of vision, then he heard a shout and human voices, none of them Calypso's. Overwhelmed with nausea and dizziness, his vision blurred and he closed his eyes.

"Over there," a male voice shouted.

"Where?"

"Right next to that big log. See? Halfway into the water."

"My God!"

"You think he's still alive?"

"Who knows? He looked okay when Bernie spotted him from the plane, but nobody lasts long in this territory."

English, he thought groggily. How could they speak English here?

He heard the splash of oars and again the voices of two men, their words underscored by subdued monotonous vibrations farther out in the river. It must be a motor boat, he thought with sudden lucidity. Maybe his signals had worked.   Opening his eyes Jackson saw, sharply and clearly, a transparent canoe sliding toward him propelled by a massive, blond, bearded man. A smaller, leaner version of the giant manned the oars behind; Jackson suddenly realized this wasn't a man at all but Calypso, again swathed in a luminous fabric. Both occupants of the boat were staring at him with strange, unreadable expressions.

"His eyes are open. I hope it doesn't mean he's dead."

"He can't weigh more than seventy pounds. And look at that *shoulder*, for God's sake."

Funny that Calypso should speak in a man's voice, he thought, reassured by her angelic and tender smile. He closed his eyes, feeling comfortable and light, as though floating on clouds, safe and happy with Calypso nearby. There was a jolt as the canoe lodged in thick mud.

"Hey, he just shut his eyes. Hop out, Al."

"Wow, something's wrong with his foot."

Why is she called Al, he wondered fuzzily, unless there was a third, invisible person in the boat?

"Poor sucker. Man, this place gives me the creeps."

"Bob, don't get water inside your boots. There're leeches and all kinds of crap in the river just waiting for fresh meat."

There was a brief, snorted chuckle. "Yeah, well if this guy can go to sleep in the stuff, I'm not going to worry too much about a couple of drops."

A sudden roar shook the ground and rattled the undergrowth around them. Jackson's eyes flew open in alarm and he saw twin streaks of silver directly overhead that faded almost immediately from his vision as the thunderous din diminished into a comforting, distant drone: a plane—maybe two. He took a deep breath and began to cough in uncontrollable, strangled gasps that tore at his chest and pulled his heart.

Beside him on the riverbank, Calypso and the blond man hastily unrolled a canvas stretcher supported on each side by wooden poles. Once again, metal flashed overhead just above the treetops and then vanished. The large man squatted down and bent close.

"I'm Dr. Bob Gossett; I'm with the medical team out here. Can you understand me?" he asked in a gentle voice.

Tears prickled the back of Jackson's eyes but he was too dehydrated to cry. Weakly, he lifted a hand and reached for Calypso as he opened his mouth and tried to speak. He couldn't make a sound.

"Can you tell me your name?" asked the doctor, pressing the man's other bony hand sympathetically between his two palms. "Just that much."

Jackson inhaled then heard the air whistle through his wind pipe in a choked, throttled noise but he was unable to utter a single word. Frantically, he tried again, clinging to Calypso's hand. Long ago, when this nightmare began, he'd talked to himself, even carried on conversations to raise his spirits, but that had ended with the appearance of the native arrows. Voices were as much a target as a red shirt or flare gun. His mind wavered and lost focus.

Dr. Gossett twisted to look at his companion.

"He's in bad shape, Al, and he either doesn't understand English or can't speak. Get on the radio and tell Bernie to fly low and keep a sharp lookout until we get underway. And let Warren know what's happening and have him ready to land about quarter of a mile downstream, but not till we're in the boat. We don't want his plane bobbing around as a possible target."

"Right."

Calypso turned away, her robe enveloping him in a warm, comforting mist and Jackson again closed his eyes, secure in a wave of safety and love. Dr. Gossett bent closer, examining Jackson's shoulder wound and touching it gently at the edges, before sitting back on his haunches and rummaging in a back-pack. As he extracted a few items, he again spoke to his companion.

"Bernie and Warren okay with everything?"

"Yes."

A frown creased the doctor's forehead before he spoke again.

"Take a look in that metal box and see if you can find an I.D."

"I'm on it right now." There was a brief pause. "Not a thing. This is a survival kit, but it's pretty depleted. Just a flare gun without flares, a pistol with no ammo and a signal mirror. Couple of other things."

No ammo, he wondered. All this time guarding the gun and he'd lost the last bullet. It didn't matter. Calypso was here to protect and help him.

Dr. Gossett bent over him again. "I'm going to give you a little injection and then we'll take you out to the launch. It's a fast boat that we've been using to search the riverbank and there's an amphibious plane waiting just downstream. You'll be in a hospital ICU hooked up to about a dozen tubes and machines in no time at all. We need to get some fluids and antibiotics in you."

Dr. Gossett picked up Jackson's arm and began to rub icy alcohol on the skin. He scarcely felt the sting of the needle but heard the doctor's words very clearly.

"Bernie spotted your signals but his plane doesn't have pontoons for a water landing, and this territory's not well mapped. We weren't absolutely sure of your location or we'd have been here sooner."

His body was buoyant, weightless. At some point, he was lifted onto the stretcher and wedged carefully into the canoe where he heard meaningless words drift by on the moist, still air.

"Maybe he's from the Dryson wreck they found day before yesterday."

Jackson watched Calypso float to his side, take both his hands and pull him to his feet. Her tangled, curly hair, unrestrained, wrapped around him as they began to dance, out of the boat and across the water, faster and faster, rising into the air until they were spinning among the clouds. In the boat, the two men continued their conversation.

"Impossible. The Dryson plane went down three or four months ago over a hundred miles upriver, and the animals got everyone. Only left some well-chewed bones."

"Al, it was the same river. That tells us something."

"Tells *me* that white folks have no business being there *or* here, and if we don't haul ass, we could become tasty cannibal roasts."

A smothered chortle mixed with the muted splash of oars in water. Still spinning in Calypso's arms, Jackson felt warm and numb, happy and safe and, comforted by the gentle rocking of the canoe, slipped into unconsciousness.

"I wonder who he is."

"That's something we may never know. His chances are very slim."

TWENTY-SEVEN—GUANAJUATO, MEXICO

*P*erspiring heavily after the exertion of her uphill climb, Calypso stepped into the cool, musty church and paused to catch her breath. Leaning against the wall, she glanced around the interior, lifted her eyes to the vaulted ceiling and was stunned by the unexpected sight of several enormous crystal chandeliers. As she moved slowly down the nave toward the altar, still gazing upward, more arches came into view along with additional chandeliers.

Mesmerized, she stumbled against a wooden pew and her concentration snapped. Dizzy and off-balance, she sank wearily onto the hard bench. Taking a deep breath, Calypso bent forward, leaned her forehead against the back of the next pew and closed her eyes. In the comforting peace and tranquility of the church she might have dozed, or perhaps only drifted into an area of mental serenity, but she was roused by the muffled slap of worn leather sandals on the floor nearby. Slowly straightening, she found herself staring at a wizened old woman in a shapeless black dress who had stopped a few feet away and now returned Calypso's cautious gaze. A small triangle of black lace had been arranged on the woman's ashen hair, emphasizing her dedication both to the Church and to old fashioned, conservative precepts. With unreadable black eyes and deeply wrinkled, mahogany skin, only a pair of delicate gold and coral earrings adorning her withered ear lobes saved her from an austere and forbidding appearance.

Raised as a Catholic attending mass in Brazilian churches similar to this one, Calypso suspected that her observer was one of the ancient widowed faithful whose lives were now centered upon prayer and service to the Church. These were the ladies who washed and ironed the priests' vestments and altar linen, swept and cleaned the church and sacristy, replaced the altar flowers and arrived an hour before each mass to ensure that every necessary item was in place. If her guess was correct, then this woman would likely know where the priests could be found at almost any moment of the day or night.

"*Boa tarde*," Calypso whispered. "I'm looking for Father Juan Xavier. Do you know where I might find him?" She spoke in slow, careful Portuguese, choosing words that were similar or identical in both Spanish and her native language. Although she had no difficulty in comprehending Spanish, speaking it was another matter.

Without moving or appearing to have heard or understood, the woman continued to study Calypso with her black, unblinking eyes. After a long time, the woman's lips parted slightly and she rasped in Spanish, "Wait here."

As those antiquated jaws slowly opened and closed and the tiny figure turned toward the sacristy, Calypso imagined she heard the distinct rattle of old bones. Sliding to the edge of the pew, she looked up at the chandeliers once more, and then scrutinized the Stations of the Cross, windows, niches and saints. Almost at once, her attention was captured by a female saint standing on a base of silver-toned metal and, pulled as though by magnetic force, she stood and moved across the church. Amazing, she thought, stepping very near. The statue was carved of wood and dressed in cloth robes encrusted with stones that were either real gems or excellent paste imitations, and the base looked like silver. It even seemed to be slightly in need of polish around the edges. Spellbound by the saint, she froze at the unexpected sound of a man's hushed voice just behind her.

"Beautiful, isn't she?"

Breath lodged in her throat, Calypso slowly turned. For one silent, shocked moment she studied the man who wore a short sleeved blue shirt and clerical collar, baggy cotton pants and huaraches. With soft brown eyes sparking a face that was memorable for kindness and sympathy rather than stunning good looks, the man could have been Seth's twin.

"I'm sorry if I startled you," he apologized in Spanish.

Heated blood flooded Calypso's face.

"You speak English." It was not a question. Extracting a handkerchief from her handbag, she dabbed at perspiration around her hairline.

"Of course," he replied in a broad, American accent. "It's my native language."

He smiled. Calypso turned toward the statue, hiding her emotions. Her throat felt tight and constricted. It was Seth's smile, and, in English, his voice.

The priest followed her gaze, misinterpreting her interest. "The Church was named for her. Our Lady of Guanajuato. She dates from the seventh century in Spain and was revered there until Felipe II presented her to our city in 1557. She's the oldest Christian figure in Mexico."

Regaining her composure, Calypso focused on the Virgin and pedestal.

"Is the base made of silver or tin? Or maybe an alloy?" she asked.

"Sterling silver. From the Valenciana mine not far from

here. Until the mid-nineteenth century, a quarter of the world's silver came from that mine alone so a little chunk like this was not a big deal." He paused. "And those stones in her gown are real, as well. She's valuable in a number of ways."

Calypso frowned.

"Is Guanajuato safe enough to leave her unguarded in an open church?"

He chuckled. "No. Tomorrow we celebrate Our Lady's coronation as Patron Saint of the City. She's out here for a spruce-up, and I can assure you that no armed guard is as vigilant as Senora Ramirez."

As though summoned, the ancient woman in black shuffled around a corner, her back bent with the weight of a basket she carried in both hands.

"She doesn't look like one of the ground troops," commented Calypso.

"You haven't heard her voice when sounding an alarm. Birds drop from the sky and our mummies over in the catacombs return to life. I've thought of using her instead of the church bell on Sunday." His smile faded and he looked at her narrowly. "I'm Father Juan Xavier; Senora Ramirez said you wanted to speak with me. Was it about Our Lady?"

"No."

"I thought not. We can talk either in my study or out here. Mrs. Ramirez would probably be more comfortable if she can watch both you and the Virgin."

Calypso smiled in spite of her sudden flutter of anxiety. "This is fine. And it shouldn't take too long."

"I have more time than anything else."

They retreated several feet down the aisle and he gestured toward a pew. Calypso slid onto the bench, followed by the priest. For a few moments they watched Mrs. Ramirez unload her basket and align cleaning materials on the floor at the feet of the Virgin. Father Juan turned to face his visitor.

"How can I help you?"

Calypso took a deep breath, then expelled it and inhaled again. "I don't know where to start."

He spread the fingers of both hands and lifted the palms upward while raising his shoulders and eyebrows in a gesture of helplessness.

"My name is Calypso Laskar, and my husband has called himself Seth Laskar." Only a slight tension in the priest's jaw muscles indicated his familiarity with the name. "Recently, I discovered that the real Seth was captured in Vietnam, and then lived for years as a drug addict and street person." Again, Father Juan's jaw muscles tightened briefly before relaxing. "My husband and his three partners were in a chartered plane that disappeared in a storm some time ago. No flight plan was filed but they left Caracas headed for São Paulo, so the aircraft almost certainly went down somewhere in the Amazon. No trace of either the plane or the men has been found, even though there was a massive search over a large area."

Reaching into her handbag for a linen handkerchief, Calypso failed to notice that, for a moment, the priest's tanned face crumpled. Nervously, she twisted the bit of fine cloth between her fingers.

"My husband may never turn up, and I need to know his real identity. When I discovered that he'd sent regular monetary payments to someone named Norma Drefan for many years, I hired a private investigator that told me the money is managed by Norma's sister, Bonny King. He also gave me the King address, which is where Norma lives."

Calypso's voice wavered and she closed her eyes, holding the handkerchief over the lids for a few moments. Clearing her throat, she opened her eyes and gazed directly at Father Juan.

"I paid a visit to Bonny, who told me about her brothers. Although she'd lost contact with both Ralph and Earle, she said Junior was dead, Chester back in San Quintin and Duke was a priest somewhere in Mexico." She paused and studied Father Juan intently. "I spoke with Chester and he told me that Duke had become a priest, Father Juan Xavier. For the past eight years, Father Juan has served the Basilica of Our Lady of Guanajuato." Calypso's eyes followed the movements of Mrs. Ramirez as she industriously polished the silver pedestal. "Bonny resembles Seth, but you could be his twin."

For a long time they both watched Mrs. Ramirez as she lovingly rubbed the metal, then energetically buffed it to a higher sheen. Finally, Father Juan shifted on the pew, turned to face Calypso, and laced his fingers together. The expression on his surprisingly boyish face was identical to the one Seth wore when he was worried or apprehensive, and Calypso's heart lurched painfully at this jarring reminder of her husband.

"Under any other circumstances I would never disclose information about my brother, but you already know about his stolen identity and you certainly have the right to the truth about the man you married."

Another ancient lady in black bustled into the church, followed by two slightly younger females carrying stacks of ironed linen. The three paused for a short conference with Mrs. Ramirez, each of them closely examining her progress with the silver base and gesturing helpfully toward Our Lady. After reverently rearranging the Virgin's jeweled robe, the trio marched toward the sacristy, disappearing from view as they filed through a doorway.

"Your husband's legal name is Earle Drefan. We were eight children, raised in trailer parks in Stockton, Vallejo, Daly City...wherever Dad could find work. He was an uneducated, good man, a Jack-of-all-trades, who died in a factory fire when Earle was nine."

"And you're Duke?" Calypso asked, anxious to confirm the man's identity. Father Juan's face rounded in a quiet smile identical to Seth's. "I'm Duke, a year younger than Earle."

"Forty eight? You don't look it."

"Healthy living and hard work." The smile faded. "After Dad died, Ma tried to support us as a laundress and then as a waitress at a truck stop café, but she had a hard time and finally quit trying. When Earle was thirteen she told him he was the man of the family and she went off with a trucker named Bud Baker. We never heard from her again."

Calypso was stunned. "You mean not *ever*?"

Father Juan shook his head. "That was it."

She felt totally empty.

"I'm so humiliated and insulted."

"Why?" He was taken aback.

"Obviously, Seth thought I'd leave if I knew his real story."

"That's part of it," the priest said. "He wanted to tell you, believe me." He reached over and took her hands, awkwardly clasping them between his own. "When Ma left, there were still four of us at home—Norma, Sharon, Earle and me. Earle raised us with a great deal of help from the parish Altar Society. He worked at all kinds of jobs. Supermarket bagger, theater usher, gas station attendant, construction worker—I can't remember them all. He was a serious, hard worker though. When he was twenty-one, he was offered a job as a Brinks guard in San Francisco. By then, I was in the seminary and Sharon was a Playboy Bunny, so he persuaded Bonny to take Norma into her own home, which she didn't want to do, since she already had five children, but Norma's not quite right and can't live on her own. Earle's always sent Bonny money for her care."

"Brink's guard?" Calypso echoed faintly, withdrawing her hands and pulling the wrinkled handkerchief taut. More visitors had gathered around the statue, enthralled by Mrs. Ramirez, who seemed to be delivering a lecture.

"Earle stayed with the company for three years. One day when he was twenty-four he filled a champagne case he'd brought on board with cash while the armored truck made its rounds. Since he was in the back, the driver and guard riding shotgun couldn't see what he was doing. The last stop was a fancy restaurant and he and the other guard brought out the bag of checks and cash from the office. Then he put the champagne case on a hand truck, told his colleagues that the wine was a present for his girlfriend who worked in the restaurant and he'd be right out. He wheeled half a million dollars into the building and disappeared."

Slumping against the hard, wooden back of the pew, Calypso raised her eyes and studied flashes of light caught on the chandeliers. What had happened to her happy, well-ordered life as a respected professor? She should be at home in Claremont with her books and papers and adored and adoring husband. Instead, she was in Guanajuato, carrying a baby of uncertain paternity and discovering that she was married to a thief. Lowering her eyes, she stared dejectedly at the crowd clustered around the Virgin.

"This can't be true," she whispered. "Seth was a professor and a very successful businessman with a degree from UCLA and an MBA from Claremont. I've *seen* the degrees and they're for Seth Laskar." Turning to face him, her expression was one of profound distress.

Father Juan inhaled deeply. Hands resting lightly on his knees, he studied his visitor quietly before speaking again.

"Yes, they are. Seth Laskar was our high school chum who disappeared on duty in Vietnam and was presumed dead. After the theft, Earle assumed his identity and moved to Chicago, where he got a job as an office clerk at Price Waterhouse. Except for that one little lapse..."

Calypso's eyes widened. "You mean the half million dollar one?"

A broad smile lit Father Juan's face and Calypso caught her breath. He and Seth could indeed be twins.

"Except for that tiny indiscretion, Earle was always very, very smart. And practical. He knew that he couldn't go far with only a high school degree, so when the

271

accounting firm transferred him to the L.A. branch, he enrolled in UCLA." His back straightened against the hard, wooden pew. "Graduated Summa Cum Laude, did you know that?"

Clearly, he was proud of his brother. Suddenly, nothing was real to Calypso but the vivid memory of the loving, gentle man she had married. At that moment, she yearned to touch him once more, hear him laugh and see that special look reserved only for her. Tears collected in her eyes.

The priest's attention shifted to the growing crowd and his smile vanished. With an air of importance, Senora Ramirez was speaking to a rapt audience and pointing in his direction.

"Oh-oh."

Several women, heads draped with black mantillas, stared at them while listening to Mrs. Ramirez. After a few vigorous nods, the group started to move in their direction.

"You've been recognized," Calypso commented.

"I'm afraid so. Let's go outside," Father Juan proposed, quickly standing.

"I should leave so you can concentrate on the celebration tomorrow."

His eyes sparkled mischievously. "Mrs. Ramirez and her minions do it all. Come on," he urged, "this delegation probably wants to know where to put the flowers, and they'll have eight suggestions and debate each one until supper time. And then Mrs. Ramirez will decide."

Calypso laughed, rising to her feet and hurrying after him. After the dim, temperate church interior, the heat outside was thermal and, as they stepped into the sun, Calypso felt dizzy. Father Juan's forehead furrowed in concern.

"Are you all right? I should have offered you a drink of water at least."

"I'll be fine. It's just so hot."

Calypso had worn a long, flared linen jumper in order to conceal her pregnancy from the priest. The last issue she wanted under discussion in this inherently painful meeting was her approaching maternity.

After eyeing her curiously, Father Juan grasped Calypso's elbow and guided her down the steps of the Basilica.

"Perhaps it's the altitude or your climb to the church. Let's sit in the plaza where it's shady and we can get bottled water or juice from one of the vendors."

With his firm hand under her elbow, Calypso could almost imagine she was with Seth. Resolutely, she pushed the thought from her mind.

"This is a beautiful town," she commented, pausing for a moment to rest and absorb the sight of the bright, colonial buildings, their iron balconies adorned with the brilliant flowers that also crowded the steep slopes of the canyon. "But walking any of these streets is harder than climbing mountains."

He chuckled. "Keeps us in shape. You don't see any fat people here and we don't need health clubs." Moving slowly into the shady plaza, they ambled toward a nearby bench.

"Before you leave town, you should see our theater. It's famous and very close by, on the other side of Jardin de la Union."

"I know. I'm meeting my friends, Virginia and Maybelleen, there at noon." She paused, then explained: "They both had husbands on Seth's plane."

"I'm so very sorry."

They settled onto a bench and he twisted toward Calypso. "Now that you know Earle's story, it's important that you understand how he felt about his past and his family."

"I think I do."

Raising both eyebrows, he slowly shook his head. "You have no idea. You probably know that he worked as a

Price Waterhouse CPA after graduating and, after AT&T hired him as a controller, he was awarded a company-sponsored fellowship for an MBA at Claremont. Certainly you've heard that cover story about a Montana family and Chicago Aunt, but you can't imagine how guilty and full of regrets Earle has been. He never stopped wishing he could own up and confess, but both of us knew that that was impossible unless he was prepared to spend years in jail, lose his job and forfeit the respect of his colleagues, friends and the community. When he fell in love with you, he was tormented by this fabric of lies he'd woven for himself."

"He should have told me the truth."

Father Juan smiled at her innocence.

"Of course he should have, and that's what I told him to do, but our perceptions don't always coincide with reality. He couldn't risk losing you, so he decided to continue with the deception."

Calypso felt her face flush. Perspiration soaked her pony tail, shrinking the long strands into corkscrews, and trickled in two small streams down her cheeks and throat. What had her suspicions and jealousies done to their lives?

Father Juan rubbed his hands absently together, and lifted his eyes to the leafy canopy overhead. "Are you a Catholic?"

"Yes."

Shifting his gaze, Father Juan regarded Calypso with soft, brown eyes identical to Seth's, and Calypso felt her eyes begin to sting with tears.

"I hope you don't feel that I'm negligent in my priestly duties."

She frowned. "How so?"

"I've known about the theft for years and never counseled him to confess to the authorities. Because his conscience wouldn't allow it, he spent very little of the stolen money and I helped him channel the rest of it anonymously into social causes just as I arranged Norma's monthly support payments to be sent from one bank to another to avoid detection of the source. Quarterly reports from the private investigator were my idea as well."

The priest extracted a packet of cigarettes from his shirt pocket, shook one out and offered it to Calypso.

"No thanks. I've never smoke, but please go ahead."

While he lit a cigarette and inhaled deeply, Calypso dabbed at her temples with a paper tissue, fighting nausea and queasiness and resolving to see Dr. Callahan when she got back to L.A. Two streams of smoke spurted from the priest's nostrils before he delicately lifted a piece of tobacco from his tongue and turned back toward Calypso.

"Earle worked like a dog to raise the family." He paused and blew a few imperfect smoke rings. "His was not a happy adolescence and he's spent his adult life agonizing over the theft, his inability to be honest with you and the fact that he couldn't keep our mentally handicapped sister at home."

"But he could have," Calypso cried. "I would have been happy to have her there."

"Are you sure? It would have meant dealing with Norma and facing Earle's real history. You might have seen him quite differently." Calypso frowned, staring at her yellow and white gold wedding band, seeing only the Seth she knew and loved. "My brother regretted the theft almost the minute it was committed, but unfortunately we can't undo our actions."

Calypso paled. "No."

"We're all sinners. My job is to encourage repentance and change so that the same sins aren't repeated. Earle repented, he changed and I know God forgave him a long time ago. Unfortunately, even though he'd used the money for charitable causes, he couldn't forgive himself."

With her head lowered, Father Juan was unable to read her expression but he heard Calypso's muffled comment. "I can understand that."

Abruptly, he looked at his watch, discarded the

cigarette and crushed it under the heel of one sandal. "Nearly noon," he announced in a tone that, while still friendly and warm, indicated that the interview was over.

They stood and Calypso stretched out her hand, her eyes puffed with unshed tears.

"Thank you so much, Father. When and if I have news of Seth, I'll let you know."

Waving her hand away, the priest offered his arm.

"I'll escort you."

"That's not at all necessary."

"Of course it is."

Grateful for his presence, and leaning heavily on his arm, Calypso allowed Father Juan to guide her slowly out of the park. His low-pitched, melodic voice was soothing, like the splash of a waterfall, but she was mentally shattered and unable to concentrate on his words as he related the history of Guanajuato. Seth was a reformed, absolved thief, but she had been the real offender, leaping to jealous and erroneous suspicions and conclusions, then compounding these failings by committing adultery rather than confronting her husband directly.

Why hadn't she just come right out and asked her husband about the bank deposits and the mysterious Bonny and Norma? Rather than risk a response she couldn't handle, she'd destroyed a nearly perfect marriage and could now be carrying another man's child. Or, by some miraculous touch of God, might it be Seth's?

TWENTY-EIGHT—FREMONT CASTLE WINERY, CALIFORNIA

*W*earing scuffed work boots, a man's plaid shirt and a pair of shabby jeans, Virginia followed Ferguson into the cavernous interior of the vatting room. Pungent with the odor of fermenting wine, the air hummed and rumbled as pumps forced vertical recycling of the fluid through thick hoses affixed to the sides of huge oak barrels lining both sides of the cool room. Her forehead bunched in disapproval, Virginia squinted at a hose and then turned to her former husband.

"You're not punching the chapeau down manually?"

Ferguson shook his head, watching as one of his employees checked the lower spigot on a vat.

"Up by Ukiah, Eddie Garza had a man fall in and he died, so I decided to use pumps like the French do."

"Wasted in Dago-red! Dude showed class," Vince exclaimed, enthusiastically pumping both fists in the air and circling one of the barrels in admiration.

"Oh, for God's sake," Virginia said crossly. "To suffocate in three feet of grape skins and a thousand gallons of wine is hardly a glorious death." Still scowling, she turned back to Ferguson. "I remember we talked about those pumps and decided that manual was by far better." Her tone was sharp and authoritarian.

For a moment Ferguson stood, hands in pockets, slouched against a wine vat and then he straightened and shook his head.

"Virginia, we can't start off like this." Virginia felt her face flush with embarrassment and pressed the fingers of both hands to her lips. "One of the reasons we couldn't make a go of our marriage was because you were so bossy and I wasn't about to fight with you over every little thing. I haven't changed but I thought you had."

Clearing her throat and stepping closer, she whispered, "I'm trying."

Tension left his face but his smile was thin.

"Well, that's good to know. You're very stubborn, and when you make up your mind about something you're sure to succeed. You're the one love of my life, which is why I never remarried or even had a serious affair, but I don't like to be pushed around or dictated to. That might work with Pete and others," he shot a quick look in the direction of Vince who had disappeared behind a vat, "but it didn't work for me."

The muscles of her stomach knotted and she folded both hands tightly together. "That's the truth."

"Also, you'll find that the wine business has marched ahead while you've been on sabbatical, so things like the pump that weren't worth considering are now the best options. You'll just have to bow to my better judgment and take it on faith."

Relaxing slightly, Virginia managed a wan smile. "I'll try."

Vincent appeared, moved to one of the vats and tested a spigot.

"How about a little taste?"

"Don't touch that," snapped Virginia.

"This is just skin, pulp and juice beginning to ferment, but the Tasting Room has finished samples of all our wines," interjected Ferguson calmly. "You're very welcome to try them out."

Vincent wheeled about and loped toward the exit. "Later, Sweets."

"Before you get tanked up, remember you're the designated driver," Virginia called. Staring at his retreating form, she shook her head. "I must have been insane."

"To hire him? Not at all. He's devoted to you, smart and capable. He just likes to get your goat." Ferguson stepped closer, lifted her chin and scanned her face. "Welcome back."

At Ferguson's unexpected demonstration of interest and possible affection, Virginia felt blood flood the surface of her face and arms. After a moment, she cleared her throat.

"Thank you." Straightening, she turned slightly and they began to walk the length of the room. "Since we're going back into business together, I guess I should see what changes you've made here in the last few years. You've really made incredible progress, especially considering the fact that you have no wife or partner."

"It wasn't easy. But you're wrong about the wife and partner."

She stopped, suddenly clammy with fear. When she spoke, her voice rose on a metallic note.

"What? You certainly never mentioned an associate. And you've said several times that you're single."

"Legally, I am. However, you're my partner who's been absent for a while, and you're the only wife I'll ever have."

Accustomed to communicating through sharp, witty remarks and dealing confrontationally with any divergence of opinion, Virginia automatically searched for a suitably caustic retort to deflect the guilty sting of Ferguson's kind words. To her horror she felt tears thicken her throat and she covered her mouth with one hand to conceal lips that had begun to tremble. As they resumed walking, Virginia swallowed several times while focusing intently on two workmen who were adjusting a hose.

"I really blew it. I feel terrible," she confessed.

Ferguson grasped her free hand and squeezed it with powerful, calloused fingers, then gently folded it into his palm.

"So you've made mistakes. Everybody has things they wish they could erase."

"Even you?"

He chuckled. "Oh, please. Let me off this pedestal." His smile faded as he watched the two struggling laborers. "Be right back," he told Virginia, releasing her hand and striding across the cement floor where he huddled with his employees.

Virginia wiped sweaty palms on her jeans, and then ran one index finger under each eye. Pressing her lips together, she inhaled deeply several times, patted her hair and moved toward the nearest vat. This was what she wanted, what she intended to work for, but what if she was just being a fool and the relationship was dead? With Ferguson, she wasn't sure if he was just being his usual kindly, nice self or was really willing to forgive her and start in where they'd left off.

Hearing Ferguson's footsteps behind her, Virginia swung around and scrutinized the familiar, lined face.

"There's something I have to explain," she began in a soft, strained voice, stumbling ineptly over her words. "Over the past few years I've discovered a lot of things about myself including the fact that life in the country with you was exciting and fun and that life without you is empty and unsatisfactory, no matter where I am or who I'm with." She paused and stared at the nearby vat. "I guess when I left you I was only committed to myself and what I thought I wanted, but I hope I'll have another chance." There was a long pause; she shifted her gaze to Ferguson. "I just wanted to tell you that."

"I'm glad you did." His voice was gentle and sympathetic.

"And I'm going to make every effort to change being bossy and snappish. Maybe even with Vincent."

"I have a suggestion," he said. "One that you won't like..."

She felt a twinge of apprehension mixed with annoyance. If she wouldn't like it, and he knew it, why even bring it up?

"Oh?"

"We discussed this years ago. A therapist." Virginia opened her mouth and he held up one hand. "I know as well or better than you the real legacy your grandmother left, and you need to see someone to help you straighten that out from the ground up. You and Vince may enjoy sniping at one another, but you do it with everyone else too. Others who don't necessarily like it."

"I know what I have to do," she said waspishly, knowing that it was exactly the wrong tone and yet somehow unable to control her voice, "and it doesn't include a shrink."

"You can call him or her a counselor if that makes you feel better, but I think that once a week is a good investment in the future. Our future."

In spite of her smoldering anger, Virginia's heart leapt.

"I doubt there are too many *counselors* in the badlands of Baja."

"If not, you could make a weekly excursion into T.J."

Reluctantly, Virginia chuckled and then laughed aloud. "Oh please. I might consider it if we upgrade to National City where they more or less speak English."

"If we're going for a border town on the north, we may as well think San Diego."

Sobering, she nodded. Pressing her lips together she raised her eyes to Ferguson's and then, after a few moments, looked at the two workmen.

"Problems over there?" she inquired in an even, clear

tone. The web of intimacy snapped; both Ferguson and Virginia moved away from one another.

"Not really. Boy on the left's a new hire." He tilted his head to one side. "Want to take a look at the racking room?"

A broad smile spread across Virginia's face. "Do you still rack when the moon is full, the wind in the north and the weather clear?"

The years of separation vanished and they were again easy, best friends.

Ferguson raised his eyebrows. "You always thought that that was just superstition, but Jesse Holtman over at UC Davis says it's scientifically sound. When those conditions prevail, atmospheric pressure is high and wine at its least active, so the lees tend to stay in the old barrels."

"And you hang around waiting for these perfect circumstances?"

"Of course not. What vineyard can afford that?"

They both laughed. Emerging into the sun, Virginia slipped on her dark glasses. "I'll give the racking room a miss this time but I'd like to taste the new Zinfandel."

"It's good."

Nothing here had changed, Virginia thought, observing her surroundings with pleasure. The flagstone path over which they strolled was still shaded by huge oaks and edged on both sides by pansies and jumping-jacks. To the right, an expanse of smooth, well-tended lawn stretched to a low, stone wall nearly hidden by a border of lavender. On their left, a few redwood tables and benches were occupied by picnickers unloading elegant hampers of food and indulging in *Fremont Castle* wine.

"What on earth are those?" asked Virginia, staring at the woven baskets.

"Gourmet grub for luncheon alfresco. It's big business up here now. Bed and Breakfast guests can order a take-out lunch which is usually fresh asparagus, pate, oeufs

Printanieres..."

"Nobody has crackers and cheese or peanut butter sandwiches in a paper bag these days?" To her own ears she sounded crabby; why on earth, she wondered unhappily, would Ferguson ever want to restart their life together?

"Only the locals out spying on the competition."

Virginia twisted her mouth in wry amusement. "Interesting, but is it progress?" She glanced at her former spouse with sharp curiosity. "I hear both our Zinfandel and Cabernet Sauvignon are the best around."

"I think so, but my opinion isn't really objective."

Virginia studied the flower beds for a moment and then turned to Ferguson. "You know, when we went to France for those first cuttings we were accidentally very astute."

"Babies and idiots."

"That is absolutely true. Any recent experiments with other hybrids?"

He grinned. "That's why we're going to Baja, if you remember." They reached the arching French doors of the Tasting Room and paused. Scanning Virginia's wary expression, Ferguson spoke with ease and confidence. "It's not as risky a venture as you may think. Most of the Mexican vineyards are located in Baja within a hundred miles of the border and not far from our property."

She liked the use of the word 'our'. It was somehow comforting and encouraging. "Well, that cheers me up even though we're only talking about five competitors ."

"Maybe six, if we include the esteemed Santa Tomas."

Grasping one of the brass knobs, he swung the door open and waited for Virginia to enter. "Our odds in the south are considerably improved by the fact that the Mexican government now supplies growers with information and healthy stock varieties from the Oenological Department at UC Davis. I understand Jesse's even set up a lab down there."

"Wonderful," she commented, again aware of her

caustic tone and wondering if a therapist could really help her with this problem.

"Makes *me* feel better. You know how often we run over to Davis with soil or vine samples, but it's a whole different ball game if we're trying to take them back and forth across the border."

"I suppose."

Stepping over the threshold onto the flagstone floor, Virginia glanced around the room, her attention immediately captured by a massive English bar on her left. The wall behind it supported an old, very flawed mirror in which the room was reflected. Several bottles bearing the label, *Fremont Castle*, were aligned on glass shelves, and on top of the carefully polished piece of solid mahogany a number of small, clean wine glasses had been arranged on a linen towel imprinted with a British flag. Checked curtains framed the beveled glass windows while small, round marble tables and iron chairs invited potential customers to rest and revitalize.

Vincent, the only other occupant of the room, had planted himself mid-way down the bar. A cluster of open bottles and used glasses in front of him attested to the fact that Virginia's driver was taking his sampling very seriously.

"Okay, Dad," he instructed the bartender who was about his age, "now let's have some of your really *expensive* plonk."

After glancing in his direction, Virginia turned her attention to the light, spacious room and looked in surprise at Ferguson. "This is totally new."

"You like it?"

"I don't know. I loved the old sawhorses and wood planks we had out in the shed."

"It was a necessary change. Customers now arrive with hundred dollar picnic baskets and great expectations, instead of tuna sandwiches in a paper bag."

Suddenly transfixed, Virginia pointed toward an open

archway on her right where a discreet sign announced, *Virginia's Table.*

"I assume that's a restaurant."

Grimacing slightly, Ferguson ducked his head in embarrassment.

"For the folks with expectations and no basket. I thought using your name was alright since the vineyard's still half yours, but I guess I should've asked."

"No, no, I'm flattered." Her cheeks were slightly flushed and a smile of pleasure lit her face. "If Virginia really has a table in there, maybe we should go there to eat."

"Good thought. Why don't—"

A shrill, if muffled jangle interrupted them and Virginia began scrabbling through her large handbag. "Damn! I thought I turned it off," she muttered, plucking out several items and hurling them back into the purse. Stepping to a table, she turned the handbag upside down, pawed through the contents and finally located her phone. Pressing it to one ear, she ran the fingers of her free hand over her short, chic haircut. "Virginia here." In the silence, her eyes flashed toward Ferguson and then she weakly lowered herself into a chair. "Maybelleen, are you *sure*? Do they know who it is?"

Ferguson slipped into another chair, pulled it close and studied Virginia with anxiety.

Without disconnecting the phone, Virginia dropped it in her lap and, with an ashen face, turned to her former husband. "I have to leave. They've found a survivor of the plane crash."

Although her voice was controlled and her expression set, Virginia felt her stomach clench with fear and anger. Peachy had a knack for doing the wrong thing at the wrong time and she had a strong premonition that it was he who had been resurrected from the unknown. It would be just like him to kill any chance she might have, however slim, of a renewed romance with Ferguson.

TWENTY-NINE—MANAUS, BRAZIL

The door of a private room in the Hospital of Tropical Medicine opened slowly and a nurse, dressed in pristine white with a perky cap on her black hair, stepped out.

"You may come in now," she announced in Portuguese. "When he was brought in, Senhor Jackson was clearly hallucinating but since yesterday he's been quite lucid. However", she warned, "his condition is still grave, and we don't want him to tire or experience any emotional trauma." Flashing a brief, impersonal smile, she waited for Calypso, seated on a sagging vinyl sofa between Maybelleen and Virginia, to translate.

Calypso turned to her companions and, in a strained tone, repeated the nurse's announcement, her mind wandering. Ever since the unnerving phone call reporting the discovery of Jackson, she had waited for a similar call telling her Seth had also been found. Every day she had awakened nervous and edgy, jumping hopefully when the phone rang, and each night she had been depressed and despondent. This, she knew, was the end of her uncertainty, since Jackson would surely know the fate of his companions.

Previously, the trio had been outwardly calm but now they were clearly unsettled and anxious. Virginia and Calypso stumbled to their feet; Calypso leaned down and stretched out a hand to Maybelleen. "We're all here together," she said gently. "You don't need to be afraid."

"But I am," protested Maybelleen, struggling to stand up, "and I don't know whether I'm afraid that Wheeler's alive or dead."

I know what you mean, Virginia thought, as they began to move toward the nurse.

Across the room, Starr rose slowly from a worn steel and canvas arm chair, her skin tanned to a creamy bronze, and paused for a dramatic moment. The center of attention, she smoothed her extremely short, coral linen skirt, adjusted the thin straps of her tight, matching tee-shirt, then folded *Vogue* and tucked it into her Coach handbag. As she checked the details of her make-up in a small compact, her hair, drawn into a thick, single platinum plait, gold hoop earrings, bracelets and many rings glinted in the diffuse light.

Closing the compact with a decisive click, Starr pivoted slowly and sauntered across the Spartan waiting room on coral-toned, four inch high stiletto sandals. Aware of their stares, she joined the other women waiting outside the open door.

"Since you were so anxious to join us *for the very first time*, I think you should lead, Starr," whispered Maybelleen. Uncharacteristically waspish, her nervousness was betrayed by fingers that incessantly primped and fluffed her glinting curls. In a halter-top, polka-dot dress with a voluminous skirt, she looked exactly like Marilyn Monroe.

Starr's eyes strayed to the faces of her traveling companions; to her satisfaction, she detected apprehension and fear. Assured that she was in command and captain of this ship, she tilted her head in gracious assent. "I'd be happy to."

On long, trim, tanned legs, she strode into the hospital room, hesitantly followed by Virginia, Maybelleen and Calypso. At the foot of the bed, they halted. For a few stunned moments the four stared at the gaunt figure, then Calypso's tear-filled eyes lifted to the plastic bags suspended, like multi-colored balloons, from a metal IV hook. Her chest contorted with pain and she squeezed her eyes shut. Until this moment there had always been a chance, just the remotest possibility, that the survivor was Seth and there had been a mistake in identification. Now, with a calmness she could never have anticipated, she felt the death of hope. This wasn't Seth and there had been no incredulous announcement of her husband's survival; almost certainly he was dead. Her grief was acute but mixed with a flicker of happiness that she hadn't expected. At least Jackson was alive. As she stared at his helpless, emaciated frame and gaunt face that seemed to have aged thirty years, she silently prayed that he, at least, would live through this ordeal.

Virginia's eyelids squeezed shut and she rocked with dizziness. Before their arrival in Manaus, river port city of one million residents in the heart of the Amazon, she was sure that Pete was the survivor even though it didn't seem feasible that her husband, who couldn't even turn on the computer successfully, could live for weeks alone in the jungle. Thank you God, she silently prayed, for giving me a chance to win back the life I threw away with Ferguson. Wondering if it was quite appropriate to be grateful for a spouse's death, she quickly amended her thanksgiving. Thank you God, for bringing my dear cousin Jackson back to us and may he return to normal very soon. Her mind caught on the word normal and her eyes strayed to the man on the hospital bed. In this maelstrom of lies, tangled half-truths and hidden agendas, what did that word mean? And was Pete actually dead or just hiding in the bushes, waiting to spring one more unpleasant surprise on her?

Maybelleen stood just inside the doorway staring at the reclining figure. "Jackson," she mouthed silently as she moved closer to the bed. Not Wheeler, who had told her all those lies and forgotten to tell her about all the other wives he had cheated, but kind, loving and loveable Jackson. Wheeler might still be alive; maybe Jackson's rescuers were bringing him in now, she thought with a glimmer of hope. But she was so glad Jackson had survived. If they did find Wheeler, as soon as he was well enough to go back to California, her Daddy could make him sorry he'd been so sneaky and untruthful.

Bending over Jackson, Maybelleen shook her head in worry at his condition. Her glance flicked to a machine with dials, knobs and many buttons, flanked by a screen with a moving green line that jumped and skipped and was accompanied by a rather comforting periodic ring. Like the IV bags, everything was attached to various parts of the man's body by an alarming array of tubes and wires. Her eyes lifted and lingered for a moment on the expanse of clear, aquamarine sky visible through the room's one large window before she looked again at the motionless, supine figure. This is going to require one of God's miracles, she thought, immediately asking Him for one.

"I just *knew* God had more plans for you on earth," she said softly, intertwining her fingers in Jackson's.

Forcing herself to breathe deeply, Starr noticed how very old and unattractive her husband had become. Moving to the bed, she placed one hand on his inert, nearly transparent arm. "Hello, Jackson," she said, her voice tight and icy. For a moment the two exchanged unfriendly stares and then Starr spoke again.

"I'd like an explanation of how you managed to live and what you and your buddies were really up to." Calypso sucked in her breath at the calloused rudeness of the demand.

"For pity's sake, Starr, let the man rest," Maybelleen said sharply. Squeezing his hand gently, Maybelleen bent toward Jackson. "At church we had a Prayer Circle for you and even Punky and Blossom joined in although they're not members of the congregation. None of us lost faith for a single minute."

A suggestion of a smile curved his lips. "Thank you." His eyes moved to encompass the other three. "Thank you all." Briefly interrupted by a spate of coughing, he gratefully accepted a few sips of water from a glass Calypso held to his lips.

"Don't try to speak," Virginia urged.

"No, Starr was right. You deserve a full and truthful explanation." His voice was hoarse and low, the words forced through dehydrated vocal chords. "First, I'm sorry but your husbands didn't make it."

Calypso felt a clench of pain in her chest that was almost physical. "I hope Seth didn't suffer," she murmured in a broken voice.

With an effort, Jackson turned his head and allowed his eyes to rest on hers. His curly hair, beard and mustache had turned completely white during his recent ordeal and he now looked twenty years older than his fifty-six years, extremely frail and very ill.

"None of them did."

"Praise God for that," said Maybelleen, "even though I've found out that Wheeler cheated and stole and told huge fibs as well as marrying me when he was already married. That's a felony, you know." Her blue eyes flashed indignantly behind the screen of black lashes. "Of course," she added more mildly, "no one should have a nasty death."

With a jolt, Calypso realized how much her two friends had changed. As Maybelleen gradually acknowledged the truth about Wheeler's devious character and unethical background, resentment had replaced blind trust, and was later supplanted by concern for the future. Similarly, Virginia had accepted responsibility for the direction in which her life was headed and had taken steps to drastically alter its course. A great deal of their readjustment had been accomplished through talking and listening to each other. Father Juan's face floated into focus and she remembered his words, "We're all sinners. My job is to encourage repentance and change so the same sins aren't repeated."

"Are you all right, Calypso?"

Abruptly, her mind was tugged back to the hospital room where she found herself the center of concern. Maybelleen gently eased her into an uncomfortable metal chair.

"Yes, of course. I'm sorry. My mind just didn't focus for a minute."

A female figure in white appeared beside Starr, frowned sternly at the group and made an announcement in Portuguese.

"What did she say?"

"Except for the wife, we all have to leave," translated Calypso. "She doesn't want Jackson to get too tired."

Virginia straightened and glared at the nurse.

"Tell her he's hallucinating again and now we're not really sure who he is. We'll go when we've identified him."

"Wait just one damned minute," Starr said brusquely. *I'm* the wife here and maybe I don't want you to share our private moments."

After a quick glance at Starr, Calypso interpreted a modified version of Virginia's statement and watched the uniformed woman leave the room. Obviously fuming, Starr glared at each of her companions and then stormed to the door.

"Nurse," she demanded. "Nurse, come back here."

After a few moments, the nurse brushed past Starr and looked enquiringly at Calypso.

"Senhora, que aconteceu?"

"Nothing," replied Calypso in Portuguese. "She's just excited at finding one of the men alive."

"Well, tell her if she makes more noise, I'll have

Security escort her out."

The nurse disappeared and Calypso turned to Starr. "She said to tell you to calm down or you'll have to leave."

Her skin pale under her tan, Starr glared at Calypso.

"You're despicable. All of you." She swiveled and encompassed the other occupants of the room with a cold glare, then focused on her husband. "So, how come you survived but the others didn't?" Starr asked abruptly.

Jackson looked steadily at his wife, raising a warning palm to ward off protests from the other women. When he spoke, his voice was raspy. "I don't know. Luck, I guess. Although I never really doubted I'd somehow come through." He paused and struggled for breath. "Maybe the fact that I was an Outward Bound leader helped. Certainly my experience in tracking and surveillance came in handy."

Calypso leaned forward, rested her elbows on the bed and gazed levelly into the man's coffee-brown eyes.

"Whatever the reason, we're all happy you're here and we just want you to get better."

For a moment she thought of that night in Claremont, but the picture was oddly skewed and out of focus. It was a long time ago and those were two different people. Jackson's eyes held hers for a moment before speaking softly.

"I know you were hoping they'd made a mistake in identification."

"No. I prayed that Seth had been found too."

The heavy, awkward silence was finally broken by Starr's harsh voice.

"I hate to break into this tender scene, but you were going to illuminate the past few weeks for us."

Jackson turned his head on the pillow. His dark eyes were unwavering and forceful as he looked at his wife, reminding them all that, in spite of his physical infirmities, his mind and will were unbroken.

"Don't worry. I plan to tell all right now. I shook hands with death and there's still a chance that I might not make it out of this hospital."

"Don't even think that," Maybelleen cautioned in alarm.

"We have to be honest. Among other, minor problems, something's gone wrong with my heart, there's a lot of infection and I have a collapsed lung. I can't even transfer to UCLA Hospital until I'm in better shape."

Calypso and Virginia exchanged glances and Maybelleen stroked Jackson's white hair, curling the strands around her crimson-tipped fingers, and then unwinding them again. Starr raised her eyebrows.

"We're waiting..."

Jackson took a deep, ragged breath. "You all know that California Consultants was hired to help Brazil identify their telecom needs and locate a vendor. We identified Globaltrac, which was forty-five percent owned by California Consultants, as the firm best suited to provide the services required."

Maybelleen frowned. "Is that *legal?*"

"Probably not; it's certainly unethical."

Jackson continued: "Key Brazilian officials were then bribed so that Globaltrac would actually be selected, and we similarly convinced influential members of the US Department of Commerce to loan the Brazilian government money for the project. Then we bought the support of landowners in areas where we planned to install the system."

"You *bribed* the government? Jackson, you know very well that's wrong," Maybelleen stated emphatically.

"Yes, I do know, and I have absolutely no excuse except desperation and greed." For a moment, his eyes locked with Starr's, and then his lids closed.

"But why was the US government interested?" Virginia was baffled.

Jackson opened his eyes. "They *said* it was to help monitor cross-border drug trade and possible terrorist movements, but it was basically economics. It would benefit a lot of American banks and businesses. The Brazilians, of course, thought the deal would help them get a permanent seat in the UN Security Council and bring more power in the fields of world trade and technology."

Shifting his frail body slightly, he paused to clear his throat.

"Our technology goals, if not our methods, were public knowledge. The real, very secret intention of California Consultants was to identify, through satellite photographs, potential alexandrite mines so that we could buy these properties through dummy corporations and tie up the mining rights before anyone else discovered the lodes."

Maybelleen shook her head slowly from side to side. Calypso frowned and tilted her head to one side.

"Most of the world's alexandrites come from the state of Minas Gerais."

"At the moment, but experts are certain that there are huge deposits in Goias and Matto Grosso in the Amazon Basin, where our system was to be located. Since the area's pretty desolate, we figured we could keep a mine hidden for a long time."

"Then what were you doing in Minas?" Virginia's face reflected her confusion.

"We were learning about mining and mines, studying alexandrites and the people who buy and sell them so we wouldn't be completely ignorant. We were prepared to invest in land once the system was up and running and we'd spotted a likely deposit."

Starr's voice grated the silence. "You mean you found nothing at all? You just spent money you didn't have and hoped for the ace?"

"I'm afraid so."

"A woman named Sally Jacobson kept turning up in L.A.," said Virginia, "claiming she was from the DEA, but Vincent found she really worked for a ring of international jewel thieves. Since a number of people seemed to know about your plan, it can't have been as clandestine as you like to think."

"As a little tyke during the Second World War, I remember a saying, 'Loose Lips Sink Ships'. Excuse me, Virginia, but Pete's loose lips could sink just about anything. He thought we didn't know about Sally and the service he was presumably performing for the DEA." He coughed softly, and then wheezed shallowly. "I mean we *had* a lot of contacts who couldn't wait to tell us that Sally was a jewel smuggler, although not a very good one. Wheeler, Seth and I spent a lot of time throwing out red herrings and roping Peachy back in, kind of like a bad comedy."

Jackson winced in pain as his parched lips cracked and began to bleed. Maybelleen grasped a water pitcher and tumbler on the bed tray, poured out the liquid, then bent down and held the glass and straw while Jackson took a long drink. Framed by the window, an airplane drifted into view and sliced the azure sky into two neat halves with its vapor trail before slipping out of sight. In the corridor, a trolley rolled past and a muffled argument could be heard in the reception salon; inside Jackson's hospital room, it was very quiet.

Maybelleen replaced the tumbler on the tray, then fussily straightened Jackson's hospital gown and smoothed his pillow. Starr's grating voice filled the small room.

"We found a big pile of alexandrites in the bank vault. What are those all about?"

Slowly he rolled his head, the nearly transparent skin stretched taut over prominent facial bones, from side to side.

"We paid two *garimpeiros* to smuggle those stones out of a Minas mine and then we had them cut and polished. It was an investment and, at the price, a good one."

"Garimpeiros? You *have* gone completely native," commented his wife sourly.

"Miners," Calypso's interpreted mildly, severely tempted to call the nurse to ask for Starr to be barred from the premises.

Jackson's emaciated body seemed to shrink into the hard, hospital bed. His eyelids fluttered shut, opened again, and he gazed at each of them in turn, his eyes finally resting on Starr. His voice, when he spoke, trembled uncertainly.

"I'll confess that I lost my values, my ethics and my sense of direction—everything that was most important. I got *way* off the track because I was greedy and saw only the possibility of vast wealth no matter what the price." His head slowly revolved on the pillow and his eyes turned to Virginia. "My family and our grandmother would be humiliated and ashamed of me, but no more so than I am of myself."

"You have been absolutely terrible," said Maybelleen primly, "but God gives everybody a second chance, and so do we."

Calypso again heard Father Juan's voice as though they still sat on the bench outside his church; she remembered Seth's flashes of anxiety, his rare grammatical errors and occasional insecurity in social situations that she only understood after her visit to Guanajuato. Seth had a second chance but it didn't bring him peace or tranquility.

"The first thing you have to do is to get better," said Virginia, patting one of Jackson's nearly transparent hands.

"In a way I'm lucky. Since our company partnership no longer exists, the contracts are null and void and so is the scam. I imagine other firms are already bidding to replace California Consultants." A rough rumble in his throat announced an incipient chuckle or a hollow cough. "I just hope the next guy is more honest than we were. Brazil desperately needs a telecom system, but one that's value for money, not built on secret agendas, bribes and payoffs and outright theft."

Starr's hazel eyes snapped yellow sparks. "At least we still have the alexandrites."

"No, we don't. They belong to the company and will be

sold to cover huge debts."

"Jackson, think. If the company declares bankruptcy, we can sell the stones and keep the money." Her voice rose.

"I can't do that," he said flatly. "If there's any cash left over, we'll divide it four ways, but we owe a fortune, and then there's the matter of the kited checks. Business ran at a loss for a couple of years, Starr. You'll have to live on your own income and savings."

Silently contemplating her husband, Starr smoothed the muscles of her throat with tangerine-tipped fingers. Abruptly she turned and stepped toward the window, coral heels clicking decisively, her designer handbag clenched in one fist. A shaft of sunlight stretched obliquely across the room and struck her hair, jewelry and smooth, golden skin. For a moment, Starr glittered and glowed like an exquisite, celestial being and then she pivoted, as though on a runway, and returned to the bed.

"That's just fantastic. My protector and provider turns out to be a gigantic failure."

"Stop that, Starr," ordered Virginia. "This is *not* the time for unpleasant theatrics."

Calypso rose and headed for the door, intending to call the nurse.

"Oh, you're all such soppy do-gooders," Starr said acidly. "I can't live on my savings or my income because there isn't any. I've been running *Starr's Stars* on household money for a long time, hoping it would pick up." She advanced threateningly toward the hospital bed. "Not only are you an unethical, criminal business failure, you didn't even have the grace to die so that I could collect the insurance money. *They*," she flung one arm out to indicate the other women, "are going to be rich. And what about *me*?"

Calypso, Maybelleen and Virginia stared at one another. None of them had thought of insurance because they had always imagined that the men would be found alive.

"I hope my late departed carried life insurance," commented Virginia, trying not to rejoice internally. She couldn't help thinking that it was poetic justice that Peachy, who had blundered self-centeredly through her life, bringing nothing but humiliation and problems might, through his demise, finally deliver something positive in the form of money. She tried to be fittingly sad, failed and finally concluded that she would hold a very elegant memorial service for her deceased spouse to ease her conscience.

"Insurance?" whispered Maybelleen dazedly, one hand on her throat. "But I don't need more money. I have a wonderful job as an airline mechanic and friends I love dearly." She thought for a moment and mused, "Land sakes, insurance money. Can you beat that? I guess this is what you could call the silver lining."

Angrily, Starr leaned over the bed. "It's all very well for you to be honorable and noble and sell the alexandrites to clear your precious name—"

"Not just Jackson's," interjected Calypso, "It's for all of us."

Starr continued as though Calypso hadn't spoken: "We are broke, with a lot of personal debts. Since you're being so righteous, what about me?" One index finger stabbed the air in Calypso's direction. "At least *she* can sell her alexandrites if she needs to."

Calypso frowned. "What alexandrites?"

"The big ones you wore to my house the night we met Maybelleen."

The room reeled and Calypso steadied herself with one hand on the wall, staring at Starr in disbelief. "I thought you knew those are faux. They're much too big to be real. If they were genuine, I'd have to keep them in a vault."

Jackson's translucent skin flushed crimson and then paled to bleached alabaster. Raising his head slightly off the pillow, he stared at Calypso.

"You mean false gemstones inspired Wheeler to hatch

the alexandrite scheme? The scam that ruined the company, destroyed our integrity and killed most of us?"

Appalled, the five stared at one another and then Starr's voice filled the room.

"You ladies will be rich, but dear Jackson managed to live. What am I going to do now? What about *me*?"

EPILOGUE—THREE YEARS LATER

CLAREMONT

*I*gnoring the stack of books and papers on the nearby table, Calypso sat on the green and white glider on her front porch watching her son Paulo and two neighborhood children skimming down the slide in the front garden. Shouting excitedly, they scrambled back up the ladder to hurtle downward once again. Beside her on the swing, Jackson sipped ice tea and smiled.

"The amount of energy small children have is truly daunting."

"And they seem to keep it up until they collapse or decide they're hungry."

One of Paulo's small companions apparently lost interest in the slide and climbed up the porch steps to mount a wooden rocking horse. As though on cue, the two remaining boys also abandoned their activity, clambered up the porch stairs and dove underneath a card table draped with a sheet that served as a playhouse.

"It's amazing how much Paulo looks like you. A very beautiful child."

Calypso smiled and shrugged disparagingly. "Thank you but he's the exact image of my father, for whom he's named." She paused thoughtfully. "I'm very lucky that he has such a happy disposition. And he seems to be quite smart and inventive."

"He has very good genes."

For the first year after Paulo's birth, Calypso was very tempted to check his DNA and identify the father. It would have been easy enough, since Jackson spent a great deal of time in her Claremont home and had even stayed in the guest room, where he kept a razor and change of clothing, a few times. At first she thought he was desperately lonely, since Starr had divorced him, sold the San Marino house and moved to Brazil where she was rumored to be involved with a shady politician. However, it gradually became clear that he was romantically interested in her and that this was a courtship, although a very gentlemanly and deliberately circumspect one. And with this knowledge came the realization that she didn't really want to know the identity of her child, information that would, however subtly, color her view of Jackson, Seth and Paulo.

"And a wonderful mother who is also the ideal role model," he continued.

"I'll never live up to your idea of me," she protested.

"I know how hard it must be for you to teach, be a single parent, work on the Father Juan project that you founded and have any kind of a social life. I'd like nothing more than to share my life with you and try to make yours easier."

Calypso turned to face him and covered one of his hands with hers. "You are a good, kind man, Jackson, and you've really rehabilitated yourself since the accident. I'm very fond of you. I always have been, but we've been through this before, and I'm just not ready to make any kind of commitment."

In the distance they heard the throb of a motorcycle that swiftly drew closer and louder. They exchanged amused glances, the moment of intimacy gone.

"Wonder who?" Jackson said.

"Wouldn't it surprise us both if it turned out to be a tattooed man with long gray hair in a pony-tail and studs all over his black leather gear."

Less than a second later, a yellow Harley Davidson thundered around the corner, leapt the curb and eased noisily up the front walkway. Dressed in a matching yellow outfit, Maybelleen switched off the machine and dismounted as Paulo batted his way out of the playhouse and ran to greet her.

"Auntie May, Auntie May, can I have a ride?" he asked flinging himself into her arms and kissing her loudly and sloppily. After hugging him fiercely, Maybelleen sat him back on his feet, removed her helmet and shook out her platinum curls.

"Silly boy, of course not, especially since I see you have guests. Hello boys," she said, climbing the porch steps and waving to the two gawking youngsters. "Go on playing and maybe we'll all have some ice cream later on, if Calypso says it's all right."

"Ice cream," they all chorused reverently, running down the steps to the slide.

Moving to the glider, Maybelleen bent to kiss Calypso on the cheek as Jackson stood up. "Sit down, Jackson."

"I have to be going anyway." He kissed her on both cheeks. "How're you getting along?"

"Super dandy. In *fact*, I have something to show you both."

Pulling off her yellow leather gloves, she held up her left hand, fingers spread, so that they could see the rather small diamond on her ring finger. Calypso jumped to her feet, clearly thrilled by her friend's obvious happiness.

"Gil?" she asked.

Maybelleen nodded. "I've thought about it a lot—for two whole years, in fact—because I don't want to make the same mistake again." She frowned and her lips thinned in disgust. "Not much chance of *that* happening."

Shortly after discovery of the plane wreck and verification, through dental charts of the crash victims, Maybelleen, Virginia and Calypso had applied for payment of their husbands' life insurance. Not only did Maybelleen discover that Wheeler had carried no insurance; she found that she was not legally married to him. In the State of California, a duly signed marriage certificate must be returned to the Recorder's office within three days or the union is invalid. Wheeler had simply not mailed in the certificate, as was the case in several of his other marriages.

"Another poor lady turned up last week, hunting for Wheeler who had married and deserted her," Maybelleen continued. "It's like a club, just dozens of us, and I doubt that he ever really, truly married anyone."

"Don't worry, Gil's not anything like that," Jackson reassured her. "He's solid and honest and he loves you."

Maybelleen smiled broadly and tossed her curls. "Isn't that the truth... Blossom and Punky like him. *And* we're both airline mechanics and belong to the same union and share lunch pails." She waved toward the swing. "Sit down, both of you."

"No, no I have to get back to work," Jackson said, turning and kissing Calypso lightly. "Dinner tonight?"

Calypso gestured to the books and papers on the table and shook her head. "I have to get through all those and I haven't even started. But tomorrow night would be wonderful. Paulo," she called to the group in the garden, "kiss your uncle goodbye."

As Jackson made his way across the lawn, both women sank onto the glider. Calypso gave a push with one foot and it began to swing gently back and forth.

"I think you'll be very happy with Gil," she said.

"I think so too. And how about you and Jackson? He's just crazy about you; any fool can see that."

Calypso watched Jackson lift her son, gently tousle his curly hair and kiss him on both cheeks and on the forehead while Paulo shouted with joyous laughter.

"We'll see."

PARIS

Virginia watched a uniformed bellboy haul their suitcases into the reception area of L'Hotel as Ferguson bent backward and allowed his eyes to travel slowly upward.

"There's the plaque."

He gestured to a polished brass oval, high on the left of the building, proclaiming the fact that Oscar Wilde had lived there. After scrutinizing the engraved piece of metal, Virginia and Ferguson exchanged pleased glances.

"That's why it's the most chic little hotel in Paris."

"Oh, I don't know if it's the *only* reason." Opening the hotel brochure, he began to read. "We're located a block from the incomparably beautiful Seine, close to trendy Beau Mich with its gourmet restaurants and famous artists' hangouts and almost next door to the Beaux Arts." He looked up with a grin. "Just in case we want to take a course in advanced sculpture or painting. Add the ghost of old Oscar and it's a package you just can't beat."

Handing the keys of their rented Peugeot to the doorman, Ferguson slipped one arm around his wife. "Let's walk down to the river and unpack later," he suggested.

At a leisurely pace, the pair strolled hand in hand along the shady sidewalk above Quay Malaquais, then turned and leaned their forearms on the stone balustrade. Behind them, horns shrieked, brakes protested and overloaded trucks rumbled along the cobblestones, but their view of the river was bucolically tranquil. A bateaux-mouche, the linen-draped tables on its lower deck occupied by patrons combining sightseeing with consumption of French food and wine, slipped slowly through the opaque water toward the Ile de la Cite. On both sides of the waterway, fishermen sat on the stone embankments and lethargically dangled lines in the water while watching three shells race down the center of the Seine, their oars dipping and lifting in perfect unison. Along the embankment directly beneath Virginia and Ferguson, a young woman carrying a string shopping bag followed three schoolgirls wearing white blouses, navy skirts, sweaters and knee socks. Their voices raised in laughter, the girls clasped hands and skipped in unison, their long braids flying.

"I don't see any lovers. Aren't there supposed to be hundreds of them jammed together all along the Seine, kissing and hugging?"

"It's the middle of a work day, Virginia."

"I didn't think that bothered the French."

"That's a stereotype."

Virginia fanned one hand dramatically in front of her face. "What *are* we doing in all this noise and traffic, Ferguson? Let's go down by the water."

"Suits me."

Arms around one another, they strolled toward a ramp leading to the embankment. Overhead, patches of fluffy white clouds billowed rapidly through the sky, propelled by a wind imperceptible to those below. Two bateaux-mouches passed in opposite directions, the lower decks of both crowded with diners, the flat roof section of one filled with cheerfully waving tourists.

"I'd like to stop at the kiosk up ahead to buy a postcard for Maybelleen."

"That's a bit silly. We're going back in two days. Why don't we take her some snapshots instead?"

"I promised I'd send a postcard from Paris, Ferguson. You know how disappointed she'd be."

He smiled and squeezed Virginia around the waist.

"Maybelleen could come over herself on an air pass."

"Do you think she gets them?"

"Probably," he replied. "I've heard that mechanics for major airlines have great travel benefits. She could bring all her Motor Maid buddies."

The couple stopped at the kiosk. Virginia glanced cursorily at the vast array of postcards and then began to peruse them more seriously. "I'd better get cards for Calypso and Paulo as well."

"Good idea."

Virginia extracted two cards and then replaced them. "Did I tell you Gil Givens has started line dancing at the Buttons and Bows with Maybelleen and Blossom?"

"You didn't, but I'm not too astounded."

Selecting three cards, Virginia paused, gazing reflectively at the river. "I wonder if she'll actually marry Gil."

"I don't see her rushing to the altar."

"It's hardly a rush since they've been going out for over two years."

"Since he was Wheeler's buddy, she's probably very cautious."

"Undoubtedly."

Smiling contentedly, Virginia rummaged in her handbag for change while Ferguson scanned the display of newspapers.

"Well, what'd know? Here's the *Herald Tribune*." As he plucked one of the papers from the rack, the proprietor's vigilant eyes darted from the postcards in Virginia's hand to the newspaper. "I haven't seen one of these for a long time."

Virginia paid for their purchases and they turned down the stone ramp, descending to the embankment in companionable silence. As they ambled toward a bench, Ferguson scanned the front page. "Nothing good here."

Virginia dusted off the bench with one hand, examined her palm and shrugged before settling onto the stone. Ferguson grinned and seated himself very close to her.

"Not up to our standards?"

"It's the reason travel wardrobes are always black, navy or brown."

Ferguson opened the paper to the second page and glanced at it briefly.

"This was a waste of three dollars."

She scanned it over his shoulder. Suddenly, she grasped his forearm. "Ferguson, look at the bottom of the page. That's Starr and some man."

"My word, it is," he exclaimed, folding the paper in half, then half again. Bending low over the photograph, they read the headline and article.

American and Brazilian Senator Murdered in Sao Paulo

Early yesterday morning, Starr Bailey, 52, of Los Angeles, California, and São Paulo, Brazil, and Senator Jorge Jucá were shot and killed in Senator Jucá's BMW as they waited at a stop light in the Morumbi section of the city. Three men wearing black crash helmets and dark clothing and driving motorcycles without license plates surrounded the vehicle, ordered the couple out and shot them several times. No motive for the crime has been established, although robbery appears unlikely. According to police, the assailants fled immediately and could not be identified by the sole witness who observed the murder from a nearby bus stop.

Mrs. Bailey is the former wife of bestselling author, Jackson Bailey. The only survivor of a plane crash in the Amazon Basin that killed his partners, Mr. Bailey made headlines three years ago when he exposed his company's scheme to illegally locate and acquire Brazilian alexandrite deposits and mining rights under the guise of performing telecommunications services. The ensuing scandal, which revealed international bribes on the highest levels and triggered several resignations, arrests and convictions of officials in the U.S., Brazil, Columbia and Venezuela, was the basis of Mr. Bailey's first book, "Stealth". Later, it was made into a feature film of the same name, which he scripted and co-produced, that won four Academy Awards.

Starr Bailey, beautiful businesswoman, actress and socialite, attained fame when she publicly fought Mr. Bailey for the lead in "Stealth". Awarded only a supporting role, critics claimed that her mediocre performance caused the film to lose a fifth Oscar for Best Picture. For the past three years, she has been the constant companion of Senator Jucá, owner of a number of hotels and apartment buildings throughout Brazil and Florida and President of Jucá Construções, a building firm founded by his father. Although he was indicted numerous times for criminal activities, charges were always dropped.

Brazilian law mandates burial within twenty-four hours of death but Mrs. Bailey's son, Roger, 30, who arrived in Sao Paulo this morning, asked that his mother be returned to California. Tonight, Roger will accompany Starr Bailey on her final airplane trip to Los Angeles where funeral arrangements are being made.

Both Virginia and Ferguson stared fixedly at the newspaper for a moment, deaf to the sounds of Paris. As Virginia lifted her head, her face reflecting shocked disbelief, and gazed at the river, Ferguson gently stroked her hair and shoulders. A teenage couple passed the bench, arms intertwined and eyes on one another, followed by a group of chattering, closely chaperoned schoolgirls and three businessmen wearing pinstriped suits and solemn ties.

Pressing one hand to her collar-bone, Virginia shook her head from side to side.

"I'm stunned, but not that surprised. She was a selfish gold digger, who nearly wrecked Jackson's life."

Slipping one arm around his wife's shoulders, Ferguson pulled her close. Virginia dropped her hand and twisted toward him, her face clouded with anger.

"And he seemed to be a nasty piece of work. According to the papers and magazines, Jucá is a crook who's confiscated over half of his employees' salaries and extorted bribes from every street vendor and shop in his constituency. He's famous for all the wrong things, and it sounds like they were the perfect couple."

"I knew Starr very slightly," Ferguson commented, "and only because she was married to your cousin, but she always liked being in the limelight, having nice things and lots of cash." He paused for a moment. "She just never got over Jackson selling those alexandrites to cover the company debts."

"He was lucky he could do it." Frowning, Virginia looked into her husband's eyes. "If it wasn't robbery, then what was it about?"

Ferguson shook his head. "I can't even begin to guess. Juça was hated by a lot of people, and she antagonized just about everyone with her airs and arrogance."

"The perfect couple..."

The slightest hint of a smile flitted across Ferguson's weathered face. "Possibly, although this might just be an example of being in the wrong place at the wrong time."

Two pudgy, middle-aged women wearing straw hats, polo shirts, trousers and tennis shoes and draped with cameras, bottles of water, neck pillows and back packs approached. One of the women was reading from a guide book and both paused from time to time to gaze and point at buildings on the opposite embankment.

"I know Jackson won't be too upset, but we should go back to L.A. for the funeral, to show him our support."

Ferguson stood, and then bent down to help his wife to her feet. "I suppose you´re right, but for now let's just walk. The bags are still packed and we can probably get a flight tonight; we need to soak up some French air and atmosphere to take back with us."

Silently and slowly they ambled along the embankment, passing motionless fishermen and occasionally meeting other tourists and Parisians of all ages. Benches were occupied by older men reading newspapers while teenage lovers with intertwined limbs pressed against the wall. A young boy at the edge of the quay tore pieces of baguette and tossed them into the river where they were snapped up immediately by eager fish. No one was in a hurry; even the breeze was languid as it stirred the leaves overhead and the surface of the water.

On the opposite side of the river, a trio of old men sat on a bench, talking. All three wore suits and ties; the face of one was shaded by a Panama hat while his companion on the right leaned both hands on a walking stick. A very chubby woman in her sixties wearing a short, tight skirt and striped tee-shirt and carrying a basket loaded with vegetables approached their bench, and the men broke off their conversation. All three stared fixedly and silently at the woman as she passed in front of them and then, when she had moved down the embankment, they began to stamp their aged feet, whistle and yodel. The Panama hat yelled "Bravo!", a cry taken up by the other two; it was a cheer that only faded when the woman had disappeared from view.

A smile tipped the corners of Virginia's mouth; Ferguson affectionately squeezed her hand.

"A long time ago you told me some things never change. You were right, Virginia. Some things never do."